DATE DUE

**LACKAWANNA COUNTY
LIBRARY SYSTEM
PENNSYLVANIA**

DEMCO

THE
IMMORTALS

THE IMMORTALS

Tracy Hickman

A ROC BOOK

ROC
Published by the Penguin Group
Penguin Books USA Inc., 375 Hudson Street,
New York, New York 10014, U.S.A.
Penguin Books Ltd, 27 Wrights Lane,
London W8 5TZ, England
Penguin Books Australia Ltd, Ringwood,
Victoria, Australia
Penguin Books Canada Ltd, 10 Alcorn Avenue,
Toronto, Ontario, Canada M4V 3B2
Penguin Books (N.Z.) Ltd, 182-190 Wairau Road,
Auckland 10, New Zealand

Penguin Books Ltd, Registered Offices:
Harmondsworth, Middlesex, England

First published by Roc, an imprint of Dutton Signet,
a division of Penguin Books USA Inc.

First Printing May, 1996
10 9 8 7 6 5 4 3 2 1

 REGISTERED TRADEMARK—MARCA REGISTRADA

Library of Congress Cataloging-in-Publication Data

Hickman, Tracy.
   The immortals / Tracy Hickman.
      p.   cm.
   ISBN 0-451-45402-2
   1. Communicable diseases—Fiction.   2. Quarantine—Fiction.
I. Title.
PS3558.I2297I56   1996
813'.54—dc20   95-25758
                                                                         CIP

Printed in the United States of America
Set in Sabon
Designed by Leonard Telesca

WILD COVE

Wild Horse Corral

ERIS

LONG VALLEY

Wah Wah Hardpan

LAKEVIEW

Pitchfork Spring

Wah Wah Cove

Long Valley

INDIAN QUEEN

KELLEYS PLACE

DUTCHMAN

Crystal Spring

Horse Spring

Kelley's Place

CRYSTAL SPRING

San Francisco Range

Indian Queen

RANCH COMPLEX

Cactus

Wah Wah Springs

NEWHOUSE

Imperial

Frisco (Abandoned)

Quartz Creek

SR-21

Cupric

King David

Horn Silver

RANCH SPRINGS

Lulu

QUARTZ CREEK

Willow Creek

ANTELOPE SPRINGS

WILLOW CREEK

WAH WAH VALLEY
Installations
ERIS US ARMY 6TH V-CIDS
RELOCATION DISTRICT

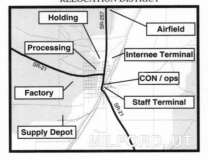

Holding

SR-257

Airfield

Processing

SR-21

Internee Terminal

CON / ops

Factory

Staff Terminal

SR-21

Supply Depot

MILFORD, UT

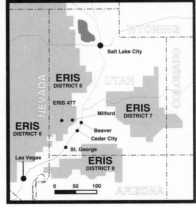

WYOMING

Salt Lake City

NEVADA

ERIS
DISTRICT 6

UTAH

COLORADO

ERIS 477

Milford

ERIS
DISTRICT 7

ERIS
DISTRICT 6

Beaver

Cedar City

Las Vegas

St. George

ERIS
DISTRICT 8

0   50   100

ARIZONA

Abandoned Foundations

Gate 'Delta'

Gate 'Echo'

Abandoned Foundations

G/L Barracks X-Z

Gate 'Charlie'

Hospice & Nursery

Hydroponics 1

Women's Barracks A-H Blocks

Gate 'Fox'

Warehouse

Water Tank

Com Tower

Pump House

Rec Field

Sanitation Unit

Married Barracks J-N Blocks

5340 feet

Mess/Info Hall

Gate 'Bravo'

Hydroponics 2

5320 feet

-38° 28'30"

Power/AG/Guide Cable to Milford HQ

Main Gate

Gate 'Alpha'

Men's Barracks P-W Blocks

5160 feet

5280 feet

5120 feet

5200 feet

5240 feet

113°20"

1,320'   2,640'   3,960'

ERIS

NEWHOUSE CENTER
Camp 477 -- Elev. 5143 ft.
UNITED STATES ARMY 6TH CIDS RELOCATION DISTRICT
SCALE 1:12 000

Topographical Data Source:
    United States Geological Survey
Controled by: USGS, NOS/NOAA
Compiled by Aerial Photographs Taken 1953
Planetable Surveys: 1959
Limited revision from Aerial Photographs: 1984
Field Checked: 1986 / Map Edited 1989
Projection: Lambert Conformal Conic
    Grid: 100 meter division of Universal
Transverse Mercator Zone 12
1989 Magnetic North Declination: 14' East

660'   165' 82' 0 100'   330'   660'

CONTOUR INTERVAL 40 FEET

To convert feet to meters multiply by .3048
To convert meters to feet multiply by 3.2808

Overture

"Then Peter said, Silver and gold have I none; but such as I have give I thee: In the name of Jesus Christ of Nazareth rise up and walk.

And he took him by the right hand, and lifted him up: and immediately his feet and ankle bones received strength.

And he leaping up stood, and walked, and entered with them into the temple, walking, and leaping, and praising God.

And all the people saw him walking and praising God:

And they knew that it was he which sat for alms at the Beautiful gate of the temple: and they were filled with wonder and amazement at that which had happened unto him."

—Acts 3:1–10

PROLOGUE
Fox and Geese

February 2, 2010 / 0330 hrs
Lake Havasu, Arizona

Jason Barris slept fitfully. The mattress in the motel wasn't the worst he'd tried and was a far cry better than the stone-cold ground he'd been using recently. He was tired to the bone, but sleep never came naturally any longer.

It was the eyes of the desk lady that haunted him in his half-consciousness. In a not quite dream, his mind replayed the scene in agonizing detail, searching for where he might have made a mistake. The vision floated before him as his mind looked on like an impartial yet critical observer.

"Evening," he said again to the woman.

"Evening. What can I do for ya?" Her face loomed menacingly in front of him, tilting back like a hound sniffing for the scent of him. She rather looked like a hound, he thought; big jowls sagging down from her spotted cheeks and sad, watery eyes. The motel business couldn't be very good with all the county and zone restrictions on travel. It all showed in her face. A hound in a hair net. Funny that he'd remember her that way.

"Need a room for the night," he spoke again to the woman.

She sniffed again, eyeing his battered satchel. She could smell it, Jason thought. Smell it or taste it on him. He punched down the panic welling inside him. He'd certainly learned how to do that well enough. Survival either taught quickly or never at all.

"I, uh, just broke down the road a piece." Jason shook his head thoughtfully. "You just can't get good parts for the 'wheelers' since the 'gravs' got popular." Suddenly, a new twist on his old speech occurred to him. "Say, you wouldn't know any place that's open this late, would you? I mean, maybe they could just fix it quickly, and I wouldn't have to trouble you . . ." The lie sounded hollow as he looked back on it. Was money enough to suspend this woman's disbelief?

The eyes under the hair net widened. She caught his drift. If Jason really had a wheeled car and could get it fixed, then the garage would be just as happy, but she could have one less rented room for the night. The hound started talking all at once. "No! . . . not this late, at any rate. Be happy to set you up in the mornin', though, mister. Jack Spafford's got a little place down the road that does lots of 'wheelers.' Best you get some rest tonight."

The motel register floated into his vision. The pen felt cold in his hands, but they didn't shake. Never, ever shake, he reminded himself.

The flat-faced old woman grinned hideously at him. "That'll be seventy-nine in advance for the night. No paper an' no plastic— you gotta have New Coin 'cause old money don't carry no weight out here no more."

The key sparkled and danced in his mind, dangling before him the promise of four walls and a bed. He fumbled through the over-size steel dollars in his pocket. They slid from his hand to ring on the countertop.

She dropped the key just as he reached for it. She dropped it so she wouldn't have to touch him.

She knows! his mind screamed, but he just turned and walked out onto the rain-slicked asphalt parking lot. The peeling paint of the door to his room swam toward him with agonized slowness.

The keypad sounds of a Touch-Tone phone blared suddenly in his mind. Eleven notes banged through his head. It was like a song, the tones those numbers made. He could almost sing them. They were a requiem for him and for everyone like him. For whom the bell toll calls? Was the woman calling him in even as he walked?

Yet somehow he couldn't look back, couldn't stop. Through the window next to the motel door he saw, in his fitful dream, a green park in the sunshine. Running across the park, waving at him through the motel window, was his father. Jason cried. He'd been lost in that park once and here was Dad—he'd found him. He'd take him home. Just the other side of the door.

He'd take him home.

As he reached for the ragged, ugly door, it suddenly exploded into darkness. Black hands reached for him, dragging him into the Nothing beyond. He was being swallowed up into a limitless darkness that got smaller and smaller until there would be nothing left of him.

His scream just wouldn't come . . .

He sat upright, the wet sheets clinging to his body.

His breath pounded into the chill room. It hung in staccato clouds before him, lit from the too bright street lamp outside the motel room window. He shivered in his own sweat. Clasping his hands together, he rested his forehead against them and tensed. The light pain he felt broke the fear in his mind, and when at last he released, he blinked twice and came back to reality.

He kicked aside the covers and rolled out of bed. "Damn," he muttered into the night. The sheets were useless now, and he wouldn't dare call down for a fresh set. He walked over to the window and looked to the east.

The sunrise was still a full half hour away, but the thinning of the night had already been working for some time.

Two more days, he thought. Just two more days and I'm home.

He smiled wryly into the darkness. Home. What a joke. He really had no home, and if he did have one, it certainly wasn't with his father. He'd left him and his mother a long time ago, and their relationship had gone pretty much downhill from that moment on. Yet the one thing he could count on was that his father always knew just what to do no matter how much trouble Jason could get himself into. The man loved charging to the rescue—probably the only thing, Jason reflected, that his father did love. Dad would charge in like some knight in full armor and plume, righting wrongs as he saw them. He just wasn't much good at dealing with the results afterward.

Jason hated his father for that. He hated the "rightness" of his father. He hated the quiet, smug self-assurance that sat at the root of every argument they had ever had. Jason knew that his father had failed him in every important aspect of his life and, as far as Jason was concerned, had done so from the top of some shining ethical tower—untouched and unsullied by a son who had only wanted to be accepted and comforted.

Time only widened the chasm between them, which Jason had eventually turned into a physical one—distancing himself by moving out of the house as soon as an excuse could be found. There never seemed to be enough space between them. Blocks became miles. It wasn't until Jason found himself entering the University of Wisconsin at Madison that the rage he felt at his father's "rightness" subsided to a tolerable level. Strange, he thought, to think that he'd fled California to find friends and, ultimately, himself in the gay community of the Midwest. There he could finally put words to the distance he felt toward his own family, and understood himself at last. With their support, he had come out of the closet.

His father had reacted typically.

His father wondered how his gay son could be *fixed*.

As if Jason were broken. As if Jason were somehow defective. His father had again leaped on his knight's horse to right a perceived wrong. Jason couldn't make his father understand that he didn't *need* fixing.

He hated his father all over again.

Then the sky fell. His friends vanished suddenly either to the new plague or were dragged forcibly away to places that were only whispered about and from which no one ever returned. Suddenly alone and hunted, Jason turned again to the one man who could possibly, in his mind, *fix* it.

Of course, Dad would be there for him. Dad would be home. Jason had called him, knowing full well that the lines were being monitored. Dad had said come home—typically, without saying how. Jason had hit the road, leaving Wisconsin only two days before the Minnesota Cordon closed the last free border out of the state. He was left with nowhere to run except toward the cold embrace of the one man he hated most.

Jason stared out the window of the claustrophobic motel room. He could picture the scene in his mind even now. He would explain what had happened to him and, yes, they would fight and yell and dredge up ancient, dead wrongs and insults as only fathers and sons can. They would both hurt each other with their own blundering prides. Dad would look at him as though he were still twelve years old—some kind of perpetual myopia peculiar to fathers. Jason, no matter how adult he would start the conversation, would end up sulking as though he really were twelve again.

Yet, in the end, Dad would know what to do. Dad would fix it—and Jason would hate him all the more for it.

Jason sighed toward the sunrise. Does Dad know the whole story? he wondered. Had someone contacted him? Almost certainly they had . . . where else would they start looking for him? What did they tell him? What would he think? Would they tell him all the details of how his son came down with the plague or, more likely, would they just leave it to his imagination . . .

All he knew was that he had to get home. Humiliating or not, he had nowhere else left to run.

Jason wandered into the bathroom and pawed groggily at the light switch. The stark white tile blinded him. His clothes were hanging there and were still somewhat damp from being washed in the tub. He put them on anyway. They would dry, he knew, and it beat looking like you had been running for a month—which, of course, he had.

He flicked off the all too bright light and staggered back into the dark room. A high-pitched whine buzzed in his ear. He had been a photographer and started to smile at leaving his flash attachment on.

Then he remembered he hadn't brought his camera.

His eyes widened in the mirror. Animal senses still left within him took hold. Conscious thought fled before the raw terror that suddenly engulfed him. His instincts took his life in their hands. He crouched to spring.

The door to the motel room exploded with the impact of two huge men. Wood splinters shot into the room. The black uniforms had rushed from the parking lot beyond as though nothing had stood or could stand between them and their prey. Jason turned on instinct alone. He leaped. The black figures had misjudged, crossing each other in the small doorjamb. Their huge hands grasped at air as Jason sprang backward.

Flight. His mind was alert. More alert than he ever could recall. Part of him exulted in the chase, the adrenaline whipping his mind and body into a fiery state.

One more step, the animal within commanded, and then the rear window. The glass between him and freedom never entered into the thought.

Behind him, a soft pop reminded him of his pump air gun when he was a child. He could see out the window. The dawn had not yet broken above the desert plain . . . and the world went suddenly and painfully white inside his eyes.

Time had passed. He was sure of that; something inside him recognized the discontinuity of his life. His arms and legs again became a part of him, as though returned from far away. Moving them was out of the question. His mind slowly came back together from the great distance to which it had been so suddenly blown.

Two National Guardsmen stood over him, barely more than silhouettes in their black fiber-cloth body armor. The armor was tough, sealed, and disposable. "If you move, sir, we'll have to stop your clock again." The electric TASER gun glinted in the light pouring through the broken door.

Things were moving around him, but he couldn't turn his head to examine them. In a single frame of his fixed vision, he watched his sheets and mattress leave the room.

Two sets of viselike hands hoisted him off the floor, their rubber-synthetic gloves chafing his raw skin. They half lifted, half dragged him back into the cold early dawn. *The parking lot is still wet,* he thought slowly. It was all Jason could see as his head swayed against his chest to the rhythm of the Guardsmen's metered steps.

One of the gloved, iron hands pulled his forehead up carefully. A colonel in another black fiber-cloth uniform, the spidery ERIS patch clearly visible on his shoulder, stared through him with piercing green eyes. The colonel's voice spoke in a forced whisper behind the sealed facial mask.

"Jason Lee Barris . . ."

They all began moving again toward the black van hovering at the far side of the lot. He could almost feel the hum of the grav packs under the new armored vehicle.

". . . In accordance with Executive Order A632294, you are being placed under protective custody . . ."

The motel keeper stood in the damp morning air signing the voucher. Behind him, he knew dully that they were piling the mattress and furniture from his room onto a Woodchuck trailer to be burned. She'd never feel the loss: the government would see to that. The flat face of the old woman grinned at him.

". . . By order of the President of the United States . . ."

Dad, oh, Dad! I was coming home. How will I ever come home now?

". . . As a suspected carrier of the V-CIDS plague virus. Your rights . . ."

Can I cry? They'll burn everything I touched. Would they burn my tears as well?

". . . Under the Constitution are hereby suspended pending verification . . ."

The doors of the van rang of cold steel as they opened. Black hands reached for him from within. He was being swallowed into an eternity of darkness.

Freedom

Tuesday, April 13, 2010 / 0900 hrs
Newhouse Center / 477th ERIS District
Wah Wah Valley, West Beaver County, Utah

The chill wind rushed from the western desert and rustled eastward in desperate haste. It was no harbinger of spring. The constant, blustering gale flowed with frigid purpose across the Pine Valley Hardpan and over the Wah Wah Mountains. It cleared the sharp peaks and dropped down the easily receding slope to the Wah Wah Valley itself, crossing the ten miles of gentle desert floor before being confronted with the towering San Francisco Range. Those barren rocks were no friend either. The air itself seemed to recognize the inhospitable sentinels as an enemy to its very breath and pushed itself with renewed vigor. The wind never stops. It is a ghost of a life, condemned here to always blow over the desolate ground, forever hastening in fury to pass from the dead face of West Beaver County to lands and places more fertile and alive, which lie beyond.

The wind has always been here—it will always be here. It has seen man come and set about putting his mark on the face of the Wah Wah Valley. It has seen his seeds spring up and die. Man comes to the Wah Wah to seek the copper and the lead and the silver that are in the hills. Man lives hard in the Wah Wah, often dies in the Wah Wah, and inevitably, man always leaves the Wah Wah at best breaking even. Men come and go—but the wind never stops.

P.T. sat on a wooden fruit crate as he gazed down the access road, the wind pushing his matted hair about his head. The Indian blanket draped over his shoulders flapped wildly in the gusts, threatening to fly away from him and everything in the camp. He didn't notice—fashion was not on his mind. His front-buttoned shirt may have once been white—small tears were noticeable in its fabric. It had a tailored look about it, but P.T. no longer filled it properly. The slacks were battered Armani, now secured precariously around his thinned waist with a tied cotton cord. The shoes may have also been Armani, but their leather was dull and cut in so many places as to make it impossible to tell. His ensemble was bizarre—in any event, it was completely inadequate in the cold flowing uncaring about him—but P.T. never took any notice of such things.

There was a watery brightness to P.T.'s eyes. One could almost forget to notice the three circles that discolored the center of his forehead. That faint mark was his common bond with all the other cattle in the camps. The rings were the mark of his kind— the sign of the beast—and marked that place where they had given him a gift. He reveled in the thought that in his forehead was a blessing that touched the sky. The satellites orbiting overhead could look down on this world and, lo, from the heavens, they did see *him*! The omnipresent electronic eye was always watching him. The brand made him special, but the device made him one with the cosmos.

His lower lip trembled slightly amid the gray stubble bristling on his face. P.T. rocked back and forth, his hand clutching a carved wooden slate in one hand while the fingertips of his other hand danced across its surface in sharp, purposeful patterns.

"Ref logit dbase datenow," he stuttered to himself in the cold, his eyes a fixed stare down the access road as he tapped the board in rhythm to his words. "Internees arrived gravlev train log systime. Log datenow, name, intcode, ref dbase omnet central."

The untrimmed nails clattered against the board. P.T.'s eyes flicked down from the road stretching to the south and fixed on the board. The dried pine had grayed over the last two months, and the details P.T. had carved so carefully into its surface had worn somewhat smooth with use. Yet they were, in his mind, as clear-edged and bright as new plastic.

P.T.'s eyes widened as he stared at the flat gray blankness of the board until the glistening whites could be seen all around the pupil. His jaw started working excitedly, uttering no sound in his excitement. His rocking became even more agitated as he suddenly found his voice.

"He . . . he's coming! He's coming!" P.T. wheezed to himself before succumbing to sudden uncontrollable giggles.

P.T. looked up sharply. His gaze fixed again past the three pairs of pillars that bracketed the road before him. *Gates to the promised land,* he thought. The Nul-gravity fencing that extended to either side of the gates itself was invisible, of course, but its presence was all too easily discerned by the debris that had blown into it. Tumbleweeds, sticks, and even the dust itself hung suspended in a surreal curtain, especially on the outer-perimeter line. Occasionally, the powers-that-be would turn off the fences in sequence, using alternating attractor-presser pulses to clear out the debris and keep the fencing invisible. But it never remained clear for long. The wind told him that she wouldn't allow it.

The wind whispered to him often, but P.T. never trusted her. "Trust the Omnet," he giggled again. *"The world's knowledge at your command."* Then he remembered again what he had seen in the blank wooden screen. He stood suddenly, his gaze still fixed down the road to the south.

The broad expanse of the desert beyond the dirty invisibility of the camp's fence was rimmed by mountains whose gray was so dark as to give the appearance of soot. Despite the wind, nothing beyond the perimeter fence gave any sign of movement. There were no trees to bow or rustle in the wind. Even the sagebrush that grew was so stiff and obstinate that it only vibrated against the rustling gale. P.T. could see other camps in the valley, each just like his own. They dotted the valley floor with great brown ovals. The nearest was over three miles away—too far for anyone else in the camp to see if there were anyone alive or dead. Yet P.T. could see that far. P.T.'s sight was far indeed.

Only the clouds moved with the wind over the valley, their dry puffiness dragging long shadows across the mountains and valley below. P.T. was patient. P.T. knew.

There! A slight swirl of dust between the mountains! A flicker of light! The old highway was bringing them in, bringing P.T. his world and his work. The gaunt scarecrow danced a little jig, the blanket flying from his shoulders, flapping down to the black-brown dirt landing yards from him and his crate.

The great dark worm on the highway slowed to a crawl and then turned toward him. The billowing dust suddenly became far more pronounced as the gravlev pallets left the broken paved highway for the straight line of the dirt access road.

P.T. stood on the crate and stretched his arms wide, his face pitched suddenly to the sky. The wind ruffled his shirt with frigid claws as he seemed in his own mind to fly. His upturned face screamed into the wind an incoherent cry merging smoothly into repeated words.

"Freedom!"

A tumbleweed stuck itself to the invisible fence.

"Freedom!"

The red lights atop the outer gateposts began flashing with the approaching pallets.

"Freedom!"

The grav modules affixed to the bottom of the transfer pallets increased their hum slightly as they slowed the momentum of the train. Dark figures huddled against the low railing of the pallet, its protection insufficient against the cold wind. Others stood in the center of the pallets, there being no room to do otherwise. Fifteen pallets in all, each ten feet wide and thirty feet long. The first two pallets, as always, contained children and therefore more than the usual hundred and twenty per unit.

"Freedom!" P.T. screamed at them.

The pallets floated slowly past the outer pillars and stopped. The red flashing lights of the outside perimeter stopped.

"Freedom!"

The flashing lights atop the inner and middle perimeters began to flash. For a moment the shivering sobs from the pallets nearly covered P.T.'s voice in the wind. The faces were new. The faces were the same. Round eyes watering in the wind. Tears flowing from eyes that had thought they had cried their last. Foreheads all marked—making them one with P.T.

Keening wails flowed from most of the pallets, but not from the first two. These were filled with children. The children were always silent and wary, drawn back into their secret places far inside themselves. Not even the cold blue bodies of the children who had died on the way could touch them. Dead or not, the children were always silent.

And the children shall lead them. P.T. smiled at the thought.

The gravlev train hummed ever so slightly louder and slid between the last two gates. P.T. leaped down from his crate and snatched up his blanket from the dirt. He threw it over his shoulders without dusting it off, unknowing and uncaring about the cloud he raised about him. He stood, suddenly erect and with great dignity, clutching his weathered piece of carefully carved wood as though it were the tablets from Mount Sinai. He spoke in great sonorous and self-important tones. His audience of despair was drifting past him.

"Welcome to the promised land."

Newhouse

Tuesday, April 13, 2010 / 0930 hrs
Newhouse Center / 477th ERIS District
Wah Wah Valley, West Beaver County, Utah

Michael Barris gazed at the madman for a long time as he drifted on the pallet into the camp. He stood gripping the low rail around the outside of the pallet. His hands hurt with sharp, needlelike pains. For the last hour he had been on this flat slab of fitted wood, pressed and jostled by the men and women who had been unceremoniously packed onto every square inch of its surface. It had been all he could do to remain with the train.

At one point as they traveled west, a man and woman had jumped from his pallet, causing three others to tumble from the platform after them. The grav train had slowed, just as it was cresting a steep grade on an old two-lane highway where the train power guides had been laid. How the couple had gotten up the courage to do it, Michael couldn't imagine. The place they had jumped was itself littered with bodies in various states of decay. The grisly sight should have been enough to freeze everyone in place, but it was the first time the grav train had slowed since they had been loaded. *At least the birds were eating well,* Michael thought crazily.

Yet the five people had cascaded off the pallet like a small group of lemmings. The couple had jumped on purpose, Michael was certain, while the others just sort of fell from the couple's momentum.

The man and woman had barely touched the ground when they started to run.

Within their first two steps Michael's eye caught a flash from the southern hills. Third step was accompanied by the simultaneous sounds of rifle reports and that of wet melons dropped against the pavement. The running couple's heads flashed with a gray-pink mist. Their heads snapped back in unison as their legs collapsed under them. When they slid to a stop, their hands were both still intertwined. Clean holes pressed through the centers of their foreheads while large, ragged holes exited the back of their heads. A crimson stain began soaking into the parched desert ground beneath them. Both of them had come to rest among many other dead that littered the ground. They weren't the first to die here. Neither their ideas nor their results had been unique.

The three others who had fallen from the pallet had just gotten their feet under them when the first couple died. Panicked, they charged up the hill, desperate to get back on the pallets, which were just picking up speed again. They stumbled over the bodies, kicking decaying limbs loose from their sockets in their haste. The two men, who were trailing the woman, heard the report from the hills and turned instinctively to face it. Both suddenly kicked sideways, the guided slugs slamming neatly into the center of the three rings marking their foreheads.

Michael could feel nearly everyone reach up silently and touch their brands. The implants they had been given had marked each forehead with three interlinking circles. Michael's own brow was covered by a bandanna. He knew, however, what everyone on the pallet was thinking: Was it possible that the bullets actually *saw* their brands?

The remaining woman kept running, her eyes locked on the last of the pallets. Michael remembered her. He'd talked to her in an old high school stadium where they'd been held the night before. He seemed to remember her being from Riverside. She'd been worried about her six-year-old daughter. They'd been at the Alpha Beta Market together when the Guardsmen had taken her. She didn't know what they had done with her. The woman's name was Elizabeth Becton; the daughter was Amy.

The pallets continued to pick up speed, but the woman named Elizabeth didn't seem to notice, increasing her pace to sprint up the hill. She was within three yards when the third report sounded.

Elizabeth didn't turn toward the sound. Her hands stretched out in front of her. Michael was ready to reach out to her.

The slug didn't have a good angle on the implant and so didn't enter the head cleanly from the front. It ripped across her forehead, shattering bone as it transited. Blood erupted into her short, honey-colored hair.

She fell forward on her hands, sliding across the ancient, broken asphalt. Michael could only stare as they crested the hill. Elizabeth Becton was pushing herself up from the pavement with one hand, the other pressed against her wet, shattered forehead. She disappeared from view as the pallet crested the hill and began again to pick up speed.

Someone behind Michael murmured, "They'll come and help her, won't they? I mean, they won't just leave her there, will they?"

Michael looked up and saw crows gathering in the sky. *Sorry, Amy,* he thought, *Mommy's not coming back.*

From that moment he never let go of the railing. The packed pallet compressed even more toward the center, if that were possible. No one dared fall off.

Now, as the pallet slid to a quiet stop, he had to force his fingers open from the wooden railing. The muscles had cramped closed against the constant pressure of the jostling people behind him. Now aching, he pulled them free. He'd been so preoccupied with raw survival that he had taken little notice of anything but his most immediate surroundings.

They'd pulled onto a siding of sorts. The pallets had left the main road and moved between a set of warehouse buildings on one side and dorm barracks on the other. Some of the barracks, he noticed, were three stories tall, others only a single story, yet each was identical in its architecture. All wood. Even the roofs, which he thought for convenience alone would have been made of some Quonset-hut sheet metal, were crafted in wood. Only the spindly pyramid structure on the north side of the train grade was of a different construction. The sleek, thirty-foot tower was gleaming white, painted concrete. Beyond that, the world looked like housing design had just dropped back about a hundred years.

He wanted to stand on the pallet to get a better look around, but suddenly the pressure of his fellow passengers pushed him to jump from the pallet just to get out of the way. The ground was already warm as he landed. There was a charcoal quality to the dirt. It clung to everything.

On either side of the pallet train, the right-of-way was bordered by large men—each wielding a length of two-by-four. There was no uniform; each man was attired in the same style that he had come to think of as "Early Roust," meaning whatever they were wearing at the time. They were obviously some of his fellow detainees, but their demeanor had the distinct air of authority. In any event, no one, least of all Michael, was interested in questioning that authority at the moment. The guards were pointing at people and waving their sticks less in threatening ways than as traffic cops. It didn't take long to get the idea.

Michael looked up the road—if you could call it that. It was an open space between the buildings with a slight rise to it—an ancient railway grading he guessed. They were nearly nine hundred people in all on this particular caravan, counting the nearly three hundred or so children on the first pallets. All of them shuffled forward as directed toward a large open space just around the end of the barracks and up the hill.

The trampled roadway ran almost directly up the slope. The low, one-story barracks they had seen coming through the gate towers as they entered the camp were somewhat dwarfed by two-story complexes behind them and even a series of three-story buildings he could see farther up the road. Michael had been to New Hong Kong in '01. It was his last trip to Asia before all the trouble began. He'd wondered just how all those people could live so close together and not get on each other's nerves. He supposed he was about to find out. Considering the size of the buildings and the crowding on the pallets, he could only assume that the camp wasn't much more spacious in its accommodations. That would suggest a huge number of internees in this one camp alone.

He was carried up the road more by the momentum of the crowd around him than by his own volition. *Processing, I suppose that's what they'll call it,* he thought to himself. *Let's get it over with . . . I've got other things to do.*

He found the sluggish human river, in which he was only a drop, drifting around the two-story barracks and into a large open area. Barracks surrounded the flat, trampled dirt of the field on two sides. A huge, low building could just be discerned over the heads of the people around him to the east. Other smaller buildings were to the north. It felt like the center of things around here to Michael.

A man suddenly appeared above the crowd, standing, it would seem, on a box. Space cleared magically around him, assisted, no doubt, by the rather large men who were encouraging the crowd to back up slightly.

He seemed like an odd man, his bald pate shining in the sun, giving a gleaming, almost clean quality to the three red circles marring his forehead. It branded this man just as it branded everyone around Michael, but somehow on him it seemed different. Perhaps it was the crops of wisping hair that framed it so gracefully. Or maybe it was the deep-set, burning emerald eyes. Chin up and confident, he was the antithesis of all he surveyed.

The man on the box shrugged into his gray-smudged black coat, as if somehow to seat it better as some mantle on his shoulders.

"Ladies and Gentlemen," his voice boomed in the morning air. A deep voice, accustomed to speaking and probably in love with itself, Michael thought. "May I have your attention for a few minutes."

He did. There really wasn't anything else they wanted to look at.

"I am Quinton Weston. Reverend Weston if you like. As the appointed administrator of this facility, it is my honor to stand before you today and bid you welcome. Welcome, I say, to Newhouse Center!"

You must be joking, Michael thought as he stared.

There was a smattering of dazed applause rippling through the large crowd. Reverend Weston smiled warmly toward its meager offering, milking it for all he could.

"Yes, welcome! These are desperate times requiring desperate measures," Reverend Weston intoned in his best doomsday voice, normally reserved for more distant apocalypses safely ensconced in the Old Testament. "Our nation finds itself in the grip of peril—even from ourselves. This plague has ravaged the land even as it ravages our bodies now. We are here that others will not have to be. We are here, quarantined from the rest of our fellows so that the plague in our bodies will not destroy them as well. Our sacrifice here makes for a stronger nation—and a stronger humanity."

Michael smiled suddenly at this. So far, most of the reverend's quotes were taken directly from the President's speeches over the last six months—not that there was anyone left to quote *other* than the President these days.

"Under the direction of the President, the ERIS centers like this one were established in the desolate western deserts to quarantine us and our terrible virus from the healthy world until such time as a cure for our malady may be found." The reverend's voice turned suddenly cold as his words spat out forcefully. "Make no mistake. You are interned here, and here you will stay—for your own good and for the greater good that lies outside that fence. If you stay here, you will continue to live. If you leave, except as invited by ERIS and their programs—you will die. Some of you have already disobeyed this commandment on the way here. No one would want to see the results of that tragic mistake repeated again."

Michael looked up sharply, Elizabeth's face flashing crimson through his mind. *How did he know so soon?* he thought.

"Now, a few important things before you get processed and settled into your homes." Reverend Weston spoke through a smile again. It was as though a church social had just begun again. "There are some things you need to know right away for your own safety. First, this center is surrounded by several rings of Nul-gravity fencing. They tell me that the fence is dynamically stable and inertially reinforced. All that fancy talk means that if you try to cross the chalk line around the camp, you'll end up floating about five feet above the ground with nothing to hang onto. You'll stay there until someone notices you and throws you a rope to drag you back in. Coils of hemp rope are located at the end of all barracks facing the inner fence just for this purpose. By the way, if you do find someone stuck in the fence, don't try to bring 'em in yourself. You'll need a couple of people on the rope with you to haul them in. It's the only kind of fishing we've got, but when you catch 'em, they're always big ones."

A smattering of chuckles rippled through the crowd as the joke fell flat. To Michael, the reverend appeared as if he always wondered why no one got his joke. This must not have been the first time he's given this speech.

"Back up the hill here"—Weston gestured grandly up toward the east—"is the Commons Building, where meals are served and all worship meetings take place. We also work in that building, each man and woman's time occupied to support research for our cure. You will each be assigned a work function there to support either this great effort or the need of the community directly. First, however, across the hill here to the north"—his hand swept grandly around like some human compass—"is the Hospice. The children are already there being checked and assigned by our Hospice staff to their nursery quarters."

Hospice staff? Michael thought.

"When they are finished, you will first be processed and treated there and then sent up to the Commons to get your building assignment and other duties."

The reverend then looked sternly down into the crowd. "You are here because you are a danger to society and humanity. You will leave here only when the danger is passed. You can work here to help end that danger and suffering. If you cooperate, if you obey the rules of the Center, then your time here will be pleasant."

And what if we don't, Michael thought.

"Your country needs you." The reverend droned on.

In Michael's mind, red flashed across Elizabeth's forehead.

"We are here to serve," the reverend intoned.

That beautiful white forehead ripping into a frothy crimson mist.

"If we obey, nothing bad will happen to us."

The blue eyes, life flickering out alone in the desert wastes.

Before he could turn and run, what remained of Michael's meager breakfast coated the back of the short bearded man standing in front of him.

Reverend Weston turned toward the interruption. He was not amused.

Nurse

Tuesday, April 13, 2010 / 1920 hrs
Newhouse Center / 477th ERIS District
Wah Wah Valley, West Beaver County, Utah

Nurse Olivia Codgebury, RN.

She paused for a moment and thought on that. RN. It seemed so little, so small sitting there at the end of her name like some afterthought. It wasn't very reflective of who she was, that little RN.

It had been enough, to be sure, when she had started in Boston. She liked the city and found it genuinely beautiful in places. The Commons in Boston—now there was a real common! She loved to take lunch there, especially in the fall. The executive types didn't much care for the chill and the wind, but she reveled in it. It was a perfect counterpoint to her life in ER at Boston General. That place had been crowded and exciting—everything that the Commons was not in the late fall. Even when the hospital was finally seized by the military and its cordons turned away thousands from the perimeter three blocks out, she still managed to get away to that place that was all hers, whether there were other people nearby or not.

Her family had all been Yorkshire born and raised, but she had wanted to take her medical training in "The States." She had simply stayed on, somehow not finding any reason to go home—to her family's great sadness. She was the youngest, however, and her sisters were all gone from the house, having their own lives. Her parents loved her, but Dad had always been a bit heavy-handed with the kids. She was just as glad to live her life a few thousand miles away. The Commons, it seemed to her, was always a short trip to a few thousand miles from anywhere.

It was there in her Boston Commons, in fact, that they took her when her time came. Olivia supposed it was inevitable, since she continued to treat anyone coming through the door. They had simply crossed into her own private Boston Commons and swallowed her away to hell. Now the Commons was like some fairy story in her mind: too beautiful to be remembered and somehow all done in the blurred watercolors of her mind.

Olivia Codgebury, RN. May as well add a few other letters to it now, she thought, considering all that she was expected to do. How about MD for the appendectomy she had to perform with plastic knives? Surely she earned those few letters just for attempting that one. Perhaps GYN would be tacked on for the stillborns she had to clear out of their dying mothers and figure out how to dispose of. Then there was DDS—oh, yes, and just how was she supposed to perform dentistry with the limited tools they had given her in the Hospice kit? Toss me a PhG for dispensing whatever few drugs I have to those who need more than I've got. What about a DSO—the Distinguished Service Order—for meritorious conduct in defending that same drug cabinet against the junkie from south Chicago who had the shakes so bad that he could barely hold the board with the nail in it that he kept swinging at her and so she had to kill the little bugger. Killed him! Her, the little RN with the little RN initials after her name because she was so goddamned scared, and she would have given him the drugs if she hadn't needed them for that goddamned appendectomy in the morning, which had gone badly and the goddamned girl died anyway. . . .

Olivia Codgebury clapped her hands together tightly, but they still shook in the clear, unwavering light of the fiber-optic lamps that ran around the ceiling of the examination room. She exhaled a shuddering breath, almost a laugh, as she muttered into the rapidly cooling room. "Olivia Codgebury, MD, DDS, RN, GYN, PhD, PhG, DSO—BS!

She jumped slightly at the gentle knocking on the door behind her. It was show time. As the head of Care in Newhouse Center, she was the ruler of all things medical. Now she had to face down another fool in a parade of fools, which never seemed to end and which never ceased to amaze her. Why couldn't they just leave her to die like the rest of the place, she wondered.

There was another sharp set of taps against the thin plywood door.

Her head jerked up. "Yes!"

A square, handsome head slipped through the open door, its owner keeping the plywood somehow between himself and the rest of the room. "Nurse Codgebury? Everyone has been cleared out except that last one. I've held him back just as you asked. Are you ready to see him now?"

Codgebury had to think about that one for a moment. Did she really want to see this man? What could he tell her that would possibly make any difference? The man represented a mystery to her—in Newhouse, mysteries could kill you.

"Yes, Gene, bring him in but do me a favor and stay with us, will you? I may need your help with this one."

Gene's smile was broad and perfect. "Of course, ma'am. Happy to help in any way I can."

I'll just bet you are, Gene, she thought as he disappeared again.

Codgebury picked up the thin folder from her desk and began leafing through it just as Gene returned with a man who was nearly as tall as himself. With a quick little jump, she sat on the edge of the high wooden table, causing its legs to slide a noisy inch across the plywood floor. Gene motioned the man in the direction of a short wooden stool. The man sat automatically and only then noticed that his head was actually below the nurse's eye level.

Olivia never looked up from the folder as she spoke.

"You are my last examination today. Let's cooperate and everything will get completed in short order. Name please?"

"Michael Johnson."

"Former residence?"

"Laguna Beach, California."

Olivia snorted quietly. "Date you tumbled to Vic?"

Michael blinked. "I beg your pardon?"

Olivia looked up languidly from behind the sheaf of forms. "Date you became V-CIDS positive?"

"Ah, I see what you mean. It was, ah, November of '09."

"You're sure of that?" Olivia said, her eyes still fixed on the man.

He looked away from her. "Yes, ma'am, that was it."

"How did you get it?"

"Huh?"

"I suspect your hearing remains pretty much intact. I said how did you get it?"

"Oh, you know," Michael hemmed a little, looking again at the floor. "My wife—I got it from my wife."

Olivia arched her imperious eyebrows. "Now, that would be a trick since she died in '99."

The man looked up sharply, his eyes bright and fearful.

"Here, let me help you. You are not Michael Johnson, but rather you are Michael Albert Barris, senior executive of—pardon me, *former* senior executive of the I-Net. You might occasionally go to Laguna Beach, but your residence is in Beverly Hills. Your wife, one"—Olivia glanced momentarily down at the thin papers—"Kasandra Evanston Barris, died as a result of a car jacking in '03. Her death remains an open case with no real suspect leads. Before that you were in the Marines as part of the Cuban Expeditionary Force in '02, making you one very dangerous guy in your time, although by the looks of you, your conditioning's shot. You gave up smoking and drinking in"—another downward glance—" '06, you have never done drugs more powerful than Extra-strength Tylenol, you had a broken arm when you were seven, and you have never had your appendix out." Olivia suddenly slammed the folder down on the table. "You didn't 'tumble' to 'Vic' because you haven't a clue what 'tumble' or even 'Victor' means. You weren't infected in November of '09 or any other year for that matter either. The blood running through your veins is 'good soup' as we used to say. In short, Mr. Barris, you're healthy, damn you!"

Michael glanced back toward the door.

"Look at me when I'm talking to you." Olivia used the same powerfully quiet voice her Welsh mother had used on her whenever she even contemplated the least degree of disobedience. It commanded, demanded, and always got both attention and obedience. "Gene here works for me. The man may be a faggot but don't let his manners fool you—he's not only capable but willing to kill you if I say so. There's so much death here now that one more isn't going to matter to anyone—least of all him. There's only one reason you're still able to walk and breathe. I suspect you're valuable somehow, and no one here throws away anything that's valuable, even if they happen to be a lying bastard. I'm even willing to bet that if you remove that rather ridiculous red bandanna from your head, that we'll see something we haven't seen in a long time. So, do you cooperate with me or do I have Gene take care of your worthless carcass?"

Slowly, Michael reached up with his right hand and lifted the sweat-soaked circle of cloth from his head.

Olivia gasped. So often had she seen the red mark of the three interlocked circles branding everyone's head, that it had become a permanent human fixture. Now, Michael's smooth, unmarked brow threatened to take her mind back to kinder times—simpler times. She had to shake her head in a sudden shudder to bring her back to the present.

"Good Lord!" Gene whispered. He, too, had become suddenly entranced by Michael's clear forehead—so much so that his hand was actually reaching out tentatively to touch it.

"Gene!" Olivia said, lengthening out the word almost comically. "Get your little pansy ass back over to the door. Remember? You're suppose to be my guardian angel?"

"Oh, sure!" Gene's muscular frame moved easily toward the door as he spoke. "As though *you* need it. This has been one of the most 'butch' performances I've ever been privileged to witness from you. Are you sure you're not playing for the wrong team, Olivia?"

"Oh, thanks, Gene! Let's just leave dykedom out of this for the time being."

Michael blinked at them, bewildered.

"Look at this, Gene! I swear, the man is going to need a translator!" Olivia smiled rather coldly at Michael. "What is it you really want, Mr. Michael Albert Barris? First of all, how did you avoid getting branded?"

"I . . . I couldn't get the brand," Michael stammered. "I mean, it wasn't that I wasn't willing; it's just that I had to be sure I was coming to the right ERIS center. That meant sneaking onto the train directly rather than going through the branding process. If I'd allowed myself to go through the system, there's no way I could be certain I'd come to the Wah Wah camps."

Olivia leaned forward, perched on the edge of the table. "And why, Mr. Beverly Hills Barris, was it so urgent that you fight your way into this graveyard?"

Michael hesitated.

"Mr. Barris?"

"I'm looking for someone."

"Really?" She spoke coolly. "Anyone in particular?"

"Yes. My son."

Olivia rolled her eyes up in disbelief. "Oh, God!" she exclaimed, jumping down from the table and pacing the room.

"No, really." Michael, tired as he was, became suddenly animated. "Look, my son was taken last February somewhere in Arizona—I think. They took him directly to the ERIS Quarantine Center in Las Vegas. My sources tell me . . ."

"Your sources!"

". . . that he was sent to the District 6, 477 ERIS camps—the Newhouse Center to be exact. Most of that was easy, but the ERIS Command is terribly tight-lipped about its operations. This was the last transport being sent to this camp—so it was now or never. I figured if I could just find my son . . . talk to him . . ."

Olivia suddenly turned on him. "Then everything would be just like the happy ending to a nursery story. Did you ever think that your sources might have been wrong? This kid"—she grabbed the folder from the table and eyed it feverishly—"this Jason Lee Barris is your son, and you say he's in the centers. Is he straight, bi, or gay?"

Michael blinked as though he'd just been hit unexpectedly by a damp mop. All he could manage was an indescript sound of "Ahhhhh."

"Well, is he straight, bi, or gay?"

Michael looked away again. "He's gay."

Olivia turned to her assistant. "Gene, have you ever heard of this Jason Lee Barris?"

"Well, now, ma'am, you know how crowded it is over in Z block. It might take me awhile just to find out if he's in there or not."

Olivia had begun waving her hand during the middle of his reply. "Fine, fine! You go ask the Dark Queen for permission to tell us one way or the other—Sweet Mary, Gene, don't you ever do anything on your own?"

Michael interrupted. "Excuse me, the 'Dark Queen'?"

Olivia turned back to him. "Yes, deary, the Dark Queen. None of us hetros are supposed to know who he is. He runs things over in the G/L barracks—oh, don't look so pathetically baffled, that's Gay/Lesbian barracks to you. He occasionally holds court—God only knows where. The man's got ears in every corner of this camp and is supreme ruler of the X, Y, and Z blocks in the compound—believe *that* no matter what the Right Reverend Weston may say to the contrary. If your son's gay, he's in one of those blocks, and if he's in one of those blocks, then you'd best stay the hell away from him. Hetros like yourself go poking about Z block and all that happens is that the body count escalates."

She suddenly noticed the deep pain in Michael's eyes. *Grand,* she thought, *another bleeding tragedy for me to sort out.* "Check back with me. Gene here is a spy for the Dark Queen . . ."

"Well, I never!" Gene chirped.

". . . and he'll find some sneaky way to let me know if your son's in the camp. Don't get your hopes up. There are at least twelve other camps in this valley—maybe even a few more up the way that we can't see—and there is no guarantee that your boy didn't end up in one of those camps even if he did end up in this one ERIS grouping. Of course, whether he did or not isn't going to make any difference now."

"Why?" The long day was beginning to show on Michael's face. "What do you mean?"

"This is the end of your road, Mr. Barris. If he isn't here, that's it. There's only two ways I know of out of this camp: getting a ticket to the NIH research facility, which is about as likely as you sprouting wings or just dying on your own. How did you figure you'd get out of here anyway?"

"I . . . well, I hadn't worked all of that out." Michael's brow furrowed. "I thought that you, as medical head of the facility would let the ERIS command people know that I wasn't infected, and they would pull me out of the camps. What's so funny?"

Olivia continued her dark chuckle. "Deary, almost five percent of the people brought into this camp don't have the V-CIDS virus when they arrive. Most of those aren't even sick."

Michael blinked again, trying to concentrate on what she was saying.

Olivia brandished the folder aloft, jabbing at it as she made each point. "How do you think I know so much about you? How do you think I came by such information? Do you see any I-Net access in this room? Do you even see a machine capable of such communication? I got this from Reverend Weston himself today— and he got it from ERIS Central."

"You mean . . ."

"Yes, bright boy," Olivia smiled. "They already know you're here. They know all about you, Mr. Television Executive. You're here only because they want you here."

Michael drew in a long breath.

Olivia smiled sadly. "Welcome to my parlor said the spider to the fly."

The Reverend and the Bulldog

4

Tuesday, April 13, 2010 / 1947 hrs
The Cathedral
Newhouse Center / 477th ERIS District
Wah Wah Valley, West Beaver County, Utah

The night air was chill as Michael and the nurse walked up the dimly lit road, a third large figure following a few steps behind. Darkness had fully descended, yet the street—if the wide dirt path could be called that—was still filled with people shuffling about. Processing the new internees had taken the bulk of the day, and many were only now finding their newly assigned quarters. Lamps made a pretense of lighting the way between the buildings. They stood as dim sentinels to either side. Many of the windows were lit with the same dull glow. Not even the light was warm—it did not burn from an incandescent bulb but shone coldly from optic network emitters. Michael's breath drifted around him as he walked into their hanging puffs of spent steam.

Michael wound his way up the gentle slope between the dark figures milling in the road. He was unable to catch the eye of a single person as he moved, everyone else seemingly fascinated by the freezing dust underfoot.

"Thank you for showing me the way," he said idly.

"Not at all." Nurse Codgebury spoke flatly, meaning every

word. "I've been instructed by the reverend to deliver you when I was finished. We'd been worried you were here for some nefarious purpose—I suspect it was that Marine entry that spooked Weston. Now I know you've come for simple, sentimental reasons, stupidly misguided as they may be. I doubt you'll give us any trouble, Mr. Barris. We may even be able to help you with your little personal quest."

"Thank you, Nurse." Michael stopped and sighed a great cloud of breath. The lights in the windows continued their cold glow into the night. Only then, through the shuffling crowd around him, did he notice the dark figures slumped against the foundations of the buildings. Sometimes singly but often in twos and threes huddled together. Michael was touched by the companionship evident in the way they so peacefully leaned into each other. "By the way, shouldn't you do something about those people?"

Frozen as the night was, the words of Nurse Codgebury beside him were colder still.

"If you can wake them up, you're welcome to move them back inside. They aren't asleep, Mr. Barris—they're dead."

"They're— my God! You can't be serious!"

Nurse Codgebury didn't meet Michael's eyes, her gaze remaining vaguely directed toward the still figures against the wall. "Each night we lose about one percent of the camp to any number of minor diseases. Reverend Weston's group estimates the maximum capacity of this camp to be about twelve thousand people. That equates to approximately one to two hundred people each night. ERIS sends a pallet every morning to pick them up and drag them down to that central facility a couple miles west of here in the bottom of the valley. The Ranch they call it. They must be doing quite a business—smoke is pouring out of that thing all the time. Occasionally, the wind shifts drastically, and the smell drifts over the camp like . . . hey, you all right?"

Michael was paler than even the frigid light of the optic emitters could account for. "All these people are dying from V-CIDS?"

"No, all these people are dying from the most common of diseases and maladies—colds or flu mostly."

"Colds or flu?" Michael was astonished. "Two hundred people a night from colds? How can you stand to . . ."

"Mr. Barris, this is an ERIS Quarantine camp for convicted V-CIDs carriers. Here, you're either dead, dying, crazy, or just don't care. Death and crazy hold little appeal to me."

"But you're a doctor—well, medical professional at any rate!" Codgebury didn't even flinch at his words. "I'd have thought that you'd *have* to care!"

"Gene?" Codgebury's gaze didn't shift. "Isn't that Richard Hengrath?"

Michael felt Gene's shadow cover him. Silhouetted against the bare lamp, the tall man looked like a harbinger of death himself.

"Yes, Ms. Codgebury. I believe it is."

The small woman's lips drew tight as she started again to walk up the roadway. Michael followed quickly as did Gene. "I'd better go tell Patty Hengrath her husband's died. She's over in the women's barracks, somewhere in 12-F, isn't she?"

Gene shook his head. "You can't be in the compound at night without me."

Michael watched Codgebury's smile appear intermittently between the passing downcast faces as they continued up the dry dirt road. The number of people around them were rapidly dwindling.

"How chivalrous of you, Gene," she said grimly. "Are you acting on behalf of the Queen or the greater interests of the governor reverend?"

Gene gave no reply.

"No matter," she continued. "Once you've seen my virgin self safely home, you can tend to it. I've a list of others that will need to be notified as well. You're going to have another busy night."

The road opened onto a large clearing reminiscent of a town square but which, in fact, had little in common with the name. Firstly, it wasn't square, but a roundabout, similar to those circuses that were so common in Europe. The road branched into two dimly lit streets lined by row after row of barracks. To his right, the large Commons, as he had heard them call it, curved around in nearly a half circle. To his left, a smaller building curved around the circle as well, bearing the stencil-sprayed lettering "ADMINISTRATION." Small, decorative lava rock filled the garden area in the center of the circle. Across from that, set between the fork in the two roads, was a large, barnlike building. Its large barn doors were open, light spilling into the circle.

The nurse changed course slightly and began crossing the lava rock directly toward the open doors.

"Patty Hengrath lost her child last week. This isn't going to go well with her." Codgebury continued to talk, somehow knowing that Gene would be listening to each of her instructions. "You'd better take along some strong help so she doesn't create too large a fuss in the women's complex. Let me see, what else? Oh, yes. Five children died in the nursery this morning; the Ladies Aid Society worker on duty broke down and ran from the Hospice—I think her name is Mrs. Barker from somewhere in G block. See how she's doing, and find someone to take her shift tomorrow . . ."

Michael stopped for a moment while Nurse Codgebury continued her clinical litany of the dead. The barracks were dark hulks against the clear April sky, which shone overhead with brilliant intensity. He marveled at the glory blazing above him. He remembered, for a moment, the times when he would lay out on the front lawn of their Minnesota home, his grandmother's blanket spread beneath them, and spend hours talking while they looked at the stars. They had seemed glorious and beckoning to him then; yet they couldn't compare to the clarity and glory of the desert sky unfettered by smog and bright city lights. He puzzled for a moment at a smudgy band of dim luminance that crossed the sky until he suddenly, wondrously realized that it was the Milky Way.

There was something about those stars—so high above this hell into which he had fallen, so untouched by death, that seemed to call to him. The stars were speaking to him, and he couldn't hear. There was a poem or song, he thought, in the back of his mind, but the words were muttered by the starlight as dim and unclear as the Milky Way overhead.

"Mr. Barris?"

Michael's mind, soaring among the stars, suddenly fell back to reality. "Yes?"

Olivia Codgebury looked at him carefully. "The reverend wishes to see you now. Are you sure you are all right?"

"I thought you didn't care?" Michael said as he turned toward the open door.

"Make no mistake, Mr. Barris," she said evenly. "I don't."

Michael braced himself for a moment before entering. He'd tried lying to these people: it hadn't worked. He'd tried being openly honest with them: it had left him vulnerable. He was walking into the center of hell. He wouldn't make either mistake again.

". . . were separated at the last stop. I don't know how it happened but we were. Kevin went to see about getting some blankets or something for the children—they were so cold in the morning, you see. We stayed where we were, waiting just where he said to but he didn't come back before they forced us onto the . . . the . . . oh, you know! . . . onto those . . ."

Nurse Codgebury had called it the Cathedral, and, Michael supposed as he entered the hall, they probably weren't far wrong about that. It was a barnlike structure with a high-vaulted ceiling. Rows of smoothly painted benches sat in two neat rows on either side. Powerful optic lamps lit the room from just below the rafters better than any he had seen in the camps so far. Michael guessed that the building had originally been intended as some sort of community meeting hall and may still serve that purpose from time to time, but the trappings now had a distinctly religious bent to them. There was a plywood altar on the elevated platform at the far end. A cross had been assembled and mounted to the far wall. The reverend had apparently other uses for the building in mind.

At the far end of the large room, in front of the altar, a woman and two small boys stood with their backs to Michael. The woman's voice was reasonably factual in tone, but there was an hysterical edge to it that belied the panic raging inside her.

Beyond her, behind the altar, the Reverend Quinton Weston sat on a rough-hewn chair, listening with his eyes closed. He only spoke occasionally; more, it seemed to Michael to encourage the woman to get on with her story than out of any real concern.

"Grav trains, sister. They are called grav trains. Please do go on."

"Well, we were forced onto the, uh, grav trains, and I haven't seen Kevin since. I don't even know if he got on the train. It isn't like Kevin. He was so concerned about the boys that he just had to do something. Isn't there any way you can find him?"

Michael sat down on one of the back benches to await his audience. Somehow he hoped to himself that his indiscretion during the reverend's previous speech would somehow be forgotten. It was then that he noticed the huge man leaning in the shadowy corner of the hall, not far from the reverend.

The reverend, sensing that the woman had finally come to the point, opened his eyes and moved forward in his chair. "Sister—Barns, isn't it?—Sister Barns, we are doing everything we can to help you with your problem. Please understand that this camp, as with many of the ERIS centers, is very large and understaffed. We do what we can to help our people, but especially on new arrival days there is always some confusion. Currently, there are nearly twelve thousand people in Newhouse Center alone. We have no computers here—all our records must be kept on paper, and so mistakes are inevitable."

Michael listened to the preacher lecture the woman in soothing tones, but kept his eye on the large man. Even in shadow as he was, his eyes still shone brightly, not so much with intelligence, Michael thought, but more with intensity. Those were the eyes of a hawk.

"So, Sister Barns, my advice is to just be patient. Our experience is that these things tend to sort themselves out after a few days. Your Kevin will probably surface from being misplaced in the single men's barracks, and you'll be able to get on with your life together. In the meantime"—the reverend looked down over his glasses as he leafed through several pages on his too full clipboard—"we can assign you and your boys to 17-L, Room 2B. There's another family in that room right now, but it will only be temporary housing until we find your husband. In the meanwhile, it will give you a place to lay your children down and get some rest yourself."

The reverend smiled graciously as he looked up at her. She didn't budge, however, and answered him with a cold and determined look.

"Oh, please Mrs. Barns, be reasonable," Weston sighed, folding the clipboard into his lap. "We'll find out what has happened to your husband. It's just going to take some patience on your part."

Michael noticed the woman's shoulders fall slightly in submission. She murmured a "thank you" and turned cradling one boy under each arm. They walked back down the aisle past Michael, all three of them turning to look at him as they passed. As though through some unseen signal, the light in all of their eyes dimmed to shocked resignation beneath the three red circles on their foreheads as he watched them pass.

It was like watching three people die.

"Mr. Barris" came the warm, chilling tones of the reverend. "I believe you are the last problem I have to deal with tonight."

Michael felt the eyes of the hawk focused at once upon him. He stood slowly and walked between the benches toward the altar and Reverend Weston.

"Reverend, how did you come to become governor of this center?" Michael had been in broadcasting enough to know how to make his voice heard. His words carried through the hall. "Were you elected? If so, by whom?"

"Mr. Barris, you need not concern yourself with that." Weston changed gears into his "strict father" tone of sin proclamation and denouncement, giving Michael what he probably considered to be a withering gaze over his glasses. "Of more importance is what we are going to do with you. Why has such an important figure in interactive television networks decided to grace our little camp?"

Michael continued to walk forward casually, his hands in his pockets. "Then, if you weren't elected, you must have been appointed. Who appointed you?"

"God appointed me to my ministry, if that's what you mean." Weston eyed him cautiously. "Have you come here to ask questions? It will do you no good, you know. Any answers you may get will just die with you in this camp—right along with the rest of us."

Michael smiled. "True enough—so why am I here?"

"Only you know the answer to that, Mr. Barris!" the reverend snapped irritably.

Movement caught the corner of Michael's eye. The shadowed

man had moved. He was no longer leaning against the wall but was standing with his arms across his chest.

"Also true. I'm looking for someone—my reasons for doing so are my own," Michael said cautiously. He was being strong-armed subtly and didn't like it. These men were dangerous, he knew. Perhaps, he thought, he needed to hold his cards a little closer to his chest until he knew the rules of the game better. "When I find them, then my reason for being here will be complete and, I should think, obvious."

"Ah," said Reverend Weston as he stood behind the altar and walked around it. The reverend stepped off the platform and moved conspiratorially close to Michael. Too close for his liking. The man's breath was even more repulsive than his smell. A vision of the Cathedral Hall during the heat of day reminded him something of an oven. It may indeed have been a long day for the reverend. Yet the man's closeness was itself a challenge. Michael resisted urgently the strong desire to take a step back. To do so would be to demonstrate weakness—something he sensed he couldn't afford with this man nor the silent man in the corner. So he let the red face of the balding man fill his vision and allowed the stinking breath to wash over his own face in gusty waves.

"We may be in a position to help you there, Mr. Barris. As appointed governor of Newhouse Center, I pretty much know where everyone is in our little village."

Michael held his ground, speaking into the reverend's close face with tones of intrigue equal to his host's. "I thought you just told 'Sister' Barns that her husband was lost in your paper shuffle?"

"Ah, yes, sadly that was something of a misstatement on my part." The reverend smiled sadly back at him. "Her husband has been dead since seven o'clock this morning."

Michael blinked, staring into the cherubic face that suddenly in his mind had turned into an infinitely dark well. For a moment his concentration wavered, but he regained it with a vengeance. *Don't let them take you!* he thought. The reverend's eyes were searching his face for the weakness he would not allow to be seen.

The reverend looked away first.

"Quite tragic, really," Weston said, shaking his head as he sat down on the foremost bench in the room. "As I understand it, he had gone in search of blankets for his ailing sons. Like yourself, Mr. Barns was not V-CIDs positive, though his wife and children are. When the officer in charge refused to hear his complaints, well, he just snapped." He snapped his fingers in graphic demonstration. The sound he had made seemed to startle even the reverend. Weston turned to look at his fingers.

As though the right hand knoweth not what the left hand doeth, Michael thought.

"Please, Mr. Barris—may I call you Michael or do you prefer Mike? Michael it is, then. Michael, please sit and let's talk man to man for a moment." Michael followed the reverend's gesturing hand to the bench opposite his own.

Weston inhaled deeply and continued. "It happens sometimes. He was making such an unreasonable fuss that the group around him was getting agitated. He forced the duty guards to kill him, really. He left them no choice."

As Michael listened, he sensed the reverend building a sermon to him. He wondered for a moment if the sermon was the point of this encounter or whether the reverend, just out of habit, was weaving the lecture out of their conversation. It was difficult to judge. Other things were distracting Michael's attention: most notably the fact that the large man had quietly left the corner. Michael could sense the hulk moving closer behind him.

"We all have choices," Weston intoned solemnly. "We can either cooperate—with a chance to beat this thing—or we can fight authority and simply add to the tragedy. So, in the final analysis, Michael, whatever your reasons, you are the one who must choose. What kind of man are you, Michael? Are you the kind of man who looks for trouble on a sunny day? I'd rather think you were the kind of man who would help us build a better America—perhaps even a better world out of so much tragedy. If that is the kind of man you are, then I feel sure I can help you."

"Well, Reverend—may I call you Quinton or do you prefer Quint?" Michael replied straight-faced.

"Most prefer to call me Reverend or Father." Weston's smile was relaxed, but Michael's glib words had kindled a cold fire behind the eyes. "I'm fairly nondenominational and informal about such things."

"Well, Reverend," Michael spoke with practiced ease, "you haven't introduced me to your friend yet. He's standing close enough now to touch me if he wants to, and I'd prefer to be formally introduced before he asks me to dance with him."

Reverend Weston hesitated only a moment. Michael saw the eyes flick to the figure he knew was behind him for confirmation before he spoke. "Of course, how rude of me. Michael, this is Will Bullock—a member of the Administrative Council in this camp."

Michael turned slowly with forced casualness. The man was wide-shouldered and muscular, though his beer belly, which he had apparently spent many summers accumulating, remained as something of a sad legacy. The broad red face was topped by raggedly crew-cut rust hair. His appearance seemed oxlike, yet his movement was graceful and easy despite his apparent mass. Then there were those gray eyes that told an even deeper story. There was real cunning there.

"So, I'm being called Michael, and the reverend now has a name. What do I call you?"

"Bulldog."

Michael nodded. "Simple, direct. I like it. What is it you do around here, Bulldog?"

"I fix problems, Barris. Any problems the reverend here sees fit to correct." The gargantuan arms folded again across the massive chest. A Cheshire grin split the wide face. Bullock towered over Michael as he sat.

"I'm sure you do, Bull," Michael replied carefully.

Bullock's smile fell into an intense scowl. "It's Bullock or Bulldog, Barris! No one ever calls me—"

Weston spoke suddenly, drawing Michael back around to face the minister. "Michael, we're here to help. ERIS has their hands full taking care of hundreds of camps like this one. Inside the gravity fence is left pretty much up to us. We need help to keep our civilization in order. We need help from people like you, Michael, to maintain the standards and values that make America great. Scratch my back and I'll scratch yours. Do we have a deal?"

"I'll do everything I can to help," Michael said.

"That's all we ask." Weston smiled as he stood. "You son is, indeed, in this camp, Michael—in Barracks 10-Y-2D or E, if memory serves me correctly. If you have not yet been so informed, that's in the very heart of that collection of homosexuals and perverts known as the G/L blocks. You would be well advised to avoid entering that area alone, especially during evening and nighttime hours."

"You consider it a dangerous place, then?"

The reverend leaned back, looking for words among the rafters of the Cathedral. "Michael, most of the people in this camp are decent folks. They were hardworking people who were caught up in V-CIDS through no fault of their own. They are the innocents. They are the true victims here. Such is not the case with the perverted heathens in the G/L blocks. They *caused* this, Michael. V-CIDS came from them—they spawned it. They are the ones who are in need of punishment! They are the ones who have brought this curse on us all. It is a judgment from God, and it is his justice that we administer in this camp. The sodomite corrupt are kept strictly separate from the righteous here, Michael. They stay within the law and boundaries we have set for them."

"And if they don't?" Michael asked quietly.

"Then, their punishment is sure if not swift."

"You murder them?" Michael's voice sounded strangely calm in his own ears.

"We execute them as publicly and as painfully as possible," the reverend said easily. "It has proven to be a most effective deterrent. They are, after all, not *really* human like you and I. They have squandered away their humanity on their own carnal and base desires. Our policy just keeps the animals in their place."

Michael couldn't decide whether to laugh or choke at the vile absurdity of the statement. "I take it that these, uh, animals, don't much care for your policy. That's why the G/L barracks are avoided?"

"It is, indeed, a dangerous place, Michael. Not even Brother Bullock here goes in there at night. However, I suspect that you will, indeed, enter into that unholy flock to find such a wayward son." The reverend leaned forward, the cold fire again alight in his eyes. "And when you do, you will, of course, let us know anything you may hear that may be of use to us. There are certain deviant elements in this camp—centered in those blocks—which would propose to bring about the destruction of our entire social order. Their unenlightened and pagan viewpoints are contrary not only to our traditional values but the will of God. If you were to hear of any such elements meeting or where their leaders might be found, would you keep such knowledge from us? Would you perpetuate disharmony and destructive evil in our midst?"

Michael looked up into the minister's face. *This man is foreign to me,* he thought. *He's speaking a language that I can barely understand.* Acutely aware of his danger, Michael reached into his mind, trying to construct a sentence that would be in a similar language to what he was hearing and yet would convey what he felt. It took a few moments before he could compose and deliver it properly.

"I'll do everything I can to serve God's people," he heard himself say.

That night, Michael believed he had understood clearly the meaning of his own words.

He was wrong.

The Powers That Be

5

Tuesday, April 13, 2010 / 2110 hrs
Command & Control Center / 477th ERIS District Command
Milford, West Beaver County, Utah

"*. . . traditional values but the will of God. If you were to hear of any such elements meeting or where their leaders might be found, would you keep such knowledge from us? Would you perpetuate disharmony and destructive evil in our midst?*"

The words rang with slight distortion into the dark space enclosed by glass. Distant glimmers of monitor screens and the Christmas-colored dance of control panel lights were the brightest lighting in the dim room beyond the glass, whose main features were three large projection screens. On the center and largest of these screens was projected a map of the Wah Wah Valley with several triangles branching from what appeared to be roads. Within the glass room itself, panel lights from the sweeping arch of the console illuminated the two uniformed men from below, giving them a sinister aspect. They were silent as they absorbed everything that was taking place some thirty miles distant to the west.

"*I'll do everything I can to serve God's people.*"

"Seems OK to me, Colonel," said the younger man. His uniform was somewhat rumpled, a sharp contrast with his superior officer standing next to him. "I don't think he's going to be much of a problem."

"Captain, first rule around here is to never underestimate the dead." The colonel reached for the jar on his desk and selected a mint. Its sweetness hung in the slowly circulating, heavily conditioned air in the room. "This Barris fellow broke *in* to the camp system—that means he's looking for something he thinks is here. His story checks out—he does have a son in the camp. If that's all he's looking for, then the only thing he's found is their own joint deaths. However . . . well, damn it, man, you've read the brief on him, haven't you?"

The captain responded at once. "Yes, sir."

The colonel's eyes fixed on the blurry image fed to him through the remote fiber-optic camera. "The man was an executive with the I-Net Television Network before we nationalized communication systems. He's been pretty much running things over there for us since then—done a fine job, too, by all reports. Reasonably cooperative with the FCC mandates and so forth. Still, he used to work in the news division, and I just don't trust anyone even smelling like a reporter."

"You don't suppose he has confederates on the outside, do you, sir?" The captain moved only his eyes to gauge his superior's response.

"Difficult to say, Captain. Difficult indeed. Still, we'll take another look at perimeter security and make sure it's up to the task. I don't want anyone in this military district that doesn't belong." The colonel rolled the mint around in his mouth as he thought. "You're new to this post, aren't you, Captain?"

"Yes, sir. Arrived tonight, sir."

The colonel smiled in the flickering blue-gray light of the screen. "Sharp, son. Very sharp."

They lapsed into silence again, watching the grainy flicker of images on the monitor. Barris stood up, shook hands with the reverend, and quickly left the camera's field of view, only to be followed a moment later by the man identified as Bullock. Reverend Weston, still under the gaze of the monitor, stood silently still for a moment, then turned back under the camera, reaching down for his jacket and a few small items he had left on the chair at the back of the hall.

The colonel reached forward and touched a button on the console. "Governor, this is Overlord. That was fine, Governor Weston, just fine."

The figure on the grainy monitor jerked his head up suddenly in response to the sound. "Yes, sir. Th-thank you, sir. You startled me. I didn't think you'd be monitoring this late."

The colonel let the implications of that slide for the time being. "What is your evaluation of Mr. Barris, Governor?"

The distant distorted voice rumbled in the room. "He is no threat to the harmony of this camp, Overlord. In fact, he may yet be of some use to us here."

"Very well, Governor. My faith in you is as firm as ever. There's only one man I trust to keep this camp under control, and that is you. Keep an eye on Barris for the time being until we are sure of his motives. Otherwise, you've earned yourself a good night's sleep. I am happy to inform you that this is the last allotment of detainees in your camp. The gates are now shut. There will be no more coming."

"Yes, Overlord" came the distant reply.

"I am counting on you to bring these people through this, Reverend. I'm sure you can keep a lid on things until we can develop a cure for you and everyone else in the camp." The colonel's tones were calm and gentle. "CDC tells me that they are going to need a few more test subjects soon, but otherwise what you have is what you are going to keep. Bring them through the fire, Reverend, keep them calm so that they don't hurt themselves or others, and we'll all soon be free to live our lives—right, Father?"

"With God's help, Overlord." The response sounded like it came from the bottom of a well. "I had best be getting on to bed. Tomorrow promises to be a rather long day."

"Of course, Weston. Get on back to your bed and a well-deserved rest. Just remember: we're depending on you to hold everyone together until we're through."

It was difficult to tell from the grainy fiber-optic feed, but the reverend may have smiled just before he left.

The colonel released the contact button, its light dying as he did so. "Amazing, isn't it, Captain. He actually believes it."

"Sir?"

"Damn the dead." The colonel began sucking on the mint in earnest now, as though fortifying himself with its dubious nourishment as he awoke to the captain's presence. "Oh, I forgot, you just arrived. The governor of Newhouse—that reverend fellow— actually believes they're going to make it out of there one day."

"Then, there's no hope for them, sir?" The captain's tired eyes were difficult to read for any emotion.

The colonel shook his head slowly. "Homos, perverts, and leeches, every one of 'em, Captain. They've got the Victor-CIDS— they deserve what's happening to 'em."

The captain could only stare as he spoke. "How long do those people have?"

"How long? Oh, that's easy," said the colonel. His great shadow turned in the dark room to a binder and flipped open its cover. The sound of rustling paper whispered through the room. "Everyone in that camp dies on . . ." His finger passed down the page. "On May 21. That means that they have almost thirty-four days before we pull the plug."

The captain gazed through watery, tired eyes. "Sir? 'Pull the plug'? And what's this business about 'Overlord,' sir?"

"It's all right, Captain: I know you've had a long day." The colonel held up his hand in feeble resignation. "I wish I could give you a little more time. Unfortunately, that isn't going to be possible right now."

The colonel's still upraised hand motioned slightly. The door opened to the room at once. Two large MPs appeared in the instant.

"I'm hearing charges in the morning," the colonel said as he rubbed his face with both hands. "Desertion, sabotage, failure to carry out orders, willful disobedience, and the like. I'll have to get through quite a number of those if the executions are going to be conducted before noon—so I've got to get some rest."

"Executions? Sir!?" There was noticeable stress in the captain's voice.

The colonel continued, pretending not to notice. His eyes

gleamed brightly even in the darkness. "We're here to do an important job, Captain. Perhaps the most important job this country has ever known. For decades now, our country has been sick—sick to the heart with a moral cancer that has destroyed our nation's greatness. There were signs, oh, sure, many signs of the coming downfall, but who could have predicted God's hand in all this? AIDS came to ravage the land, but did we learn from it? No—not a thing. Then came the social programs and V-CIDS. They failed because the people weren't just physically sick, they were spiritually sick as well. The cancer has grown, Captain, until the patient is in danger. We, Captain, are the surgeons. We will cut out the dead flesh of society, and in the end, we shall be stronger and healthier for it."

"Colonel, the people in those camps . . ."

". . . were already dead when they entered the gate," the Colonel finished. "Talk to them, and you're talking to the dead—corpses who just don't know that they've already passed on."

The captain blinked, his ramrod attention beginning to slacken—something the captain had never before allowed in himself. "Sir . . ."

"Your questions will be answered, Captain. These two gentlemen"—he gestured to the MPs standing by the door—"will accompany you to the conference room, where you will read through the operational orders of this command."

"Sir, I—I reviewed the operational orders before I arrived."

The older man's smile blazed white from his shadowed face, even in the dim light of the command center. "Very diligent, Captain. Well, son, you *thought* you reviewed the operational orders. You were mistaken—do you understand?"

"Sir! Yes, sir!" the captain barked.

"Very well." The colonel turned to the two large MPs. "Gentlemen, accompany this man to the conference room under Protocol Omega. Inform me when the gentleman is finished." The colonel turned and sat at the luxurious chair facing the console, pressed the selector, and viewed yet another camp.

The captain sat in a large, windowless room somewhere in the heart of the Command Center. He couldn't remember how long it had been since he had seen daylight. He was wondering if he would ever see it again.

The guards stood to either side of the door. They led the captain here and followed him in—then immediately drew their 9mm semiautomatic side arms, leveling their wide muzzles in his direction. Now the captain sat, occasionally wondering what "Protocol Omega" was, if it had anything to do with the guns leveled at his chest and head, and if he really wanted to find the answer out in the massive loose-leaf books set on the large conference table.

Before him, four oversize binders lay open; each filled with the operational orders of every aspect of the 477th ERIS Camp within the US Army 6th ERIS District. ERIS utilized the latest MCOP-IV programming in their command computers, which cross-referenced automatically all orders for the command. As a result, all entries were fully and carefully cross-referenced between the reports and the standing orders. He continued to stare blankly at the montage of words, paragraphs, graphs, and schematics swimming before him. The tapestry was woven of nightmarish segments that, to him, had begun to reference back to themselves in a loop of frighteningly coherent logic. His eyes would focus from time to time on fragments of the pages. Understanding was dawning red in his mind with each new piece of the puzzle.

One fragment began:

Staff Study Report
Optimum ERIS Camp Design

Problem

Optimization of ERIS (Emergency Relocation & Isolation Service) camp design for the efficient internment and sanitized termination of said camps.

What does "sanitized termination" mean? the captain wondered. He skipped farther down in the report through the *Criteria* section of the staff report.

Criteria
    (1) The solution must meet the goals of Presidential Executive Order #A632294. Specifically, these criteria include (but are not limited to):

    (a) Relocation internment of suspected V-CIDS victims in ~~humane~~ facilities that are safely isolated from designated "free-zone" communities.

A footnote to the crossed-out word "humane" read: "[Change authorization #OVL-Alpha5288]". The captain checked the order, which basically stated that due to problems in defining the word "humane" to the various ERIS region commanders, the word had been eliminated from usage.

The captain returned to his original text.

    (b) Economically viable systems for the ongoing construction and support of such camps in order to minimize the fiscal and industrial capacity exposure of the United States of America.
    (c) Support and Termination procedures for internment camps that will both sanitize the location from the effects of the contamination and provide ERIS personnel the optimum protection from exposure to the V-CIDS virus.

    (2) Details of implementing a solution to the problem may result in conflicts between the goals of several criteria. The solution should represent the optimum solution toward achieving the criteria.

Discussion
    (1) The United States is currently in the grip of a health and medical crisis precipitated by the unexpected autoimmune effects of the V-CIDS virus. V-CIDS is a highly contagious disease spread by direct contact between individuals and, to a lesser extent, via airborne particulate over limited distances. Mortality rates for the virus have not yet been

determined accurately but are believed to be between 97–99.4 percent.

(2) It has been the determination of the President of the United States, in consultation with the National Institute of Health (NIH) and the Centers for Disease Control (CDC) that the isolated relocation of infected citizens is the best case solution to the rapid spread of the V-CIDS virus. Regions for the location of relocation camps were set aside under martial law by the President on Friday, March 13, 2009. These regions are primarily located but not limited to Nevada central desert regions under federal control, eastern California, and Utah except the I-15 corridor and the Salt Lake Metroplex.

(3) It is the stated objective under Presidential Order #632294 to "isolate and contain this (V-CIDS) virus" and "pursue its destruction by the isolation and ~~natural~~ attrition of its carriers until such time as a cure may be found."

The footnote to the crossed-out word "natural" read: "[Change authorization #OVL-Alpha6395]."

Sweat trickled in a single river from the back of the captain's neatly trimmed hairline, burning under his collar to collect in a pool under the shirt of his lower back. "Natural" attrition was no longer a consideration. As if trying to convince himself of something else, he flipped through the second operational book, detailing general orders in the Command Diary, until he came upon #OVL-Alpha6395, double-checked its reference, and scanned down to the applicable section. He read again . . .

IIa. Pursuant to ERIS general directive 977, henceforth, all orders that specifically state "natural attrition" will be modified by striking the word "natural" and read simply "attrition." Specifically, this is to be understood that "forced attrition" [SEE composite command glossary AP-201] will be practiced by this command from time to time as directed by ERIS CinC or in order to meet the various mission goals of each command.

Again, the captain flipped to the composite glossary in the fourth binder to look up "forced attrition."

"My God!" he murmured to himself.

ATTRITION, CAMP: the reduction of ERIS INTERNEE numbers in a camp or camp system through death of the internees. ATTRITION may be either FORCED ATTRITION OR NATURAL ATTRITION. (9/7/09)

ATTRITION, FORCED: the reduction of ERIS INTERNEE numbers in a camp or camp system by means of termination with extreme prejudice. As opposed to NATURAL ATTRITION, which is the gradual reduction in ERIS INTERNEES through natural death or death caused by complications resulting from the V-CIDS virus. (9/7/09)

Termination with extreme prejudice had only one meaning in any military context. Still, he had to be sure. The logs were maintained by an open-architecture computer base that automatically referenced anything entered into it. In the past, he had bemoaned the thorough record keeping as the ultimate in paper proliferation. Even simple order structures became exponentially huge by the time the government-contracted software engine milled it into a completely referenced work. Tonight was different, however. Tonight he needed everything to get a picture of what was actually happening in this command.

Again, he leafed quickly through the pages of the fourth book to the index. The dutifully over-complete referencing software told him that "ATTRITION, FORCED" had nearly four hundred references under its various headings. He drew his clammy finger down the index page, scanning the various headings. Some drew his attention more than others, with titles of "CAMP DESIGN," "PROSCRIBED MEANS," "PROTOCOLS, RECOMMENDED," and "SCHEDULES." He wrote down a few of the reference numbers of each, and turned to them in the various books arrayed before him.

Solutions

(1) Holworth Design Group Concentration Centers provide a system of internment that meets the maximum

needs of the presidential mandate. Each camp design allows not only for the housing and care of the internees but for the termination of each camp when ~~natural~~ attrition requires the sanitation of the campsite itself. The life cycle of these camps would be as follows:

(a) Establishment of the camp-support infrastructure: Concentration Centers would be established around a branching system of AGLL-47M Gravitic Train Guides, which could be laid along any existing road-bed or passage meeting minimum type 8 standards. This would allow Concentration Center establishment along most undeveloped grades not exceeding 15 percent and any developed grades less than category 6 (4-wheel drive). Command and Control Center, Security and Support Companies, Attrition Disposal Facility would serve a number of these camps from a central location.

(b) Relocation Center construction: These camps are located at the terminals of the Gravitic Train Guides. Each is designed in a roughly circular design to maximize the impact of fuel air explosives (FAEs). Created entirely out of wood and flammable materials, this allows command to terminate and sanitize the campsites while minimizing area denial effects for camp replacement.

FAEs? the Captain thought furiously. *They're using fuel air explosives on these camps?* Fuel air bombs were an old but surprisingly simple and effective affair. Every elementary school graduate knows that for a fire to burn, it needs three things: oxygen, fuel to burn, and heat. Take away any of those and the candle goes out. FAEs, on the other hand, operate on the other extreme. If the fuel is flammable enough—oh, say properly atomized nitromethane—and it is mixed with the atmosphere itself in just the right quantities, then the *air itself* becomes explosive. All you need then is one little spark and—pop goes the FAE! The resulting explosion is so effective that the atmospheric blast pressures at the center of some fuel air explosions have been measured *in excess* of atomic bombs.

The camps, by the description in "Camp Design" were made *entirely* out of flammable materials—mostly wood, but even the windowpanes were made of flammable plastic. The fiber-optic audio links were of lower resolution but required *no metal parts* to function. When an FAE was used against such structures, nothing would resist it. Everything—everyone—would burn quite suddenly to the ground . . .

. . . at which time the camp would be considered "sanitized." The charred remains would be bulldozed under within two days. A new camp, the specifications noted, could be delivered and operational within ten days to the same site.

My God! the captain thought, sweat streaming down his face. *The Nazis were bush league amateurs compared to this!*

The question came again to him as it had before: why? Why kill them? Why not just build more camps if they were building the buildings anyway? And, as before, the answer hovered before him as he turned back and found Directive 977.

1. WHEREAS the operations budget for support of the camp system is fixed under the general emergency funds allocation #726265 on an annual basis and whereas the transfer funds under the Global Health Act of 2004 having been exhausted in 2008 and
2. WHEREAS the President of the United States has determined that other methods of funding will be detrimental to the security of the United States of America under the Fiscal Security Act of 1998 and
3. THEREFORE IT IS SO ORDERED that the maximum number of camps established under Presidential Order #A632294 shall be twelve (12) per ERIS district and that the maximum number of districts operational shall be forty-five (45).

So the government wasn't building any more camps because they couldn't afford to maintain them? That didn't make sense: they were the lousy government, they could just print more bills, couldn't they?

In any event, section 4 of 977 was the most telling.

4. All Internees are decreed to be "predeceased" for all legal purposes of the applicable laws of the United States of America. Such appellation shall be defined as follows: Predeceased persons are those who are diagnosed as terminal and whose presence and proximity would endanger the general populace. Predeceased persons are to be considered dead for all purposes of law until such time as their status may be reversed. Predeceased persons may be subject to Forced Attrition in order to satisfy the support requirements of individual ERIS districts and to avoid overcrowding and taxing of facilities due to the arrival of additional internees. The stated purpose of Presidential Order #A623394 is to preserve the health of the general populace before pursuing the health of the internees. Forced Attrition of surplus internees is therefore ordered as an operational imperative.

Predeceased? The internees were to be considered casualties before the fact just because they couldn't build any more huts in the desert? The camps themselves were set up so cleanly, were filled so quickly, and then could kill so efficiently. All for the good of the general populace. All for the good of . . .

Just how many people were they talking about? He turned the book to the combined internee processing chart.

Internment Ledger
(To Date)

Operational Start Date: April 20, 2009
Last Reporting Date: March 31, 2010

Internees Processed to Date	410,035
Current Internee Total	158,475
~~**Natural**~~ **Attrition to Date**	251,560
Average Inflow Per Month	13,572
Average ~~Natural~~ Attrition Per Month	13,573

ERIS 477, at maximum capacity, should detain and quarantine 168,896 internees if the twelve camps were filled to capacity. However, the internment general ledger showed the camp as having received and processed over four hundred thousand internees since the district had become operational in April of '09. The inflow and attrition levels were almost identical. Moreover, when he checked the month-by-month performance charts, the attrition rates rose hand in hand with the Inflow rates after the camps had achieved maximum capacity.

One camp was being blown to the ground every two weeks. A new camp had six months before its rotation came around again to be destroyed—whether the internees in them were dead or not. Six months and any predeceased remaining gain a more permanent status. Six months, ready or not, and you have to make room for a new camp to be built on your ashes.

The last ledger indicated an inflow of 23,652 for the previous month.

The attrition rate was listed as 23,654.

If the 477th was filled to capacity, then the other forty-four districts must be in similar conditions. Directive 977 was issued from the Central ERIS command, so all the districts would be operating under the same rules. He could assume, then, that all forty-five districts had similar attrition figures.

Overall attrition for all camps since they had been established would therefore be in excess of ten million people.

And, of course, the word "natural" was always crossed out.

Down the Abyss

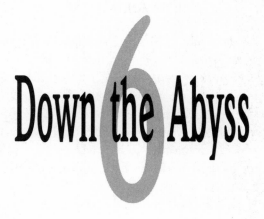

Tuesday, April 13, 2010 / 2133 hrs
Barracks 7-R
Newhouse Center / 477th ERIS District
Wah Wah Valley, West Beaver County, Utah

Barris stepped gratefully back into the chill night air. He drew a deep breath and blew it out slowly, as if somehow it would take with it all the tension and threat he had found in the Cathedral. Yet as the tension left him, so did his strength. He couldn't remember being this tired.

"You left without your barracks assignment, Barris."

The sound of Bullock's voice behind him shot enough adrenaline through Michael to keep him moving. He turned slowly to look up into the tall man's face. "I thought I'd just check into a local hotel for the night. Know one around here that takes American Express?"

"Your plastic ain't no more than that here, Mr. Barris—just plastic. You may be rich as Midas outside them gates, but it won't buy you a cup of warm water from me." Bullock spoke in lazy, almost bored tones. "Your place is in 7-R, bunk E-106 the reverend tells me. Them barracks are across the Recreation Field in Block R. I'll be showin' you the way."

"Well, Bulldog, that's very neighborly of you, but I think I can find it," Michael said with forced casualness. "You wouldn't want to carry my bags, would you?"

Bullock snorted. "Are you always this clever, Barris? I once killed a clever man. Took both hands. I always liked to think that it was his brain that died last." The huge man stepped past Michael without a glance into the nearly deserted camp square. "You'll want my company, Barris. This camp ain't no place to be strollin' about at night."

"Uh-huh." Michael's words were flat, but he followed anyway.

The temperature had dropped precipitously even as the wind had picked up. Michael drew up the collar on his lined jacket and held the front closed as he trotted to catch up with Bulldog. The fiber-optic emitters were woefully inadequate to the task of lighting the "streets" of the camp. They seemed almost pathetic as they dropped from the wooden poles feebly casting their allotment of light on the buildings. It may be just as well, Michael thought. The dark huddled shapes leaning against the walls were growing in number and occasionally their faces were all too plain even in this poor light.

They passed the Commons Building and crossed the large field under the frozen sky, its lights holding place against the gusting wind. Not even his jacket protected him against the April night. Bullock thundered down the slope in front of him apparently more used to the night than Michael was.

The two-story barracks of Block R were neatly spaced with little more than ten feet of clearance between them—thin canyons of blackness that even the emitters didn't seem to penetrate except in small pools of gloom. Bullock marched into one such canyon without looking back and in the moment was lost to Michael's vision.

"Bullock?" Michael called out as he stopped suddenly. "Bulldog?"

Only the sighing wind answered back.

"Shit!" Michael muttered to himself. Somehow the word vented his frustrations. He knew he had to go in and find his precious prescribed bed in his carefully assigned space—some pigeonhole called 7-R, E-106. "Shit!" he said again, and the repeated word somehow began dispelling the black fear that was gripping him. Crazily, he thought of an old locomotive, building up headway as he repeated the words faster and faster with more conviction.

"Shit! Shit! Shit!"

His steam built up, he suddenly plunged into the darkness of the alleyway.

A procession of black walls rose labyrinthian around him, separated by chasms of darkness leading everywhere. *I can't see, damn it!* he thought furiously. *Where the hell is Bullock?*

The huge numbers painted on the building to the right of the intersection couldn't be read. He turned left at a sound of footfalls and began trotting down the alleyway. Black walls rushed past him in his swift gait.

Another intersection and suddenly a broken emitter blinded him for a moment as its light struck him in the eyes undiffused. He looked down the alley to his right and left, but the buildings weren't set exactly on the square and each way only offered the view of another wall. Ahead of him, the alley continued, but he noticed black lumps leaning against the outside walls and knew that his feet couldn't take him that way.

He turned right again, then left, his feet pounding the blackness faster and faster in his rising panic. He turned to the left this time, then right, trying to find some place where his view down the alleys wouldn't be so restricted and he might catch a glimpse of the huge Bulldog somewhere in the maze of Block R.

Suddenly, Bullock's voice floated through the abyss. It rebounded off the darkened walls, echoing seemingly from all directions at once.

"Hey, Barris!"

Michael wheeled, trying to catch the direction of the sound. The voice continued but was distant and incoherent. More on instinct than as any fact, Michael turned around, and ran at full gait down the alley. The blackness closed in around him, the very darkness itself difficult to breathe.

The voice came again—still indistinct yet, he thought, somehow louder—louder to the left. Again he wheeled, now thoroughly confused in the darkness, unsure where he had come from let alone where he was going. He lunged forward again, his legs pumping under him. Rage began building inside him: rage at Bullock for so clearly leaving him behind; rage at himself for being so stupid as to get lost among the buildings; rage at the terror that threatened to take him. The voice was closer now, he was sure of it somehow as he turned the corner again.

Something caught his foot. Michael fell forward . . . forward in an endless motion through darkness. His mind screamed that the ground wouldn't be there, that the darkness of the alleyway would open up under him and he would fall forever down . . . down into the darkness that always threatened to take him. Down into his own grave. An oblivion from which he would never again be known or remembered.

Suddenly, a cold softness broke his fall. His hands outstretched before him slipped between the dark round folds as his face pressed against the yielding obstruction. The chill of the night was nothing compared to the iciness his hands finally closed around. Michael lifted his head . . .

. . . and stared into the foggy gray eyes of the dead.

The woman must not have been more than thirty, yet the face that surrounded the blank, open eyes was blotched. Thick mucus clung in rubbery strings from her nose and gaping mouth. Some of it clung obstinately to his own face as he struggled to press his face away from her frigid, firm breasts. Only then did he notice the other bodies stacked against her that seemed in his burning mind to cling to him as he labored to get himself free of the dead.

Eyes wide, Michael fell backward against the opposite wall. His mouth gulped down the night air. He shuddered suddenly, clawing his face to strip the woman's snot that had come away with him. He sat, shaking in the night that had suddenly seemed colder than he remembered.

After a time, his breath became more regular. Michael simply sat in the darkness, staring at the woman sitting sprawled among the bodies around her. He wondered idly who she had been and who would miss her. Was her mother still living somewhere in the sane world outside? Did she wonder where her daughter was? What would she think of her precious one coming to such an end?

And there was something else, something wrong about her being here.

"My God," Michael murmured aloud to the dead woman. "What are you doing among the men's barracks?"

In response, the corpse next to her spoke.

"She is beautiful, no?"

Michael blinked furiously, his mind reeling.

The corpse stretched a thin hand toward him, beckoning him with its thin wrist. "She is beautiful, as beautiful as I found her. You can have her—I will share."

Michael slowly began to rise, sliding his back up the wall he had fallen against. *This cannot be real! This cannot be real!*

The corpse slipped his right arm under the arms of the woman and stood. The woman's head lolled backward, her gray frosted eyes staring into heaven. The corpse approached Michael in labored steps, dragging the woman's feet, already badly mauled, across the alley toward him.

Michael couldn't move, couldn't accept the reality of it.

The corpse's face came within a foot of his own. It grinned hideously, white teeth gleaming in the night. "She's wonderful! Tasty breasts! Firm thighs! and"—the corpse suddenly giggled like a hyena—"she's most cooperative."

Michael could only manage a single, faltering sound as he shook violently.

A great darkness fell over them. "It's your turn, friend!" the corpse mouthed. "I'll just watch. I'll just help you and . . ."

The corpse's head jerked suddenly upward and to the right. Michael had once stepped on a sheet of plastic packing. The sound didn't seem that different.

The switch had been thrown. The horribly animated dead and his frozen companion both tumbled to the ground at his feet with a quiet wheeze. Still shaking, the darkness reached out and grabbed Michael by his jacket.

"Barris!" Bullock's voice was filled with contempt. Michael suddenly knew the big man had found him. Bullock had seen fear stop Michael cold.

Bullock looked down at the man who Michael had feverishly

assumed had been a corpse—and who now seemed to be obliging his delusion.

"Damn corpse-fucker," Bullock spat. Then he turned back to Michael—who was still held in both the big man's hands. "Barris, it's time I tucked you in your little beddy-bye. You gonna cooperate now?"

Michael couldn't stop shaking—but managed to nod twice.

Michael couldn't make out the number on the building Bullock dragged him to, but was sure it was 7-R. Not that it mattered. All he wanted was to be out of the alleys and into a bed. He needed sleep, although after today he wondered just how welcome his dreams would be.

The door, identical with all the others in Block R, stood at the top of a steep set of wooden steps. This one, however, was open, feeble light spilling into the alley, illuminating the four corpses stacked unceremoniously next to the steps.

Bullock bellowed into the lit opening. "Hey, Sid! Get out here!"

Feet shuffled on the wood-planked floors. In a moment a man appeared, his long, dirty hair silhouetted in the door frame. The man's shirtsleeves were rolled up almost to the edges of his open vest. He stood casually with his hands in his pockets. "Yeah, Bulldog, it's late and we've got things to do. What do ya want?"

Bullock shoved Michael abruptly toward the stairs, speaking in rough, jeering tones. "This is Mr. Michael Barris—he'd like to rent the penthouse suite for the duration of his stay. *He's* got American Express."

Michael looked up at the man standing atop the steep stairs above him. Sid's face was framed by matted hair and a beard that had been far better kept in former times. The face was broad behind the beard, all framing a pair of very large, sleepy eyes. He might have been in his mid-thirties or early forties; his looks made it impossible to tell.

As he watched, two men came up behind Sid, both struggling with the body of yet another man. One of them murmured, " 'Scuse us, Sid." Sid leaned back against the door frame to get out of their way. On the count of two, the men heaved the body onto the pile below and disappeared back into the barracks.

Sid looked down at the corpse and then into Michael's face.

"We have just had a cancellation," Sid said. "It would appear we have room."

Nobody Lives Here

Tuesday, April 13, 2010 / 2133 hrs
Barracks 7-R
Newhouse Center / 477th ERIS District
Wah Wah Valley, West Beaver County, Utah

Sid flattened himself against the wall as Michael tumbled past him into the narrow, softly lit corridor. The hallway was bisected by corridors leading to the left and right. A set of stairs also climbed to the next floor above. The hall itself appeared to run the complete twenty-foot width of the barracks, ending in another door marked "EXIT" in large, red stenciled letters. Otherwise, the walls, floors, and ceilings were bare wood under a gloss finish. The strong odor of chlorine bleach mixed with a hint of the resin finish and a touch of deadly sickness nearly choked him.

"Take a left down the hall, Barris," Sid said as he combed his fingers back through his hair. The gesture did little good, as his thick matted mass resisted the act with all the vehemence of a briar patch. "Your place's down that way. Oh, and, uh, don't mind the smell—you get used to it."

Michael shuddered. The stench was unbelievable, almost physical in its assault. He could believe he was swimming through it as he moved deeper into the corridor. *How many oxygen molecules could exist here?* he thought to himself. Almost at once another thought came to him. *How many people are living here?*

"So," Michael managed to choke out as he lifted his bag over his shoulder. Its weight had increased to become almost unbearable as the day wore on. Now Michael found himself struggling with it as he moved down the hall. "You run this place?"

"Yeah, I run this place." Sid dug his hands down into his Levi pockets, his head tilting up to assume an attitude. "I'm the officially designated den mother of Newhouse 7-R, dutifully appointed by our lord, his holiness, Reverend Weston. Is there some problem?"

"No, sir. Mr. . . . ?" Michael let the word hang in the air like a question mark. Yet the man just let the question hang there, dangling without any hope of support. An uncomfortable eternity passed until Sid shrugged again and spoke.

"Most people call me Sid until they piss me off."

"So . . . what do I call you?"

"Well, you got me outta bed pretty late at night. On the other hand, you seem to have twisted the Bull's tail and, from what I gather, the reverend thinks you're some kind of subversive." A smile cracked amid the scraggly beard. "That counts for something with me. So until you piss me off again—call me Sid."

Michael smiled weakly and wondered vaguely what he'd have to call him if he *did* piss Sid off. He followed Sid's gesturing hand into the left corridor. As he moved down the short hall, he noticed a door in each wall. Even in the dim fiber-optics light spilling from the room ahead of him, he could read the carefully stenciled words on the doors. One said "GAME ROOM," the other, "LIBRARY."

Michael glanced back at Sid. "Library?"

Sid snorted. "Pilgrim, the first thing you gotta learn is not to believe everything you read. In here, don't believe *anything* you read. It requires sort of a gift for translation is all. Just a little compromise of the mind. 'Library' means Sid's room. It's all mine—no one goes in unless I take 'em myself. That's all you need to know."

"The game room—who takes that?" Michael asked.

"Oh, no one sleeps in there. Sometimes people get really inconsiderate and 'crash out' after the body brigade has made their morning rounds."

"Crash-out?"

Sid smiled and shook his head. "Boy, you are new at this, aren't you? It's slang for 'crash and bleed out.' It's when your body finally admits that it's had enough and blows your guts out both ends. You'll learn that people die in all sorts of ways—not like the vids. Some just sort of pass out and never wake up: that's nice when it happens, which ain't often. Usually people leave this ol' world kicking and screaming. Whatever it is that finally nabs 'em . . . Karposi sarcoma, cancer, colds, flu, whatever . . . can often take 'em in a pretty ugly way. Sometimes they just flat out explode with puke and blood everywhere. All that mess they throw about is 'hot' with whatever sickness finally crashed them. Touch that stuff and you can get whatever they had in a heartbeat—pretty serious shit in a place where you can die of the sniffles in about a week. So when a guy starts to go down for the count, we bag 'em and toss 'em in there till night. Down here it's cool enough that they can die in their own time and keep well enough during the day. That's one room we know how to clean. Upstairs is a different problem. It can get to be one hot griddle up there around two in the afternoon. You're lucky Gerry Yeatts checked out today—otherwise I'd have had to put you in one of the ovens upstairs. —Oh, occasionally, there's even a day when no one kicks, and the room remains empty. If no one dies and if someone can actually convince a woman to come into the men's barracks—then the room is used for other things."

Michael stood halfway down the hallway staring at Sid. The man had spoken so calmly, his voice so flat and without emotion. Michael wasn't sure he'd heard him correctly—and was rather fearful at asking for clarification.

Sid chuckled to himself. "Hey, judge not that ye be not judged, baby. There's not much else for recreation at this club." Sid may have had the long hair and beard, but couldn't possibly have been mistaken for a renaissance Jesus any longer. Sid gestured toward the larger room at the end of the hall, then stepped around Michael to lead him forward.

"Suppose we continue the tour." Sid's voice sounded like an operator from one of those long distance phone carriers. The room he entered was about fifteen feet square on a side with five wooden doors leading to the surrounding rooms. Overhead a seven-foot square in the ceiling was filled with a milky white panel, coated with a thin layer of red dust, casting an even, thin light down on the room. Scattered about the room, four or five men lay on the floor or slumped squat against the wall. No one moved as they entered the room nor even so much as lifted their heads.

Sid moved around them as he spoke, gesturing wildly and speaking in smooth, salesman tones. Only Michael seemed to be paying any attention to him.

"The Emergency Relocation Internment Camp-Regency provides the finest accommodations in the world—which, incidentally, ends at the camp's inner perimeter line." Sid recited in his singsong voice, sweeping in exaggerated movements around the room. "Here we have the door to Suite A . . . a smaller accommodation that's about ten by twelve deep. It usually sleeps four—sometimes five or six counting the closet—but since Vance caught the sniffles, we've pretty much left him there to die on his own. The doc thinks it's an Ebola-Reston virus, which means that he'll probably convulse and paint the room with his own blood by the time he 'crashes-out.' We may have to rename it the red room. Still, the nice thing about getting sick around here is that you get to enjoy a lot more spaciousness in your accommodations than you might otherwise get—available for a very limited time only. By the way Mick—it is Mick, isn't it?"

"Michael," he replied in something of a tired daze.

"Right, Mick, like I said, you'll know when you're on your way out when people start giving you all the room you want." Sid's arm swept along the wall. "Here, then, is Suite B, C, and—tah-dah! Suite D for our lucky winner tonight! Jack Friendly, tell him what he's won!"

The old man sat against the wall as Sid reached down and raised his chin. The eyes were feverishly bright yet unfocussed. His slack jaw never moved, and he never uttered a sound.

Sid turned, shrugged and once again thrust his hands deep into his pockets. "The guy's gone toxi on us, Mick. He won't be much of a conversationalist for a while."

The smile lingered at the corners of Sid's mouth, but there was a dark fire in his eyes. He turned and walked slowly and purposefully toward Michael as he spoke, his words with the edge of glass. "Suite D is a six-bunk cell just like B and C. Yeatt's bed is now officially yours, since he's now officially dead. It's the bottom bunk against the outside wall. Community kitchen is closed until seven. You are your own maid service. Everyone does their own laundry, and there's no room service after November of last year. So, do you have any questions?"

Michael sighed. "Just one—where's the bathroom?"

Sid twisted his face again into a smile that spoke volumes without saying anything at all. "The communal bathhouse and toilet facilities are out the door you came in and one building beyond—if you can get that far at night. The public buildings aren't disinfected until six in the morning, and the chance of catching a bug in there increases dramatically throughout the day. I wouldn't go until morning if I were you."

Michael's eyes scanned Sid slowly once more, measuring the man. He felt that he was looking into a deep well—dark and empty. He wondered if there was anything to find in the man's depths but hollow darkness. He nodded tiredly and spoke with a slight chill. "Thanks for the bed, Sid. 'Night."

Michael turned to enter the door marked "D," but Sid's hand flashed to his arm and turned him gently back. He turned to find the lines of Sid's face somehow softer. The steel and ice eyes were averted.

"Ah . . . Michael . . ."

Michael's eyebrows arched as the man used his name.

"We had a guy come through here a couple of weeks ago. He said that the government nuked Houston. I used to live there, and I was just, well, you know . . ."

"Yeah, I know," Michael sighed. "Sorry, Sid, but it's true. The I-Net played it up as a 'surgical strike' to, as they said, 'cauterize a region of acute-and-security-threatening infection.' They claimed that the region was evacuated—lots of I-Net shots of people in evacuation columns beforehand—and everyone on the 'Net bought it. The return approval for the strike was eighty-seven percent with an abstaining rate of only four points. Everyone on the network loved the show. We discovered that the video they used on the net was digitally composited from the Denver Exodus of '06, and the news division wasn't able to find a single one of those supposed evacuees. But, since the net's been nationalized, there wasn't a prayer of getting that information out."

"Lord O' Mighty," Sid whispered. "Didn't anyone do anything?"

"Texas seceded from the Union and is now under blockade. There's been talk about the Mexican army shooting anyone crossing the border into their country. Seventy-six percent of the nation approves of the President's handling of these 'upstart Texans.' "

"Damn this country!" Sid spat the words with venom. "Damn it and everyone in it!"

"Well, Sid, you might damn the country, but it isn't the people's fault, Sid. Remember the I-Net ads back in '03? *Your voice will be heard!* Everyone jumped on what they used to call the 'information highway' at the same time and caused an information traffic jam. With all those people talking at once—who had time to listen? No one's making good decisions these days. Hey, look where I ended up?"

"People make bad decisions—and a city of people die. Well, hell! You'd better turn in. The major achievement for every individual in this camp is finding themselves awake every morning. It's a different world in here—do you think you'll cut it?"

"Yeah, Sid, I think I've got it. 'Library' means no admittance to Sid's room. 'Game room' means place where people either die or try to forget that they are dying. 'Crash-out' means to die in a hard way. 'Exit' means there really isn't one at all."

Michael looked at Sid, and then his eyes drifted upward to the wall behind the long-haired man. Sid turned briefly to follow his gaze, reading the red stenciled words fading on the wall beyond. Huge black gashes of soot had been raked repeatedly across the letters until new words were formed.

DYING ROOM.

Sid chuckled as he followed Michael's gaze to the sign. "You're catching on, Mick. Yes, this is the dying room . . . because no one, but absolutely no one, *lives* here."

Dawning

Wednesday, April 14, 2010 / 0630 hrs
Barracks 7-R
Newhouse Center / 477th ERIS District
Wah Wah Valley, West Beaver County, Utah

The snow drifted down about him. He was cold as he stood only in a long lumberjack shirt. It was night but the moon must have been out, for the tall pinewoods all around him were lit up with bright blue light.

The boy stood on the ridgeline just below him. He was twelve years old, by the look of him—all bundled in a parka and mittens. The coat's hood was drawn up over his head and tied tightly around his face, which remained in shadows. He walked slowly in the snow toward Michael. Each step made a deep impression on the curl of snow that supported him over the abyss below.

"Jason!" Michael's voice rang out brightly and painfully loud in the night.

The boy looked up as if searching for him.

Suddenly, the ledge of snow under him gave way, its grip on the mountain shattered by the sound of Michael's voice. The snow wall crumbled into an avalanche falling quickly away from Michael, carrying Jason with him.

"Jason!" Michael screamed. Yet this time, stubbornly, no sound came. He pressed forward but found his legs plowing through snow quickly rising to his waist. The more he struggled, the deeper and wetter the snow became.

The boy rode the avalanche without making a move, seemingly unaware of the dark fortune engulfing him. Snow billowed around to cover him in waves as his small body cascaded down the face toward an endlessly deep crevasse below.

Michael screamed silently again, reaching out, powerless to reach his son. Powerless to save him. Powerless to join him . . .

"Hey, mister, wake up!"

Michael's eyelids sprang open. Sweat poured off his brow as he surfaced quickly from the nightmare and tried to reorient himself. His arms flailed against the rough blankets covering. His breath pounded into great billowing clouds in the chill air around him.

A face that was not quite a boy nor yet quite that of a man receded from his vision to a safe distance. "Sorry, sir. It's just morning, sir!"

"Who the hell are you?" Michael gasped. *Lord,* he thought, *the air is cold!*

The gaunt figure hunched next to his bed suddenly raised an eyebrow and eyed him askance. "Who do you think I am?"

Michael could only stare at him. His own breath hung between them like a fog.

The boy was probably fifteen: all arms and awkward legs. His hollow eyes looked sideways slyly, as though checking for others paying too close attention to their conversation. The task, it seemed to Michael, should be easy considering that there was no one left in the bunks of the deserted room. The young teen leaned closer to Michael.

"I am Spiritwing, Defender of Truth. It is a secret identity that I carry with me all my days. Only the select have heard me utter it. Only the chosen may know this great secret." The youth whispered a bit too loudly for any real security of this dire classified information. "I am but in disguise now—walking among men in the guise of a common man named William Vanhorne. Use only the name 'John' while I am in this guise."

Another loon, Michael thought, *poor kid.* But he only said slowly, "Right. Forgive me, mighty Spiritwing . . ."

"John," the youth smiled his reminder. "Just call me John when dressed as common men, lest others discern my true identity!"

"Yes, well, forgive me, *John,* but why are you here and where is everyone else?"

The boy awkwardly stood, his long limbs showing all the grace of someone who had recently grown too fast and his reflexes were still trying to catch up. The blond explosion of hair atop the thin face of the boy, too long neglected, now seemed to have a mind of its own. Long strands of it seemed to float without weight in silhouette against the dim light of the window behind him. It was only then that Michael noticed the dark lesions beneath each ear—a bad sign for someone deep in V-CIDS.

"Sid, the Nightshadow and sometimes known as the Puppeteer, has sent me to awaken you and lead you to the morning repast posthaste."

Michael shook his head to clear it with little effect. "What?"

"Hey, it's breakfast, mister-man! You gotta get up to breakfast!"

Michael sat up slowly on the edge of the bed. He'd slept the night in his clothes, too tired to do anything else when he was shown his bunk the night before. Now he was just as glad that he did. *You could hang meat in a room this cold,* he thought then suddenly realized that that was exactly what happened from time to time in the game room.

Michael shook suddenly.

John laughed. "Yeah, it does get pretty cold awful quickly around here when they turn off the heat panels. They usually pull the plug on 'em all across the camp around four in the morning. I guess they figure it'll get us out of the sack quicker. Hey! Come on, mister-man!" The boy suddenly grabbed Michael's arm. "We gotta get up to the Commons quick before breakfast is over!"

Michael snatched his arm free, the anger and adrenaline rush from being leeched onto so unexpectedly by this strange kid suddenly slamming him into a full wakeful state. "Don't do that! I'm not hungry!"

The boy's eyes looked at him with undeterred brightness and a sense of puzzlement. "It ain't the breakfast mister-man! Darn it all to heck, mister-man, if we all had our way, we'd rather not have breakfast here either. It's just that everyone's work assignments are given there, and if you miss yours, you can take all kinds of heat from the Bull!"

Michael looked up from under his eyebrows with his own disbelief. " 'Darn it all to heck'?"

"Oh, sure," John said with as honestly simple an expression on his face as he could muster. "Real superheros don't ever say hell and damn and shit like that. It makes 'em look like assholes when they do."

Michael appeared speechless at this blinding logic. He pushed back the cold leather of his shoes and put them on in silence.

"Hey, mister-man," John said after a few moments. "I really like your bandanna on your head. Is it, like, some kind of statement, or what?"

"Well," muttered Michael, "I guess we all get to have our own little secret identities."

He grabbed his Levi's jacket and stood up.

Dawn had not improved the camp, Michael thought as he hugged himself against the cold. Gazing up between the other three-story buildings surrounding 7-R, all he could see lay in a purplish shadow beneath a bright blue, clear sky overhead.

The dead that had littered the alleyways the night before were now conveniently gone.

Michael had emerged from the barracks with this kid still practically joined to him at the hip. He had, of necessity, found the bathhouse where even the urinals were made of fitted wood and the mirrors were of some kind of plastic. Rows of shower stalls were constructed of wood with each carefully finished in some kind of resin. They were both simple and beautiful to look at—artistic in a reductionist sort of way. He would have liked to examine them closer but the smell of chlorine bleach was overpowering. It's a wonder, he thought, that these people's clothes aren't whiter than they are just from the fumes.

Now both Michael and his newfound sidekick made their way up once more across the packed-dirt expanse of the large recreational field toward the mess and information hall—apparently known as the Commons, as John put it. The boy's chatter never ceased.

" . . . comes in shifts, one every twenty minutes, so you have to eat really quickly. We're SM4—you'll need to remember that— which means that this week we eat at 6:20 A.M. for breakfast and 11:40 A.M. for lunch and once again at 6:40 for dinner. You can look up the schedule on any of the camp notice boards—there's one nailed to every bathhouse. It changes every week, so you gotta be up on the schedule for your group. . . ."

Michael turned at the top of the slope and looked back over the buildings. From here he could see the west side of the valley more clearly. He gauged the gentle slope of the valley to be about ten miles across, but the estimate could easily be wrong even by his own admission. Light filled the west side of the valley on the opposite slope but would not reach Newhouse, he guessed, until late in the morning due to the huge shadow cast by the mountain jutting from the ground directly to the east. The towering, barren face of the peak rose abruptly from the valley floor into the sky no more than a mile or so behind him, blocking the warmth and light of the sun from him.

"What is that down there at the bottom of the valley," Michael asked as he pointed, not even considering where John might be in his discourse.

"Oh, that's called Wah Wah Ranch—beats me as why. The ovens are there, and we also think that . . ."

Michael shuddered at the word. "Ovens?"

John just shrugged. "Yeah, how else can they get rid of all the dead lumber we're producing every night?"

"Lumber?" Michael repeated weakly.

"Oh, Jeez, mister-man, get with it. A guy dies in the night, he's lumber—you know, stiff as a board?"

Thin curls of smoke drifted in faint vertical lines from several other developments in the valley. He could see that there were numerous buildings at these locations as well but could make out no details at this distance. "What about those?"

"Those?" John giggled to himself with a slightly superior edge. "Those are some of the other camps, just like this one. That one

past the ranch on the right is, uh, Kelley's Place. The one to the left is Ranch Springs. That one farther north on the other side—that's Lone Valley or Long Valley—something like that. North of here is Dutchman, and that one south of here, that's Antelope Springs. There's a bunch more, but those are the ones I remember."

"How come you know so much?" Michael asked casually.

"Remember"—John suddenly did his best to look sly and confidential—"I'm Spiritwing, Defender of the Galactic Light. No unseen thing escapes my sight or knowledge!"

Michael was rapidly losing patience. "All right, Wonderboy. Look, I don't suppose that as the crusader of the Galactic Light . . ."

"Defender of the Galactic Light," John corrected earnestly.

". . . that you might have some idea as to where this place is in the United States."

John snorted his derision. "Stupid! We're west of Milford!" he said obviously, and then, shaking his head, the boy stalked up the slope, waving Michael on to follow.

"Great," Michael muttered to himself. "So where the hell is Milford?"

Virgil

Wednesday, April 14, 2010 / 1720 hrs
El Bambi Café / Beaver City
Beaver Valley, Beaver County, Utah

"Virgil! By Gawd! Git yer skinny little butt down here!"

The nasal voice cut across the El Bambi Café like a hunting knife—bright, clean, and sharp. You could take a whetstone to that tone and not come up with a keener edge. The voice was used for urging wayward cattle back into the herd and calling dogs from a mile or two away. There was nothing quiet about the ranch hand's life—a good set of lungs was one of the first things you developed, next to a thick hide and a stubbornness to equal and surpass any critter, wild or domestic, that might have the misfortune of crossing your path.

Virgil snatched the broad-brimmed straw cowboy hat off his head and slapped it several times against his Levi's, raising a small cloud of dust just outside the entrance to the café. Virgil's smile flashed as bright as the sun at noon. With the exception of their rather jagged unevenness, his teeth seemed as though some dentist had just polished them against the deep brown skin of his broad face. His eyes were small and bright, nearly buried behind the habitual and perpetual squint. The black hair had a grayness to it under the tinting of dust and sun. But more than anything else, it was the size of the man that was Virgil's most impressive quality. He wasn't so much overweight as just rolled muscle hung from a huge frame of bones that might have done a Clydesdale horse proud. Virgil was "mountain," meaning that he was as at ease on a rock up on Old Baldy or Big John Flat as any bed in town—not a few of which he had visited from time to time. He could out hunt, out fish, and just about out anything anyone in town. The only sign of decay on Virgil was the slight belly he sported— evidence of a few too many beers, which habit, if left unchecked, might someday blossom into something really pronounced in his profile.

Virgil Wayne Johnston was the wildest of the wild, twenty- three years old and raised mostly by his father, Emmett. His mother was a churchwoman of First Ward who had tried to do her best by her boy, but God had seen fit to take her in a car rollover on I-15. Since that rather unjustified act, neither Emmett nor his boy had quite been on speaking terms with God. Emmett himself finally made up his mind to join his wife and used a twelve-gauge shotgun to hurry the process, whether God thought it was his time or not. Virgil was seventeen at the time. Folks said that Emmett had been drunk out of his mind and that it was a terrible shame. It didn't matter much to Virgil. Emmett had left Virgil two things: an independent will and the knowledge of the mountain which no other person alive possessed.

Of course, Bishop Peters of First Ward took the boy in as an act of charity, hoping that his own four boys might be a saving influ- ence on the Johnston boy. It turned out to be something of a draw. After a two-year-long exercise in frustration and rage, the first of the Peters boys barely managed to keep himself out of trouble enough to go on a mission, and Virgil, now nineteen and his own man, celebrated by going to the Renegade Lounge—and never went back.

In Beaver, there were three kinds of people: church people, which might include those civilized folk of all denominations but which, in reality, meant Mormons. Mormons founded the town and by divine right were its owners—a fact that no amount of questioning by anyone would ever shake.

Then there were the "renegades" or the "wild ones"—usually

from among the youth who sprang into this world only to discover that they had entered it in a place where there was really
nothing to do—interactive television and direct satellite not with-
standing. The Firmage theater—the only screen in town—only
opened once a month now, and no one had ever bothered to equip
it for interactive displays or virtual immersion cinema. All it
played were the old flat screen movies, which were becoming increasingly difficult to find. So the youth either buried themselves in
farmwork and church, or they cruised up and down Main Street
in a time-honored tradition staunchly maintained down the long
years. The truly restless boys wore their outlaw status as something of a badge, gathering at the Renegade Lounge—the one
place you could get a drink and play a little notorious pool in the
town—and were generally too loud, too proud, and too charged
with their own manhood to give many mothers and fathers much
decent sleep when their daughters were loose.

Outsiders might make the mistake of thinking that they could
get some advantage in playing the wild young people against the
church folk or vice versa. It was a mistake not often repeated.
Such ruckuses were always viewed as "nobody else's business" and
were always "kept to ourselves."

The reason for this was the "outsiders" themselves. The only
thing that the good church people and the renegades had in common was their mutual disdain for outsiders. The term was reserved for anyone who hadn't been born, bred, and raised in the
rocky ground that relinquished crops in the Beaver Valley only
under the greatest of protests. Outsiders might on first blush find
in Beaver a friendly community and its people genuinely kind, but
after a while even the dullest of visitors would discover a silent
and invisible barrier beyond which it was impossible to become
part of the community. Whether wild or righteous, everyone in
Beaver maintained the quiet and unspoken circling of the wagons
that had become a way of life. It was as old as their pioneer an-
cestors who fled religious persecution in the east; they haven't
trusted such outsiders since.

The line is razor-sharp and hard as a rifle's blue steel.

Virgil swung his hat back on his head, giving a quick brush
with his hands in a vain apology to the brim of his hat. The brim

continued to hold its shape only by the thinnest margin of effort. In quick succession, the pointed-toe boots crossed the linoleum tile in the bowlegged swagger that apologized for nothing.

"Well, Harl, you som'bitch," Virgil rumbled in a deep bass that would never be trained to sing anything presentable in mixed company. "What are you doin' sittin' here with these other horse-faced mama's boys?"

Virgil didn't deign to notice the other patrons in the café as he strolled past them, his own voice booming entirely too loud for the confined space. If he noticed the tension rising in the booths as he passed, he didn't let on.

Harlan Murphy's smile was trouble easily recognized by the other locals in the café. He was in the booth with the Lowell and Louis McNeil twins. Outsiders who crossed paths with any one of those boys alone might think they had encountered one of the shyest and most polite people they ever met. They might even think that the "cowboy" they encountered was sensitive and "well in touch with his feminine side." Voicing of such an opinion, however, would be a mistake, and the consequences might not be questioned in any court in the county.

By themselves they were just considered one of "those boys." However, put more than one of them together in any one place and there could be hell to pay. Several cups of coffee were hurried along, and a few burgers were downed a bit quicker than might otherwise have been expected. Quietly and without a fuss, the El Bambi began emptying very quickly.

"You look like a sack o' shit left out in the rain!" Louis chirped. The laughter in his voice almost had an hysterical edge to it. "Where have you been the last week, Virg?"

Virgil flopped back into the newly vacated booth opposite Harlan. A half-eaten burger and some cold fries remained on the plate. Virgil casually reached over, smelled at the sandwich, and started downing it. The act left his diction slurred. Some muffled syllables tumbled from his mouth, accompanied by a number of bread crumbs.

"What you say, Virg?"

Lowell punched his brother in the arm. "Shut up, Louis! Let the man eat, will ya?"

Virgil tossed the rest of the burger down in a single shot, gave a moment's contemplation, and then gave a belch that shook the windows. "Damn local beef tastes like shit!" Virgil pronounced the last with the characteristic drawl that pulled the word into a form which sounded more like "shee-it." "Might as well be venison for all the game to it. What are them boys out at Parkinson's feedin' them cattle these days: tree bark?"

"Ah, Virg"—Harlan tipped his own hat back on his head and leaned over the table—"thar ain't been no decent feed supplements since the interstate's shut down. The Ag department rep says that all the decent feed is being sent to the Midwest."

Virgil tossed a handful of cold fries at Harlan. "That's bullshit, Harl. Just plain bullshit. It's on account of Milford, ain't it?"

Harlan took his hat off and scratched at his head. The distraction didn't fool Virgil for a moment. Both the McNeils were looking down at the table as well.

"Well," Virgil demanded, "it's Milford, ain't it?"

"Ah, hell, Virgil, thar ain't nobody who knows that fer sure."

"Bull*shee-it*!" Virgil drew the word out in emphasis. The big frame dragged itself upright in the booth, pointing a hard-callused finger at Harlan. "Ever since the government emergency—or whatever the hell they call it—thar ain't been no decent commerce through Beaver. Hell, the truckers and lifters just flat dried up on I-15, and nothin's got through fer months. No feed. No grocery. The AP ain't had a shipment of canned goods in weeks 'cept fer the stuff Anna Sue bought off the army surplus. I hear tell that ol' Randall's gonna use that McDonald's of his out on the interstate to start storing hay."

Lowell's head bobbed up and down like it was on a loose spring. "Damn rights! It's this disease, by Gawd. I hear tell that L.A.'s just about deserted between the refugees and the dead lying all over the streets."

"Now, where the hell would you hear that?" Harlan scoffed.

"I heard it!" Lowell affirmed. "Ol' Jim Halver's boy been working for the army. He come by just a few weeks ago on leave. Hell of a time gettin' here, too, so I hear. You need state papers just to cross the county line now and unless you know someone or are in the army, you can kiss crossing a state line good-bye. He told his pa that central L.A.'s pretty much emptied out as well as south-central and East L.A.—wherever the hell that is."

"Gawddamn perverts, that's what they were." Lowell intoned his moral judgment swift and sure. "They got the Vee-Kids, and they paid the price."

"Damn rights!" Louis seconded the judgment.

"Well," Virgil leaned forward, resting his arms on his knees, "I don't know about that. But I'll bet the Halver boy didn't get home comin' up I-15. I'll just bet you he got here down the Milford road."

Lowell blinked. "Now, how in hell did you know that?"

" 'Cause thar ain't been no Greyhounds on I-15 for over a year, moron!" Virgil was working himself up into a fine rage. " 'Cause everything that's moving in this country comes up the old rail line out of Vegas or down out of Salt Lake through Delta . . . and that means it comes into pissant little Milford. The damn place was a dried-up tumbleweed of a place till this emergency hit. Now you want fruit, you gotta get it from Milford. You want cloth, you gotta get it from Milford! Decent beer all the way from Denver, you gotta get it from Milford! You want any job that's not behind either a plow or a cow, you gotta go to Milford."

Appropriate scowls rippled across the faces of all the boys. The rivalry between Milford and Beaver went back, it would seem, to the moment both towns were settled. Beaver was the county seat, but Milford had the rail line—and jobs. Then, when the interstate went through Beaver (or within reasonably close proximity) and rail travel no longer required crews to be spelled as often, the balance of things shifted back toward Beaver and Milford was left with their pride to hang onto. If Beaver got a new high school— well, Milford marched right up to the state house and made sure that it got one, too. If Milford was granted a new stadium, well Beaver would just have to go up and lobby for one of its own— just as big and just as well appointed.

The new century was looking bright for little Beaver with a number of high-tech industries looking to build on the interstate. Then V-CIDS came and plunged the country into reeling chaos. The industries quickly closed when the interstate was shut down by the national guard.

Yet the cruelest blow of all was Milford. Suddenly, the army came into Milford, took over the town, and set up its own factories and industries. Milford was a boomtown, a mecca that was now the only hope for living a life even close to anything before the emergency.

Now it was Beaver's turn to hang like a dried fruit on a dead vine. It stuck in every craw in town.

"What the hell is so la-de-dah special about Milford anyway?" Louis whined.

"Yeah." Harlan bobbed his own head, his Adam's apple following suit. "Just what the hell do they think they're doing over there anyway that makes them so special?"

"Yeah!" chorused the McNeils.

Virgil kicked back into the booth and folded his huge arms across his barrel chest. "Well, boys, I don't know but I was just thinkin'."

Back in the kitchen Neil Abbott, who had been listening in on the conversation, winced visibly. When Virgil started thinking, it was never a good sign. Neil quietly began looking for the phone book to find Bishop Peter's phone number.

Virgil looked up toward the acoustic ceiling tile. The act seemed to help him think better. "You know that they've been shipping all them buildings and stuff they been making out toward the Wah Wah Valley, right."

"Well, hell, Virg, everyone knows that!"

"Talk's been that they're buildin' cities out there for all them Vee-Kids people." Virgil mused. "I also hear they been sendin' about a thousand people a week out there."

Louis was doing his best to follow but wasn't doing too well. "Yeah, so what, Virgil."

"So." Virgil looked the McNeil boy straight in the eye. "So I'm thinkin' that all them people in those cities out there have to get their milk and cheese and meat from somewhere—probably Milford, and they're probably payin' Milford prices for it. But if a few of us good ol' Beaver boys were to get their fat asses out into the Wah Wah—we might be able to sell 'em some good ol' Beaver cheese at a slightly better price."

Harlan shook his head doubtfully, though part of him wanted

to believe it—his father owned the dairy and cheese factory in town. "The Wah Wah is closed, Virgil. The army don't let no one into the valley. There's road blocks and shit like that!"

Virgil groaned, pained to explain such a simple plan to a kid like Harlan. "We ain't gonna go down the highway, Harlan. We'll go up north a ways then come down the back roads. There's a pass over the north end of the San Francisco Range down to the Wah Wah Hardpan. We'll cross in there. Hell, I'll bet those people would be glad to see even a face as ugly as Lowell's if we were to offer them some decent trade. Why the hell should Milford get all the goods?"

Lowell slapped his brother on the back. "That's talking, Virg!"

Louis had turned a little white. "But—well, what about the Vee-Kids and diseases and shit like that?"

"You ain't gonna get no Vee-Kids, Louis!" Virgil stood up slowly, massaging his fists. "Vee-Kids is a disease for perverts. You ain't no pervert, are you, now, little Louis Wayne?"

The red in Louis's face erupted right to his big ears. Only Lowell's very firm hand held him back from making a very big mistake. "You damn well know I'm not, Virgil!"

"Then what say we go up to the Renegade Lounge and kick back a few, boys." Virgil stuck his hat back on his head firmly, the brim down low enough as to make him look and feel dangerous. "It's gonna be a cold one, and I think we'll all need a little warmth before the night's done."

The deep tanned hide of Virgil's face broke into another pearly grin. "I think it's time we see what's happenin' in that valley, by Gawd, and show them Milford som'bitches what Beaver boys are made of."

Heigh-ho

Wednesday, April 14, 2010 / 0925 hrs
Factory Commons
Newhouse Center / 477th ERIS District
Wah Wah Valley, West Beaver County, Utah

Michael Barris sat silently in the vast tomb and wondered just what he was doing here.

Thanks to John's help, Michael had figured out when to report for breakfast. He'd stood in line with gray people in gray clothes wearing gray expressions and had received this little slip of paper with its cryptic little words. Then he had dutifully stood in another gray line and sat with gray, incommunicative people eating gray-brown food from gray-brown paper trays and plastic forks.

In the midst of hundreds of people, he had never felt so utterly alone.

Then when breakfast was over he checked the schedule again, converted the military time, and realized that he needed somehow to be at his work assignment. His questions were answered curtly by each person in turn, but eventually he found his way to the adjoining section of the Commons Building that was most commonly known as the factory.

Michael stared again down at the flimsy paper he had been given. The type was faded, but he could still make out the words. It was a form letter with each of the blank spaces filled in by hand. It was like a road map through a bad dream. He had, so far, followed the schedule, having completed breakfast and had, as much out of curiosity as anything else, reported for work as instructed.

Now, sitting at his bench in the factory annex of the Commons, he reviewed the schedule and wondered at it again.

TO: <u>MR. MICHAEL BARRIS / SM4-WSAD27-874-56-9732</u>

FROM: SHIFT ADMINISTRATOR / <u>NEWHOUSE</u>

RE: WORK ASSIGNMENT

Dear Camp Worker;

You are hereby assigned a position in the ERIS RELIEF SUPPORT MANUFACTURING EFFORT (ERIS/RSME). You are assigned to the following schedule.

Meal Service (check service board for time): _____ <u>SM4</u>

Work shift: _____ <u>WSAD27 (Assembly) 0800-1700hrs</u>

where you will report to: ___ <u>Virginia Thorley (Team Leader)</u>

Your designated education & recreation time is: <u>1830-2030 hrs</u>
when you will report to your R&E director: ___ <u>Preston Duffy</u>

Your service assignment is:_____ <u>NYD</u>
in which capacity you will report to:_____ <u>NYD</u>

You are subject to curfew during the hours of: <u>2200-0600hrs.</u>

Those who do not show to their assigned posts and who are not on signed medical waiver from the infirmary are subject to disciplinary action by the security staff.

May your efforts contribute to the cure of our disease. Remember, every effort you make brings us that much closer to a cure.

Have a nice day.

Avril Tanner
Shift Administrator

Now he sat on another bench before yet another table in a room filled with an endless procession of tables and benches. Everyone around him sat here in silence, waiting for . . . what? Each person had a set of tools set before them—lightweight polymer composite tools with small blades and keen edges.

And still he had no clue why they were all here.

"Excuse me?"

The bright voice intruded on Michael's thoughts. It had an edge to it, sharp as the instruments in front of him and, he thought, too bright for such a shadowy place as this. For a moment he resented being bothered by anyone, but he was new in the camp and humanity had not yet left him. He looked up.

Next to him stood the woman he had seen last night in the Cathedral with her two children. *Damn! What was her name?*

"Sorry to bother you, but they said I should come and sit over here." There was a quiver in her voice and a moist distance in her eyes. Michael remembered seeing the look in a rabbit's eyes just before he pulled the trigger.

"Uh, sure," he choked out. "Please, sit." He looked down and away from her.

"I guess they've put all of us new people together," the woman said with a thin smile. She seemed to collapse slightly, however, when she carefully sat down. She needed sleep. "Mary Elizabeth— she's the woman our family is rooming with right now—she says we'll have a teacher or trainer or something today, and then we'll be ready to do whatever it is we're supposed to do. I'd have been here earlier, but I had to get my boys settled at their workstations. Did you know that they ask the children to work as well? Oh, I see you got one of those assignment things, too."

My God, Michael thought, *they still haven't told her?*

"Hi, I'm Miriam Barns. Have we met somewhere before?"

Michael blinked and took the outstretched hand. It was cold to his touch, soft with a limp grip. She had looked right at Michael the night before, and now she couldn't place him. It must have been a bad night for her. "Well, it doesn't matter, people are always thinking that they've seen someone somewhere before, aren't they?" Her eyes settled back on the page Michael was still gripping. "Mary Elizabeth—the one I told you about—she told me how to read the page they gave you. Do you understand it?"

Michael sighed deeply. He really didn't want to talk to this woman, knowing what he did. "Yes, thank you, I think I do."

"Oh." Miriam paused a moment, her hands rubbing together more out of nervousness than the chill in the air. She glanced down at the tools in front of her and then fixed her gaze on them as though they were unfriendly objects. She looked up again and looked up and down the table nervously. There seeming to be no more likely candidates, she turned again to Michael.

"I'm sorry if I'm bothering you." She spoke it half toward Michael and half toward the universe at large. "I know I talk too much. My husband, Kevin . . ." Then she shuddered visibly, her voice catching in her throat before she blinked furiously and continued on. ". . . he says that I really just can't shut up when I'm upset. I suppose I'm upset. Do you think I'm upset?"

Michael turned to her, looked her in the eye, and said, "Yes."

Miriam stopped under Michael's gaze.

"Oh."

Startled silence hung between them, Miriam withering under Michael's look and Michael doing his best to put brakes to the conversation. However, motion beyond her caught his eye, and he looked up.

A huge woman waddled her way toward them. Her five-foot-four-inch height resonated with at least three hundred pounds of flesh stuffed into, of all things, a jumpsuit. Her hair was pulled back severely into a bun so tight as to seem to make her face stretch upward.

It took Michael a moment to realize that she was not alone. Behind her, another figure followed—a man with close-cut blond hair who was so slight and wiry as to nearly be eclipsed by the large woman. When at last she came to a halt at the end of the table, the man behind her stopped short and then, in a feat reminiscent of Magellan, circumnavigated her, clipboard in hand.

"Good afternoon, brothers and sisters."

Well, hallelujah! Michael thought. *Who the hell are you?*

"I am Brother Charles Lukin—shift training supervisor. This"—he gestured to the woman looming as an ominous backdrop behind him—"is Sister Virginia Thorley, who, as you know, will be your team leader."

Not for long, Michael thought. He could see the dark splotches at the woman's neckline and the fogged look in her eyes. *I'd give her something like a week on the outside before she's one very large stack of lumber.*

"The ERIS Relief Support Manufacturing Effort is a program where, through your labors while at this facility, you can directly contribute to the search for a V-CIDS cure and, thereby, your return to healthy society." Lukin's voice droned on in a speech that he apparently had given one too many times. "The equipment you assemble here today will be sold, and the proceeds thereof will be applied directly toward the research foundation. In addition, the most productive and cooperative members of each shift will be given additional privileges in the Newhouse Relocation Center as well as consideration for special assignments outside the camp." Lukin looked down at his clipboard. "Are there any questions?"

Several hands went up.

"If not, then let's proceed." Lukin turned and shouted to the side of the room. "Brother Tomkins! Let's do it!"

Suddenly, the eight great doors that lined the side of the hall opened as one, their squeal shrieking through the vast room. In rolled several massive carts, each laden with colored plastic boxes filled with parts. Several teams of younger people made their way to the carts and began distributing the boxes through the hall. In moments, several plastic boxes were sitting in front of Michael as well as everyone else at the table.

"The process is simple. Each person takes the frame from the box labeled '1.' Set it in front of you like this. Then you take the support frame from the box labeled '2' and set it on the first one like so. Take four screws from the box labeled '3' and use them to secure this frame to the base. Now, when you have done this, you take the bearing washers from the box labeled '4' and . . ."

"Excuse me," Michael interrupted.

". . . slide them over a shaft from the box labeled . . ."

"Excuse me." Michael spoke more insistently.

". . . At this point, you place the bearings and shaft on the framework so that they—"

Michael stood so suddenly that he almost knocked the other people sitting on his bench to the floor. Reaching across the table, he placed his hand over the assembly, directly in Lukin's way.

"Excuse me!" Michael's voice carried a strong edge. "Just what are we assembling?"

Lukin looked up at Michael, meeting his gaze evenly.

"Does it matter?"

Ten rows and four tables down from where Michael was learning a new trade, Mrs. Helen Casler smiled through unfocused eyes at the completed mechanism before her—the forty-seventh one today by her own count. To her, that mechanism had become a god to be worshiped and adored—a sacred idol of her own personal salvation.

Helen had come into the camp nearly four weeks ago—making her an old timer so far as anyone else in the camp was concerned. Even P.T. referred to her as "the old one," though Helen was only this year staring down thirty-nine. Maybe P.T. saw something in her brilliant blue eyes that so often looked beyond the fence perimeter and the bowl of the valley horizon itself that gave her the look of Methuselah. Perhaps P.T. was drawn to the iron gray hair that had been hers at so unfortunate an age as nineteen but had still managed to win the heart of Martin Casler, the finest dentist in all of Portland. She had the frail look of a grandmother, a wisp of a thing whom you might hold only as gently as a fallen robin so as not to break her even through some accident. Yet those who knew Helen inside understood that her thin, tiny bones were made of steel that would never bend or break. Helen had a soul.

That soul had brought her through Martin's philandering with patients, wildly sensual and, in many respects to Helen, deeply disgusting far beyond the adultery they implied. That soul had also carried her through their divorce with grace and secured her support and that of their children. That same soul had borne up under Martin's long, slow plunge to death of the V-CIDS.

Now it maintained her through her own death watch. She knew nothing of what had happened to her children—the ERIS security men that took her as she arrived late for her church auxiliary meeting hadn't allowed her to notify the schools or even her mother in Tacoma. Still she knew—even through her two separate bouts with the mumps since she arrived in the camp—that everything would be all right. Jacob was fifteen and remarkably adept for his age. He'd know what to do with the four younger ones. She could still picture them through the hope that was the driving force of her soul as sitting around their table, working quietly on their homework while Jacob finished the dishes and wondered when Mom would be home. Emily might whine a little and complain, but Jacob would comfort her and tell her that Mom would be home soon.

"Mom will be home soon," Helen murmured to herself.

She knew she would, too. The work that the factory gave her to do was furthering the research effort. The money the government was saving by having them assemble these devices was going directly toward research for the cure. Mr. Lukin—*Brother* Lukin—said so each morning in his rousing speeches. "Every device you make brings us all that much closer to going home."

"Every device brings us closer to going home." Helen smiled again, her eyes still unfocused.

Then, quite suddenly, her eyes focused into a laser-sharp clarity, her smile fierce and determined. She recalled reading in high school how in decades now long cold and buried, munitions factory workers had inscribed their handiwork with phrases and names. It had been a way of sending some of themselves directly to the enemy in person, so to speak. She had quickly seized on the idea as a way that she could, somehow, send a message beyond the perimeter fence and beyond the valley walled with mountains. A message that she was still here, that she was still alive, and that she would be coming home someday.

As she had with every device since that day, Helen picked up a scribe tool and with a series of practiced, swift moves, etched two words into the black casing near the bottom. She always put it in the same place, and in the 94 days of her internment and the 5,372 devices she had assembled, she never missed one.

She smiled at the words, "To Emily."

Then she set the device in its case and moved on to her 5,373rd device.

Sixty miles eastward in Milford, the captain buried his head under his pillow. The rifle volley came with clean precision following the usual three count.

His own shift wouldn't be starting until late in the afternoon in the CON/Ops Center. He should get some sleep but knew somewhere within himself that the sleep wouldn't come and that the sound of the execution squad's carbines would ring in his ears and mind for a long time.

It was the seventh such volley he'd heard today.

Lukin's words rattled around in Michael's brain.

"Does it matter?"

For the nine hours after hearing them, Michael pondered the answer to that question. The assembly of the widget or wodget or whatever it was they were making soon became a ritual of box 1 and box 2, with a hypnotic rhythm of its own. Virginia Thorley watched over them with the concept of a mother hen and the execution of her duties as a slave master. Soon enough, however, the new people at the table came to understand the hows of the assembly if not the whys. Time slid into a nonexistence of frames, bolts, and bearing washers. Slowly, the drug of repetition sedated them, quieted them, and kept them occupied through yet another day.

In the end he was told they had had a very good day. The good news was that only forty died during the shift. The bad news was that Virginia Thorley wasn't one of them.

Recreation

Wednesday, April 14, 2010 / 1310 hrs
Barracks 12-Q
Newhouse Center / 477th ERIS District
Wah Wah Valley, West Beaver County, Utah

An exhausted and depressed Michael Barris dutifully presented himself for recreation and instruction under the watchful eye of Preston Duffy, camp morale officer.

Preston Duffy, it turned out, had been dead for at least a week. Not that anyone was concerned. Indeed, there were those who would swear that, as one of the senior camp morale and activities officers, he had improved considerably since his demise. So pleased was everyone that the jocular and effervescent Duffy had passed on, that everyone in his group decided to keep the fact to themselves.

Preston had been the kind of fellow that you could always count on to have a sunny disposition even in the worst of times. When the trains of new internees would tumble into the main street of the camp, Preston was always there to offer encouraging words and his glittering smile. If you were separated from your family, Preston couldn't find them for you but he would throw his arm around your shoulders and offer his moral support and words of hope. If your life had suddenly been pulled out from under you and everything that gave your existence meaning had suddenly vanished in a well of despair, Preston was incapable of changing any of that but would give you a friendly sock in the arm and let you know that others stood with you in much the same predicament and that therefore you were not alone. If you were dying— well, hey, who wasn't? Hang in there, he would say, and things were bound to improve.

Death, rape, murder, hangings, torture . . . Preston was always there with his legendary "indomitable spirit," as he so often called it. Nothing would get him down, by gosh and golly. He worked under the direction of Reverend Weston and with the full support of Bullock's people; recreation was mandatory. He was a beacon of hope in a world of black despair and made sure that everyone was going to be actively engaged in diverting activities whether they wanted to be or not.

He was unquestionably the most hated person in the camp— and shrugged off the fact with his own "indefatigable good nature."

So when Preston began coughing and having difficulty breathing after any exertion, there was a mildly elevated interest in the camp. Several pools were hastily formed by Carl Emmett, a member of the Recreational Crafts Staff who shared the general sentiments of the camp regarding his boss. The prize of which generally promised to include several personal articles of Preston's to be divided upon the conclusion of the contest. Preston developed a slowly creeping case of Pneumocystis carinii pneumonia—PCP for those who understood it—and, as the infection steadily grew to drown him in his own lungs, his activities and presence at camp functions became more and more rare.

Without intending it, Preston gained in his last hours of mortality the very thing that he had strived for over the three weeks of his reign—actual diverting interest in the camp. The worse Preston's health, the more interested people were in his death. The proliferating betting pools began to actually donate items from around the camp to "sweeten the pot" until one of the most impressive collections of worldly wealth known in Newhouse had been collected in Preston's room.

Unfortunately for some lucky soul, the exact time of death

came into dispute. It seems that Nurse Codgebury was called to Preston's bedside not only out of protocol but as something of an official timekeeper to establish the exact time of death. She unfortunately arrived just moments after Preston drew his last gasp (according to some witnesses) and by those same accounts attempted to revive him out of sheer habit. Much to everyone's surprise and considerable dismay, she actually managed to bring him around. It was at this juncture that Nurse Codgebury was called away (some have said spuriously) to another emergency case. Whereupon Preston had the bad grace to die yet again some forty-seven minutes after his first passing.

This left Carl Emmett with a dilemma. Again, according to the accounts later circulated in whispers among those who were in on the pool, Carl ruled, from the head of the bed in which Preston now lay quite cold and quite gray, that the time of death was in dispute, and therefore, no prize could be awarded until an official time of death could be determined by Nurse Codgebury. In the interim, however, the prize winnings would be held in a sort of escrow to be awarded when the hospice director gave a final and official time of death.

He then conveniently forgot to tell Codgebury that Preston had died at all.

Whenever anyone asked about the "treasure"—for so they had all come to regard it—Carl would take them to Preston's room and show it to them. It was all still there. Then, as Carl showed them out, he would always echo the sentiments of most people in the camp: "You know, if the administration finds out about Preston, they'll just put someone else in *just like him.*"

"... hope you'll appreciate the wonderful gift your recreation staff has just given you. Let's take a moment to go over the points one more time."

Michael shook his head, frantically trying to stay awake and get what was being said. The group crowded into the north living room—excuse me, dying room, he reminded himself with a scowl—of building Q9 were apparently all people who had just arrived. Michael thought he recognized several of the faces from the pallets he rode in on yesterday. It was the end of a day of mean-

ingless and frustrating labor at the factory. Michael had not come
to the camp for any purpose but his own, and being so close to his
goal, he was anxious to get on with it.

In front of them stood Carl Emmett, who, he had explained,
would give them the real facts about the camp and how to survive
it. Carl had a head like a box with a ragged crew cut whose uneven golden bristles stood out at odd angles. The skin around the
square head, however, was skull-tight, the lingering effects of a de-
hydration problem that he simply couldn't shake.

"Now, who is your recreation director?"

A few feeble voices managed to mumble out a name.

"Look, people, this may be called recreation but another word
for that here is survival. Now, with some feeling from all of you:
who is your recreation director?"

"PRESTON DUFFY." The chorus was ragged but at least everyone was participating.

"Right! Where is Preston?"

"SICK!"

"Who is your recreation director?"

"PRESTON DUFFY!"

"Where is Preston?"

"SICK!"

"Right! Now: one of Bullock's men stops you and asks you
what you're doing. What do you say?"

"BASKET WEAVING!"

"And what if they ask you where your basket is?"

"I'M STILL GATHERING MATERIALS!"

Carl's smile stretched across his blocky face into a ghoulish
grin. "Very good, people. Now, the leader of our community, the
Right Reverend Weston, requires that all members of this camp
submit themselves to meaningless recreation for the full length of
their period and requires that I report on that recreation each
night. To that end, you will go to the Commons Building at the beginning of your recreation period and report to one of our staff.
You'll get a green recreation slip of paper. Hang on to it, because
if one of the Bulls catches you milling about without one of these
slips they may just beat you or they may kill you, depending on
their mood."

Someone near the back of the room snorted.

"Funny, eh? Thirty-five people died last week of unnatural causes in the camp, and nearly two-thirds of those were 'security related.' You were all read your rights when you were arrested and that amounted to the fact that you no longer have any. You've all been declared 'predeceased,' which means that you're already dead so far as anyone outside this camp is concerned—or inside it either."

Michael's blood began to run hot in his face. *This is the morale officer? What do they do when they really want to cheer us up—bury a cat alive?*

"Some of you will be required to play baseball so that our leaders will feel that we are all doing our jobs. At the end of the recreation period, you return the green card to me and I get the honor of filling out a report that says you're all happy. You then get to go to bed so that you can start again in the morning."

"So," Michael snapped. "Just what the hell do we do for our recreation time?"

Carl looked squarely at Michael, a thin smile parting his cadaverous lips as he moved to stand directly before him.

"Why, survive, Mr. Barris. Just learn to survive."

"You know," Michael said in a flat tone, his own eyes locked with those of Carl's, "I feel so out of place with everyone knowing my name. Have we met—formally, I mean?"

Carl turned nonchalantly away, continuing as though he had heard nothing. "My advice right now is the last thing that you'll get for free in this camp. Survival is the name of the game here. It's a losing game. Ms. Bryson, the map, please."

A tall, willowy woman with sleepy eyes lifted a large piece of plywood with deceptive ease and held it against the wall. On it, a map of the camp had been carefully rendered in pencil.

"Here is the main camp road, it runs from the warehouses and the Com Tower roughly southeastward through the center of the Commons and out gate 'Bravo.' It's officially known as 'Main Street' and often is officially referred to as 'the street' but this only has real meaning for the administrators. For you and me, however, it's simply called 'the line.' "

"The line?" piped in an accountant type with broken glasses just behind Michael.

"That's right, the line." Carl turned cold at the interruption in his speech. "It's what divides the camp. This side of the line you deal with other men like yourselves. This side of the line are just other hardworking boys like yourselves and a few families that somehow managed to come as a complete family unit into hell. The map says blocks J through N are 'Married Barracks'—don't believe it. There are a few families in Block J, but they are rare and seldom seen out together. The rest of this side of the line are men.

"Across the line, E block is reserved for administration people—that's anyone who agrees with the Right Reverend and his policies enough to brownnose a cushy job. If you're looking for career opportunities—that's where you might end up if you are willing to pay the price. You degrade and debase yourself enough and you may end up over there. If you don't belong there, avoid it. There's tales of percs over there, but if the Bull catches you, the game is over once and for all.

"Blocks A through H—except Block F, of course—are the women's barracks. Rape is a common practice here, and if you're willing to trade what's left of your life to bang some bitch, that's up to you. My caution, however, is that the women in those blocks have developed a strong sense of fight over flight and have learned to prowl in packs. You cross the line into their territory after dark without a very willing escort and you'll never see sunrise—if you're lucky. There's a picket of sharp sticks along the line by F block, and the berries that are hanging from the sharp ends of those sticks are not exactly dried fruit. The sight will bring your knees together very quickly—I recommend that you strongly consider looking at those trophies long and hard before crossing the line into those blocks.

"That leaves Blocks X, Y, and Z. On the official map they are noted as 'G/L barracks'—that's gay and lesbian to you. If there's a faggot, queer, fairy queen, or butch in the camp, that's where they are kept. Their schedules seldom cross yours, and where they do cross they are confined to their blocks. Don't take them lightly. Occupancy per square foot in those three blocks is easily double that of the rest of the camp. Conditions over there are beyond crowded, and the health risks there are a factorial increase. They have their own separate and mostly autonomous branches for nearly every service in the camp. They take care of their own dead, their own cleaning, their own shifts, and their own cooking. In short, they take care of their own in every way. Even Bullock's men don't actually enter the alleys in the blocks themselves, although they do patrol around them heavily. Don't bother them and they won't bother you. Cross the line into their blocks—and the rest of us won't even bother looking for your pieces."

Michael had had enough. "So, I suppose life on this side of the line is ever so much better?"

Carl smiled again, the smile of the damned. "Why, no, Mr. Barris—you haven't been paying attention. There is no *life* on this side of the line or otherwise. We're all dead, or did you miss that part? But if you would rather be one of the walking dead than the lumber heading every morning to the furnace, then you had better learn the ropes on this side of the line as well. Kiss civilization good-bye now and you'll live longer here." Carl cocked his head suddenly to one side, as though examining an issue with a scalpel. "A woman falls at your feet face first into the mud with convulsions, what do you do, Mr. Barris?"

"Well, if the convulsions are extreme, then—"

"No!" Carl snapped. His voice carried loudly to every ear in the room. "You leave her alone. You let her die right there at your feet. If you have to, step over her in order to get away from her. A woman that sick with anything—KS, PCP, mumps, measles, whatever—will drag you down into the great dark with her more surely than a knife blade in your stomach. It's not just health issues either. There are people on this side of the line who will kill you just because the shoes you happened to wear into the camp remind them of shoes that they once owned."

A long silence fell over the room. Carl seemed to have run out of things to say. Michael wasn't sure whether it was simply that he had run out of advice or that he couldn't possibly give enough advice to be helpful to anyone.

Finally, Carl spoke again. "During your recreation shift, unless you are assigned to a sporting event for the reverend's amusement, learn the skills you'll need to survive and, most of all, stay out of the Bull's way. If you can't think of anything to do, come and see either myself or Ms. Bryson, and we'll provide you with 'meaningful and exciting recreational opportunities.' If you need anything more than that, you can, of course, go through official channels and request it, or you may call on me and actually have a chance of getting what you need. My prices are reasonable. Now, get up to the Commons like good little campers, get your green paper, and get lost for the next few hours. Try to keep breathing until the end of the recreation shift. I hate tracking down dead people—it's a lot more paperwork. Now, go!"

Not exactly Knutt Rockney, Michael thought. After a few moments of shocked silence, one or two in the back resigned themselves with a shrug and began exiting the room. The log jam broken, the crowded room soon emptied of the depressed audience until only Michael stood in the room facing the recreational director.

"Well, Mr. Barris: bored so quickly?" Carl said wryly. "Can't think of anything to do? Perhaps you need some instruction in basket weaving?"

"You're cute, Carl . . ."

"You'd best be careful with an accusation like that!"

". . . but I need some help, and I suspect you're just the kind of guy to give it."

Carl cocked his head slightly and shrugged without commitment. "Many things are possible. It depends on just how much you have to exchange."

"Well," said Michael with what he hoped was an equal air of ambiguity, "as you said, many things are possible."

Carl moved to cross to the opposite end of the building, nodding to Michael to follow him. Just across the hall they turned to a door on which had been scrawled "PRESTON DUFFY" and "DO NOT DISTURB" above the fading label of "GAME ROOM." Michael involuntarily shuddered, remembering what the appellation implied in his own barracks.

Two guards stood on either side of the door, making way for Carl as he approached. Carl barely seemed to notice them as he reached down and opened the door.

"Come in, Mr. Barris, where we can talk." With that he stepped inside, followed at once by Michael.

The room had taken on the aspects of a shrine. Opposite the door sat a chair with a shirt, jacket, and pants that had been stuffed with cotton batting from a mattress. The right arm was propped up as though in a greeting. A badly battered and thoroughly deflated volleyball took the place of the head, which had been carefully molded into an abstract of a smiling face. About this figure was arrayed an amazing collection of watches, chocolate bars, stacks of hundred-dollar bills, diamonds, carved figures, and jewelry of all kinds and description. All of these were carefully arranged in displays about the stuffed clothes piled on the floor, tacked on the walls, and even nailed to the ceiling. Michael was dumbfounded. The room was filled with icons of another time and life—a life that he himself had participated in fully not a few days before. Yet even after so short a time here, he was coming to realize just how far from that life he had come—and how meaningless it all seemed to him now.

"I take it that this is all that's left of Mr. Duffy?" Michael muttered.

Carl leaned casually against a gold-encrusted wall, folding his arms across his chest. "Mr. Preston Duffy has yet to have an official declaration of the time of his death. While his predeceased status means that such a declaration is meaningless, we nevertheless maintain this illusion for the benefit of the camp administration."

"I would have thought that you were part of that administration, Mr. Emmett," Michael said calmly.

"You pay attention, Mr. Barris, I like that." Carl looked sleepily toward the silhouetted figure in the chair. "I'm on the administration roster, and I do my job—at least so far as their reports are concerned. More important, the camp has remained calm for the most part, which seems to be what the administration is actually concerned with. Still, we don't see eye to eye on a number of things. My methods may be of occasional use to them, but they nevertheless do not always approve of them."

Michael snorted. "You sound like someone who gets things done—and one of the few who understands what's really happening here."

Carl Emmett looked at Michael with a sudden burning suspicion in his eyes. The smile fell from his face. "What is it you want, Barris? You specifically came to this camp. Despite your ridiculous bandanna act, you were discovered before you ever arrived at the Milford Depot. Reverend Weston and the Bull have been using everyone they can touch in this camp—officially or otherwise—to figure out your motives for coming here. You're a dangerous one, you are, and you've got someone up there very frightened."

Carl stood suddenly. Michael again stood his ground.

"I don't care what your motives are, Barris. I don't grovel for the most righteous reverend or his righteous brood. I serve me. If you want whatever it is you're after badly enough to come here, then I'm here to tell you that I'm the only one who can get it for you. Everything comes with a price—it just depends on what you want and if you can afford to pay. So, Mr. Michael Barris of the I-Net Information Service, what is it you want?"

Michael looked the recreational director squarely in the eye. He'd heard many things since he came into the camp, but this was the first time he'd heard the truth.

"I just want to cross the line."

The Twilight Man

Thursday, April 15, 2010 / 0013 hrs
Newhouse Center / 477th ERIS District 6
Wah Wah Valley, West Beaver County, Utah

Gene Lovett stood under the cold stars shining in the cloudless sky overhead, his own moment of stillness blanketing the camp. It was Gene's moment—a moment of quiet and peace. It was the between time; that instant that was the demarcation between two worlds, neither one at rest.

Gene was the exception to the rules of the camp—the gay who was also a trained EMT. The line that cut the camp was clearest to him because he stood above it, straddling the line. One foot was safely planted in the hospice where Nurse Codgebury protected him during the day. The other stood firmly in the courts of the Dark Queen at night. His medical skills were too valuable to the straights in the camp to murder him for being abroad in the day. His ability to walk in the sunlight made him valuable to the Dark Queen. So he became the Twilight Man, standing in the light and the dark at once, his comfort coming to him as he stood between the worlds here in the middle of the night.

The last of the factory's night-shift workers had left the Commons an hour before. A few suspended panels that had lit the larger passageways of the camp quite silently died, relinquishing the camp to any light the sky might wish to offer. Even the guards of Bullock's security force had abandoned the camp streets to the unending piles of the nightly dead. For the moment, all was quiet. For the moment, there was peace—Gene's only peace—and he drank it in like waters from a clear mountain stream.

Then Gene sighed: the moment passed, carried away with the witching hour. As if by some silent signal, a tide of dark emptied into the night. It spilled into the star-shadowed passageways between the buildings like arterial blood from a gaping wound centered squarely in the center of Block Y. It poured with two thousand pairs of light-blinded eyes into the open doors of the Commons or the warehouse or the hydroponics buildings waiting vacantly to swallow them up again.

Silent as the night enveloping them, Gene watched the G/L barracks empty into the camp to begin their designated graveyard shift. Only Gene and the stars in the brilliant, cold firmament above them watched the proceedings. This shift's crew was known by the hetros of the camp, but none of them were truly *known*. The shifts were all carefully arranged by Weston's administrators, the schedules all worked out and the assignments insured that none of the right-thinking, straight members in the camp would ever see—let alone be confronted by—the visage of a gay man or lesbian woman. The line was narrow and firmly drawn.

Gene had seen the results of someone crossing the line. Melinda Hodges—Mel to her friends—had just gone buggy one day: she just flipped out. She had wanted to walk in the sunshine. All she wanted was to see the sun, she said, from the wide-open field behind the Commons. She hadn't passed the line more than eight steps before the first of Bulldog's security goons swung his stick with both hands into the small of her back. Gene could still picture the hideous grin on the man's face . . . could still hear the words the man had spat into her face. *"Hey, you butch-bitch! Crawl back in your hole right now! I said now . . . before you make all these decent folks puke!"*

Mel looked back at him.

"I said, move your perverted, diseased ass across the line, god-damn it!" Then he hit her again with the board, this time in the stomach, doubling her over and dropping her to one knee. She

looked up. More security men were arriving, a pack of hideous wolves. A crowd was forming, curious and detached at once.

She looked up, uttering a single, barely audible word.

"No."

She died long before the men had finished with her. Bullock had put her unrecognizable head on a pole above the body, but friends had stolen it and the body in the night. Many in the G/L barracks had wanted to bury her under Y barracks, but the Dark Queen said no—the "hetties" would still locate her remains from the satellite transponder in her forehead and just put her back up on the pole. In the end, they snuck her onto the death pallets quietly in the night, which was the most decent funeral they could give her.

Since that day, Gene had watched his friends become this faceless, nameless tide, closeted once again in a cage fashioned from fear and resentment—segregated from a daylight majority that wouldn't or couldn't understand them.

The last of the graveyard shift shuffled past Gene, leaving him alone once more. It was the same song, he reflected, and always the same refrain. In the eyes of the "natural" world—as the majority so often enthroned itself—the homosexuals were freakish and dangerous, a threat to the natural order of humanity. Over the march of centuries, that same watchful patriarchal eye of western civilization turned on the whim of history its gaze in alternating turns of amusement, disgust, pity, hatred, tolerance, anger, indifference, and raging, murderous violence.

Yet Gene knew this history was not fully his. The gays and lesbians shared an occult culture and history that was their own—even the word "occult" was misunderstood as being demonic and evil rather than its original meaning: "hidden." For hidden truly represented their roots—roots from which they all too often felt cut off and alone. Their past was not written in books but carried on through oral traditions of dubious reliability. Those parts that were not passed on by word of mouth were left only to be guessed at from the shadows of texts whose nuances were purposely left unclear. Hidden was their culture, which through ages as old as mankind developed into a civilization of secret signs and rituals—not for the calling down of some dark power, but simply to identify one another and communicate with a language that was their own. Such communication, whether through small symbols in meaningful places, verbal keywords that were meaningless to the hostiles about them or subtle gestures of recognition, became as integral a part of who they were as the air they shared with all life. Only with the supposed cultural enlightenment of the last half of the twentieth century did gays and lesbians attempt to forward that culture openly, hoping that their roots could be established in the sunshine at last.

The eye that had followed them with suspicion for so long did not look so threatening as once it had—but it was still watching.

In the Decade of Excuses, as the end of the twentieth century was later known, there were concerted efforts, connected with the AIDS research of the time, to discover the "cause" of homosexuality. To this now advanced and scientifically liberal patriarchal eye, finding some reason or cause for a person's sexual preference would "excuse" the fact and make it more palatable for "real" society. Sexual preference could then easily be categorized like someone suffering from some physical or societal defect—suffering and defect being the unspoken operative words—which, now understood, could be excused.

Excused—but never understood and, certainly, never ever accepted.

Despite the provocative research, no single, underlying cause for this "abnormal" behavior—a behavior that some people placed as affecting as many as ten percent of the male population in the United States—was ever accepted by the mass audience of the great eye of media. All problems were explainable in three-and-a-half-minute reports. All comments worth hearing were never longer than thirty seconds of sound bite. All the world's knowledge *worth knowing* could be learned while standing on one foot. If not, thought the mass audience of the patriarchal eye, then it just was too complicated to be worth knowing. Gays and lesbians were hard to explain in twenty-five words or less.

There were behaviorists who claimed that they had found the behavioral roots of gays, and there were geneticists who claimed to have discovered "defective" strands in the genetic code that determined lesbian proclivities. Each in turn proclaimed it possible to "cure" these behaviors.

No one ever asked if they should.

Nor did they want, really, to know. So when the V-CIDS detonated in the gay community like a mushroom cloud, it evaporated with it all the tentative steps that had been made toward understanding, and blasted it with a vengeance back into the closet. The sound bites and the three-minute "in-depth coverage" quickly and efficiently tagged the gays with the same stigma that AIDS had done over a decade earlier. V-CIDS was not only a gay problem, but had somehow been caused by gays as well. Only occasionally did anyone ask the question "Why?" and as the reasons were clouded in a research trail and government red tape, no clear answer ever was able to fit into the news format. The leaders of the gay community were stunned at the swiftness with which the western eye had turned suddenly against them. Finally, they tried to rally support with the Great Frisco March, which became the San Francisco Massacre. That march quite inadvertently provided the excuse that the great majority needed to change its hateful mind again—this time to surer, swifter ways of hiding the gays from their sight.

So it was that in the nearly five hundred camps set carefully in places beyond the sight of the mass eye, this same tide of dark figures emerged each night to work, to eat, and to slowly die. They shared the darkness and a brotherhood whose very concept was sniggered at by the powers that had always been and now were openly murdered when they tried to walk in the light. They were faceless, without identity in the minds of those who ruled.

Who wants to look into the face of sin, Gene thought grimly, when it so often turns out to be a mirror.

Scott Johnson, the graveyard shift supervisor, walked the factory floor. He knew his time was limited despite the assurances of Nurse Codgebury. The KC was taking him slowly, and he recognized all the signs. He'd worked in the gay clinic in San Diego too long to ignore the obvious. He may have been something of a romantic in his time, but he had come to learn the virtues of realism. Still, he wouldn't give up without a fight. He owed Lee that much.

Just the thought of the name brought him up short. Lee had been the quiet one between them, adding that dimension to Scott's life that gave it meaning. It was as though cosmic confluences had somehow conspired to bring the two of them together—two shattered individuals who both knew they were missing their better half. Scott had been working a bar, trying to find something within himself that he thought he had lost. Lee had come in that night torn up because his lover had left him in a flurry of harsh language and hurtful feelings. They were both lost, but somehow that evening they both realized they had started something more complete and fulfilling than either of them had hoped for in all the dark and lonely years before.

Could that have been only a year ago? Scott had only seven months before the V-CIDS took Lee from him forever, yet it was hard for him to imagine any life other than that heady and empowering time. Scott fought the internment—Lee would have wanted it that way—and had actually survived in the underground for two and a half months before the weakness of a friend betrayed him and landed him in the camps. Through that time Scott had maintained his strong looks and his chiseled physique. He looked like a natural leader.

That was why the Dark Queen had placed him where he was.

Scott casually walked between the tables, watching as the units were slowly taking shape, each mechanism identical to the one previously assembled; each assembly identical to that which had been performed on uncounted nights before. He occasionally stopped and inspected the various components. They all passed his eye. He wasn't all that sure what he would see wrong even if there was anything amiss. It wasn't why he was really here.

"Mr. Johnson! Could we see you for a moment?"

Ira Mason waved him toward the fourth-row table seven in from the door. The back of Ira's hand was turned toward him as he beckoned. Scott understood the signal and came at once.

"Yes, Mr. Mason, what seems to be the trouble?" Scott and Ira were actually quite close and would normally have laughed at the starchy formality they placed between themselves on the factory floor. Familiarity even in simple friendship, however, was a luxury that no one on the floor could afford. Scott's eyes were leveled at Ira's, but his awareness was elsewhere. The common areas of the camp had been fitted with optical and fiber resonance cables.

Someone, somewhere was always watching—a state with which Scott and his people were all keenly aware.

"Well, sir, we seem to be having a little trouble with these fittings."

"Let's take a look, shall we?" Scott gestured, leaning over with Ira while putting his right arm around the other man's back.

The left hand crossed to snatch the torn scrap of paper held by Ira between them.

Scott turned and nodded with practiced ease at Ira, then left. Within minutes he again made an innocuous contact with another worker—this time one of the many faceless laborers in the transportation detail, casually dropping the paper into her pocket in a move so graceful as to be unnoticed by any of the eyes looking through the fiber-optics monitors.

The transport captain—a butch lesbian who was known only as Marc—stuffed both hands in the pockets of her baggy pants, touching the paper as she did so to make sure that it was secure, and moved outside of the factory. With a few quiet gestures to her team, Marc and her fellow workers turned to the great wheeled pallet and began guiding it down the slope to the warehouse buildings below.

Within ten minutes the message was passed in succession through the shift inventory officer, the shift coordinator, the quality control inspector, and through four separate inspection group leaders.

When at last it came to rest, the ragged-edged paper sat before a lone, large man moving the various parts of the mechanism on a test bench. He was only one of a thousand different faces, indistinguishable from the others in the room by first glance. His hair was a brilliant white, raggedly cut and shaggy. There was nothing in his broad features that suggested he was out of the ordinary. Indeed, his saving grace was that his visage continued to be so ordinary as to never be remembered. His was the kind of face one could never remember in a crowd except for the faintest hint of softer lines and kinder disposition. His eyes, however, were a frighteningly shocking giveaway, for to look into their palest of blue was to understand your own soul. Those eyes the man studiously avoided using.

Seated carefully in one of the few places where the optics could not reach, the man calmly raised his hand and formed a quick succession of signs that caused the inspection foreman to quickly exit the hall. He never once looked up from his work.

Within ten minutes there wasn't a person on shift who hadn't received—clearly and accurately—the message from this one obscure man working an unimportant post in the quality control division. Quietly, silently, members of the shift began disappearing into the star-lit dimness of the streets, crossing the line back into the G/L blocks. Nearly a hundred had slipped into the three barracks' blocks within half an hour.

And not a single eye reporting to the control room at ERIS ever noticed anything amiss.

"You realize that this is a really stupid idea, don't you, Barris?" Carl rumbled under his breath as he crouched at the corner of the A-7 barracks. His eyes were wet blue orbs as he stared out across the baseball diamond to the thin cracks of light that defined the door entries to the Commons factory.

"Look, my son's got to be working one of those shifts right now: he's just got to be in one of them."

"Fine! So now what's your plan?" Carl snapped. "Gonna walk onto that factory floor and yell, 'Scuse me! I'm a straight guy who's looking for his faggot son!' You do that and I'm not gonna bother to even look for your body parts in the morning."

"Now, why would anyone want to do that to harmless old me?" Michael said in the easiest voice he could manage.

"Because," Carl said sweetly back, "that's exactly what happens to them whenever they cross the line during the day. It's nothing personal, you understand."

"Thanks, Carl," Michael snorted nervously, "you're a real moral support. No, I'll just 'recon' a little and then decide how best to proceed."

Carl shook his head. "You really just don't get this, do you? Well, I said that each person should figure out what they want to do for their own recreational activities, and I suppose that this could qualify." Carl looked around the corner. The recreation field stretched as an icy blue field under the starlight, leading up to the

Commons factory above. The brilliant carpet overhead cast the camp barracks in sharp contrast of dim flat roofs supported by shadows blacker than the night above, their defining detail lost in impenetrable darkness. "Why couldn't you have just taken up basket weaving."

Michael turned his face toward Carl and smiled, his features looking somewhat demonic in the stark light overhead. "I may yet if this doesn't work."

"So," Carl said in as disinterested a manner as he could manage. "You think you'll try the factory first?"

"It's as good a place to start as any."

"Well"—Carl looked down as his watch—one of several different watches Carl had worn over the last few hours—"the Bulldogs are all back in their pens by now. They pretty much let the queers have the run of things until the change of shift in the morning. You can yell nine-one-one all you want. There ain't no cavalry that's gonna come at the last minute to pull your ass out of the fire. You walk their turf—you walk it alone: understand?"

Michael nodded just once and then turned again to face the silvery gentle slope leading up to the factory. He couldn't remember a time when the stars seemed too brilliant and yet the night so dark.

"Well, wish me luck," Michael murmured, half to himself.

"Luck" was all Carl said.

Michael began quickly moving across the intervening ground. The starlight seemed like a searchlight as he moved. He was halfway across the field when he began wondering why he was crouching down as he moved. He suddenly felt awkward and foolish. Just what was it he was trying to hide from? He couldn't put a face or a name to it yet, but there was something out there that part of him knew was stalking him.

Michael shrugged the notion off. The black nothing of the factory was near now. Soon he'd be in the light.

Michael suddenly stopped in his tracks.

From the dark black under the factory eaves, a tall figure slowly emerged into the starlight. Shining eyes glinted from the shadowed face. A hideous smile slit his features seemingly from ear to ear. The scarecrow of a man, nearly half a head taller than

Michael, held a single gray board before him in his left hand while his long nails clattered, typing against the wood.

Michael stood slowly from his crouch. "Do I know you?"

"Not now," the scarecrow replied through his grin.

"But"—Michael gazed as well as he could into those impossible eyes—"I think that you know me?"

"Omnet! Omnet!" the man screamed loudly to the night with deep religious fervor. His words echoed unchallenged from the walls of the camp. "The world's knowledge at your command!" His head lowered, his eyes now trying to burn into the wood slab that he held in his hand. The other hand clattered again against the board. "I know you, Michael Barris! I know you better than you know yourself. The future comes on your wings! The judgment rests on your shoulders! Mortality and immortality are in your fates. You come to die and live forever! You are freedom, Michael Barris!"

Michael took two careful steps back from the man. "What the hell are you talking about?"

"P.T. knows all!" The gaunt man leaned toward him, his tattered Indian blanket whipping behind him in a chilling gust of wind. He held up the carved, blank board. "See? See? It's in the net—it's destiny. Who are you, Michael, to deny the prophets as well as yourself?"

Michael stood frozen, his eyes wide on the man.

P.T. suddenly smiled again, his wrath vanishing with the gust spent about him. Quite suddenly, softly, he began to sing.

"Hello—I must be going . . ."

Michael blinked. "What?"

". . . I have to stay,
I hate to say,
I must be going."

Michael's eyes were transfixed by the bizarre man retreating now before him, oblivious to the motion behind him.

"I'll stay a week or two,
I'll stay the summer through,
But I am telling you,
I must be . . . going!"

Carl watched Michael stand suddenly as he approached the darkness of the factory wall. Suddenly, shadows shifted on shadows, a black wave of figures rose up from the ground and swept toward Michael like a tide.

Carl nearly cried out in warning, but the words stuck in his throat. What was the use? Why get involved?

The tide broke over Michael, dragging him down to the ground. The sounds of brief struggle drifted unheeded down the compound. In moments the stillness of the night reasserted itself. Nothing moved. Nothing was out of place.

Carl sighed. He knew it was the last he'd see of Barris. Too bad, he thought, he seemed like such a nice—if stupid—guy.

Revelers

Thursday, April 15, 2010 / 0042 hrs
Barracks 6-Y
Newhouse Center / 477th ERIS District
Wah Wah Valley, West Beaver County, Utah

A blur of impressions, all black on black.

The hands, many hands, skilled hands, all coming at him from the ground as though reaching up for him from the grave.

They drag him down, quietly taking their prey in the night. He sinks in the darkness toward the cold hard ground. The blackness closes over him, covering his eyes, his ears, his mouth.

He tumbles in darkness, now hooded with a sack whose draw-string forms a noose-like collar around his neck. He utters a cry, and the collar is yanked so violently that for a time breathing is hard and the world's reality begins to fade from consciousness. Choke chain, he recalls vaguely and learns that it is time to heel not heal.

Voices on voices in the void, murmuring about the solitude of his sacked head. He is passed quickly high overhead and moving atop a sea of hands all pressing up against him and rushing him toward the unknown.

Then, suddenly, savagely, more hands pulling at his clothes. He struggles against the unseen hands, cursing the hood that blocks out the world around him. Yet the hands of the beast are numerous and turn him over and over, head to heel as piece by piece his shirt, shoes, pants, briefs, and dignity are stripped from him. His bandanna raked from his head. Exposed. Naked he tumbles now into the freezing darkness. His feet suddenly find floor as he is pushed to stand.

The hood suddenly flew from his head.

He stood suspended by his arms between two support posts. Three brightly burning torches were set uncomfortably close to his face, one directly before him and one each on either side. It was difficult to tell much about what lay behind them: the flames were brilliant in his face compared to the darkness beyond.

His arms had been tied so that he hung bare naked between two support posts. By looking up, he discovered that he was lashed to the center of a dying room but greatly changed from the one in his own barracks. The ceiling here and on the floors above it had been torn out, leaving a vertical shaft clear up through the center of the building's wing. Only a makeshift walkway was at each of the above levels. He dimly realized beyond the brilliant flames about him that each level was lined with people—all looking down toward him.

The walls surrounding the floor he found himself on, he thought, were lined as well—forms and partial faces obscured by the flames. He tried to move, tried to step back away from the flaring brilliance that filled his vision and kept the rest of the world in shadows, but his feet had been bound as well. He stumbled against the ropes, losing his balance and falling forward toward the torches, the ropes cutting, burning into his flesh.

"Ooh, now we can't have *that* in our home, can we, Mr. Barris?" The honey-smooth tenor voice drifted over him from beyond the torchlight. On instinct, Michael looked up toward the voice, but all he could see was the torch ablaze in his vision. From somewhere beyond the light, a long, delicately black hand reached toward him from a red silk kimono and pushed against his chest just hard enough to allow him to regain his balance. "Burnt offerings come later in the program."

A roar of laughter and hooting rang through the great hollow of the hall.

Michael blinked furiously. The smoke from the torches stung his weary eyes. "I . . . I can't see you."

"Ah, but isn't that the point, Mr. Barris? I mean, really, hasn't that *always* been the point? You never saw any of us in the past even if you had even thought to want to. Why should you see us now? And, oh, do let me call you Mr. Barris," the high male voice crooned with deadly sap. "It will make the rest of the proceedings ever so much more formal."

Michael closed his eyes, allowing his tears to cleanse them for a moment before he tried opening them again. "Proceedings? What proceedings?"

"Mr. Barris, I am shocked! Come to trial and not even have your own attorney?" The fire flashed off the silk as it moved around the torches. The voice carried behind him as well, circling his staked-out prey, yet try as he might, Michael could never get a look at the face of his accuser. The voice shouted into the well above him. "Well, are there any lawyers in the house?"

"Yes!" came the distant chorus of many voices overhead.

"So, will any of you defend this poor, wretched, and obviously guilty creature?"

"No!" came the resounding choral reply.

This set off another set of howls, cheers, and laughter.

The voice waited for the laughter to die down. His timing was excellent. "Oh, but just look at the poor thing, shivering in the cold! This straight 'arrow' could use a little warmth—hum, come to look at him, I wouldn't mind having him in my quiver!"

The crowd roared.

He could suddenly feel the breath of the man close behind him. His voice whispered loud enough for the hall to appreciate his words.

"So, how about it, Sitting Bull? Care to go a hunting?"

The silk ran softly down his bare back. Michael closed his eyes again and shuddered. Peals of laughter rang through the hall— only to be silenced by the delicate hands held up from the kimono.

"Alas; there's none to defend him. He stands naked and alone—defenseless."

A beat of silence lapsed. Michael shivered despite the heat from the torches. The voice spoke with quiet, deep contempt.

"So, defend yourself, Mr. Barris."

Only the rustling of the flames spoke in the following moments: that and Michael's labored breath.

"Defend myself from what?"

"Why, from accusations of ignorance, intolerance, slander, treason, as well as accessory to murder and genocide." There was a smiling lilt in the voice.

"So, what's the punishment for these crimes?"

"Sadly, our state is a lenient one. I personally would prefer punishments that were more in keeping with the crimes mentioned, but, oh, honey, you can't have everything you want in life!" The voice sighed with mocking sadness. "I'm afraid that all of these offenses only carry a light sentence—death."

"What!" Michael's voice actually squealed.

The crowd chuckled lowly. The slender dark hands reached in between the torches, caressing his face gently as he spoke. "Oh, Bunny-Barris, don't be that way! You're gonna die here anyway—just think of it as an early parole, huh, sugah?" Suddenly, the hands flew to Michael's throat, the long, unkempt nails digging into his flesh. He struggled backward but the cords held him. Michael could feel his own blood begin to trickle down his chest. He thrashed about for breath . . .

"Stop."

The baritone voice rang into the hall with such force as to echo in its confines. Instantly, the hands released their grip. Groans of protest filled the hall. Michael struggled, off balance as he was, to see who had spoken. All he could make out was a dark figure beyond the torches obscured by heat and smoke.

"You can play the queen-bitch later, Lucian," the baritone said from the darkness. "But for now you know what I want."

The voice—Lucian—pulled his hands back beyond the fire. "So," Lucian continued with some pique, "you crossed the line tonight. Just what were you looking for?"

Michael shivered again. *Damn,* he thought, *it's cold in here!* He was acutely aware of the eyes, hundreds of eyes, staring at him, exposed utterly before them. He was humiliated, and knowing that didn't help him deal with it in the least. All that was left was to answer the questions and hope for the best.

"I need to get in touch with the gay community . . ."

"Well, honey, I'd say you found it!"

The crowd went wild.

Michael finally got his feet back under him. "I'm looking for someone!" he shouted over the noise.

Again, Lucian silenced the crowd. "Oh, he's looking for someone! I suppose you aren't just looking for just any ol' faggot, fairy, butch, or queer, are you? You are probably looking for that limp-wristed son of yours, sweet-cheeks?"

Michael leaned forward, hope in his eyes. "Yes, my son, if I could just . . ."

Lucian remained behind the flickering light—one hand reached in and grasped Michael firmly by the jaw, shaking his head back and forth as Lucian spoke. "If you could just what, Mr. Straight-man in Fairyland? Maybe you could be a real father to him instead of the guy who gave him a name and split?"

"No," Michael muttered through Lucian's hand, "that's not it at all, I just . . ."

"Maybe you feel bad about your queer son dying on you before you could set him straight—and I do mean straight?"

"No, damn it, that's not it either, I just—"

Lucian slapped Michael hard across the face. The strength of the blow surprised Michael, blurring his vision and nearly knocking him off his feet again.

"You, Mr. Barris, run the biggest information network in the United States—all that wealth, all that power—and you just happen to turn up in an ERIS isolation camp so you can chat with your little baby boy? Sweet-thing, a man that stupid *deserves* to die."

The crowd roared again.

Lucian waited for the crowd again. "So, Mr. Michael Barris . . ."

"Fine," Michael said flatly through the stinging pain.

" 'Fine'? 'Fine' what?"

"Fine," Michael said, "fine. Kill me. You seem so intent on doing it anyway, then kill me."

Silence again. This bunny wasn't playing the game right. Somehow the fun had suddenly left, for the crowd evaporated into a puzzled seriousness.

Lucian tried to recover. He spoke slowly, unsure of his words for the first time. "Far be it from me to deny a man his last request . . ."

"Then grant me mine—*let me see my son.*"

Another hesitant pause. Michael sensed that he had suddenly, somehow, changed the rules of their game.

"Pretty good, Mr. Barris: but what makes you think your son wants to see you?"

Naked and cold, humiliated and ridiculed. Utterly alone. Michael wondered with a sudden insight if these things were not just a matter of show to these people but items of real significance. Did they humiliate him here because they felt humiliated in his world? Did they ridicule him now because they were shamed in his world? Were they utterly alone?

And what made it "his world" to begin with?

"I have to talk to my son," Michael said simply. "He may not wish to hear me, he may not even understand what I have to say— and God knows I may not understand his answers either—but I must speak with him anyway."

The distant baritone spoke from beyond the light. "Mr. Barris, what do you have to say to your son?"

Michael looked up. Could it possibly be that Jason was actually out there in the darkness? So close, could his words reach him?

"Jason?"

His voice sounded hollow in the huge space above. His own brightly lit form small at the bottom of a well of darkness. Only silence answered him.

"Jason?"

His voice seemed to carry past the top-most floors and to the stars themselves.

"Jason, I . . . I don't know you, son. My life tastes sour in my mouth. The things I thought were important are crumbling into the dust—and that's OK: it's where they belong. Maybe you don't want a father, or a brother, or a friend—but I need to at least know you and be a part of who you are. Help me to understand what we have in common and set aside our differences."

He looked again into the night stars through the roof overhead. He spoke loudly and with passion.

"Jason, I don't know you, but I want to. I'd like to love you for whoever you are."

His voice carried into the night and was swallowed by it. The night gave no reply.

Only the baritone from beyond the wall of flaming light answered him.

"Fine words, Barris," the baritone voice of the Dark Queen came in reply. "Fine words—for last words."

Joyride

Thursday, April 15, 2010 / 0107 hrs
Wah Wah Hardpan Military Zone / 477th ERIS District
Wah Wah Valley, West Beaver County, Utah

"By Gawd, we sure 'nuff showed them som'bitches!"

Whoops and joyful yells shot unheard into the dark of the night. Harlan and the McNeil twins were standing behind the cab of the truck, holding on with one hand to the roll bar while waving their hats in the other. Beneath them, the bed of the truck was bucking over the open ground. They could barely keep their feet under them. But broncs are all part of the cowboy life, whether they are muscle or steel, and to feel the motion was pure joy.

Virgil, piloting the expedition, was feeling mighty good himself. It just didn't get much better than this, boys! Sure, it would have been better if they had come up with some Coors but, hell, no one was getting much foreign produce since the interstates were all choked down. Old Frank Small's home brew was about all you could get at the Renegade Lounge these days. It was powerful stuff most of the time and certainly did the job, but it lacked, well, smoothness. Occasionally, Frank got some Coors out of Milford, but somehow that did something to the taste. So they had to make do on Small's kickapoo juice and trust that quantity would make up for quality.

It generally did—just like tonight.

Virgil had rolled the "old boys" out of the El Bambi and piled them into the back of his "Dolly." It was an '05 GMC Renegade/AG that Virgil had bought two years ago from Mack Sullivan just before he joined the army. Mack had taken good care of the truck, but his devotion to it never came close to Virgil's. Virgil loved that truck more than any girl in town—or out of it for that matter either. It showed. The body may have been five years old, but it shined like black diamonds—rust was a bad word around Virgil. The GMC was one of the first anti-gravitic service trucks produced in the United States and, true to form, it was overpowered. Six separate lifters bulged the chassis between the chromed rail skids on both sides, while two more powerful A/G thrust housings gave the truck's flanks a muscular appearance. The '05 GMCs were all muscle; back then no one really understood the more delicate points of gravitics and so, true to the American way, they simply built their vehicles so as to overcome any obstacle with raw, brute force. The GMC's power plant was a 388-cubic-inch, turbo-charged Cyclone generator—big enough to power all the A/G projectors directly at 110 percent rated cruise—coupled with dual ultrahigh-yield Delco Capacitors that Virgil had installed himself. It wasn't delicate. It didn't hum sweetly like the little subcompacts that Virgil sneered at so often on the road. When Dolly moved, she rumbled the ground with a deep resonance that you could feel more than hear.

They had rumbled down to the Renegade Lounge—talk was cheap so far but courage needed a little assistance. It was about eleven before the four boys had all the assistance that they needed.

It was like a hunt, Virgil told them. It was like moving through hostile injun territory the way their great-grandfathers did thousands of years ago. That wasn't exactly true. The local settlers were actually on pretty good terms with the Native Americans when they moved in and the thousand-years part may have been a stretch of the truth. Still, it sounded awfully important and exciting to say it through the fog of the beer.

They thundered alone up Interstate 15 heedless of the traffic since there was none to heed. The elegant stretch of road had once been immaculately kept even after the advent of grav-lifters so as to provide the smoothest possible surface to travel on. As late as '07, you could still travel the freeway in a "wheeler" and never have to worry about a bump in your suspension—let alone a hole to swallow you up. Those days were gone now. Road crews hadn't been working since '08, and traffic had dwindled pretty much to nothing by later that same year. Now weather and time were rapidly reclaiming what millions of man hours and billions of dollars had tried to carefully put in place.

They had headed north and then jumped off I-15 and turned west. The roads here were now barely visible—all the worse since there was no moon up, and Virgil, for stealth reasons of his own, had decided to drive with the lights off.

It had seemed pretty reasonable. They crossed the Milford Valley about thirty miles to the north of the town itself and then beat the old dirt jeep trails over the end of the San Francisco Range. They had seen several checkpoints along the way and had always studiously slipped around them. Occasionally, when distance on the road didn't permit a wide berth, Virgil would shut down the power plant completely and switch the lifters directly to the capacitors, and they'd glide like a black ghost through the moonless night.

Civilian vehicles weren't supposed to be able to do that, but Virgil minded his Dolly well and thought that it might just come in useful. There were a number of fathers in Beaver County who had wished those capacitors hadn't held their charge quite as well as they did. Of course, driving your vehicle on capacitors alone was illegal. Just as illegal, in fact, as disconnecting the transponder—which Virgil had done as a matter of course.

To be honest, it wasn't skill alone that brought them to crest the northern slopes of the San Francisco Range and charge full bore down toward the Wah Wah Hardpan. A herd of antelope were playing havoc with three of the SASAR-88 stationary recon robots hovering at the two-thousand-foot level in the northeast perimeter. The relief for the two guard details had been delayed coming out of Milford, and the details already in place were too busy grousing about the fact to notice the silent black truck moving against the night. Not even the heat bloom of Dolly's power plant—and it was considerable—was noticed by the outpost sentries with their long infrared eyes and coordinated weapon packages. Their attentions had been turned momentarily to an unscheduled transport arrival that had to be covered. It was momentary only—but momentary enough.

In the end it may just have been fate.

"Captain, who's up to bat tonight?"

The captain hadn't slept well—not that he'd let the colonel see that. He had dressed and polished himself to the point where he looked parade presentable. Still, for a career army man, there was too much to think about going on around him.

Now he stood again with the colonel in the Operations Center—a timeless place that looked the same regardless of the hour or season outside the walls. He found himself staring at the oversize wall displays in the large room beyond. *We're protecting our nation,* he thought to himself in what had become a mantra over the last two days. *We're protecting the nation from a deadly invader.*

"Captain?" the colonel looked at him questioningly.

"Yes, sir," the captain snapped at once. He pulled the operations schedule from under his arm and opened the loose-leaf binder smartly to the appropriate page. Some part of him wondered if he was really doing this. "The morning supply train arrived early. Four teams have been assigned to supervise its off-loading. Delta Squads have been alerted for security cover. SASAR's Echo-5 through Echo-7 are giving bad data; I've called them down for repairs. There were some transport problems with some of Beta Squad's sentry groups, but they have been solved and all the graveyard assets are in place and reporting."

The colonel absorbed all this. Waiting. "And what else, Captain?"

"Wild Cove is scheduled for sterilization, sir."

"Very good, Captain. Let's get this over with." The colonel sat down at his command station and reclined into the tall back of the office chair. He pulled the microphone on its boom stand toward him and threw a switch. "Duty officer, what's the status of Whiskey-Charlie?"

Through the glass, the captain saw the duty officer stand in the room beyond and turn toward them. "Whiskey-Charlie has been operating under Shutdown Protocol since 0600 hours yesterday, sir!"

The colonel had been here before. He continued to stare at the ceiling as he spoke and listened. "Monitors shutdown?"

"Yes, sir!"

"Power feeds uncoupled?"

"Yes, sir!"

"What about the factory pallets?"

"Rerouted as of yesterday, sir!"

"Very well, Lieutenant." The colonel pulled a cigar from his coat and smelled it. "Is the camp perimeter secure?"

"Yes, sir. We are getting positive feeds from the perimeter. All is secure."

The captain blinked. *If all the people in the camp are dead, why are they so worried about the perimeter?*

"Something the matter, Captain?"

The colonel rarely missed a trick. "No, sir. I . . . I was just thinking about all those dead, sir. What a tragedy it is, I mean, sir."

"Yes, isn't it."

WHAM!

"My hell-o-mighty, Virgil, take it easy, will ya?"

Virgil slipped the truck sideways. The stabilizers whined as they fought to keep the truck upright. The tall cowboy grinned in the cab, glancing back to see his buddies all a jumble of boots and spit in the truck bed, trying to stand up yet again. Still, they would have to fend for themselves.

Under the stars, Virgil, traveling across the Wah Wah Hardpan, had spotted a jackrabbit.

Chasing down a rabbit is one of the oldest traditions in Beaver County. You get your truck, find a rabbit, and do your best to run him down. It may not sound like much in the way of entertainment compared to the tri-videos and interactive worlds on the I-Net, but it's high sport in the open air, simple and impossible. You can get close, but you just can't catch the rabbit.

Virgil, however, had his own ideas about that subject. It seemed to him that the problem wasn't in being faster or turning sharper than the rabbit—that was flat-out impossible for a pickup. The real trick was to know which way the rabbit was going to turn *before* the rabbit himself did.

You had to think like a rabbit.

Virgil, slamming down another of Frank Small's souped-up beers with one hand while abruptly spinning the wheel with the other, was beginning to think that he was approaching the mind of a rabbit very rapidly.

Somehow, the vaunted goal of bringing fresh Beaver produce to the new citizens of the Wah Wah Valley had vanished the moment Virgil saw that rabbit in the flat, dried-up lake bed before him. Now he slammed down the accelerator again, let out a whoop, and glanced back into the flatbed.

"You boys like the ride?"

None of them heard him. They were too busy yelling themselves while trying to hang onto the bucking truck.

Virgil turned around smiling, then vaguely realized that something was wrong.

The dry lake was suddenly coming to an end, an end with a wall of volcanic rocks jumbled across it.

Virgil's eyes grew wide. He slammed the lift select to full. "Shee-it!"

Dolly's front began to lift slightly as the rocks came up. The lifters managed to keep the chassis from making any direct contact with the stone, but the abrupt change in elevation shot the GMC into the air like a cannon, its considerable momentum sailing forward into the black night sky.

"Yee-hah!" Harlan howled, oblivious to the hard ground rushing toward them.

The GMC arched over in the blackness, the gentle slope of the ground rising to meet it. The forward lifters felt the earth's resistance and drew power to compensate. The grav truck was an early model, however, and what it had in power it lacked in grace. The truck may have appeared to float over the ground, but lifters were tuned rock-hard. Dolly simply had a hard suspension. Worse, Dolly was rolling slightly, causing the forward lifters to contact the ground unevenly.

"Damn it!" Virgil cursed through set teeth as the truck leaped back into the air not unlike the jackrabbit he'd been chasing a moment ago. He gripped the wheel until he thought he might just break it off. Feedback through the steering column let him know that the truck was very quickly rushing out of his control.

The GMC strained sideways, the stabilizers threatening to off-line as the truck began to slide through the air. Virgil turned the wheel into the skid, kicked the spare lifters on-line, and tried to recover. He didn't mind the slide—hell, making snow donuts was a winter sport—but if Dolly flipped out here in no man's land, there would be a whole lot of trouble for his boys in the back.

The added thrust righted the truck but exaggerated the skid in the opposite direction. The back end of the GMC flipped around, overcompensating as the stabilizers screamed again. Back end first, her momentum spent, Dolly slammed evenly down onto the hillside. The impact smashed the joyriders flat into the truck bed. The Cyclone generator suddenly died, and the lifters, engaged to safety mode, spooled out the last of the energy and settled the truck gently the remaining two and a half feet to the ground.

Virgil found himself pulling his hat up from where the cab of the truck had pressed it down over his eyes. He threw open the door of the truck and jumped out. "You boys all right back thar? Harl? Louis?"

The jumble of Levi's began to move. "Gawddamn! What a ride, partner!" Harlan moaned.

"You boys hurt?" Virgil was sobering up awful fast.

"Hell, no, we ain't hurt," Louis exclaimed. "But I ain't feeling so good neither."

Virgil grinned and shook his head. "Well, don't go pukin' in my Dolly or you damn well will be hurt. I'll be damned. I was sure someone back here had broke somethin'."

"Hell, no! It'll take more'n a little bronc to take a McNeil down." Lowell jumped down from the truck bed, but his feet weren't quite under him yet. He fell flat on his ass.

Virgil laughed to the stars. "I do believe you boys are just too damn drunk to get hurt."

"Damn rights!" The McNeil boys said it like it was a chorus.

Virgil knew better. "Well, boys, looks like the fun's over for the night. Climb on in and let's get goin'." The big man climbed back into the cab of the truck and turned the starter over. The Cyclone cranked but wouldn't kick in. After the third try, Virgil quit.

Harlan leaned over the side of the truck's bed. "Hey, Virgil, how we gonna get outta here?"

Virgil squinted into the sky despite the night. It was just part of his thinking process. "Something must of knocked loose when we took that last bounce. Maybe the breakers from the feedback, maybe just some connectors. I'll get her running, boys." Virgil stepped up on the open cab door, grabbed the roof, and took a look around. "This whole valley's just plumb full of little settlements! Hell, Harlan, there's one just up the hill a piece—maybe half a mile."

Harlan and the McNeils turned to where Virgil pointed. Sure enough, the black box outlines of buildings were clearly visible.

"You boys go on up there and see if you can get any help. Hell, we're supposed to be here to sell them folks stuff anyway." Virgil looked them all in the eye. "Don't you worry about Dolly: she ain't never failed me yet. I'll get her runnin'."

Virgil saw the agreement in their eyes. They'd never question him. He never even considered that they might.

Virgil lowered himself to the ground, popped open the hood, and grabbed the flashlight from behind the cab seat. By the time he turned around, the three boys were already moving up the slope between the scattered sagebrush.

It didn't take them more than ten minutes to reach the perimeter of Wild Cove.

Thunder in My Soul

April 15, 2010 / 0125 hrs
Perimeter 3
Wild Cove Center / 477th ERIS District
Wah Wah Valley, West Beaver County, Utah

Harlan was tired. The beer was wearing off pretty quickly in the cold night breeze. Picking his way among the sage was getting tiresome. There weren't even any lights in the town ahead of him. All asleep, he thought. That sounded pretty good to him.

What had seemed like a good idea in the warmth of the El Bambi Café was turning sour in his mind. The buildings ahead of him were getting closer and still no light. He'd have thought that at least one or two would be up this late—even in Beaver some folks are up past midnight—but only black windows stared back at him no matter how hard he looked.

The wind kicked some sand up into his eye, the low moaning increasing. "Damn! Louis, you see anything in there?"

"No, no I don't." Louis's voice sounded quiet. The McNeils were probably losing the glow from earlier in the evening as well. There was something ahead that Louis didn't understand, and it worried him.

"Ah, hell!" Louis wiped his eyes just as the wind died down for a moment.

He heard crying.

Not just one woman sobbing or a couple of people but a whole bunch of them. They sounded like the wind to him, and he realized that's why he hadn't heard them before. But close as he was now, he could hear the agony of the individual voices. The sound froze him where he stood about five hundred feet from the nearest of the buildings.

Harlan squinted. In the starlight he could barely make out figures now moving against the two- and three-story buildings of the town—if that's what it was. Hundreds of them, he thought. It was difficult to tell.

"What in the name of hell are they doin' to them people." It was as close to the sound of a prayer as Harlan had ever heard Lowell utter.

It had all seemed so simple: just dodge the army, run out here, and set up a little trade with the natives, that's all. The sound of the cries wasn't simply pain or anger. The sounds he heard were agony from the depths of another's soul. They cut to his heart. Women's screams. Men's sobbing. Children—*by Gawd,* he thought, *there's even children making that damnable sound!* It had been such a simple idea! Now here they were, hip-deep in manure and scared shitless.

"What . . . what'll we do, Harl?"

Harlan turned to Louis. How was he supposed to know? He wasn't Virgil. Virgil would know what to do. Virgil always knew what to do. But Virgil wasn't here, so Harlan guessed it probably was up to him.

Maybe.

"I don't know, Lowell. Something terrible's goin' on up thar, and it just don't seem right. Maybe we aughta get up thar and ask one of 'em what's their problem. Then maybe we can help 'em."

The McNeils just looked at him.

"Well, damn it, we can't help nobody if we don't know what their problem is, can we?" Harlan yelled.

Lowell jumped at that. "Damn rights!" Lowell began marching up through the brush again, his Levi's rustling against the dry branches. He began calling out. "Hey, you in thar! What's yer problem. Maybe we can help out!"

They were getting closer. Lowell was determined, a good thirty feet ahead of either Harlan or Louis. It looked like he was beginning to attract attention—in fact, quite a lot of attention. The sounds from the camp were getting louder, and a huge crowd was gathering.

Harlan was puzzled. *Why aren't they coming out to meet us?*

"YEOW!"

Lowell, shouting and waving his hat, suddenly shot straight into the air.

The checklist was finished. The colonel noted the neighboring camp monitors to be sure they were secure, and isolated the remaining auxiliary feeds to the camp. That done, he pulled his key from around his neck and inserted it into one of twelve similar keyholes in his command console.

"Lieutenant, prepare to turn safeties key."

"Affirmative, sir."

"On my mark: three, two, one, turn!"

"We have a red light with safeties off on Whiskey-Charlie." The lieutenant's voice was even. He'd done this many times before.

"Safeties off. Ejector is charging. Detonation in five minutes." The colonel leaned back again in his chair. "Well, Captain, I suppose that's all that—"

The lieutenant on the other side of the glass turned suddenly back toward them.

"Colonel! We have a Perimeter Three alarm at Whiskey-Charlie!"

The colonel looked up sharply. "What is it, Lieutenant? More antelope?"

"Negative, sir! We read it as a single man."

The captain turned to the colonel. "Good Lord! You mean there's someone out there?"

The colonel ignored the remark. "Why didn't we get interior perimeter alarms?"

This didn't make sense to the captain. The camps were each ringed by a succession of three anti-grav fences. Each was not only capable of lifting anyone attempting to leave the camp off the ground, but feeding back the fact as a security alarm to the Operations Center. If someone were trying to leave the camp, the first fence—Perimeter One—should have tripped. Even if they made it past the first fence somehow, Perimeter Two should have picked them up. To trip the Perimeter Three alarm, someone would either have to come from the inside past two other fences or . . .

The lieutenant was sweating despite the cool air in the room. "I don't know, sir. The systems are all checking out as normal."

"Bring the Wild Cove monitors back up." The colonel was aggravated.

The timer display for detonation suddenly burned into the captain's mind. "Sir, shouldn't we abort the count?"

The colonel didn't turn away from the bank of monitors suddenly lighting up in front of him. The fiber-optic feeds were giving him IR enhanced images, grainy but readable. Blank desert was in the distance, but in the center of the picture was the warm figure of a man hanging in the air. Beyond him, on the ground, two other figures flared brightly in the infrared.

"We have a security breach in the vicinity of Wild Cove Camp." The colonel stared at the monitor. "Alert posts Sierra 5, 7, and 8 to stop any egress. Captain, who's in the bull pen?"

The captain was on the phone. "Gold Squad reports prep and dispersal in two minutes."

"Time on site for Gold Squad?"

"Eight minutes, sir."

"Very well." The colonel glanced at the timer display and then leaned back in his chair. "Inform Gold Squad that they are to wait for my instructions before leaving."

"Sir?"

"You heard me, Captain, hold the security team until I say so."

"Sir, what about the detonation?"

The colonel made no move.

"Gawddamn it! Get me the hell down from here!"

Harlan didn't know what to do. If he stepped forward to help Lowell, he'd just end up hanging in the sky like he was. It wasn't like the man could climb down out of the air—or could he?

"Louis!" Harlan had to shout to be heard over the cacophony of noise pouring from the camp. It seemed that word had quickly spread that they were out here. By now there must have been a couple of thousand people screaming at him from the houses only five hundred feet from where he stood. He didn't understand it. All he wanted now was to get the hell away from the camp. "Louis! Get back to the truck and get a rope. We'll lasso the som'bitch and get out of here!"

Louis didn't wait to answer. He just turned and ran down the slope toward where the truck had been left behind.

The captain caught some movement on another monitor just as he spoke into the phone. The lieutenant had dutifully brought the monitors from the camp back on-line, but in his rush had brought all the feeds back from all over the camp. The bank of monitors displayed a number of areas in the camp. Just as he finished his call, the captain leaned closer to examine the monitor.

"Colonel!"

"What is it, son?"

"Sir! There are people alive in that camp! There must be thousands of them! We've got to stop the count—there's been some horrible mistake!"

The colonel turned to look at him with a cool, slow movement.

"There's no one alive in that camp, Captain. They have all been declared dead by the United States government. You *did* read the operational orders of this command, didn't you, Captain?"

Three minutes.

Virgil was facedown under the hood. The flashlight kept slipping from its precarious perch, slamming down on Virgil's right hand every time he reached for the loose fitting. It wasn't so much painful as frustrating. Virgil howled every time, as though the flashlight was trying to do him personal injury.

He never even heard Louis coming.

"Virgil!"

Virgil's head slammed up against the truck's hood. Swearing mightily under his breath, Virgil jumped back from the bumper and landed on his feet, doubled over and holding his head. "Louis, what in the hell are you doing?"

"Virgil, you all right?"

"Yes, Louis. What the hell do you want?" Virgil continued rubbing his head but stopped suddenly at the look on the McNeil boy's face. He'd seen Louis sober, drunk, shamed, mad, giddy, serious, and unconscious, but never before now had he seen him terrified.

"What is it, Louis?"

"Gawd almighty, Virgil, it's terrible up thar! They got about a hundred thousand people up in that thar place. I swear to Gawd! They's all screamin' and yellin' and Lowell got hisself caught in a gravity fence . . ."

"You're shittin' me!"

"No, Virgil, it's true, I swear! Harl sent me back here to get a rope so's we can haul him on down!"

Virgil began moving before Louis had stopped talking. He reached back into the cab and started fishing behind the seat. Never go anywhere without a good rope, his daddy told him. He never did.

Louis kept right on talking. "You ain't seen nothing like this, Virgil! Thar's women and children in there, all of 'em wailing like banshees! Some of 'em saw us out thar, and before you knowed it they was all comin' out and yellin' at us. Damned if I know what they were yellin', but they sure was yellin'!"

Virgil took it all in as he fished about for the rope. His hand finally connected with the harsh bite of the hemp, and he pulled the rope clear of the cab. He stuck it in Louis's hands.

"You git yer ass up the slope and pull Lowell free of the fence. Sounds like he's pretty far up, so be careful that he don't break nothin' coming down. I figured out the problem with Dolly, and I'll be thar just as soon as I can. We're up to our necks in dog shit, Louis. Somethin' wrong's goin' on out here. We gotta get our asses home before anyone finds us. Now git!"

Louis jumped. He ran full tilt up the slope tripping over a sage now and then as he dashed through the moonlight.

Virgil jumped back up on the front bumper of the GMC and reached in too quickly. The generator was still hot.

"I got no time for this!" Virgil shouted as he groped for the wayward power fitting.

* * *

The captain stared blankly at the colonel.

"Yes, sir," he murmured. "I read the operational orders, sir."

"Then perhaps I must conclude that you question my judgment in this matter, Captain. Or perhaps you are questioning the operational orders themselves?"

The captain again could feel the sweat gathering between his shoulder blades. "No, sir! Not at all, sir."

One minute.

"Here's the rope!" Louis shouted through his burning lungs. "I think I got about fifty feet of it."

Harl was spooked. He'd waited forever for Louis to return with that rope. The mob by the buildings had grown enormous. Harl couldn't remember seeing that many people up close before in the same place. For someone used to quiet streets and wide space, it was truly terrifying.

"Jesus! Harl, get me the hell down from here, will ya!" There was real panic in Lowell's voice. Harl looked up again at his friend suspended thirty feet in the air.

"Jest hold yer horses, Lowell!" Harlan grabbed the rope and began casting about for a rock to tie it to. He didn't have to actually throw the rope—he'd figured that much out. All he had to do was get the rock into the gravity fence, and the fence would take the rope up to Lowell.

"It won't take me but a second."

"Lieutenant, close down the monitors."

"Yes, sir, Colonel. Monitors are now shut down. Whiskey-Charlie is now isolated."

Ten seconds.

Virgil leaped into the driver's seat and turned the ignition. The Cyclone rumbled to life. The capacitors showed positive charging. The lifters gently pushed the GMC off its skids.

"Jeez, Dolly! Thank you, darlin'!" Virgil actually kissed the dashboard. "Here comes the cavalry, boys!" he shouted, and threw the select into drive.

He was about to jam the accelerator all the way to the fire wall when he heard a low thump, rather like the sound fireworks make just when they're launched. He hesitated, unsure for the moment whether it was something outside or another problem with the truck.

It didn't matter, he shrugged and jammed the accelerator down anyway, prepared to turn the truck around . . .

Many in the camp heard the dull report of the canister launch, though others were too absorbed in their own misery and wailing to hear.

Louis looked up at the sound. He saw a single lozenge flying through the air, starlight glinting off its surface.

The FAE arched upward along a path calculated to bring it to just the right position over Wild Cove Camp. The camp itself had been designed to fit neatly and completely inside the footprint of the explosion. The jacket blew apart, forcing the fuel to mix completely with the open air encasing the camp.

The pressures at the heart of a fuel air blast are in excess of those at the center of a nuclear blast. Those who were breathing in at the moment of dispersal were literally blown apart. Those who were breathing out were crushed. The footprint of the blast extended at least a hundred feet beyond the Perimeter Three fence that held—for only a moment longer—the body of Lowell McNeil.

All this happened in a matter of moments above a camp where absolutely everything was made to burn.

Night evaporated around Virgil. The lightbulb flash behind him blinded him instantly. Instinctively, Virgil let go of the wheel and covered his eyes.

Before his arms could cover his face, the pressure wave hit. Air, compressed by the explosion until it was nearly solid, slammed into the back of the levitating GMC with such force that Virgil's head snapped back hard. Only the headrest saved him from breaking his neck. He had the vague sensation that he was riding a rocket.

The GMC actually rode the pressure wave for a moment before it passed the truck by. By that time the wave had imparted considerable velocity to what was left of the truck, for the entire rear end was smashed in as though it had been hit by a train. The Cyclone died yet again and with it the lifters, and yet the Renegade still flew, end over end through the air. Virgil, dazed and in shock, watched the world spin around him for a few moments.

He wondered what his daddy thought of death.

It was the last thought he had before the crumpled remains of the GMC slammed into the gully wall over a thousand feet from where he started.

"Lieutenant, I want two more follow-up bursts and an incendiary spread over the next five minutes. After that, you may release Gold Squad. Have them evaluate Whiskey-Charlie and make sure that there are no longer any intruders loose in the area."

The lieutenant nodded. He knew the job actually belonged to the captain. It was a bad sign.

"Captain, would you join me in my office. We have a few things to discuss."

As the colonel and the captain left their Operations Suite, the lieutenant turned back to his console and shook his head. He wondered if anyone would ever see the captain again.

16 Son

April 15, 2010 / 0125 hrs
Barracks 6-Y
Newhouse Center / 477th ERIS District
Wah Wah Valley, West Beaver County, Utah

The building shook visibly, causing dust to filter down like thin snow from the exposed floors above. Within a matter of seconds, a second concussion of sound rattled the walls again. A collective cry went up from the crowd. Feet pounded the boards until they vibrated from the successive impacts. In moments, the building was empty.

Except for Michael.

Forgotten, he slumped against the rough ropes securing him to the support poles in the center of the dying room, naked in the night, which was cold despite the torches flaring before him.

He felt none of it, heard none of it.

It had been a desperate chance, calculated to be sure, but a chance nonetheless. He'd pulled every favor he had just to help a boy who was a stranger to him. What had he hoped to gain? Respect? Joy? Friendship? Love? Forgiveness?

Whatever else, surely forgiveness. Forgiveness for some crime he suspected himself of having committed and yet remained unsure just when and where he had committed it. His son was gay, something which he had had to admit to himself with some shame at first—wondering where as a parent he had gone wrong and as a father he had utterly failed. As he saw the distance between them widen over the years, Michael had wondered at the time whether the problems between him and Jason's mother had somehow caused their son to grow up "wrong." For a long time he engaged in a tortured search for answers. Long wakeful nights and years of worry later, there was still no answer, no cause, and no crime of which he could determine himself guilty.

Then came a day when at last he did understand that he could never understand. There were no answers to be found—not in genetics, nor behavioral psychology, nor his own memories—both real and imagined. His son was gay. That was all there ever would be to it.

He had a son whom he simply didn't know at all. Their thinking was divergent in so many ways that they could barely even talk. Yet it wasn't until Jason had long gone to college and was working in the Midwest that he began to realize something more: that he had spent so much time looking at their differences that he had forgotten to look at all the ways in which they were alike.

He remembered many things from when Jason was growing up. Things that they had shared even though his work had pulled him from home, while at the same time, his wife seemed to be driving him away. He'd been riding herd on the Fourth of July festivities in the centennial year, which had become just another holiday that he had or could be away from home. He'd been working since three in the morning and hadn't come back through the door until six that night. Yet there was Michael—that strange boy of his—waiting for him. Michael had made a point of taking Jason to every liberty fireworks display since he was old enough to talk. He wasn't sure why—perhaps because it was one of the few things he could count on his own father doing for him as he grew up. Yet on that huge day, all he really wanted was some quiet and to be left alone.

Then he looked into the bright eyes of his son, and all he could see was the anticipation.

"We can't miss the fireworks, Dad," Jason had said.

Michael had opened his mouth to protest, to lay down his arguments, and if necessary, to lay down the law in order to stay home and . . . but his eyes couldn't leave those of his son. It was the only time he remembered his son using the word "we" with him. So instead, Michael just smiled.

And Jason smiled back.

That smile carried him through the night. He could no longer remember the bright eruptions of color in the sky or if he managed to stay awake through the whole program or not. Yet he never forgot that smile—that moment when somehow they had connected.

It was a notion that brought him some peace at last—a solution that brought closure to his emotional dilemma. Someday—when he could get around to it—it would solve all his relationship problems with his son. He'd find that common ground.

Then, right in the middle of the V-CIDs crisis, Michael got word that Jason was coming home. The time had come.

And Jason never arrived.

Within a week, Michael was sure that his son had disappeared into the ERIS protective isolation system, but kept running into stone walls as to exactly where. The "quarantine towns"—a name he liked to have his news division use for the camps—were sealed off completely from the prying eyes of the media. Precedents where thrown up with high-sounding moral objectives, the most plausible being that the identities of the camp people needed to be protected against possible discrimination by others later when a cure was found.

Yet there was no cure for Michael. The wound had been reopened. Anticipating the time when he could at last come to terms with Jason, Michael had been robbed of the opportunity. He had no closure. It had become for him a thing left undone—worse yet, a thing that may never be properly closed if he didn't reach his son soon. He needed Jason's forgiveness, especially now—especially with greater guilt that drove him more surely than his longing for his son that never was.

So he'd pushed and pushed—until he had pushed too far.

He had paid every price asked, nearly all of his wealth, his reputation, his position, his freedom, and now it would seem, his life as well just to have closure with his son. And it had all been for nothing. They'd kill him, Michael knew, and that would be the end of it.

The building again rattled, sifting dust and small debris over him.

"Mr. Barris?"

The voice seemed to come from the top of a well—a well that was dragging Michael deeper by the moment.

"Michael Barris!"

With ultimate effort he rose from the well of his own despair. He lifted his head, blinking into the torchlight. A figure was approaching him, blurry through his unfocused vision.

"Yes," Michael responded flatly, hopelessly. "What more do you want? Let me die."

The face penetrated the torchlight around him.

"What? And let you miss the fireworks?" Jason sneered.

Michael wept.

Michael fumbled with his pants. Only now, freed of the coarse ropes that had held him, did he feel the cold in his hands. His fingers moved clumsily over his own clothing both from the chill and his own awkward hurry. He was somehow embarrassed to be standing naked before his own son.

"I thought I'd never find you, boy." Michael's voice shook from his own excitement and relief.

"Well, you know what Mark Twain said about the reports of his own death being greatly exaggerated." Jason leaned against one wall of the room, his arms folded across his chest, his head cocked skeptically to one side. "You came close, Dad, and you're not exactly out of it yet."

"My God, it's good to see you, son. I'd about given up hope." Michael moved toward his son, but Jason instantly stood and took a step back from him.

"Look, sir, I don't know what you're here for but . . ."

Michael looked shocked. "Didn't you hear what I said?"

"Yes, sir, I heard every word. Nice words, too. I seem to remember that you used to use words in your business like a weapon." Jason stood stiffly, awkwardly, as though undecided about whether to stay or to run. "You were pretty good at it, too."

Michael sighed and took a step back, sensing somehow that putting a little physical distance between them would be more comfortable. Distance always seemed to improve their relationship in the past. "I got your message. You were on your way home. What happened?"

Jason smiled, but didn't relax. "I was making good progress until Arizona. I must have slipped up in Prescott. By the time I made it to Lake Havasu, the National Guardsmen had caught up to me. I tried to get away, but the Guardsmen leveled me. The next thing I remember, I was in the mill and being processed. They took me up to the Vegas Internment Station and sent me up here. I know why I'm here. So what's your story?"

Michael stood, studying Jason carefully. *Who is this stranger?* he thought to himself. *Even after all this time, there is still such a valley between us and I still can't find my way across.* "I waited for you. When you were about a week overdue, I started looking for you." He ventured a smile. "I guess I found you."

Jason shook his head. "Why would you want to do a stupid thing like that? Judas Priest, that was dumb!"

"You're my son, Jason!"

"I was never *your* son!"

"Now, just what is that supposed to mean?" Michael suddenly realized he was shouting and wondered why he was.

"You don't get it, do you, Dad?" Jason threw his hands up in the air in resignation. "You never did get it. You aren't my family. I never felt part of what you considered to be a *family.* I was the odd one, the different one, remember? I never fit in with your ideas of what a son was—whenever you were around to enforce them."

"That wasn't often, was it?"

"Oh," Jason mocked him, "a confession!"

This wasn't going the way Michael had pictured it. "Jason, I'm sorry, you're right. I really don't know who you are at all, do I? We lived in the same house for all those years, and we're still strangers to each other. I think we spent all our time talking *at* each other rather than *to* each other. I don't want to tell you how to live your life—I just want to get to know you, OK?"

The question hung in the air between them, as did Michael's offered hand.

Jason pressed his hands deep into his soiled Levi's.

Michael slowly took back his hand. "So," he said, "where did everybody go?"

Jason raised his eyebrows and nodded back toward the stairwell. "Come on, I'll show you."

Michael followed Jason up the loose staircase to the top floor of the barracks. Michael could see the torches they had left burning two stories below them through the gaping hole cut in the center of the floor. A makeshift ladder of broken boards lashed together with everything from twine to sneaker laces rising up to a ragged hole in the ceiling. Jason climbed into the darkness with Michael quickly following.

He stood on the roof of Barracks Y. Next to him, his son and several others from the barracks were gazing off to the northwest. Below him, along the line marking the gravity fence, Michael noticed a sea of heads—nearly two thousand, he guessed—craning in the same direction.

Then he saw it himself.

Smoke boiling a deep and angry orange rose high into the clear night. For a moment, Michael's mind was filled with the image of an atomic blast but dismissed it at once. The ground below the smoke was brilliantly ablaze in distant flashes of blues, yellows, and whites. It couldn't have been more than six, maybe seven miles away. He knew what it was even before Jason spoke.

"It's Wild Cove—poor shmucks."

"An accident?" Michael murmured hopefully.

Jason shook his head. "No, Dad, no accident. ERIS just cleaned it out."

He looked at his son. "Cleaned it out?"

"That's what Weston calls it. It happened twice before that I know of. Once just after I got here and then again about a week ago. According to Weston, after everyone dies in the camp, ERIS comes in and blows the shit out of it and then burns everything. That way, no virus gets out."

"So there was no one alive in that camp?"

Jason looked at his father quizzically. "No, of course not—why?" Michael looked pale, even in this limited light.

Jason walked Michael back to the line. No one bothered them. Indeed, Michael didn't even see another person, though he never doubted that they would suddenly appear if Jason needed them. As they came to the street bisecting the camp, Jason stopped.

"I asked that you be allowed across the line, Dad. We knew you were coming. The Queen gave permission. I guess I just wanted to hear what you had to say." Jason shrugged and looked down at the ground. "It was good to see you, crazy as you're being here is. I've thought a lot about you—and Mom, too. I'm just sorry to see you here. I'd wish a better end for you than this. You were never really bad to me, and I guess you did your best to be a father. It just didn't work with me, I guess. So, it's OK."

Michael turned to Jason. "Don't, son. Don't say good-bye."

Jason looked away, avoiding his father's eyes.

Michael struggled to keep his voice even. "I understand that they are your family now—probably more of a family to you than your mother and I ever were. Before I die, I'd just like to know who you are."

Jason's expression remained hard, but he said, "I'll talk to the Queen about the two of us meeting again. We'll see."

"Thank you."

Jason walked away, but hadn't gone more than a few steps before he turned again to face Michael. "You still haven't told me why you came."

"You were the catalyst . . ."

"The catalyst but not the reason."

The dark night was closing in on Michael. The smoke from burning Wild Cove was obliterating the stars.

"Son, I'm here for two reasons that I can no longer live with. First, the fact that you're here, and second, that I helped *build* this camp."

'Tis of Thee

April 15, 2010 / 1920 hrs
Command & Control Center / 477th ERIS District Command
Milford, West Beaver County, Utah

The captain followed the colonel into the dim room first, pressed from behind by the omnipresent MPs. The floor lamps standing to either side of the room cast light upward onto the ceiling in dull bluish patches. The neatly ordered set of bookshelves completely covered the left-hand wall, while a large map hung over a couch on the right. These flanked the mahogany desk sitting like a fortress in the center of the room. The blinds were drawn closed, keeping out the darker night beyond.

It wasn't the first time the captain had been here, but never under circumstances like this. He had never known those blinds to be anything but completely closed, regardless of the time of day or weather beyond. The colonel's office was a self-contained, ordered universe. Nothing, it would seem, would ever change here until the colonel himself changed. And the colonel never changed. He was constant and eternal.

The colonel sat behind the desk, his eyes locked on the captain with a look that threatened to turn the air solid between them. The eyes stayed on the captain as the colonel leaned back in his deep chair. The captain could hear the faint squeal of the leather as the tall officer settled in.

Silence raged between them for a single, eternal, heartbeat.

"Captain," the colonel said quietly, "I know you well enough to trust that, if I order you not to, you won't bleed on my carpet after I shoot you here."

"Yes, sir," the captain answered, still at attention before the desk. The color was gone from his face. He had seen enough to know that the colonel may just do as he says and be crazy enough to court-martial his corpse afterward if he didn't obey. "No bleeding, sir!"

The colonel's stare didn't waver from the captain, although he spoke to the MPs. "Sergeant, I don't think I'll be needing you right away. Why don't you two wait outside for a while."

The captain remained at attention, hearing the door behind him click open and shut. They were alone.

"Did you know that I served with your father during the First Gulf War back in '92? We were just a couple of pups back then, driving Abram's like they were sports cars and filling the desert with Iraqi steel and blood. *There* was a war that you could win! The objectives were clear, and all we had to do was go out and do them. Clear victory, son." The colonel reached into a box on his desk and pulled out a cigar. He didn't light it, just chewed on it. "Your father and I go that far back. When I heard that his son was coming up for assignment in the ERIS, why, I just knew I had to have you on staff."

The captain's mouth suddenly went dry.

"Damn shame," murmured the colonel.

The captain swallowed hard, trying to clear the cotton he felt was filling his mouth. "Sir, I've completed my assigned tasks to the best of my understanding. If the colonel is not satisfied with my performance—"

"I am not satisfied with your performance!" the colonel snapped. The voice was not loud, but the accusation was unmistakable. "We've got a job to do here, Captain, and it's not a pretty one. No one knows that more than I do. I can't have you questioning my orders in the Ops Center, especially at critical moments like that last stunt. You've read the operational orders, Captain! Just what do you think we're doing out here?"

The captain swallowed again. "Does the colonel wish me to answer that question, sir?"

"Yes, damn it; answer it."

The captain drew a deep breath. "Relocate and isolate suspected V-CIDS victims from designated 'free zones' until such time as a cure for the disease can be found. During that period, we are to care for the victims . . ."

"Internees," corrected the colonel.

". . . internees. Occasionally, where camps are no longer able to support themselves or be supported by us, then the camp is sanitized."

"What is sanitized, Captain?"

"Sir, we blow the camp into the ground with a short series of FAEs and then burn it."

"And anyone left in those camps?"

The captain despaired but stood straight. "We murder them, sir."

The colonel raised his eyebrows. "Murder, Captain? That's a mighty strong word."

The captain could feel his legs begin to shake under him, some part of him absurdly hoping that the shaking didn't move the careful crease in his pants. "With all due respect, sir, the killing of unarmed civilians within an enclosed space from which they have no opportunity to escape? That seems like a definition for murder, sir!"

Some other part of the captain said those words. Some part of him that had kept him up for the last two days.

The other part of him hoped that he wouldn't bleed on the carpet when the colonel shot him dead.

But the colonel only looked away, his eyes blinking in thought, his lips pursed. After a moment he stood up and walked around the desk. "Please, Captain, at ease."

The captain, a roaring in his ears, didn't move a muscle.

"Captain," the colonel said again quietly as he watched him, "*at ease!*"

The captain started and jerked his head twice like a mechanical toy jolting to life. He turned his head to look at the colonel, his eyes burning.

"Captain, please," the colonel said in a soothing voice. "Please sit down."

Slowly, like a coiled spring unwinding, the captain settled back into the offered chair, unsure about what was to follow. The colonel had transformed himself instantly from the mad commander into a saintly, fatherly figure. The captain wasn't sure which aspect was more frightening.

"Look, son, I understand how all of this must appear to you on first blush," the colonel said as he sat down casually on the corner of his desk, "but there are issues here that just don't enter into the Command Logs and that are just too subtle for even the MCOP programs to properly clarify in the operational orders. Frankly, not everything is in the operational orders. Some things are still done, well, man to man in our army. Some things are better understood that way."

Orders not in the orders, the captain thought. *What is he talking about?*

"Look, son, how do we treat cancer?"

"Well." The captain thought for a moment. "I believe that a series of modgens designed for the specific cancer type is given to the patient who—"

"Yes, yes, of course," the colonel interrupted, "we do that now because we have modgens that are designed to attack those cells and clear up the problem. But, think for a moment. What if we didn't have modgens at all? What if they hadn't been invented yet?"

"Well," the captain considered, "I suppose we'd have to go back to the old way. We'd introduce chemotherapies and radiation treatments."

"And if those didn't work?"

"Surgery, I suppose. Amputation if necessary."

The colonel smiled with bright teeth. "Exactly so! Somehow, some way, the challenge is to get the body rid of these cancerous cells. They simply have to go—for the good of the body and the healthy cells."

The captain was relaxing slightly into the easy conversation. "I'm not sure what this has to do with—"

"It has everything to do with our mission here. Look, Captain, tell me, just who do we have in these camps?"

"People who have contracted the V-CIDS virus."

"A virus which is 98 percent fatal within seven years, though usually much sooner." The colonel was forging his logic chain as he had done every day since taking command. "But just who are these people with the V-CIDS virus?"

The captain waited for the colonel to answer his own question. The colonel just smiled and reached behind him for a folder on his desk and handed it to the captain. The broken seal around it was labeled "Top Secret: Project Linebacker (Supplemental Study A6)."

"You remember AIDS?"

"Sure." The captain began thumbing through the report, looking for the major headings. "It was cured back in '02 with some sort of vaccination, wasn't it?"

"That's right." The colonel chewed the words around his unlit cigar. "Specifically with a counter-virus. Fought fire with fire, eh? The problem was that the HIV virus that caused AIDS kept shifting around every block we threw at it. We'd find a way to stop it, and the vicious thing would just mutate around it. We knew more about the HIV virus than any other virus known to man, and still we couldn't stop it. That bug had an inventive will to live. So a set of geneticists working under a DOD grant engineered a counter-virus that would mutate right along with the HIV inside the host body. Linebacker, get it?"

The captain continued to flip pages. He'd had genetics as part of his basic medical training in college. He didn't understand it all, but what he did understand was amazing. "Right. I see! Here, look." He pointed down at the report, reading the lines out loud. " 'The engineered counter-virus was designed to achieve two goals: (1) to anticipate changes in the HIV virus and destroy it before duplication and (2) to evaluate the original state of the host immune system and reset the system to those values based on statistical curves.' " The captain looked up. "They really did this?"

"Yes, Captain. The counter-virus was designed not only to destroy the HIV infection, but to set the normal immune system back up again. *That*"—the colonel tapped the report with his finger—"is the nature of the vaccine. Since it was a disease we *wanted* people to get, it was also made far more communicable than HIV ever was. Commercially, it was distributed as X-Aid, but the government originally developed it and knew it by another name—V-CIDS: Virus, Counter Immune Deficiency Syndrome."

The captain blinked, wondering if he had heard right. "V-CIDS? V-CIDS!? You mean the people in these camps are suffering from the *cure* for AIDS?"

"Sit down, Captain," the Colonel said coldly.

Shaking, he hadn't even been aware he was standing up.

The colonel pulled his cigar from his mouth, brandishing it like a swagger stick. "You can't imagine how complex genetic coding of this type can be. Especially, when you're trying to engineer heuristic traits down at the molecular level. The virus managed its first mission well, but there was a basic logic problem in the coding to reset the immune system. It reset the immune system, but it kept on resetting it, searching constantly for genetic references that were earlier and earlier in development. Pretty soon, it would reset a person's immune system to a period before it had developed any natural immunities at all. The symptoms themselves were very much like AIDS—people contracting normally harmless diseases, and their immune systems failed. The public thought it was just a new form of the old plague. Especially when it seemed to come from the gays and lesbians."

The captain looked up questioningly.

"They were the first to use the cure," the colonel said simply. "They were the first to suffer the consequences. I can remember watching the news reports. People in 'Frisco would wait for hours in line just to get the cure."

The captain was seeing it, too.

"Then, when the gays rioted in 'Frisco, that pretty well put the lid on it. The I-Net channels were jammed with the public demanding that something be done about not only V-CIDS but the gays and anyone else who had the disease as well. The government suggested that isolation and quarantine would be a prudent emergency step. The interactive networks instantly polled America and got a resounding mandate for their action. Carriers of the disease needed to be apprehended both for their own good and that of the public. America voted electronically in the vast affirmative. Of course, it was part of the secret operational orders derived from the presidential directive that actually forwarded the concept of 'predeceased.' It would save time and effort if these people were declared 'predeceased'—dead before they died—allowing their estates to continue more efficiently before they were actually gone. It was for the good of the country. The great electronic voice of America had given the President a blank check to take care of the problem. No price was too high, no measures too strong. Just get the job done and don't bother us about the details."

Price too high. Measures too strong.

"So, Captain, who are we sending into our little camps in the beyond of nowhere? Homosexuals, drug addicts, and ghetto junkies. People on the welfare doles. If they weren't to begin with, then they got it by being intimate and immoral with someone who was." The colonel saw the shock in the captain's face. "Look, Captain, the time for beating around the bush is past. The biggest problems we've had in the last hundred years have been related to these cancers, these blights on our nation! They've been bleeding this country dry, sucking the very life out of it, killing it off little by little by their own parasitic growth.

"But V-CIDS changed all that. V-CIDS was the mark of the beast, you see! You look at a person on the street, and you couldn't tell if they were straight like you and me or a homo or some other kind of pervert. You didn't know if they were a hardworking person or a leech on the welfare rolls. Yet with V-CIDS it became so simple, so direct. Justice and judgment all in a single little bug!"

The captain stared incredulously at the colonel. "You mean you can judge these people's right to live based on whether or not they have a disease? A disease *that we gave them?*"

"They have it: they're guilty," the colonel said simply.

The captain could only stare.

"And now? Now we have been given an opportunity to finally do something about our country! No more perpetuation of the welfare rolls. No more poor! No more drug trade because the user base has been wiped out! No more *cancer*, Captain! What we'll have left will be healthy tissue—an America that's alive and well. Imagine it, Captain, just imagine it! Imagine an America free of the deadweight of people who aren't pulling their share! Imagine an America free of moral decay!" The colonel pointed triumphantly at the captain. "You tell me, son. You've read the operational orders. Just what is the legal status of the people in those camps?"

Slowly, deliberately, the captain said, "They are predeceased, sir. Considered legally dead until they can be proven to be free of the V-CIDS virus."

"Exactly my point, Captain! We have no real 'people' in these camps. What we have are a bunch of corpses who are reaping the fruits of their evil behavior and just don't know that they're dead yet. Most of them are suffering from all kinds of terrible afflictions. We aren't really *murdering* anyone. Hell, boy, we're just putting them out of their misery as humanely as we can."

The captain would not allow himself to cry, though he badly wanted to. The colonel was crazy, of that he was sure, but what he couldn't be sure about was just how far that madness extended beyond him. The orders seemed clear from the President on down through command. This wasn't one runaway commander. This was a system that had grown beyond control.

"Why don't we just take them all out at once, sir?" The captain couldn't believe he was actually speaking these words, but he had to know. "Why not just pull the plug on them all at once?"

"We aren't monsters, Captain."

The captain choked, covering the sound with a cough. "Excuse me, sir?"

"I know it doesn't look like it to you, but we really aren't in the business of killing civilians. The ERIS system is set up to handle just so many people at a time. We are killing people, yes, but only so many as we have to kill to keep the system operating."

Don't run, the captain repeated over and over to himself. *Don't run from the room, or he'll pull you down dead like a fleeing animal.*

"The question is, Captain"—the colonel's face moved close to the captain's own; the commander's breath was hot and sweet—

"are you cut out for this job? Can you do your duty as mandated by the majority of people in this country, or am I going to have to do something about you?"

To run is to die. To stay is to live a lie, yet only if I live can I hope to do anything about this.

"Sir!" the captain responded sharply, automatically. "You can count on me, sir!"

"Excellent, Captain, I was hoping you'd see it our way." The colonel stood and took his hand. "Together we'll lick this cancer and be stronger and healthier for it!"

"I understand cancer, sir, and health. The problem is, sir, that it's sometimes hard to tell which cells are cancerous and which ones are healthy. What if we're killing the body just to save the cancer?"

If the colonel understood the nature of the question, he didn't show it—for the captain was still alive at dawn.

New in Town

Thursday, April 15, 2010 / 0535 hrs
Newhouse Center / 477th ERIS District
Wah Wah Valley, West Beaver County, Utah

Nancy Jensen-Smith, day shift warehouse supervisor, stood in anger at the leaden dawn. It wasn't the dawn's fault—Nancy seemed to maintain a perpetual state of rage against whatever was at hand. If you asked her, of course, she would deny it, but there was a part of her that actually liked being in the camp; there was so much here to be angry at.

Like this morning, for instance.

Her shift normally didn't start until 0700 hours, yet here she was waiting for an early parts train. Heidi Brunwald, one of Bullock's goons assigned to the women's barracks, had rousted her out of bed fifteen minutes ago with the joyful news. She pulled her blanket around her to fight off the cold as best she could and rushed outside.

Nancy made her way half awake down the slope of Main Street. The clouds had moved in about an hour before. Their gray ceiling hung low over the valley but wasn't able to obscure the column of smoke still rising from Wild Cove up the valley to the west. That angered Nancy as well. Another camp blown out. She turned at the Cathedral, passing in front of the warehouses and the elongated pyramid of the cement communications tower until at last she came to the main AG power line.

There was already a train hovering over the conduit, four flats' worth. The Death Master and her crew had had a busy night. There must have been at least three hundred bodies stacked haphazardly on the pallets. A tall woman stood supervising the last of the chains tossed over the piles and securing the bodies to the pallets. Nancy moved toward the woman.

"Morning, Meredith, looks like business is good."

The Death Master turned toward her. It rather thrilled Nancy, actually, to see her. Meredith Jernigan had held the post of Death Master for about four weeks now and had even once survived a cold to continue on in her post. She was tall with deep-set eyes and chiseled features made all the more striking by the constant physical demands of her job. Since she worked outside and at night, she had stitched together several blankets to form a warm, hooded robe. Nancy wondered if Meredith had done this just to keep warm or as some kind of joke. All together, Meredith bore a striking resemblance to the Grim Reaper that she helped.

Meredith smiled from under the shadow of her hood. "Good morning, Nancy. How nice to be alive another day!"

It was Meredith's form of greeting. Nancy didn't quite understand the humor in it, but it seemed to please Meredith. Nancy replied as neutrally as she could. "So what's the count?"

Meredith turned casually toward the stacks of cold, bluish flesh, her blanket robe shifting around her. "A bad night: three hundred and fourteen. Fifty-two single men, sixty-three single women, eight married men, five married women, forty-three children, eight infants, seventy-three gays, and sixty-two lesbians."

Nancy saw that Meredith held the reporting sheet in her hand, but never once during her litany did she even glance down at it. "That's a high figure isn't it?" Nancy offered.

"Yes, high," Meredith replied flatly. "About one-fifth of those were suicides. Wild Cove went up last night, and that always bumps up the count."

Talking to the Death Master, Nancy decided, was not the most cheerful way to start one's day. "Well, Brunwald tells me we've got an early train pulling in at around quarter to. Think you'll be clear by then?"

"Sure, we're just about . . . hey! Jerry! Pull that chain tighter before you secure it! The back end of that pile is still sliding around. Let the chains cut into the flesh a little—those corpses aren't going to feel it now! Do you want bodies trailing this train all the way to the Ranch?" The Death Master turned back to rejoin the conversation. "Sorry, Nancy, we'll be pushing this out of here in a few minutes."

"It's all right by me," Nancy sighed, the chill of the morning starting to cut through her clothes. "So what do you do next?"

"I'm going back to bed. After all," said the Grim Reaper, "I've got to get my beauty sleep. You never know who I might pick up tomorrow."

Nancy smiled at the chilling thought as Meredith moved away to inspect the train for the last time. Knowing Meredith was becoming like living in a horror film. It was different from the grim reality that she faced every day. People disappeared during the night, work assignments had to be shifted because the slots were now empty, and the reality of all that was sometimes overwhelming. That was grim. Yet there was a quality to Meredith that gave the taste of thrill and chill to what was happening. The Reaper was entertaining.

The anti-grav platforms began to hum a little louder as the train slid up the road toward the north. The inner set of pillars were already flashing just beyond the communications tower, showing that the "Fox" gate was opening for the pallets to pass through the inner perimeter. The automated pallet train would then wait for someone far from here to check that no one had escaped into the second perimeter before opening the second set of pillars for the train to pass through.

Three hundred and fourteen in a single night. Nancy was vaguely wondering if that was some kind of record when she heard footsteps approaching from the warehouse road. She turned toward the sound and suddenly found herself facing quite a contingent.

Reverend Weston was in the lead, his wispy hair drifting about him in the cold morning breeze. Nancy had never before seen the old governor up before seven. Behind him, of course, was Bullock, who was never far from the reverend when he was walking about the camp. Evan Weber was one of Bullock's flunkies and was probably on the day shift. He flanked the reverend on the other side.

Surprising Nancy more, however, was the follow-up group: Olivia Codgebury, the camp doctor; Ron Blythe, the staff director for the reverend; and Mark Haviland, the camp shrink? Just what did these people have to do with a supply train?

"Good morning, Sister Jensen-Smith," the reverend said with some difficulty. The combination of "sister" with the hyphenated last name always seemed to confuse him just a little. "I'm sorry to get you up so early, but it seems that we have something of a special delivery this morning. ERIS command tells me that they wanted to get this little package to us as soon as possible, so they've advanced your delivery today."

Something is wrong here, Nancy thought. *I wonder if I want to have anything to do with this?*

She could see the pallets carrying the dead had just cleared the last gate and were now heading down the slope toward the towering stacks of the Ranch far below them. She turned to the south. As if on cue, the tower lights on the outer perimeter poles began flashing.

"Ah," said the reverend, "it won't be long now."

The five hovering pallets skimmed over the ground like ghosts in the morning. On the leading edge of the first pallet, however, in front of the usual parts boxes, lay the figure of a large man. He still wore his wool-lined jacket and, surprisingly, still managed to retain his hat; but even from this distance it seemed that he was a bit worse for wear.

Codgebury didn't wait for the flats to slide to a stop. She pulled herself up to examine the man before the forward momentum of the train had bled away.

"He's alive."

The group waited for her to say something more.

"That's it?" Bullock snapped.

"That's about all that's important right now. It looks like he may have a bad head injury, possibly some trauma there, and a number of cuts, abrasions, and contusions. But all together he seems to be in one piece."

"Why isn't he awake, then?" Mark Haviland's expertise only went so far.

"It's a pure medical guess, but I think it's because he's asleep." Codgebury sniffed at his face once and drew back sharply. "It wouldn't be much of a guess as to why. I'd be surprised if we see anything of this guy before noon."

The councillor sniffed in disgust. "Great! A drunk! Just what are we supposed to do with this? What is he doing here anyway?"

"I believe," the reverend said, "that is why he was sent here. He had been taken to Milford for a while, at least according to ERIS headquarters. He wasn't much use to them from what I gathered. They believe he's just a joyrider that wandered into places where he didn't belong."

"I take it you don't buy that?" Ron Blythe spoke up. He rarely said much unless specifically asked to by the reverend. Nancy's opinion was that the man never had an original thought that hadn't been put there by the reverend in the first place.

"No, I don't. I believe that he was working for that I-Net fellow—Barris, isn't it?" Reverend Weston walked over to the comatose figure on the pallet. "The two of them showing up here, so close to each other under such strange circumstances."

Bullock was slow on the uptake. "You mean they're workin' together?"

Mark's mind moved a little faster. "If you're right, then what are they up to? Who are they working for—the government or themselves?"

"ERIS says they don't work for them," the reverend mused.

"Sure," Mark answered, "as if they'd just tell us if they did."

Nancy had had enough mystery. "Reverend, you got me out of bed to enjoy the rare sight of a drunk sleeping one off at five-thirty in the morning. Thank you. Now may I be excused to dig up some crew for early shifts so that we can get this train unloaded?"

The reverend looked at her coolly, but only said, "Of course, Sister Jensen-Smith. Your shipment is in, get about your work, by all means."

Nancy turned and walked past the group toward the Commons

Building. Hopefully, she could muster enough early risers to get the pallets cleared and allow herself some additional sleep time before the pallets had to be loaded with completed units. As she left, however, she couldn't help but overhear the reverend's booming voice.

"Take him up to the hospice and keep an eye on him. I want to know when he wakes up and who he's talking to. I want to know right away if he meets up with Barris . . ."

All over one drunken cowboy. Nancy just shook her head. Quite suddenly, she was wracked by a sudden cough.

Her hand came away with blood flecks on it.

"Not a good sign, Nancy," she said to herself.

Virgil realized that his eyes were closed and that, if he really wished it, he might try to open them.

It turned out to be a bad idea.

The headache sat just behind unconsciousness, waiting for its opportunity to strike. The time had come. With the decision to become fully awake came the consequences for it as well. The temple-pounding, ear-numbing, vision-blurring four-alarm headache rushed forward to assert itself as the dominant theme and purpose in his life. The bliss of slumber was suddenly no longer an option. It was time to deal with Frank Small's home brew.

Virgil swung his long legs gingerly off the table, moving slowly to sit up. Light was streaming through a window in the room, a brilliant and painful column to his left. The rest of the room was barren of anything but the examination table he sat on.

"Just where in the hell am I anyway," he said to the walls.

"You," said a deep woman's voice behind him, "are in Newhouse Center—an ERIS Quarantine Camp—which probably qualifies it as at least a part of hell."

Virgil suddenly realized that he was wearing a paper hospital gown. It wasn't quite adequate to cover the entire back. There were gentle breezes now, whereas he wasn't used to them before. In an almost schoolboy rush, Virgil wheeled around, jumping down from the table, and found himself staring into the eyes of Olivia Codgebury. He was red-faced and blinking.

"Ma'am! I'm sorry, ma'am, I didn't know you was there."

The nurse smiled. "It's OK, Cowboy, I'm the doctor around here. Yours isn't the first set of cheeks I've seen."

It may have been OK with the doctor-lady, but it certainly wasn't OK with Virgil. He continued to nervously grasp at the back of the gown, trying desperately to discover some newfound cloth that would cover up his back side. "Look, ma'am, I've had a rather poor night, so if you could just kindly hand over my clothes, I'd like to be getting home now."

Codgebury slowly shook her head. "Your clothes are being searched at this moment by Mr. Bullock, the head of our local brute squad."

Virgil looked her questioningly in the eye.

"They're convinced you are some sort of spy," she said.

The tall cowboy popped a quick, hooting laugh. "Me? Some fellers think I'm a spy? That's rich, ain't it, ma'am!" He managed to gather up enough of the tearing cloth in the back that he felt safe in waving the woman off with the newly freed hand. "You jest tell them fellers they've made a mistake. I ain't no spy, and I don't mean nobody no harm."

Suddenly, Virgil's memory started falling into place. "Besides, ma'am, I've got some things I gotta do. You wouldn't happen to know where my buddies are, would ya? Harlan and Louis and Lowell. Them last two is twins and . . ."

"Sorry, can't help you. You're it," Codgebury said, her arms folded across her chest. "Where are you from, Cowboy?"

Virgil started shuffling his feet. Having this woman stare at him practically bare-assed naked was embarrassing him. It wasn't that he'd never been seen by a woman before—nor seen a woman either for that matter—but having her dressed and him not seemed to him somehow basically indecent. "I'm from Beaver, ma'am."

"Excuse me?" Codgebury said through a barely suppressed giggle. She wasn't sure if he were naming a town or trying to convey to her some sense of his mother's anatomy.

"Beaver—it's a town about thirty miles east of here, ma'am." Virgil's eyes started looking at the corners of the ceiling with the notion that somehow if he didn't look at her, she wouldn't be looking at him.

"East of here?"

"Yes, ma'am. We're in Milford, ain't we?"

Codgebury, again, slowly shook her head.

"Well, where the hell—pardon me, ma'am—just where are we . . ." Virgil's eyes suddenly went wide. He dashed to the window, not even thinking about his skimpy hospital gown, and looked out through the plastic pane with frantic eyes. "Oh, Lordy!—Lordy! Lordy! *Lordy!*"

He wheeled around so suddenly that Codgebury was startled. The tall cowboy began moving like a caged animal, his movements nervous and quick, pacing the floor from wall to wall as though looking for some exit.

"What is it?" Codgebury was catching the very real fear coming from the tall man. "What's the matter?"

The night before came back to him in a rush, clear in his mind as the blinding light falling through the window. The truck, the night, the camp just up the slope. Louis.

"What is it, Louis?"

"Gawd almighty, Virgil, it's terrible up thar! They got about a hundred thousand people up in that thar place, I swear to Gawd! They's all screamin' and yellin', and Lowell got hisself caught in a gravity fence . . ."

"You're shittin' me!"

Virgil stopped and looked at her through laser-bright eyes. "We're in one of them camps, ain't we?" He suddenly reached across the examining table and grabbed both her upper arms, shaking her and shouting. *"Ain't we?"*

Nurse Codgebury was caught off guard. She submitted for a moment before her iron will reasserted itself. "Yes! Yes! What of it?"

Louis kept right on talking. "You ain't seen nothing like this, Virgil! Thar's women and children in there, all of 'em wailin' like banshees! Some of 'em saw us out thar, and before you knowed it they was all comin' out and yellin' at us. Damned if I know what they were yellin', but they sure was yellin'!"

Gene Lovett rushed into the room. "Nurse, are you all right?" Gene wasn't terribly large, but his body was well kept. The look on Gene's face seemed to leave no question about just how he would handle this suddenly out-of-control ranch hand—with an equal part of determination to do so if necessary.

Virgil released her, however, struggling to find the words that she could understand. "Ma'am, we gotta get outta here! We gotta get outta here right now!"

"Calm down, Cowboy, just calm down." Lord, she thought, what she wouldn't give for a decent sedative right now. One for the raving ranger and then one for herself. The cowboy was beginning to get to her. "Relax! Relax! No one here is going to hurt you! There are a lot of sick people here, and it's tough to survive but nothing you can't handle. Just do as you're told and no one is going to get hurt."

Virgil turned away from her and looked back out the window. Below him was the enclosure for the Hospice Nursery, a low fence with a pole-suspended tarpaulin for shade. Sitting or standing about the sand were about fifty-odd small children, their ragged clothing covered in dust from the sand beneath them. They listlessly reached their fingers into the sand and then let it fall from their fingers, only to scoop it up again with the same, vacant-eyed expression.

"They got about a hundred thousand people up in that thar place, I swear to Gawd! They's all screamin' . . ."

Just beyond the little fence of faded white, a tall, thin man stood, the Indian blanket around his shoulders tattered from use. His right hand clattered against a piece of board.

Night evaporated around Virgil. The lightbulb flash behind him blinded him instantly. Instinctively, Virgil let go of the wheel and covered his eyes.

Before his arms could cover his face, the pressure wave hit. Air, compressed by the explosion until it was nearly solid, slammed into the back of the levitating GMC with such force that Virgil's neck snapped back hard.

The man beyond the fence looked at Virgil.

He smiled.

"Ma'am." Virgil's voice was dry as the dust beneath the children outside. "Did you see an explosion or something like that in a camp last night—somewhere's nearby?"

Olivia Codgebury blinked then glanced at Gene before she

spoke. "Yes. Wild Cove Camp was blown last night, just up the valley." She leaned her head to one side, questioning. "It happens sometimes. When everyone in the camp is dead, the army has to . . ."

Slowly, deliberately, Virgil spoke. "No, ma'am. I was there—last night, me and my buddies. That camp was full, ma'am, plumb full of people, kids and everything."

The nurse stood frozen before him. Gene made a sound as though all the air had left him.

"And they did 'em, ma'am. They baked 'em camp and all. Just like they's gonna bake us, sure as hell!"

Virgil turned back to the window, but the thin man was no longer to be seen.

Sunshine

April 15, 2010 / 1042 hrs
Newhouse Center / 477th ERIS District
Wah Wah Valley, West Beaver County, Utah

Amanda was her name—the only name she knew.

Somewhere in the records scattered in various places locally and nationally, her name was Amanda Delany, age seven, from Oakland, California. Born January 7, 2004. Daughter of Eric Torence (deceased/V-CIDS/San Francisco) and Carolynne Delany (predeceased/V-CIDS/ERIS District 4). Diagnosed V-CIDS positive at the Hansen Memorial Orphans Home in Bakersfield, California, on February 6, 2010. Declared predeceased that same date.

Amanda knew none of that.

She sat in the dirt of the yard, her heavy jumper rustling slightly in the wind. She picked up the dirt and put it back. Picked up the dirt and put it back. She saw none of the dirt nor barely even felt the grains of sand as they slipped through her tiny, frozen fingers. She was inside herself—a world complete, vacant and apart.

This was the playtime she knew, although she barely understood what play meant now. There had been a time, part of her remembered, when play was a warm thing, a thing all sunshine and yellow and smiles. Playtime was Mommy and grass between your toes. Laughter, the deep green eyes and long lashes flashing before her face. It was tickles and squeals.

It was somewhere far from here.

Amanda didn't understand V-CIDS, quarantine, isolation, or incarceration. She didn't comprehend the high-sounding goals of her being here. She didn't accept her sacrifice on behalf of humanity. No one had asked her—and she wouldn't have answered them if they did.

They brought her here, those large people who ruled her life. She suspected that they took her mommy away from her, too. Now they shuffled her from room to room, from class to class, and droned words and pictures from the paper books at her day after day. She recognized the ducks and the mice on the pages and knew the words had meanings, but only for that time and place that was now so far away. The green fields and the top-hatted frogs were in that other place that was removed from her by unimaginable distances.

So she listened quietly and obeyed. She sat and sifted the dirt. Her body struggled through the reality that was around her, yet she never *lived* here.

Her life was in that place of sunshine that she kept so far deep within herself that the chill of the world could not reach it. Her eyes were focused inward toward those dreams that grew more impossible day by day. She lived with her mother. She lived in the grass and sunshine. She lived far away in a place and time that even she could barely imagine. She lived within herself.

And rare it was that she ever saw anything more with her deep brown eyes.

She was Amanda—that was all that she knew.

Virgil angrily pulled his second boot on and snatched his hat from the table. "Where's the mayor or marshal or whatever you call the guy in charge around here. They can't keep me in here, that's fer sure. Not till I sees my lawyer or something."

Virgil stomped out of the examination room, pushing past both Olivia and Gene.

Gene shook his head and followed him. "You just don't get it, do you, Cowboy? We've already received the paperwork on you.

Reverend Weston got the thermalfax on you before you ever arrived. You've already been declared predeceased. That means that you have no rights."

"No rights?" Virgil had moved down the hall and was looking for an exit door. He found it and stuffed his head back into his hat. "Hell, boy, everybody's got rights."

"Not here!" Gene countered, trying to keep up with the long strides of the horseman's gait. "You're predeceased. That means that you're legally already dead."

Virgil stopped short of the exit doors. "You tellin' me that I'm predeceased?"

"Yes! Everyone here is!"

"And that means that I'm dead before I'm dead, don't it?"

"Exactly!"

"Well, then, if I'm already dead, then thar ain't nothin' more they can do to me is thar?" Virgil jabbed his index finger pointedly into Gene's breastbone. "So if I decide that I'd rather git the hell out of here before they decide to fry me up like a bug in one of them bug zappers, what are they gonna do to me? *Kill me?* . . . *Again?*"

Gene opened his mouth, but somehow no logical reply came out.

Virgil flashed his "dumb-ass" crooked smile at Gene, shaking his head slightly. Then he turned, pushed open both the exit doors, and stepped through.

He stopped short and stood in slack-jawed amazement.

A comic-book hero had just landed in the middle of the playground. Dust billowed suddenly in the children's yard, stirred to life by the dashing movement of the heavy wool cape. The heroic figure stood awkwardly, trying to regain his balance on his spindly limbs before he could deliver his trademark lines.

"Fear not, followers! Spiritwing, Defender of Truth, has returned to lead you!"

Spiritwing's long red stockings were threatening to droop around his ankles as he strode purposefully across the playground. He remained undeterred by the inconsiderate leggings. Superheros are never deterred. Within moments he stood before a dejected seven-year-old boy who was generally known as Barry but who was someone entirely different to the superhero now standing spread-legged before him.

"Lugnut! The Enforcer! I, Spiritwing, have need of your services once again!" Leaning over conspiratorially, the Defender of Truth spoke in a whisper only loud enough to be heard by every child in the compound. "The evil Queen of the ogres has cast a spell over the enchanted city! Everyone believes they are in a prison, but we know better! We must rally our people and break this spell!"

"Yeah, OK." Barry's words remained distant and disinterested.

The gloved hand at the end of the gray-tan thermal underwear reached out and grasped the young boy's shoulder with affection and bonding. "It is more than even you and I alone can conquer, Lugnut! We shall need the aid of the full Alliance of Heroes before this evil may be conquered. We must search among those who are asleep, whose spirits lay dormant, and awaken the hero within them. Do you accept my quest?"

"Sure," said Barry with a yawn, not entirely sure what had just been said to him.

Virgil tipped his hat back on his head as the Avenger of Wrongs made his way across the sand, his not-entirely-trusty Lugnut at his side. A few began to move about as though they were marionettes whose strings were sluggishly, tentatively being pulled in order to dance the dance of the dead.

But not all of them. For each one that stood, many others lay still in the dust, so still that Virgil thought they must be truly dead. With a start, he realized that several of them were. Others sat in the dust or leaned against the Hospice staring into a dark void the very thought of which frightened Virgil more than the dead.

"Dance the dance of the Spiritwing!" the gangly boy cried out from behind his rough-edged mask. Several of the children had gathered around him—a puddle of semi-awareness in a sea of comatose children. "We will dispel the evil from this place. We'll fly like the eagle and be free! We'll . . ."

Suddenly, the great Defender of Truth stopped and stared directly at Virgil, slack-jawed and amazed.

"Well," Virgil answered, hooking his thumbs into the waistband of his pants and giving the kid the eye. "What are you lookin' at, Mr. Masked Avenger?"

The gangly boy bolted. He cleared the short enclosure fence in a single bound, rapidly disappearing into the alleys between the barracks.

The few children who had been dancing the spooky little dance stopped at once with the departure of the boy. Their strings had been cut. They settled to the dust again, lifeless and dull.

"Well, Virgil," he said to himself, "you really ended up in the loony bin this time."

It was about then that he became aware of an insistent tugging at the bottom of his Levi's. Virgil craned his head around and saw the matted top of a small girl's head. Her hand had grasped his jeans and was shaking them back and forth. She didn't actually look into his eyes, her own stare vacant and distant, yet her words were to him: a hollow litany from a past life.

"Mister, hey, mister. Mister, hey, mister . . ."

Virgil turned and stooped down to the level of the child. Her face was dirty beyond recognition, and her hair color could only be guessed at. Her nose ran constantly, a thin trickle of blood visible in the mucus. *This kid's got it,* Virgil thought; *this kid's gonna die.*

It was the eyes that held him. They were deep and they were brown—and they were vacant.

"What is it, littl' darlin'," Virgil said in his honey voice.

The girl glanced up at him, seeing him for only a moment before she retreated behind her eyes. "Mister, are you a for real cowboy?"

Virgil's eyes teared up. He thought he'd heard every lonesome sound there was. The girl's voice was a sound beyond tears—a sound one makes when you've cried so long you can't cry ever again. He wondered how long it had been since this small child had asked anyone anything. Words without feeling—words beyond feeling.

He quickly sniffed and wiped the moisture away from his eyes with two quick flicks of his hand. It wouldn't do for a real live cowboy to cry.

"Yes siree, bob, I sure am!" Virgil watched the girl's face as he spoke, quietly and softly. "Do you like cowboys, little missy?"

The unfocused eyes turned down toward the dirt. The girl simply stood there, doing nothing, saying nothing, yet making no motion to move away, to break the moment with him. *She's like a little doe,* Virgil thought, *too scared to leave and too afraid to stay. She'll move—but only when she's ready.*

Moments passed between them. Virgil was mountain, however, and understood silence better than most city folk understand noise. He knew he had to get out of camp, but this strange little girl held him where he knelt.

"Yes." She spoke.

"Yes, you do like cowboys—well, I like you, too." Virgil made no move, wary of frightening the wild creature so close to him. "What's your name, darlin'?"

Moments slid between them like a slow river. Virgil began to feel the sense of lazy time that the girl lived by.

"Amanda."

"Amanda," he repeated in quiet tones filled with softness. "Amanda is a beautiful name."

His time slowed to hers. Virgil felt the world growing more distant around them.

"Amanda," Virgil said, for he sensed he was coming into her secret, special place. "What can I do for you, darlin'?"

The girl looked at him. Their eyes locked, and for the moment he saw into the depths of the seven-year-old's soul. The girl's eyes filled with water, her lower lip trembled.

"Mister," she said in a quivering voice. "You smell like sunshine and grass."

Virgil smiled at her and sniffed through his own watery eyes. "Yes, ma'am, I suppose I do—though I've smelt of worse." He reached into his back pocket and pulled out his handkerchief. Almost instinctively he reached out and wiped the girl's nose. As he did, Amanda reached out for him as well, her small, dust-caked hand running down the bristles of his unshaven face slowly with barely the touch of a breeze.

"Hey, you!"

A voice from another time. Another place.

"Hey, you leave that girl alone!"

Virgil glanced up. Some old woman was yelling at him.

"You get out of here right now! These kids are all sick, and they don't need you around! Get out, you hear? Get out before I call the guard on you!"

When Virgil looked back, Amanda had turned away, her face a mask and her eyes a dull and unfocused sheen.

Virgil stood and stepped over the low fence. He looked up to where the Commons was. The nurse woman had told him to take his problems to this Weston fellow up in the church. Virgil determined to bring more to the man than just his own troubles.

"Leave kids alone!" Virgil muttered to himself. "Bullshee-it!"

The Monkey
Chased the Weasel

Friday, April 16, 2010 / 0815 hrs
Day Shift / Commons Factory
Newhouse Center / 477th ERIS District
Wah Wah Valley, West Beaver County, Utah

Helen Casler had come down with something, she was sure of that. Not to worry, she thought, just a little flu bug. She was sure she would be shrugging it off soon just as she had so many others over the years. True, she had been feeling the effects of it for the last three days, and usually she would be much better by now. It's the pressure, she kept telling herself. Just the pressure.

The parts distribution teams were busying themselves with placing the various parts into their respective assembly baskets and running them down the rows of tables. It was a thrilling moment for Helen—once again her chance to *do something* that might hasten her freedom from the tortures of the camp.

She listened attentively to Brother Lukin. He gave the same speech he always gave at the beginning of the shift. True, he always tried to change the words a little just to keep it interesting, but usually ended up using the same phrases day in and day out. It was rather like listening to those safety announcements the stewardesses give on the airlines. They know they've given it a thousand times and pretty much everyone in the plane knows the words by heart, so most people don't even pay attention. That had always bothered Helen because, to her way of thinking, you can never be too safe or pay too much attention. What if you missed something. She always paid attention to the stewardesses—she thought they might at least appreciate an attentive audience—and always looked through the safety cards in the seat back in front of her. To do otherwise, she thought, would be irresponsible.

"... with every unit that you assemble." Brother Lukin was finishing up. "So remember: 'Every device you make brings us that much closer to home.' "

Every device I make brings me that much closer to home. Helen smiled to herself.

The trays of parts were presented, and now as she sat her eyes again became unfocused as her sight turned inward with her thoughts. Her hands reached out mechanically to take the first part, the black base of the mechanism, and set it down before her. She no longer had to think about the process. It was completely automatic.

She thought of Emily. What a beautiful child—all her children! Her mind ran through multiple images of her raven-haired children. *Emily at six years old and in her class play as Snow White and the Seventeen Dwarves ... Jacob begging to drive the car around the parking lot at fourteen and getting the keys to the car ... Melanie weeping at nine when that Daryl boy had forgotten to call her ...*

Her hands moved with precision over the mechanism. Rocker bars secured to the frame. Platform held between the bars, then tightened. Six screws inserted and tightened so that the platform swung freely inside the support frame.

Emily laughed at her over her third birthday cake ... Lindia danced flat-footed at seven and then became graceful in her ballet recital at ten ... Emily pouted over the dishes in the kitchen on Sixty-third Street, her soft little sweatshirt rolled up at the sleeves ...

Fit the connectors to their respective sockets. Insert the electronic cards here, here, here, and here. Some part of her mind knew that the unit was just about finished now.

Jacob was often sullen but would surprise you now and then with—how did he used to put it—acts of random kindness. They were all beautiful, but those dark eyes of Emily's were wells of love you could get lost in.

It was finished. Helen smiled. There was just one last thing that she needed to do in order to . . .

She froze, the scribe tool quivering in her hand.

To Emily.

A stuttering, inhuman sound choked out of her throat.

To Emily.

The scribe tool fell rattling to the desktop.

To Emily.

Helen jerked suddenly and stood up, her simple wooden chair falling over behind her. She suddenly reached forward, grabbed the basket of base parts in front of her, and dumped it out on the table, spilling it into her neighbor's work. Frantically, she reached into the pile of black metal and began examining each base and tossing it aside. Something caught her eye.

She screamed.

Work had stopped as the sluggish, dull eyes of the factory workers suddenly glanced up in fear. Helen began to overturn her neighbor's baskets one after another, and then searched among the bases until she screamed again. Then again. Then again.

"Same ones! Same ones! SAME! SAME! SAME!"

Brother Lukin came puffing down the aisle between the tables, his face beet red either from the exercise or the excitement. "Sister Casler!" he called, "Sister Casler, stop this at once!"

Helen didn't stop. She moved suddenly to the next table, the workers there scurrying out of her way. She grasped another basket and tumbled bases onto the table in a loud cascade. She began reaching through them as well, then grasped one and shrieked. She drew back her thin arm and, with the strength of her rage, hurled the heavy mechanism across the hall, scattering a dozen workers from its path.

"Sister Casler!" Lukin yelled in disbelief as he rushed toward her.

She didn't hear him. She began moving to other tables, her frantic rage increasing with each stop. The other workers quickly fell below the tables, seeking cover from the terrible dervish that had erupted in their midst.

"The same!" Helen shrieked again. "THEY'RE THE SAME ONES!"

Lukin wasn't a large man, but he figured he could handle the woman even in her rage. She wasn't larger than he was and seemed frail and weak despite her newly demonstrated ability to hurl five pounds of metal across the full width of the room. He came up behind her and grabbed her by the left arm, turning her around to face him. In his rush and excitement, he still clutched his wooden clipboard in his left arm. "Sister Casler! Stop this this instant! You'll have to come with me, now, to the—"

Her fierce eyes suddenly recognized him. "LIAR!" she howled, her rage focused clearly for the first time on the round, puffy face of Charles Lukin. *Every device you make brings us that much closer to home.*

She still held the five-pound metal base in her free right hand.

She swung the base savagely across Lukin's head. The arc of the base barely slowed as it crossed the man's face. Lukin fell backward, the left side of his head suddenly transformed into a misshapen eruption of tissue and crimson fluid. His own cries were choked in a rush of blood into his mouth.

Lukin dropped to the floor, shocked by the pain and the unexpectedness of the attack. Instinctively, he held up his clipboard, talisman of his power and authority, to protect him. Somehow its special charms, he vaguely believed, would ward off the savage that had suddenly dared broach his person. Perhaps, he thought dully, the woman didn't understand just how important he was.

Helen didn't hesitate. She leaped on him, landing astride his chest, still wielding the bloodied base. She slammed the metal down again toward what had once been the shift training supervisor and which now was rapidly turning into an unrecognizable mass of broken bone.

"LIAR! LIAR!" she keened in her banshee wail. "THEY'RE ALL THE SAME ONES!"

She had struck five times before Michael Barris, working ten rows away, was able to wrestle the sticky base from her hand.

Near the bottom of the black casing were inscribed the words, "TO EMILY."

The same words that could be found on several hundred of the bases that had arrived in the camp that morning.

Olivia Codgebury stepped quietly out of the room.

"How is she?" Michael asked.

Olivia sighed. "Well, she's cried herself to sleep. That's about all the sedative I can offer her anyway. Oh, and don't bother asking. Lukin's dead."

"So I suspected." Michael covered his face with both hands, then drew them down, as if to absolve his eyes of what they had seen.

"They call her 'old one,' you know. She's probably the one who's been in the camp the longest."

"How long has she been here?"

"Maybe as long as four weeks."

Michael snorted. "Four weeks and you earn status as 'old one'?"

"I've been here three and look what it's done to me." Olivia gave a slight grin, but it faded quickly as she turned back to stare at the door she had just come through. "Strong-willed. Cheerful. Never a sign of problems. She's survived the mumps twice and a host of other illnesses as well." Olivia shook her head in wonder as she leafed through Helen Casler's file. "What ever set her off like that?"

Michael looked at the ground. "Does she have a daughter, sister—or anyone—named Emily?"

Olivia looked up in surprise. "Why, yes: a daughter. Why do you ask?"

"I checked some of the bases she was throwing around while we were cleaning up the mess." From behind him, Michael produced a black, heavy-looking piece of metal. "We assemble these same units day after day. Look here, near the bottom of this base."

Olivia took the base from him and squinted. " 'To Emily.' So?"

"So," Michael said as he took the base unit from her, "the same inscription, made in much the same way, was found on each of the base units she tossed across the room."

Olivia was puzzled. "You mean she carved this in before she threw them?"

"No: there wasn't time for that—besides, I checked several other assembly baskets on tables that she never came anywhere near. I found several more of these, inscribed in just the same way." Michael looked at the metal held in his hand as though if he looked hard enough, he could divine the future in its surface. "She kept saying 'They're the same ones.' She has been carving these words on the base of every unit that she assembles."

Olivia nodded. "Rather like a message to her daughter you mean?"

"Right," Michael agreed quietly, "only this time she found her own message coming back to her. It was bound to happen sooner or later."

"Why?"

"Because, Nurse Codgebury," Michael's anger brought a husky quiver to his voice, "our little factory isn't assembling anything. We're kept busy remaking the same things over and over again. I'm willing to bet you that there are just as many camps out there assigned to *disassembling* these damn things as there are camps like ours putting them together. What a sick joke!"

Michael dropped the frame to the floor.

Olivia jumped slightly at the sound.

"What is it, Nurse?" Michael asked. "There's something you're not telling me."

Olivia's eyes had a sleepy, far-off look. She spoke more to herself than to Michael. "You know, you work hard, you trust people to trust you, and you think that at least they'd play straight with you. Maybe that isn't even it. Maybe Weston and his whole group don't even know. Maybe Overlord is pulling their strings, too." Suddenly, she looked straight at Michael, accusing and demanding all at once. "Barris, can you get us out of here?"

"What?" The conversation had taken a strange turn.

"Can you get us out of this camp?" She suddenly moved closer to him. "Look, your accomplice came in yesterday—a huge cowboy type. He came in on the morning shipment pallet—lord only knows how he managed that—but the reverend has been keeping you two apart. If what he says is true, then we don't have much time before—"

Michael held up his hands to stop her. "Whoa! What *exactly* did he say?"

Olivia stopped and took a step back from Michael. "Well, it's like this. Every now and then one of the camps just—well it just blows up. Some kind of incendiary bomb or something. Anyway, we've always been told that it only happens when everyone in the camp has either died out of V-CIDS or has been transferred to other camps."

"OK so they burn the camp down to sterilize the site—to keep the disease from spreading. That only makes sense."

"Right," Olivia said, "only this cowboy of yours tells me that he was at the Wild Cove Camp the other night when it blew—and that the camp was full of people when the blast came."

Michael was trying to think. "This doesn't make sense. Ms. Codgebury . . ."

"Call me Olivia."

"Fine, Olivia, then; how many of these camps have you seen destroyed like this?"

The nurse considered for a moment. "Well, it was just about a week after I arrived—also a Thursday, I believe—so that would have been about two weeks before Wild Cove. That was Antelope Springs off to the south."

Michael was confused. "But I thought there was still a camp there?"

"Yes, they rebuilt it—only took them a couple of days, quite amazing really."

Michael smiled grimly. "Was there a camp blown the week before you arrived?"

"Yes," Olivia said, "Ranch Springs on the far side of the valley. Just what are you getting on about, Barris?"

Michael looked at her. She wanted to throw her allegiance behind Michael, but only because she thought he might have a way out of here for her. She was wrong—although now he wished she weren't. If they were going to get through this, then they would need her help, no matter what the reason she offered it. It may not be time for the whole truth, but certainly time for some of it.

"The interval between camps blowing up looks like about two weeks," Michael said. "We all know that there are twelve camps in this district—most anyone here can even name them. If this two-week interval holds true, then each camp will come up in natural rotation for destruction every six months—whether the people inside are dead or not."

Olivia folded her arms across her chest. "Then you had better hurry and get done whatever you came to do, Barris, because the camp records show this as being the nineteenth week of operation."

Michael let out a slow whisper.

Olivia nodded. "Next week marks the end of our fifth month. You *do* have a way out of here, don't you, Mr. Barris?"

Erik's Silence

"You sure you heard them correctly?" The baritone voice spoke incredulously. "Five weeks?"

"Yes." Gene Lovett spoke in tones of greatest respect. "I was there when the cowboy spoke to Nurse Codgebury and was just beyond the door when that Barris fellow was speaking with the nurse as well."

He stood at the bottom of the Queen's chamber in the very spot it so happened that Michael Barris had hung suspended the night before. Standing near him was a man in his mid-twenties whom Gene couldn't remember seeing before. The man hadn't said a word since Gene had entered the place. He simply leaned against the post, his arms folded across his chest, and listened. They both stood in light on the main floor speaking toward the open door of a darkened room beyond—the Queen's chamber, Gene thought—and listening to the Queen's responses from within. The floors above them were left in darkness as well, but somehow Gene knew that it was hardly devoid of eyes. The group that had been assembled for Michael Barris had been for show—designed to give him a taste of what they all felt and a scare that would keep him and anyone else on their side of "the line." The eyes above Gene now, however, were there with purpose and paying earnest attention.

The honey baritone voice drifted out of the dark chamber. "Are you certain that the cowboy and Barris aren't working together?"

"No, I don't believe so." Gene spoke, but there was a note of uncertainty in his voice. "The leaders of the 'righteous'—Weston and his group—are all paranoid about the two of them arriving at about the same time but, so far as I can tell, neither of them have tried to find each other at all. Either they're both very cool customers or they're just as big a mystery to each other as they are to us."

The baritone voice was loving but seasoned with chill. "Never underestimate an enemy, Gene. You can always deal with an opponent who is more stupid than you think."

"Yes, Queen."

Gene shuffled his feet slightly. There were those among the gays who knew the identity of the Dark Queen, but he was not among those privileged few. He could only stand outside the room, staring into the blackness and wonder with the rest of the camp as to the identity of the one person who coordinated every action of the gays and lesbians in the camp.

He was nervous, his hands clenching and unclenching as he stood alone below the open ceiling above. There were eyes watching him up there. Anxious and wary.

He had spoken but had had no reply. Now he was uncertain as to what he should do.

"My queen?" Gene spoke tentatively.

Erik Simms, the baritone voice and conducting hand of the San Francisco Philharmonic Orchestra had been the most flamboyant and beloved leader that the city had had in many years. Gifted with a talent for all music forms that was genius itself, Erik was the consummate leader, for he always knew just how far to push an issue, just how much to expect from those around him, and just how far others were willing to go to accommodate him. It was, undoubtedly, this second talent of his that allowed him to rise in respect and stature both as an accomplished violinist/conductor and as the unquestioned leader of the largest single population of gays in the United States.

His father, Douglas Simms, had been a U.S. Air Force officer who, through some mix-up in orders, had been assigned to Oslo, Norway in 1954. There he met Ilse Johannsen. The story varied depending on which of them did the telling of it, but the facts were clear enough: inside a year, Ilse was an air force bride. It was shortly thereafter that the air force straightened out Douglas's orders. He and Ilse began the roller coaster ride of an air force family in earnest. Erik was born two years later, second of what would eventually turn out to be five children.

Douglas didn't understand his sensitive, distant son. They never connected the way he had with his own father, even though his own father was away from home during much of World War II. Douglas both worried about and was simultaneously relieved about the lengths of time his work kept him separated from his son. It was a puzzling problem for him that he hoped he could solve "later." Still, when he was home, he did what he could to bring their lives into some sort of mutual understanding and participation.

However, if Douglas felt little connection to his son, it was nothing compared to the distance Erik felt between them. His father and his ways were a mystery to him by the time his father had to go on the "big trip" when he was nine—Vietnam.

Douglas Simms was among those who were returned eight years later, having spent almost seven of those in a North Vietnamese camp. Erik, now fifteen, was a stranger to his father, but, as Erik so often recalled, his father had become a stranger to himself. Douglas Simms was a changed man. The loneliness and emotion occasionally overwhelmed his father to the point of crying jags that not even his devoted Ilse could stop. On those long nights when Douglas was caught up in his own private terrors, Erik would stay up with him and care for him. It was the one thing they had in common—it was the one thing they shared. In an army brat world, the dramatic, musical, and gifted Erik was also very much alone.

The experience left him with a number of gifts. He learned that a man could push too far but that he also had to push far enough to make a difference. He was aware of his own "different" ideas about men by the time his father had returned home. The harsh world of military youth taught him both when it was time to fight and when it was time to run. It also gave him the discipline to achieve whatever he set his mind to.

Erik's greatest passion and most evident talents were in music, so that was where he applied his discipline. Through the music, his soul was free to express his needs and desires in a world where words about who he was were unacceptable. He learned that sometimes it wasn't what you say so much as how you say it. Through music, Eric could express to the world the fountain of feelings that were bottled inside without ever having to use the word "homosexual" or "gay." He passed through the seventies as a brilliant young star of both classical and pop forms, writing popular symphonies that combined art forms in a way that was pleasing to the ear and daring to the mind.

Knowing always when to push and when pushing would be too far.

It wasn't that Erik was the "King of Mediocrity," as one critic from the *Oakland Free Press* had later crowned him. Erik had passionate performances and music penned that he never showed to anyone. It was just that he knew, instinctively, just what that strange world beyond gay life was willing to listen to—and what it was not.

By the time things began unraveling in January of '09, Erik had been five years at the helm of the San Francisco Philharmonic and was an icon of the city itself and gay life. His great mane of silver hair framing his brilliant blue eyes with the grandfather twinkle and the soft, resonant baritone voice were welcome features of local and, occasionally, national I-Net cable casts. He was openly gay but perceived among the straight viewers as not being "pushy" about it. His advice was sought by every gay and lesbian group in the city—advice he always gave and causes that he occasionally participated in—the patriarch whose advice was always good and forever sought.

Of course, by that time, word of the "new AIDS" was beginning to circulate on the street. On February 3, the Centers for Disease Control made it official by publicly reporting a number of gay-community–related deaths with "symptoms similar to AIDS but not apparently caused by the HIV virus." It couldn't have come at a worse time. The third-party President had just been inaugurated two weeks before, his own election still being challenged in the Supreme Court due to the electoral college having had to convene *twice* the month before and having thus elected two different presidents on separate occasions. By Friday, February 6, the new President had already vetoed two bills challenging his authority to act and had proposed "surgical legislation" of his own to "streamline Congress." Many had claimed that the surgery amounted to amputation. By the following Monday, both the House and Senate were deep within a filibuster to prevent the President's legislation from ever clearing the floor.

Amid such turmoil, Dr. Faris MacKenzie and Dr. Jennine Lau—two Atlanta-based researchers who had done extensive fieldwork in the New York gay community—published a paper based on their own work and cooperative information coming from the National Institutes of Health in Washington. It named V-CIDS and outlined the extent of the epidemic, which by that time was growing geometrically at rates far worse than AIDS had shown. They published on the I-Net.

The news spread like a fire in the gay community, but such movements and politics had suddenly grown very personal and close to Erik Simms. His lover of ten years, Martin Keel, had been diagnosed with V-CIDS and was losing ground fast. Something had to be done, and Erik listened to the voices around him and knew that it was time to act. Some statement had to be made. The hospitals nationwide were rapidly filling up with V-CIDS patients, but the I-Net seemed preoccupied by what they called the "Ides of March" crisis in Washington, the citizens besieging Congress itself and the impeachment hearings Congress convened on the President.

For Martin's sake, for the sake of all who were suffering from the new plague, Erik coordinated the efforts of every organization in the city into a candlelight parade for March 12 of '09. The hospitals were at capacity. A plague of terrible proportions was taking place, and something had to be done to wrestle the attention of the public away from Washington, D.C.

Erik's instincts failed him at last. Turning attention away from Washington was *exactly* what the President wanted also—that, and an excuse to end the bickering once and for all.

The I-Net called it the San Francisco Riots. The video feeds were magnificently coordinated by the army feeds. To anyone on the I-Net, the streets of San Francisco were a sea of destruction and rebellion. The central telephone exchange had mysteriously failed—sabotage it was reported—and the entire city cordoned off with an efficiency that was surprising for an emergency reaction to an unexpected event. Whatever the reason, no video, audio, fax, or word escaped the cordon.

Outside the cordon, it was the San Francisco Riots. For those inside the cordon, it would forever be known as the Frisco Massacre.

For three days the army laid waste to the city. For the marchers, there was no place far enough, deep enough, or high enough to hide. War, true and open war, had been declared on the gays in the march. By the end of the third day, Martial Law had been established nationally in response to the "crisis." Presidential Order A642294 was a fact, and Congress had been "temporarily dissolved."

Erik had survived—for Erik was a survivor. He sat at the end of the third day in Griffith Park, watching the city burn itself out. The National Guardsmen around them were nervous and wary in their biological suits—each convinced that they had apprehended criminals who were trying to destroy the government of the United States and somehow completely unaware that they themselves had accomplished the very fact.

As Erik sat on that hill, the lifeless body of Martin Keel lay next to him. Erik had carried his love up the hill to the park even though he knew Martin was dead. He just couldn't leave him to be buried among the rubble.

On the other side of him lay his violin case: the symbol of his craft and soul. He had intended to play a new composition at the conclusion of the parade so many eternities ago. He could no more have left the violin behind than Martin. Now, slowly, he reached his soot-and-sweat-coated hand down and opened the case.

Erik stood up in the dark sunset, lit by the fires of the city about him. He knew that Nero hadn't actually fiddled when Rome burned but wondered if this wasn't the very image that the legend inspired.

He drew his bow across the strings. The sound made the Guardsmen jump and swing their rifles his way.

Erik played on. This was for Martin. The mournful sounds of the violin soared among the flames and over the bodies of a hundred and twenty-three thousand dead. Expert technique and years of practice culminated in the perfect conveyance for Erik's agony, defeat, and failure.

Some said that even the Guardsmen cried.

And when the last note was finished, Erik took the violin from his cheek and gazed at it for a time.

Then, taking it in both hands, he shattered it over his knee.

Erik escaped the cordon and confinement. His father, though now dead some thirty years, had one last gift for his son: the knowledge that it is never over. Erik moved through the sewers, through burned alleys, and through any hole that would keep him free. He managed to stay free for almost a year before someone arrested him in Rexburg, Idaho. He was wanted by the Feds for treason, incitement to riot, murder, accessory to murder, and interstate flight from prosecution; but they'd picked him up on a simple V-CIDS sweep. He told them he was Martin Keel, and they tossed him into ERIS 477 without a second thought.

Erik came into the camp and organized the gay community in his own way. He knew that organization without a leader was often no organization at all. He also knew from experience that being a *prominent* leader could get one shot. So he became the Dark Queen—an alter ego known only to the most essential in his organization. He could still lead from the shadows without risking Weston and his pious cronies killing him and ruining everything in his organization—not to mention what it would do to Erik himself.

So out among the workers he was Martin Keel, an older guy with a quiet smile and a perpetual case of laryngitis. It was a silent life that suited him.

His music had spoken for him before. Since the moment the violin shattered on that dark night among the flames, it was different. Now, in many ways, it was Erik's silence that spoke for him.

"Just a moment, Gene," the baritone answered. "You wouldn't want to rush this old gal, would you?"

Gene laughed nervously. "No, Queen."

"Jason," the voice turned to the young man standing near Gene, "your father says that he built these camps?"

Gene glanced over at Jason. *What's going on?*

"Yes, Queen," Jason answered, "or so he says. I honestly have no idea what he means by that."

"Hmm," purred the Queen. "I would like to know what it means. Your father suggests, if Gene has heard him correctly, that our blessed government intends to turn our camp into a faggot fryer in about five weeks whether we have the good grace to die on our own or not. It would also seem that our little efforts in the factory are meant to keep us pleasantly diverted until they pull the plug. If that is true, then we are going to have to do something about it. I for one refuse to sit around and die. I've seen far too much of that already."

"Pardon me, Queen," Jason spoke out, "but depending on my father's veracity, it may be a very big 'if.' "

"Exactly" came the Queen's soothing voice, "which is why you are going to help us determine that. Gene, you will get word to Mr. Michael Barris that his son wishes to speak with him tonight at, oh, say, eleven behind Warehouse 3. It won't require him to cross the line, and he may feel safer there."

Gene bowed slightly. "Yes, Queen!"

"And be sure that he does get there safely, Gene. If he's lying to us then we may have to kill him now and be done with it. We may not know what he's up to but if he's lying to us it cannot be for our good. On the other hand, if he isn't lying to us . . ."

Gene looked up.

"Well," the Queen said, "we'll have very little time left to do anything about it."

Detour

Friday, April 16, 2010 / 2253 hrs
Newhouse Center / 477th ERIS District
Wah Wah Valley, West Beaver County, Utah

Michael shook his head to stay awake. It wasn't helping much. His eyes moved lazily, the lids heavy with the effort.

The work shifts over the last few days had proved mentally exhausting in their mind-numbing repetitiveness. He'd tried getting some sleep during the supposed recreational periods. He discovered that Weston had his goon squad checking the barracks during each shift to make sure that they weren't occupied by those who were to be getting their recreation. So he had joined the other couple of thousand people who spent their time either in pointless activities or shuffling around the camp like listless nomads inside the fence.

Now here he was again, walking the night, trying for another glimpse of contact with his son.

Every instinct now told him how wrong it was to be out like this. When Gene had come to him about twenty minutes ago, Michael had been on the verge of collapse in his bunk. There hadn't been time to let Sid know where he was going, let alone try to enlist Carl's help—whatever that might have been. Now he was out among the dark alleys again, alone. He knew just how treacherous such a journey could be.

He left 7-R right as soon as he could, but Gene was nowhere in sight. Shivering once, Michael ran west past the bathhouse in a half crouch. Dead were already beginning to litter the alleyways, tumbled as they were out the doors of the barracks without much thought or concern. *The Tomb of the Unknown Civilian*, Michael thought, *is the open sky.*

He stopped at the edge of the R block. A twenty-foot-wide expanse separated most of the blocks in the compound, although terrain occasionally made the distance wider. Dim illumination from the dull plastic windows would continue for another five minutes or so before the optic feeds to the light panels were shut down. After that, the camp would be plunged into the darkness with the last finality of the curfew and his life would be given over to the stars overhead—if there were any to be had through the clouds that had been gathering all day. Last he had seen, the sky was solidly overcast, which meant that the camp could very quickly look like the inside of the blackest cave he'd ever seen. If he lost the light, he knew, he would be lost. He had to get to Jason before then.

Michael stood at the edge of R block and considered. The blocks at this point in the camp were slightly staggered. U block was directly north of R block and the last block before the line. Most of the children were housed in the north end of U block. V block started just south and opposite of where Michael stood. Its long rows of barracks were only two stories tall compared to the three-story affairs in R and U blocks. Beyond that was the main AG line into and out of camp with the sanitation facilities on the other side. He could cross into U block and hope that the confined spaces would give him cover from being discovered by Bullock's men but in the process put himself at risk to whatever was waiting for him in there. He knew no one in V block. He could only imagine what waited for him in there, and his imagination was pretty frightening.

He looked to his right. Down the long space between blocks he could see Warehouse 4 just past the end of V block. Gene had said to meet Jason at the north side of Warehouse 3, the one closest to the line. To get there, Michael would have to pass Warehouse 4, pass the end of U block, and cross a road to the three other warehouses northeast of the communication tower.

He felt like he was jogging to the moon for all that distance. He took a pair of quick, puffing breaths to work up his courage and ducked to the right, running his fingers lightly against the walls of R block barracks just in case the lights died early on him.

The ranks of black barracks and their dim windows slipped past him as he scurried along. He came to the end of R block and looked around the corner. There were a few lights visible from the Commons up beyond the slope of the recreation field, but no movement. He crossed quickly to U block and, still running his fingers along the barracks walls when he could, continued carefully in his crablike dash toward the bulk of Warehouse 4 near the end of the area.

His hand was suddenly arrested with such unexpected force that he thought his shoulder had been dislocated. He cried out in pain. The twisting of his arm turned him into the alley between two barracks of U block and pressed him face first against the wall. Flashes of light cascaded across Michael's vision for a moment before, and out of the corner of his eye he could see part of his assailant's fleshy pale face resting on his shoulder.

"You know," the fat man's face said, dripping sweat even in the chill of the evening, "you shouldn't be wandering about the alleys this late at night. You might disturb someone's party. We honestly can't have that, can we? It wouldn't be proper, would it?"

"No," Michael managed to say, though his articulation suffered from his face being pressed against the clapboard siding of the barracks. "I'll try not to disturb you."

"Oh"—the breath from the man was horrible—"you won't be any trouble at all. I think you *should* come to our party. You could be our honored guest, so to speak."

"Sorry"—Michael winced, the man's weight pressing him harder into the wall—"I've got a previous engagement. Perhaps some other time."

"Oh, now what's wrong?" the fat man pouted. "Don't you like our company? I'm sure you'll change your mind. Everyone likes a barbecue! We've got a nice little fire ready and some choice cuts, even if some of it is a bit stale."

Michael's eyes went wide. He suddenly stopped struggling.

"What would you like?" the sweat-drenched voice whispered in his ear. "A leg? A thigh? A breast? All carefully roasted and succulent. Oh, I suppose not." The voice turned suddenly chill. "But I know what I want—a little fresh meat!"

Michael could feel the fat man relax slightly. In a moment, he lifted his leg and slammed the outside edge of his hard boots against the fat man's calf. He connected just below the kneecap and kicked it down the length of the man's shin until it crunched into his instep.

The man howled with the pain, releasing his grip on Michael. Michael pushed backward, toppling the man into the hard dirt.

He caught movement out of the corner of his eye. Several figures were rushing toward him.

I'm going to have to ruin their party, Michael thought.

He ran.

He ran toward Warehouse 4 more out of instinct than thought. He'd been heading in that direction, and nature carried him on that alone. With the fury of adrenaline surging through his veins, he saw the other warehouses on the north side of the street beyond Warehouse 4. That was where Jason was. He could see it. He didn't slow as he passed the first warehouse.

Suddenly, several figures poured out of an alley ahead of him just short of the end of U block. The sticks and broken boards in their hands were silhouetted against the last windows of the barracks beyond them.

Michael didn't slacken his pace. He turned at once, cutting around Warehouse 4 and angling toward the Communications Tower. His feet beat against the dark ground, his own ragged breathing not quite drowning out the rumbling footfalls behind him. He could barely see from the dim illumination of the windows behind him.

Suddenly, the lights died. Eleven o'clock.

He continued to run blindly into the darkness. An instant later, someone tackled him from behind. The dark ground rose up to meet him. He half turned in the air, landing on his side, the wind knocked from his lungs as he gasped for air. He writhed in panic.

Sounds, more sounds around him. Sickly sounds. Cries and deep, wet thuds. Scuffling feet kicked dust into his face. Legs tripped over him.

Two hands reached down in the darkness and pulled Michael to his shaky feet. Though he was blind in the sudden darkness, he recognized the voice at once.

"Well, Mr. Barris," Bullock spat the words at his face. "Just where the hell do you think you're going? Taking a little stroll in the evening air?" Bullock released his right hand and slammed it into Michael's belly just below the rib cage. "That's a warning for curfew violation and this"—he drew back a fist and cracked it down across Michael's face, driving him to his knees—"is for supporting the incident with that nutcase in the Assembly Room this morning. Oh, yeah, and this . . ."

The sharp kick to the stomach again knocked the air out of Michael.

". . . This is for being such a smart-ass to me the other day."

Michael rolled onto the ground, his world all pain.

"I'm sure I'll think of something else that I owe you for later, Mr. I-Net newsman, but that'll wait." Bullock's arms waved in the darkness. "All right, get him up to the Cathedral. The reverend would like a few words with him—if he can still talk."

"Damn!" Erik muttered to himself, watching the scene below him from the roof of Warehouse 3, his own eyes adjusted to the darkness, which was not nearly so complete as Michael had assumed. Lights from the east, probably Milford, were reflecting off the clouds sufficient for them to see—barely. He lay on the roof with two of his companions where he had hoped to overhear the exchange he had set up between Michael and his son.

Things had taken a decided turn from his plans.

"Oh, let the hetro go, honey: that guy's so straight he squeaks. He's been nothing but trouble since we played our little trick on him the other night."

"Lucian, you are a queen bitch aren't you?"

Lucian purred, "Well, you've got that half right, and I'll not even admit to which half." Lucian's voice turned serious. "Well, they're dragging him up the road—off to 'Masta Weston's' I can only suppose. What now, Queen?"

Erik considered for a moment. Below he could see the security force pick Michael up and haul him up the line toward the Commons. "Lucian, where do you think they'll take him?"

"Oh, most likely it'll be to the Cathedral. It's the only place Weston can be sure that the ERIS Nazis will be listening. That man! He just *loves* an audience!" Lucian shrugged. "Besides, it's the only place in the compound that has power at this time of night—other than the warehouses and the Commons factory, that is."

"Can we get a pair of ears in the Cathedral?"

Lucian chuckled. "Honey, if you want ears in the Cathedral, you got them."

"Get them in right now and have them report to me as soon as they can." Erik considered the beefy security troop carrying the limp body of Michael Barris up the line.

"I want to know what's said in there."

Confessions

Friday, April 16, 2010 / 2320 hrs
Newhouse Center / 477th ERIS District
Wah Wah Valley, West Beaver County, Utah

Michael was dropped, gulping air past the pain, onto the floor of the Cathedral just next to the altar.

"Why, Mr. Barris, how good of you to join us." Reverend Weston stood on the other side of the plywood altar. "I honestly wasn't expecting you to be up at this hour."

Bullock moved to one side of the Cathedral. "You needn't worry about that, Reverend. He was already up and about."

The reverend's eyebrows rose in a surprise that his emerald eyes did not register. "Oh, really? A little too active tonight, Mr. Barris? Overachieving again, are we, Mr. Barris?"

Michael swallowed air and managed to rise to a kneeling position. The lights in the Cathedral were glaring after the darkness outside. He blinked furiously in the brilliance of the ceiling panels illuminating the large room from the rafters overhead.

"Reverend—Weston," Michael pushed out between gasps, "it is—imperative that we—talk."

"A-ha!" Weston said with the practiced placidity of his craft. "Oh, my dear boy, you've come to confess your sins before God and his servants! It's been a long time since I heard anyone's confession. Please go ahead, my child," the voice suddenly turning cold, "confess everything to me so that we can stop this charade and deal with one another."

Michael looked up. The reverend smiled at him through dirty teeth and those maddeningly emerald eyes. Logic and reason weren't the motivation behind those eyes. Michael knew then that the reverend ran only on feeling and instinct. What could drive a caring man to become someone like the reverend?

"Mr. Barris—rather, Brother Barris—it's a bit late for confessions, but we are not without generosity, we are not without compassion." The reverend spoke in the "royal we," but Michael remained unconvinced as to just who else Quinton Weston was actually speaking for. "You've lied to us, you've had dealings with the darkest sinners within our midst—a crime which of itself is punishable by death—and we've already discovered your conspirator who has come into our midst from the desert."

The reverend gestured to the bench at the end of the dais. Sitting on the floor, propped up against the bench, was a large man, mostly arms and legs, whose face might have been rugged if it weren't for the bruises puffing up his face. He sat rather stoically considering his injuries and the pain he must be under. His arms crossed his chest while his eyes reflected a cool and practiced disinterest from beneath what was barely recognizable as a western straw hat.

"Pleased to meet you," Michael said painfully as he sat up.

"Likewise," the cowboy offered reluctantly.

"You are?" Michael offered.

"One very pissed-off cowboy, mister."

"Ah," Michael sighed.

"I'm touched by this warm reunion," the reverend intoned, "but the time for such games is past."

"Reverend," Michael shook his head, "what makes you think I've ever even met this man?"

"Both of you arriving so near each other, so mysteriously," the reverend nodded smugly, "could not possibly have been a coincidence."

"Why not?"

The reverend gave him no answer. Michael sighed and turned

to the cowboy. "Do you have any idea what the reverend here is talking about?"

"Hell, no," the cowboy replied in a slow drawl. "He's been goin' on this way for half the night and ain't made a lick of sense yet."

"Well," Michael offered, "at least that's something you can count on. Paranoid old guy, isn't he?"

Weston had somehow lost control of the conversation. "Look, Brother Barris, it's time you and I came to an understanding. If you could just let me understand why you've come here—both of you—and what your mission is here, I could make things a lot smoother for you. There isn't an aspect of this camp that I don't control; not a place I can't get you into."

"The Dark Queen in the gay blocks might take exception to that," Michael offered quietly.

The reverend's smile fell ever so slightly. "We have everything in that side of the camp well under control, Brother Barris, I assure you. Those vile and sinful wretches are suffering the consequences of their evil. Is *that* why you're here?"

Michael looked at the reverend in silence.

The reverend stepped angrily around the podium. "Brother Barris, I do not believe you fully appreciate your situation. We are in a life-and-death struggle here, and I—I alone!—hold the keys to your salvation and continued existence! Your cowboy friend can't help you; your friends beyond this wall can't help you—just me!"

"OK," Michael said cautiously, "just what can you do for me?"

The reverend's face had become red with his anger, but he relaxed. "So perhaps there is some room for understanding after all! Well, I can get you out of here. NIH and the CDC are operating a crash program—somewhat experimental—in a new facility just west of Cheyenne. They need a supply of V-CIDS people for their therapies. I could get you onto that list—let's be honest, I can get you *there*! You and your ranch house friend here."

The reverend knelt down on one knee, his face close and intimate to Michael's. "All you need to do is be honest with me—all you need to do is tell me what you're doing here!"

Michael looked up at the reverend. "I'll tell you."

The reverend leaned closer still and bestowed on Michael his most practiced smile. "Yes, my son."

"I am in search of forgiveness," Michael whispered loudly.

The reverend drew back, standing suddenly. "How dare you mock me!"

"How dare you mock my absolution?" Michael returned with seriousness. "How dare you judge my motives without understanding them? You aren't looking for the truth! You're looking for some neat explanation that will fit into your vision of the world. No one these days wants to hear the truth!"

Weston shouted at Michael as the reverend backed up. "Truth! You talk of the truth? You talk of *your* truth, Barris, *your* truth! Not mine!"

"You wouldn't hear the truth!" Michael countered, rising to his own feet. "You wanted to know why I was here? You wanted to know what would drive a man into a death camp—yes, Reverend, a death camp!—just to find his own son? Guilt, Weston, guilt and sorrow for my own sins. Yes, dear Reverend, I confess it; I am a sinner, black to the soul! I've come here to find my own peace from the nagging, haunting torture of my awful deeds! But the terrible thing, most Reverend Father, is that you have no power, no words, no comfort to offer me, for my sin has been against nothing that you would call wicked or evil or demonic. My absolution does not lie in your hands!"

Michael moved suddenly, gathering the reverend's coat in both hands. Bullock moved quickly to stop him, but the reverend held up his hand. Bullock waited.

"You want to know why I'm here?" Michael spat the angry words into the reverend's face only inches away. "I'll tell you! I came because I own this camp! I built it board by lousy board . . . fence by lousy fence! I painted every wall, hammered every joist, and cut each piece of wood! I sent . . ." his voice cracked with raw feeling ". . . I sent every man, every husband, every wife and mother, every child with trusting eyes into this damned camp! I sent my own son! . . . My own goddamned son!"

Michael was spent. He released his hold on the reverend and slid down to sit on the edge of the dais.

Weston stood still, looking down at the man. He hadn't known what to expect—certainly not this. At last, the reverend spoke hesitantly. "Brother Barris, I don't see how that is possible."

Michael took a deep, stuttering breath, and then continued speaking to no one in particular. "Back in '97 a group of us in information management systems came together to rework the existing internet. It was all part of the information superhighway—that's what they used to call it—that everyone was so excited about. John Matthews and a number of others backed the development of broader band-communication systems with advanced digital compression using the television cable companies as channel routes into the households. By '03 nearly 90 percent of homes in the United States were fully interactive on the I-Net. The old internet died from disuse—why bother with modem communication when your television had better, faster access than your phone and did everything your phone could do anyway? The point is that I-Net became the nexus for all communication in the United States. One-stop multimedia shopping. Videophone, fax, voice, computer, television, movies—we became all that. Fully interactive—fully responsive. It was everything we'd dreamed of."

Michael turned his head to face the reverend. "The problem was that we were in such a hurry to build the technology that we didn't think what the technology would do to the people. The social impact of our vast information system was unexpected by any of us in a rush to bring newer, brighter, and faster information services to the public—whether the public wanted it or not. We had five hundred digital television channels that needed programming to fill twenty-four hours a day. That's finished information broadcasts totaling *twelve thousand hours* that had to be available each week, and a full half of *that* was interactive, requiring even more production time. The first thing we discovered was that it took the average person with a remote over *an hour and a half* just to flip through all the available channels—by which time, of course, the first program you had checked had already changed. The audience was getting confused by the sheer bombardment of information.

"So," Michael shrugged, "we had to simplify it for them. Each channel began to specialize—reflecting a certain viewpoint. That way, you could program your television to just show you what you wanted to see . . . just tell you what you wanted to hear. No more cognitive dissonance. No more having to hear those 'darn liberals' or those 'darn conservatives' or anyone else you disagreed with or who might actually change your mind. We became the rose-colored glasses to the world—telling everyone just what they wanted to hear—and with five hundred channels, everyone who needed a voice got one. All those people talking . . . and no one was listening."

Michael stood up, running his fingers through his hair. "But it wasn't enough. People decided that they not only wanted a voice, but that they wanted a say—completely different things. So, bang, full participatory democracy! Why have Congress vote for you when you could vote over your television by '04. By '06, you could provide a constant stream of your opinions, analyzed with wonderful graphics over the Harris/Nielsen Opinion Channel. Politicians kept that channel on in every office in D.C. twenty-four hours a day. They didn't make a move without consulting that channel. According to our research, by '08, they began making policy *because* of that channel."

The reverend shook his head. "I don't see what any of this has to do with your being . . ."

"We forgot two things, Reverend—and herein lie my greatest sins—we forgot, first, that people only make decisions based on what they know. You can have everyone in the country vote freely and democratically and *still* come up with the wrong answer—if the information they base that decision on is wrong. People don't want the truth, Father, when it is complicated. They don't want to spend years debating an issue. They want it homogenized, sanitized and, above all, *simplified* into terms they can understand. We told them—I told them—in our news broadcasts for nearly half a century that *any* problem—no matter how complex—could be stated clearly in a five-minute news segment; that any discussion of issues could be made clear in a ten-second sound bite. My first sin is that I let people believe that. We gave them the tools to give their voices power—then took away their ability to make free choices that gave that power meaningful responsibility."

"This is getting tedious, Brother Barris!" Weston yawned. "I was hoping that we would be able to come to terms, but I'm tired of listening to this irrelevant drivel! Do you understand what this has to do with anything?" Weston said to Bullock.

Yet before Bullock answered, an unexpected voice grumbled in the hall.

"Well, hell, yes I get it!"

Weston turned to the cowboy. "*You* get it?"

The battered rancher stretched and leaned forward a bit. "Sure. It's like if you rope a calf and stake her in the middle of a pasture. It don't matter how good the grass is just beyond that thar rope: she's gonna eat the grass she can reach." He leaned back, proud of himself. "See! Simple as that!"

"That is the end of it!" Weston had given up on subtlety. "You'll give me what I want, Barris, and you'll give it now or . . ."

"Or what?" finished the cowboy from the side. "You'll *kill* him? Was that what you were gonna say, Reverend?"

The distraction bought Michael a space to speak. "You still haven't heard my second confession. When you do, then I'll tell you why I came."

Weston leaned back. "The second confession is?"

"I committed the sin of haste. The I-Net was created to allow people to make their voices and decisions known *instantly*. Governments are often criticized for moving slowly but that deliberateness, it turns out, is their strength. They take time to think through complex problems before they act. People, however, are different. People react first from the gut and then from the head. Show a guy on television abusing workers—throw the bum in jail! See white cops beating up a black man—start a riot! A terrorist attacks the Olympics—nuke their country! We see these predigested problems on television and in a reflex rush to try, judge, convict, and sentence all in the space of a breath. But give that knee-jerk reflex real *power*—like the I-Net—to make its overwhelming will known as a national mandate *instantly*, and you can cause a 'political riot.' "

The reverend was out of patience. "What is the point!"

"Combine these sins—simplification of information and instant, visceral democratic mandates—and you lose the ability to cool down. There is no longer deliberation time between events that may or may not be true and our reaction to them. Policy becomes instinct rather than thought.

"So"—Michael drew a deep breath—"when I learned that the San Francisco rebellion was actually orchestrated by the President; when I realized that the very instrument of democracy which I thought I had built was used to give consent to the suspension of the Constitution; when I learned that the result was that my own son was sentenced to death because of it—I couldn't stay away. I truly did build this camp, Reverend, because I gave the people the ability to vote—in an instant of fear and ignorance—to build them."

Bullock snorted. "So that's why you came? Fell on the sword out of guilt?"

"No," Michael said clearly. "I came because I want to save as many of them as I can. I am responsible for this; I have to fix it. My son was the catalyst, to be sure, but I've come to help as many of these people as I can."

Bullock laughed harshly. "I don't believe it!"

"What lies can I possibly tell to you that you would accept?" Michael looked up at the reverend. "Reverend Weston, you are supposed to be the spiritual leader of this camp as well as its governor. You've got to accept responsibility for the people in this camp."

"Brother Barris, you speak the obvious."

"Very well, Reverend," Michael said carefully. "Then something must be done within five weeks or we're all dead."

"Really?" The reverend looked down from behind the podium with unmasked skepticism. "Our mortality rates have risen slightly over the last few days, but I'm confident that with a little extra diligence on the part of our sanitation staff . . ."

"No," Michael said flatly. "In five weeks, by our best estimates, this camp and everyone alive in it will be blown from the face of the earth."

Reverend Weston chuckled and shook his head. "Even if that were true—which I know it is not—just where do you see me, enacting the part of Moses, leading these people into the desert wilderness? Reno? Salt Lake? Las Vegas, perhaps? All this based on the testimony of a penitent newsman and a drunken cowboy? You're hardly the equivalent of a burning bush, Brother Barris!"

Bullock joined in. "Right, Reverend! He seems more like a smoking leaf to me!"

"Of course, you'd have to wonder just what leaf he was smoking!" The reverend, tired from the day, broke into peals of laughter.

"Can't you understand!" Michael shouted, unheard above the roaring laughs. "They're going to kill us all unless we do something about it!"

Yet there were those who heard.

A cowboy named Virgil.

The ears of the Dark Queen, unseen in the rafters above the lights who would report each word and nuance to Erik Simms within the hour.

Lastly, a captain monitoring the night shift whose tears streaming down his silent face were unseen in the darkness of the Operations Suite.

Blood

Saturday, April 17, 2010 / 0805 hrs
Newhouse Center / 477th ERIS District
Wah Wah Valley, West Beaver County, Utah

"Reverend! Reverend, wake up!"

The voice was far away. *Go away, I just want to sleep.*

The voice wouldn't go away.

"Reverend, you're needed right now!"

Quinton Weston stretched with his yawn, an action that drew protests from all the distant parts of his body. Light was beginning to intrude on his eyelids. It had been a long night. All that fuss, all that worry about a stupid idealist who wanted to assuage his conscience. As a newsman he might have been a threat to the ERIS command, as a spy he might have been a menace to Weston's own position and authority. But an idealist? That was truly laughable—and laugh he had. Before he had talked to them, the reverend had considered having both Virgil and Michael killed last night and be done with it. But after hearing Barris's tirade—most of which made little sense to the reverend—he just viewed them as pathetic and hopeless dreamers. "All talk, no shock" as they used to say on the streets. He'd just had them bundled back to their barracks by Bullock around one in the morning and went to bed.

So who wanted him to get up?

"Reverend, please, I need your help."

The reverend sat up in bed. "Wha . . . Who . . . What is it?"

A blurry face with long, straight hair started to come into focus. "It's me, sir, Melinda Rowley."

Melinda was his appointed director of factory operations. The room came into sudden, painful focus. Melinda wasn't well. The purple blotches on her face were growing together, and the cough was getting noticeably worse despite her efforts to conceal it. Weston guessed that he would have to find a new factory director soon. Behind her he could see Oscar Feinstein, whom he remembered as being the day shift coordinator and Donovan Murdock, the day shift supervisor.

What was going on?

"You've got to do something," Oscar piped up. "I don't know how to shift assignments to handle the workload."

"Wait! I've got to do something about what?" Weston said, his voice on edge.

Melinda drew a breath and glanced at the other two. They both looked down. Everyone feared to be the messenger.

"Well?"

Melinda spoke. "The graveyard shift didn't report to work. None of them, so far as we can tell."

"WHAT!" The reverend roared, jumping to his feet.

Melinda shrank back. "The graveyard shift's supply train is still in the yard. Both the breakfast supply train and day shift's train are hovering outside the outer perimeter."

Murdock shook his head. "We don't know if we should clear the parts off the graveyard shift pallets or not. If we do, we're afraid that the train will leave before we can turn the parts around, and then we'll be a full shift behind with no place to stockpile the incoming components."

Oscar sputtered to life again. "Do you want additional shifts arranged to make up the work? There isn't enough space in the Commons factory to accommodate more assemblers, and we don't have enough assembly tools to go around if we do. In any event, I can't possibly make the morning work assignments until we know which way we are going to handle . . ."

"And what about the breakfast supply train?" Murdock demanded. "People are up at the Commons right now waiting on their breakfast, and there's no—"

"*Shut up! Shut up, all of you!*" Weston bellowed. "I've got to think!" The reverend reached for the end of the bed, grabbing his smudged black slacks. Melinda hastily looked away, unprepared for the sight of the ragged boxers worn by the reverend. *Holy shorts,* she thought to herself and immediately covered the smile with her right hand and looked down.

Weston stuffed his shirt into his pants, ignored or forgot the socks, and sitting on the edge of his bed, shoved his feet into his shoes. "What about Johnson? He was in charge of that shift."

"I talked to Folleson already," Melinda said. Henry Folleson was the night shift supervisor. "He was no more happy about being woken up than you were, Reverend, but he swears he made the shift turn over to Johnson last night. He says nothing seemed out of the ordinary and that the change went pretty much like always."

Weston struggled with a knot in his shoelaces. "And this morning? What about this morning."

Murdock knew he had to field it. Shift changes were always handled personally between the shift supervisors. "I was there on time but . . . sorry, no Johnson. I found the shift packet sitting at the supervisor's desk, but it didn't even look like it had been opened. None of it was filled out—none of it."

Weston stood again. "Murdock, you get a standard crew unloading those supply pallets, then get that train clear of the AG line so that the breakfast supply can be brought in. Feinstein! You roust the Swing Shift Assignments Staff, and put everyone you can find space for to assemble those units right along with day shift. Cancel the recreation periods—we've got to get caught up. Melinda! You find Rosemary Pohlhaus—she's the swing shift supervisor—and get her working with Murdock on a double-shift schedule."

"What about you?" Melinda asked. "What are you going to do?"

"Me? I'm going to find every one of Bullock's men and put an end to this once and for all!" The reverend's voice lowered, his eyes burning with green fire. "They think they can make me look bad, do they? Think they can ruin my chances to get out of here. We'll see who leaves first, oh, yes, we'll see!"

The Reverend Weston turned to the others. "You want to know what I'm going to do, eh? I'm going to cross the line, my friends, and deal with the pestilent and petulant infestation that has too long plagued us. It's time we established who runs this camp!"

It was nine in the morning. It was still cool.

All of Newhouse was in chaos. Two shifts were trying to assemble at the same time. The breakfast schedule had been revised twice, but there was no good way of communicating that to the camp population. Conflicting schedules appeared amid an increasingly agitated crowd around the Commons' dining room. Meanwhile, shift assembly team leaders for two shifts were trying to get their crews to the right place and time based on revised orders. Most teams couldn't find more than a handful of people required.

Nowhere was this more evident than in the Recreation Field sloping westward away from the Commons itself. Shirley Sjoberg had suggested that Oscar Feinstein use the large open area as a staging ground to get the work shifts functioning. Unfortunately, the good idea in theory proved disastrous in practice. The field became a confused sea of several thousand people, confused, angry, and lost.

Into this chaos, unnoticed, appeared new people blinking into the sun. They walked in the light for the first time in what had seemed to them a long eternity of graveyard shifts. The sun's warmth was life to them, feeble as it was. They walked among the milling crowd and smiled. They were no longer in the graveyard. They had risen like Lazarus from the dead. Nearly a thousand of them passed without question amid the chaos of the field, which they secretly knew they had caused and which filled them with power and pride.

Until Willard Bullock, his nerves ugly and raw, saw Scott Johnson walking with a smile through the crowd.

A roar surged up from the people just to the north of Michael. For a moment he thought someone had started a soccer match, the sound being the image of what he had heard when he last attended the World Cup Championships in '03. It was the shout of spectacle, with a touch of blood.

He turned instinctively to see what was going on. People were running in his direction, opening a space. Michael pushed past them, fighting his way through an increasingly dense tangle of people. As he moved, through the corner of his eye, he saw one of Bullock's security people lifting his stick to strike. Another hand rose up and pulled him down into the crowd.

Michael continued to fight his way through the throng. Suddenly, almost without warning, he stopped just short of the cleared space but could see well enough. He gasped.

It was Bullock. The red hair, raggedly cut close to his blocky scalp, could belong to no one else. His fists were moving quickly and repeatedly into the midsection of a shorter, barrel-chested man. Suddenly, his rhythm was interrupted. The short man blocked Bullock's left and right combination, then slammed both cupped hands flat against Bullock's ears. Bullock howled and staggered backward.

The crowd screamed all around them.

"Stick it to the Bulldog!"

"Kill the goddamned faggot!"

"Rip his lungs out, Scott!"

Michael swayed back and forth from the press of the crowd, the people in front of him holding him back.

They don't want justice, he thought to himself, *they just smell the blood.*

The man they called "Scott" didn't waste time. He followed Bullock's backward momentum with a solid kick to the larger man's chest. Willard Bullock wasn't fast enough. The boot pressed the air out of his lungs and toppled the security chief. He rolled back across the slope, away from Michael.

The opening in the crowd moved with them, clearing the way before them, following them like circling wolves.

"Take him down! Show him who's running things!"

"Burn the fairy!"

Michael, caught in the crush, floated in the moving sea of people, following the fight with every wave.

Scott pressed forward with his attack, rage and fury making

him bolder. He jumped again, this time to slam his boots into Bullock's broad face.

Bullock was too quick for him. His arms arrested the leg as it traveled downward, using the shorter man's momentum against him, and flipped the man yelling in pain over him.

Bullock got up, a growl rising in his throat as he lunged for the smaller man now on the ground.

No one, least of all the seething crowd about the two men, took notice where they were.

Scott saw the huge security man charging on all fours toward him. He rolled quickly out of the way, and tried to scramble to his feet. Bullock reached out with both arms and tripped him before he could quite get up. The small man tumbled a few feet before he rolled again to his feet, blood running freely from a gash in his forehead.

Bullock charged him in a red, blind anger. Scott barely had time to hold his hands up against the onslaught.

The force of the impact carried them both over the small, rough-hewn fence . . .

. . . and into the children's play yard.

"NO!" Michael screamed.

The crowd roared again.

Bullock and Scott fell squarely atop a five-year-old-boy with thick black hair. He dropped beneath them without a sound. He had lived his life as he had died, anonymously quiet and without protest. When Bullock and Scott rolled away from him, the boy lay still against the ground, a red river building from his open mouth. *Lumber, you know, as in stiff as a board.*

The yard was full of children—all staring and frozen either in shock or fear or just that special world that is beyond feeling. They stood, they lay, they sat. None of them moved.

"NO!" Michael screamed again, and began clawing at the people in front of him.

Bullock and Scott rolled across the play yard, knocking five other children into the dust. The blond little girl didn't get up again.

Scott struggled against Bullock's hands at his throat. His hands flailed about for something, a weapon, anything he could use to break the bigger man's hold. His hand closed on a part of the now broken fence. The angle wasn't the best, but the rough board that smashed across Bullock's face came with a handful of desert dust. It was enough to get Scott free.

Winded, Scott staggered to his feet, hatred in his eyes. Bullock stood up unsteadily, wiping the dust from his tearing eyes. Scott quickly swung the board back for a telling blow, but the backswing of his weapon connected squarely with the face of a seven-year-old girl in an explosion of wet crimson.

Scott, the blood lust in his eyes, never noticed. He swung against Bullock's left side, connecting with the ribs in a painful, crunching sound, shattering the board.

Bullock bellowed as he arrested the remains of the board with his left arm. His right hand crossed, gathering up the front of Scotty's bloody shirt and throwing him at the side of the Hospice.

Children dropped like tenpins along the path.

Scott lay panting against the Hospice wall. He hadn't noticed that the cheering crowd had suddenly gone silent, that the entertainment had turned tragic.

Bullock, sucking air in huge, gulping breaths, turned toward his opponent. "Now, by God, . . . you homo pervert, now . . . now I'm going to kill you . . . and as many of your faggot friends as I can find!"

"NO! NO! NO!"

Bullock's head snapped forward, his eyes rolling up into his head. Michael, behind him, stood not with the thin board of the fence slats in his hand, but a solid pine support three inches thick like a baseball bat in his hands.

Scott, still blind with hate and fear, got to his feet with his broken board and charged toward Bullock's prone body. Michael swung again, yelling in his own rage, connecting across Scott's head.

He stopped and fell to the ground over Bullock.

A crow cried far overhead.

It was the only sound.

Michael stood in the center of the play yard, his fingers white from his deadly grip. His breathing was ragged from the adrenaline; he couldn't seem to bring it under control.

Then he saw them, silent, watching him.

The camp.

"THIS IS WHAT YOU WANTED ISN'T IT? DEATH!" he yelled at them, pointing to the carnage of the play yard.

His voice echoed into the distant hills.

Not one in a thousand moved.

"You . . . you believed them! They told you you were dead . . . and so you just believed them!" Michael cried out to them, his voice shaking. "You make their pretty little meaningless, *meaningless* toys to keep you busy while they wait for you to die! You kill each other and eat each other and wonder when it's going to happen to you! Big Brother tells you to please sit still while he robs you of your very breath—of everything you ever were or ever would be—and you just *do it*!"

Through his tears Michael could see the cowboy suddenly appear at the edge of the crowd. Lord knows where he's been, Michael thought, but I hope he'll help me now.

"Well, if you're dead then *fuck you*!"

At the south edge of the crowd, a tall man with sunken eyes clattered his fingers across a wooden terminal.

"We're all dying—every one of us. I'm dying, too—*but not today!*" Michael shouted at them. "I am *not* going to die *today*! Anyone can die! I want to be somebody! I want to live!"

Michael looked down.

Amanda was her name—the only name she knew.

Virgil knelt down next to her and picked her up. She lay still, her eyes open but unfocused. Her breathing was shallow.

"This ain't no life for a little girl," he said simply as he stood with the tiny child in his arms. "You want to live, Mr. Barris? Well, Amanda wants to live, too."

Michael looked at Virgil and put his hand on his shoulder. "She'll need a family."

"Well," Virgil sighed, "it don't appear that I have much else to do for the rest of my life."

Michael smiled. "Some family."

Virgil and Michael took Amanda out of the play yard and through the crowd.

They were her family.

* * *

From that moment, the play yard fence disappeared. All day long, people in twos and threes, sixes and eights, came quietly to the yard and found a child lost in their own world and took them away.

By evening, not a single child remained in the Hospice.

The assembly pallets left that night with their parts unassembled.

They never returned.

Entr' Acte

For certain is death for the born
And certain is birth for the dead;
Therefore, over the inevitable
Thou shouldst not grieve.

—Bhagavad Gita
ch. 2, sec. 27

High though his titles, proud his name,
Boundless his wealth as wish can claim;
Despite those titles, power and pelf
The wretch concentered all in self,
Living, shall forfeit fair renown,
And, doubly dying, shall go down
To the vile dust from whence he sprung,
Unwept, unhonored, and unsung.

—"The Lay of the Last Minstrel"
Sir Walter Scott

The
Children's Crusade

Saturday, April 17, 2010 / 1025 hrs
Barracks 7-R
Newhouse Center / 477th ERIS District
Wah Wah Valley, West Beaver County, Utah

Michael led the gangly cowboy into Block R. It was the only block he knew well enough to get them safely inside and out from under the eyes of the enormous crowd still milling in the recreation field.

The little girl had buried her head against the cowboy's neck and draped both arms over his shoulders. With the quiet practice which only small children have perfected, Michael knew that the girl would passively and quite effectively reject any change in her condition. The tall ranch hand was the world to her and nothing else mattered.

"Everyone here seems to think we know each other." Michael smiled, though he was still shaking and exhausted from the battle in the play yard. "I suppose we ought to be introduced." He stopped and held out his hand. "My name's Michael Barris, I'm very pleased to meet you."

The cowboy arched an eyebrow into his hat.

"Mr. Barris—m' name's Virgil. This here's Amanda."

"Pleased to meet you both. Did they give you a barracks assignment—tell you where to sleep?"

"No, sir." Virgil stood awkwardly, talking uncomfortably through the little girl's hair that occasionally drifted over his mouth. "They said somethin' about gettin' me all straightened out in the mornin', but look's like that ain't gonna be happenin' real soon."

Michael smiled. "Well, I know just the place for you two to settle down. Right this way, please!" He turned the corner and led them down the dim alleys of Block R.

What's changed in me? Michael thought. *Something's burned out of me and left something clean and solid in its place.* Even the dim canyons of Block R had taken on a better, brighter aspect than he remembered them having had before. He wasn't sure whether it was the adrenaline still banging around in his veins or whether something deeper and more basic had happened to him. Whatever it was, however, he was feeling positively light-headed.

They turned another corner and confronted the looming facade of Barracks 7-R.

Virgil looked askance at the structure. "You live in that barn?"

Michael considered the building for a moment. Three stories tall and every inch of it weathered. The desert has its own way with wood. It doesn't consume it like the ocean or forests do—there aren't enough living things out here to feed off it. Yet in the desert, the kiln-dry air pulls the life out of the wood just as surely as the wetlands. Worse, the constant wind washes the walls of the barracks consistently with sand. The once finished sides had quickly grown iron gray. What little paint had been used on signs and markers had faded to the point of being nearly indecipherable. Yes, he thought, I suppose it does look like a barn.

"I'll have you know that this is the best barn in the whole camp." Michael climbed the short steps to the entry door and swung it wide. "I like to think of it as rustic—you know, sort of . . ."

"I know what rustic is, Barris," Virgil drawled with infinite patience. He climbed the stairs easily with Amanda and passed through the open door. "Rustic is when country people get tired of their old junk and sell it to the city folk as art."

Michael smiled. "Yes, I suppose that's about right. Just down the hall and to the left there."

Virgil turned the corner in the dim hallway and ran straight into Sid Jarolscowitz.

"Hey," Virgil exclaimed, "who put the hippie here?"

"Hippie?" Sid sputtered, gazing up the six inches he required to meet Virgil's eyes. "Now, there's a term I haven't heard in about twenty years! Where've you been living, hayseed—a cave?"

Virgil considered for a moment. "Yep," he said, and then shouldered his way past Sid, continuing down the hall.

Sid turned. "Hey, this is my barracks, Cowboy! Just who the hell are you coming in here . . ."

Virgil turned and lifted a warning finger. "You mind yer language, mister! Thar's children present!"

Sid gaped for a moment before recovering. "Yeah, but who the . . . I mean . . . what in . . ."

Michael clamped Sid on the shoulder from behind and pushed past him. "Don't worry, Sid, I'm sure that you'll figure out how to speak without swearing. It just takes a little practice and some vocabulary work."

"Hey! I can speak just as well as any mother . . . well, as anyone in this camp!" Sid said. "But that's not the point! Who is that guy?"

"Well, I get the feeling that most people call him Virgil until they piss him off," Michael said simply.

"So what do they call him . . ."

Michael shook his head. "No one has ever breathed long enough to say."

Sid swallowed hard and gazed again at the great cowboy. "Hey, Barris! That guy's got a little girl with him!"

"Oh," Michael's eyebrows rose as he followed Virgil into the main room. "So you noticed?"

"So what are you guys going to do with her?" Sid asked, following behind.

Michael turned on him. "Oh, you really are sick, Sid!"

"Hey, everyone has their own tastes, Barris!" Sid shrugged. "I just want to avoid trouble with his holiness the reverend!"

Michael considered the events of the morning. Sid obviously hadn't been outside yet. "Well, Sid, I'm afraid it's a little late for that."

They were standing in the dying room. Several people from the adjoining bedrooms had opened their doors to watch the exchange. Michael suddenly realized that he didn't know any of them. These people with whom he had been sharing the deathwatch were strangers without names. That had changed. Many things for Michael had changed.

"I'll tell you exactly what we're going to do with that little girl, Sid, in intimate detail," Michael said, advancing on the longhaired supervisor with every word. "We are going to clean her up. Then we're going to comb her hair out. We are going to hold her when she cries, and hold her when she doesn't cry, and pick her up just about any time she asks. We are going to play with her—not in any smutty way that your mind can devise, but actually try to give her a taste of childhood without fear. No one's going to touch her in a bad way, because I personally will *eat the heart* of anyone who does. We are going to love her. We are going to adopt her. We're going to try being human for a change, Sid."

Sid looked at Michael soberly. "And when she gets sick?"

"We'll comfort her as best we can." Michael's voice was quiet but level.

"And when she dies?"

Michael sighed. "Then Sid, I'll promise her, we will cry."

Silence.

Michael felt a tug on his sleeve.

"Sir?"

Michael turned, expecting to see Virgil but it was a different face. The face was gaunt, the skin loose on the face as though the man had lost too much weight too quickly. He still wore the suit coat that they had taken him in; it fit him rather like a tent now. He had seen the man before, passed him often in the barracks hall. "You sleep here, don't you?"

"Yes, in the northwest corner." His voice was hesitant. "Sir, I . . . I had a little girl."

"How old was she?" Michael asked.

"About six." Tears welled up in the man's eyes. Michael could see the man struggle inside himself against emotions that he had no longer dared to feel. "Sir," he stammered, "may I . . . would it be all right if I helped you . . . you know, helped you with your little girl?"

Michael smiled sadly.

"You want to be a father again?"

"Oh, yes, sir!" the man choked out. "More than you know."

"What's your name, friend?"

"David, sir." The man sniffed. "David Yarrow."

"Michael." He shook the man's hand warmly. "My name's Michael Barris—welcome to the family!"

Suddenly, several people pressed toward Michael from all corners of the room.

"I'm Gene! Gene Muskat—please, I wanna help, too!"

"I always wanted to have a family . . ."

"Me, too! I'm Cliff . . ."

A shrill voice suddenly cut across the room.

"GIVE ME BACK THAT CHILD, BARRIS!"

Everyone turned at the sound. There, silhouetted in the hall, was the unmistakable form of Olivia Codgebury, RN. Her breathing was ragged and her voice shaking as she stood there with her hands planted determinedly on both hips.

"Give me back that child! Now!"

"She's not your child, Olivia," Michael said, turning to face her. He moved slightly to stand between her and his room, where the cowboy had taken her.

"Have you any idea what you've done?" she said raggedly. "The shifts are in complete turmoil—now no one is reporting to the factory. Other people are coming into the play yard and taking children away. God only knows what they're going to do with them! Weston's trying to get some order in the camp, but people are following your example."

"Really?" Michael raised his eyebrows. "What an interesting thought."

Olivia didn't catch his meaning, her mind too clouded with her own problems. "If you bring the girl back, we might have a chance of getting the rest of them back as well. It's our best hope of getting this camp back under control."

"What about Bullock's men?" Michael offered.

"Well, thanks to you"—Olivia's sarcasm was evident as she

folded her arms across her chest—"Bullock himself is still out cold. I'd be surprised if you hadn't given him a concussion with that bat you used on him. He's in the Hospice now and . . . don't you people laugh!" She pointed at several tittering people in the room. "Bullock's kept this camp peaceful for a long time! Without him his security people don't seem to be able to get themselves organized. We could have a major problem in this camp! A lot of people could die!"

Michael laughed heartily.

"You think that's funny?"

Michael shook his head with a sad smile. "We're all dying, Olivia! Every one of us. The question isn't whether we're going to die or not—we all are at one time or another anyway, whether V-CIDS takes us or not. The point has never been *if* we're going to die or even *when* we're going to die."

"What are you saying?"

"The point is not how we die, Olivia—it's how we lived."

Olivia was visibly shaking now. "You are being unreasonable, Barris! Give me that child!"

"No," he said simply.

Olivia motioned behind her. Two large figures filled the hall, blocking out the exterior light. The nurse had apparently managed to corner at least two of Bullock's men and enlist them under her command for the time being. "I thought you might not listen to reason. You can either give her up willingly and without a fuss or we will take her from you by force. I don't think . . ."

There was no command. There was no word. Silently, as though through one thought, the men poured from the side rooms. They stood between Michael and Olivia, a wall of defiant bodies four deep that filled the entire width of the room.

Virgil emerged from Michael's shared bedroom. "What's goin' on, Barris?"

"Not much, Virgil—and everything." Michael pushed his way carefully through the men in the room to stand face-to-face with Olivia. "Nurse Codgebury, you will not be taking the child back with you. You may consider her dead, but we refuse to allow you to bury her in that sterile grave called the Hospice while her heart still beats and her mind is still capable of thought. Furthermore, we, the dead in this room, have decided to live a real life for a while. It may not be a long one—but it will have been worth living."

Michael's eye caught sight of a chunk of charred wood in the corner. He wondered for a moment at it being here, before reaching suddenly down and grabbing it.

"Hey," Sid said indignantly, "that's mine!"

Michael walked to the side wall and using the charred end of the board, savagely struck through the scrawled word "DYING" next to the faded stencil of the word "ROOM." In quick strokes he retraced the faded word "LIVING" back into the wall, then turned back to face Olivia.

"No one *here* is dying today."

Of Command and Control

Saturday, April 17, 2010 / 1435 hrs
Commons Factory Floor
Newhouse Center / 477th ERIS District
Wah Wah Valley, West Beaver County, Utah

"Order! We must have order here!"

The momentum of the voices around him continued.

"Quiet! I said QUIET!" Quinton Weston slammed his make-shift gavel—a wood-tooled hammer—down on the assembly table.

Only the echo of sound reverberated through the nearly empty hall. Strong columns of blinding bright light slanted into the room through the windows on the west side, made nearly solid by the perpetual dust in the air. Its reflected brilliance cast strange shadows across the faces of the assembly—a small group that seemed even smaller in the vastness of the now empty factory floor.

"Please, we must have some semblance of order if we are going to get through this crisis." Weston ran a hand through his wispy hair. "We've got to get a handle on what's happening, so LET'S NOT LOSE OUR HEADS!"

They had pulled several assembly tables together in order to accommodate those gathered. Weston had managed to find most of the administration heads in the camp. Some were unavailable or missing. Some, he thought, may even be consciously avoiding it.

"Who here is going to act as scribe?"

No immediate volunteers presented themselves from the assembly.

"Brad, you're senior clerk, you keep the minutes."

"Ah, Quin, you know I don't take shorthand and . . ."

"Don't give me any trouble, Bradford," the reverend snapped, "just take these notes so we can get on with business."

Brad Garrahan shrugged and picked up the thin stack of loose papers and the pencil from the table.

"Very well, then, I call the governing assembly of Newhouse Center to order under the power and . . ."

"Slow down," Brad complained.

". . . jurisdiction of ERIS Command." The reverend finished with exasperated slowness. "Be it known that present are Ron Blythe, the staff director and Shirley Sjoberg, our communications director . . ."

Both raised their hands and waved feebly.

". . . Bradford Garrahan, the senior clerk. Melinda Rowley, the factory general director is here . . ."

Melinda sat at the opposite end of the table, quietly coughing to herself. Everyone else was making a point of keeping well clear of Melinda.

". . . with Oscar Feinstein, the assignment coordinator for our camp. We have two of the shift supervisors here, Mr. Murdock, Ms. Pohlhaus and . . ."

"Wait," Brad said, "Rosemary, how do you spell your last name?"

"P-O-H-L- . . ."

"Never mind that!" Reverend Weston groaned. "Get it later. Let's see. Mr. Folleson has not deigned to show up and so far has not been found by a search. Scott Johnson was in the Hospice after this morning's 'incident' "—the reverend spat the word out— "but has since disappeared. We can only assume he's hiding somewhere in Block Y. Mr. Ira Mason is here representing the graveyard shift, since Johnson either refuses or is unable to appear."

Ira, tall and swarthy, stood leaning back against a support post. His arms were crossed in front of him. He made no move or sign.

"Evan Weber is sitting in for Will Bullock, who is still in the Hospice and apparently will be for the rest of the afternoon."

"Hey," Oscar said, "where's Janiese?"

"She's tending to her hydroponics gardens," Evan said. "Seems like some people got a little hungry this morning when breakfast didn't show, and there were some break-ins and theft of food. We got it under control, but there was quite a bit of damage. Jake Belovich, our vaunted kitchen director, won't be here either—he's still playing catch-up with breakfast."

Weston tried to interrupt. "Can we please stick with the agenda . . ."

"OK so, where's Olivia?" Oscar continued.

"She's got more important things to do than attend this meeting!" the reverend bellowed. "There's chaos throughout the camp. I'd bet there are people out there dying right now!"

"Well, now there's a switch," Brad said to himself, but the words carried unexpectedly the length of the table.

An awkward silence filled the space.

"All right," the reverend said at last with forced patience. "Can someone tell me just where we're at right now."

Faces around the table looked at each other through the dust-filtered light.

Murdock finally spoke. "Well, we managed to get the first train unloaded—mostly with management staff; the regular crews never reported to work. That allowed the first train to exit, although we sent it out empty. The breakfast supply train then was able to enter the compound. There was one group who rushed the train for food . . ."

Evan spoke up, his face shadowed. "We took care of it. There were nineteen casualties and three fatalities—if anyone is interested."

As soon as he knew Evan was finished, Murdock continued; "Well, that's right. Anyway, the breakfast supplies were taken up to the Commons, and Food Services got to work on it, but there were conflicting shift orders . . ."

"Not my fault," chirped Oscar.

". . . and so no one has reported to work—as you can see." Murdock indicated the vacant room with a sweep of his hand.

"What about order in the camp?" Shirley Sjoberg rumbled, her throat cancer apparently getting worse by the minute. She was more afraid of personal violence than the growth that was killing her slowly. "There have been reports of fights, some killings . . ."

Evan spoke up. "We lost seven security staff in different parts of the camp this morning. They haven't reported in and, so far, only two bodies have been recovered. There have been a number of attacks registered against managerial staff in one position or another . . ."

Shirley blanched.

". . . but there's been no pattern to the violence. We are currently trying to institute a lockdown."

"A what?" Murdock said.

"A lockdown," Evan said. "It's where we just get everyone back to their assigned barracks rooms and keep them inside until we can figure out how to reestablish order here."

"Like a continuous curfew?"

"Exactly."

"Ah!" Murdock understood curfew.

"What about the work?" Oscar complained. "What do I do with the work assignments?"

"There isn't any work," Ira said.

Everyone turned to face him.

"Now, just what is that supposed to mean?" Shirley said.

"It means," Ira said as he stepped into the light, "that we've been putting together the same things over and over again. We aren't manufacturing anything at all, are we, Reverend, we're just going through the motions. We assemble them, someone else disassembles them, and then they just send the same parts back to us."

"My God!" Murdock muttered. "Is this true, Reverend?"

Quinton Weston stood. All eyes watched him.

"Yes, of course it's true."

Melinda Rowley coughed. It sounded oddly like laughter.

At last she managed to get control of herself. "You mean, we've been busting our humps on these things for weeks, and it didn't make any difference at all?"

"Don't be stupid, of course it made a difference!" Weston

snapped. He turned to Ira. "Is that what all this is about? Is that why your entire shift deserted last night? Because we're not making anything useful here?" The reverend walked around the table, approaching Ira like a cat stalking a mouse. "Homosexuals! You can't see beyond your own bloody brownnoses can you? So caught up in your animal appetites that you just can't get the picture, can you? Well, let me draw you a picture. Let me address your feeble concerns in simple terms. Are we exporting these little clockworks as piecework? No! Who do you think would possibly even touch something that passed through a camp filled with V-CIDS? Why do we make them, then? We make them, you stupid mama's boy, because they bring tranquility and hope to this camp. That's right, Mr. Ira Mason. We don't make useful widgets in this camp—we manufacture peace of mind for the suffering souls stuck here."

Brad tapped his pencil on the paper, distractedly. "Quin, that's not what you told us."

"What difference does it make what I told you!" The reverend's eyes flashed a brilliant green as he turned back to the table. "ERIS wanted you to believe everyone here was engaged in meaningful labor. We were 'meaningful' in that everyone in this camp was occupied and docile. Now, thanks to the evil degenerates in the gay blocks, the entire system is threatened. I spoke to the ERIS people just before this meeting. No more shipments—in fact, they want us to load the last of the parts back onto an empty train and get them out of here. How we keep the peace now is up to us."

"All right," Rosemary said slowly as she leaned forward. "So it's up to us. What is it you want?"

The reverend stood again at the head of the table. "We've got to find a way to keep everyone in this camp quiet and occupied until a cure can be found . . ."

"Cure?" Oscar snorted. "You must be joking!"

". . . for this terrible affliction. I know! They're working on it right now! It is coming, but we have to behave ourselves here! If we keep quiet, if we don't question those who are in authority over us, if we just hang on and cooperate—we'll survive this!"

"Great," Murdock said, "but how?"

The reverend put both hands on the table and leaned forward. "Here's what we do. Mr. Mason here is going to go back to that

Dark Queen of his and tell whoever it is to keep their people on their side of the line for tonight. Oscar, when is dinner being served?"

"Last I checked, Jake was planning on serving anyone who showed after five this afternoon."

"Fine," the reverend said. "Mason, tell your leader that his degenerate group of blasphemers can come to the Commons after nine o'clock tonight and not a minute before."

Ira was incensed. "Just who the hell do you think you are to tell us . . ."

"I won't have another incident like this morning!" The reverend literally shouted Ira down. "Everyone—and I mean everyone—will stay in their barracks except for their assigned meal time. We'll meet back here tonight at eight and come up with a program. Ron, where's Mark Haviland?"

"Sorry, haven't seen him."

"Well, find him—and Shirley, see if you can find that camp morale officer . . . what's his name . . . Preston Duffy."

Shirley shook her head. "I hear he's awful sick."

"Well, find him anyway," the reverend intoned. "I want this camp locked down until morning. By then, maybe, we'll have a plan."

"Whatever that might be," Brad sighed.

"One thing is certain," the reverend said in an unmistakable voice, "there's one person that's responsible for what's happened today. Evan, I'll need you and your boys to do a little job for me this evening. Come with me when we're done, and we'll work out the details."

Evan nodded.

"Michael Barris has caused me trouble for the last time." With that Quinton Weston banged the gavel.

Just Like Us

Saturday, April 17, 2010 / 1847 hrs
Newhouse Center / 477th ERIS District
Wah Wah Valley, West Beaver County, Utah

Barris stood on the steps of R-7 and gazed up into the patch of sunset that he could see between the towering buildings. The pale salmon colors that streaked this vibrant orange were magnificent: subtle colors, a marked and peaceful contrast to the day. The constant wind had quieted to an easy, gentle breeze—its usual fury seemingly having worn itself out.

"It can be quite beautiful sometimes, you know."

Michael was surprised to hear Sid behind him. "I didn't think you'd notice."

Sid's smile was framed by his ragged long hair. His eyes suddenly looked down shyly, reminding Michael strongly of a five-year-old. "Well, up until now they've kept us pretty busy. It's hard to take time and notice the sky when you're looking at the dirt all day."

Michael watched him in the soft light of the deepening sunset. "You know, Sid, I don't think I know you."

"Yeah, but that's the way it's been here." Sid leaned against the door frame and watched as his feet kicked dust off the step. "I've been here nearly five weeks now—a long time for anyone in the camps, I guess. At first I tried to get to know everyone, you know, network and grease the wheels the way I did on the outside. No one gave a damn. The most I ever did was annoy people who wanted to die alone. It didn't take long not to care. It was easier than throwing your heart against the wall every day."

Michael nodded slowly. "Well, something's changed. I've been here a few days now, and I don't think I even heard the names of the two other guys in my room until today."

Sid laughed sadly. "I've been here a lot longer and can say the same thing. I think I've met more people today—not just known their names, understand, but met them—than I have in all the time I've been here. It's like we all woke up at the same time from some dream and found ourselves in the shit house—yeah, I know, 'not around the young'un'!" Sid shook his head. "So how's that cow-poke buddy of yours?"

"Virgil?"

"Yeah, what's his story anyway?"

"It's a good one—though I'll bet any story ever told about Virgil is a good one." Michael shook his head and leaned his back against the door frame. "Near as I can tell, he and three of his buddies went joyriding right into the army's restricted zone. The guy's truck broke down near Wild Cove just before it was burned."

Sid's voice sounded detached. "I hear that the camp was still full of people when it went."

"That's Virgil's story. He was there."

"Do you think it could have been a mistake?"

Michael looked up into the flaming sky. "A couple of thousand people snuffed out? No, I don't think it was a mistake."

"Neither do I," Sid murmured into the breeze.

"If you'd like, you can ask him about it. He's back in the room with Amanda now."

"Nah, maybe later," Sid replied. "Say, how is that little gal doin' anyway? She doesn't seem very smart."

"She's a lot smarter than you think, Sid," Michael shifted uncomfortably with his thoughts. "Our division once did a report on abused children. Kids just shut down when they're badly abused. They protect themselves by building all kinds of barriers. Some go feral. Some go catatonic. They look stupid because it's how they survive. She'll come around, but it may take awhile."

Sid shook his head. "Time is one thing we don't have a lot of here. Five, maybe six weeks, right, that's what you said?"

"Yes—for those of us that live that long." Michael rubbed the back of his neck. "I figure that at the current mortality rates, there may be between three and five thousand of us left when the end comes, unless the smaller our camp numbers get the less the opportunity for infections. That will change, of course, if there's another influx of internees. How often do the pallets with new people come?"

"Usually, every week or two," Sid said, "although word is that yours was the last one. That Amanda of yours . . ."

"Of ours," Michael corrected.

"OK of ours . . . has the mark on her head, you know? You may have a clean brow, but she's got the V-CIDS as badly as anyone in this camp." Sid watched the sunset fade into a deep purple. "She's already got signs of a cold, Mick. She'll be leaving us soon."

"We'll all be leaving soon, Sid." Michael's voice was quiet.

"Michael! Get up!"

They always come in the night.

"Wake up, Michael! One of the goons wants to talk to you!"

"Right! All right! I'm up!" Michael sat up on the edge of his cot. "Who is it?"

Sid's voice whispered through the darkness. "It's Evan Weber."

"Who?"

"Evan Weber," Sid hissed. "Geez, you still aren't up to speed. He's Bullock's second banana. He wants you."

"You don't suppose he'd consider coming in *here* to talk to me?" Michael yawned.

"No," Sid replied quietly, "but he might just be willing to burn down the barracks in order to get you to come out!"

Michael blinked awake. He could hardly see a thing. The windows were no help. The new moon was hiding in the sky. It was hard to see at night now, even when you were used to it.

He considered waking Virgil for some backup but thought better of it. He could barely make out the cowboy on the lower bunk opposite his own. There he was sprawled over most of the bed snoring loudly. Curled next to him was Amanda, who refused to let go of the big cowboy and would awaken complaining loudly at any attempt to separate the two. No, waking Virgil would mean waking Amanda, and Michael wouldn't do that for the world.

Change of shift.

The captain's eyes felt dry as the desert sand. He sat down just as his predecessor—a man he knew only as "Falcon"—tiredly saluted and shuffled out of the room. The captain looked at the clock rolling digits above the main situation display in the next room: 0000 hours. Time to run the shift-change checklist and update the logs. Be a good soldier. Do your duty.

"Lieutenant, status report for the duty log, please."

"Yes, sir, Captain. Antelope Springs: nominal. Willow Creek: nominal. Quartz Creek: S-block riots have been suppressed internally. Four buildings in S block are burning, but the fires have been suppressed."

The captain punched halfheartedly at the monitor buttons on his console. Every camp's set of optics feeds brought him a mosaic of pictures inside the camp, in both visible and infrared bands. Everything looked depressingly the way it had looked for several nights.

The lieutenant continued his litany. "Ranch Springs: nominal. Newhouse is under lockdown following a riot this morning. Assembly Diversion Operations have been suspended as of 0900 hours this morning. Crystal Springs: nominal, with the exception of an antelope, which . . ."

The captain stopped jabbing at buttons and held down the microphone contact. "Lieutenant, didn't you just say that Newhouse was under lockdown?"

"Yes, sir."

"Then, why am I picking up movement in the camp?"

"Sir, that's not unusual." The lieutenant would have preferred to get the shift change over with as little fuss as possible. He'd wanted to get back to forgetting about what he was doing. "Even in lockdown you get a few crazies who insist on wandering the compound."

The captain hit the ID button next to the monitor that held his eye. The contact relayed a digital request through a military positioning drone suspended high over the Wah Wah Valley. The image, position data, and transponder IDs from every target infrared image on the screen were compiled by a dedicated professor. In moments, lines were drawn and figures superimposed on the image, showing the identity of every bright warm image on the screen. Six fuzzy, bright shapes—one far brighter than the others—lay on the north side of the Rec Field. All were identified instantly. The captain recognized the names, and there was nothing unusual in their being out at this time of night. Two more approached the other six from the southwest.

One of the last two images had no identification showing.

"Captain," the lieutenant said curtly, "may I continue my report?"

"Yes, Lieutenant, sorry, continue please."

"Yes, sir. As I was saying, Crystal Springs: nominal, with the exception of an antelope, which has tripped a Perimeter Three alarm. Dutchman: nominal. Kelley's Place: nominal. Indian Queen . . ."

The captain listened to the report but was no longer switching monitors.

Damn, it's dark! Michael thought. No stars overhead and the cloud base must be too high for any reflection from Milford. It was like moving through a cave. All he had to guide him was a small pool of cold, green phosphorus light that swayed in front of him. Evan Weber walked quickly in front of him holding the chemical flashlight. He followed it faithfully.

"Did Nurse Codgebury tell you what it was she wanted to see me about?" Michael said.

"No, sir, Mr. Barris." Evan's voice floated back to him through the darkness. "She just said it was urgent and had something to do with your proposition earlier."

"Well, considering that I don't recall having made *any* proposition to her, earlier or otherwise, I can't imagine what it is she wants."

A dark voice sounded behind him, making the hairs on his neck stand up.

"Perhaps you'd care to take a guess at what *I* would want, Barris!"

Michael turned to face Willard Bullock.

"Thank you, Lieutenant, that will be all." The captain was puzzled at what he saw on the IR monitor. The glowing outlines of security men were gathered around the unidentified figure. There was some sort of conference going on. There were only two people left in the camp without transponder IDs: either that Barris fellow or the Johnston man the Gold Squad had dumped into the camp the other day. But what would they be up to at midnight?

"Lieutenant, do we have a surveillance bird over Newhouse?"

"Yes, sir," the lieutenant said with an edge of reluctance. "That's where you're getting your top-down imaging from, sir."

"Do we have any audio pickup in the Newhouse Recreation Field area?"

"Yes, Captain. It's micro parabolic, so you'll have to focus it to source. You'll find the access controls just to the right of . . ."

"Thank you, Lieutenant, I've got it." The captain grabbed the imaging mouse and clicked to magnify the image. The fuzzy pixels leaped closer. The figure without ID had been knocked to the ground. The figure IDed as "(I) Bullock, W." appeared to be standing near the prone figure, delivering several swift kicks. The captain opened the audio pickups and began focusing the microphone on a second monitor.

The hiss of silence was suddenly interrupted.

". . . You think you're so fucking high and mighty . . ."

Michael curled into a ball. He was sure he had broken ribs. The pain was excruciating, making his vision red in the darkness. He wished devoutly for it to end and was terrified that the end would come all too soon.

Above him, Bullock railed at him and the night with every swing of his booted foot against Michael's side.

"You son of a bitch! You think you're some goddamn savior, don't you? You'd walk on water if we'd let you, wouldn't you, boy? You think you're so fucking high and mighty that you could just wave your little hand and get rid of the rest of us, right? Well, maybe you sucked up to those ERIS boys and maybe you think they can get you out of here, but *not before me!*"

Michael gulped air around the pain that filled his lungs. "No . . . none of us . . . getting out . . ."

Bullock stopped kicking at Michael's ribs. He reached both his oversize, meaty hands down into Michael's curled-up body and grabbed the front of his Levi's jacket on both sides. In a single move, Bullock turned Michael over, dragging the prone man's contorted face before Bullock's own. "You're wrong, Barris! There are ways out of here—not many and limited in number—and I'm taking one of them. You may think you've got it made, but you don't. All my life I've kissed butt to assholes like you. Well, now it's my turn. You sit up there on your throne like some virginal king. Every now and then you feel sorry for us 'poor slobs' down here and actually touch us with one of your gloved hands! You stir us up and give us hope, and then get the hell out because your gloves are dirty and you're tired of playing like you care! Meanwhile, you just screw it up for the rest of us!"

Michael's chest heaved, painfully trying to drag air into his lungs. "They'll . . . never let . . . you out, Bullock. They'll never let . . . any of us . . . out."

Bullock let go with his right hand, holding Michael with his left just two feet above the ground. In the faint green glow of the chemical flashlight, Michael could see the sweat pouring down the huge man's face.

The V-CIDS is taking him at last, Michael thought hazily through the pain. *I'm being killed by a dead man.*

Bullock's free hand formed a massive, rock-hard fist. It drove down into Michael's face like a falling tree. His head snapped back against the ground. The world grew distant for a few moments. Michael was dimly aware of movement over him. Bullock spoke to him from the edge of the universe.

"Well, if you *did* want to leave before me—I'm here to grant your wish. You're leaving on the morning pallets for the Ranch furnaces, Mr. 'Lumber' Barris! But before you go, I think it's more than time to bring you down where we are!"

Michael looked up. Bullock held a stick he had wrapped in twine out the end of which was a wire. It was the first metal Michael had seen since entering the camp. It was about the thickness of coat hanger wire. The end was twisted into a flattened circle.

It glowed brilliantly in the night.

"Welcome to the club, Mr. Barris." Bullock smiled.

Four of Bullock's men suddenly pinned Michael to the ground.

"You can get off your high horse of piety," Bullock sneered. "You're going to be just like us. And then—well, we'll just have to kill you."

The brilliant wire descended quickly, filling Michael's vision. The pain was immediate, electric. The sound of Michael's flesh sizzled in his ears, its acrid smoke filling his nostrils.

He screamed from the center of his soul. Then he screamed again—and again.

The captain shuddered at the sound. He checked instantly to see if the audio was on local/secure. It was. Of all the people on watch, only he heard the sound.

Steady. Steady, he told himself. *You're walking a line.*

He shut off the audio.

Bright green boxes writhed on the video monitor.

Do something!

He took a single deep breath.

"Lieutenant," he said with a level, command voice that he did not feel. "I want an immediate three-hundred-percent power-up of the Newhouse maintenance lights in grid"—he fumbled through the reference manual—"947D through 957F. Run them at three hundred percent for thirty seconds, then shut down the feeds."

"Sir?" The lieutenant sounded as though he were asked to run to the moon for ice cream. "Even when we use those light panels, we only ever run them at twenty-five percent!"

"Now, Lieutenant!" the Captain said forcefully.

* * *

Tears poured from Michael's eyes, the sobs wrenching unbidden and unchecked from his throat. Yet he opened his eyes. Some part of him wanted to see his death when it came.

He was aware of the dim form of Bullock standing astride him. The security chief held a long, thick club in his hand. Michael vaguely wondered if this was the view a golf ball has just before it's driven about two hundred yards.

Night vanished into sudden, celestial light.

Hands against Michael's shoulders and legs suddenly released him, searching to protect the eyes that were blind with brilliance.

Michael rolled. He felt the rocks strike the back of his neck where Bullock, blind and enraged, had swung the club and connected with the ground inches behind where Michael had moved. Michael felt, heard the club rise up again. He scurried from between the legs of the enraged security chief just as the club came down again.

It connected with his leg, bruising it badly and for a terrible moment, Michael thought it might have broken. The blow, however, had another effect. It literally knocked him away from between Bullock's legs.

Darkness suddenly descended, more sure than the brilliance that had just appeared. The sudden absence of light was more blinding than the light itself had been.

Michael shut his eyes against the agony that his body had become. He ran limping across the field with no direction or purpose but to get away. His only guide were the cries of Bullock's rage—which he kept always to his back as he vanished into the utter blackness of the night.

The Reins of Power

28

Sunday morning. Sabbath. The day of rest.

Olivia Codgebury leaned against the back wall of the large hall and yawned. She could see the merit in rest. Olivia pushed herself away from the wall to stand. The camp was at a standstill. She had wondered what the old preacher could say to these people. So far, it hadn't been much, but then, maybe they didn't need much.

The Cathedral was crowded, as usual, at the early service. The neatly placed rows of benches served well enough as pews for those whose faith served well enough. The cross, too, served well enough to represent whatever salvation they were all good enough to attain. The congregation itself, however, was made up almost exclusively of those who ran the camp well enough. Few of them were exceptionally bright or gifted, for such people tend to be troublesome to the majority. Nor were there any here who were stupid or foolish, for such could never be allowed to be in charge of anything. Thus, the congregation was, on the whole, made up of those who were neither superior nor inferior, neither gifted nor deprived but rather of those who were virtuously common. Indeed, many of them considered it a virtue. On the whole, they were exceptionally average in most respects, and righteously suspicious of anyone or anything that was the least bit exceptional.

The Reverend Weston had, in his weeks thus far as governor, established this special service specifically for the staff and management persons in the camp. It not only gave him the opportunity to preach a sermon to a congregation with whom he had a great many attitudes and interests in common, but it also afforded him a chance to discuss the deeper ramifications of what they were trying to accomplish in the camp.

Everyone was in their respective places by five minutes before seven. Olivia could see that the camp staff, Ron Blythe, Shirley Sjoberg, and the rest, were seated on the front left benches. Most of the factory administrators, like Donovan Murdock and Rosemary Pohlhaus, were seated on the right, directly behind Meredith Jernigan and the rest of the main support services directors. Carolyn Nichols, the maintenance supervisor, was absent and would be from now on. Meredith had loaded her onto the death pallet just a few hours ago with the rest of the lumber. And, of course, Preston Duffy wasn't here. Olivia wondered if she shouldn't look in on the man—he'd hung on at death's door for quite awhile now, it seemed.

The rest of the hall was filled with shift managers, training directors, transport captain, clerks, and supervisors. All in all, there were nearly two hundred staff people jammed between the rough halls of the Cathedral, all of them quietly complacent as cows.

Well, that was an illusion, Olivia thought to herself. After yesterday, she wondered what all of these people would do with themselves. They represented the people who were in charge of every facet of the camp—except the gay blocks and their own segregated work and meal shifts. The gays, of course, were never actually considered to be part of the right-thinking people of the camp, and thus were never invited nor tolerated in the general camp discussions and spiritual meetings. It wouldn't do, Olivia thought ruefully, to invite the prey to join the hunters, would it? If we have no one to blame for our troubles, then we might actually have to be responsible for our own actions and consequences; and we can't have *that*, can we?

The reverend, meanwhile, droned on.

". . . remarkable parallel between our lives and that of that ancient and most revered of God's children, Job. For like Job, we, too, are suffering here: suffering from a malady that was not ours and for sins that we did not commit. We read from the Book of Job: 'There was a man in the land of Uz, whose name was Job; and that man was perfect and upright, and one that feared God, and eschewed evil.' " Weston set down the dog-eared paperback Bible on the small altar before him. "Thus we see that Job was a perfect man—a man who had done no wrong in the sight of God! Yet the narrative goes on, for the Lord has in mind a test for poor Job."

So we're being tried and tested? Olivia thought. *This should really cheer everyone up!*

The reverend jabbed his finger back down at the book, as if daring the text to move under his digit. "The Lord points this up to that old devil, but what does the devil reply? 'Then Satan answered the Lord, and said, Doth Job fear God for nought? Hast not thou made an hedge about him, and about his house, and about all that he hath on every side? Thou hast blessed the work of his hands, and his substance is increased in the land. But put forth thine hand now, and touch all that he hath, and he will curse thee to thy face!' "

The reverend leaned down over the altar, his emerald eyes bright despite the dark circles under them. "What about us? Do we, when times turn hard and difficult, do we turn our backs on that authority which alone can bring salvation and life? Are we 'fair-weather friends'?"

Olivia shifted her stance. *Is he talking about God,* she thought, *or ERIS Command Authority or himself? All three like some strange triune? Maybe in here it doesn't make any difference— maybe they are the same . . .*

"Ah, but friends, there is more!" The reverend was hitting his stride now, his voice a strident gallop of emotions and diction. "The Holy Bible speaks directly to us in our time! 'Again there was a day when the sons of God came to present themselves before the Lord, and Satan came also among them to present himself before the Lord . . .' "

The great double doors next to Olivia suddenly opened with a loud bang, throwing the morning light into the main room of the Cathedral. The nurse turned sharply toward the sound and saw the stooped figure of a man silhouetted against the bright opening, his outstretched arms both holding the doors open and supporting himself. In that moment, Olivia couldn't recognize the man with the torn clothing and puffy face.

Reverend Weston frowned. He continued to quote the scripture, but his eyes never left the figure in the doorway. " 'And the Lord said unto Satan, From whence comest thou? And Satan answered the Lord, and said, From going to and fro in the earth, and from walking up and down in it.' "

The figure moved into the room, the doors swinging shut behind him. Olivia gasped. He was barely recognizable. His clothes were torn and beaten, one bare leg exposed among bloody strips of cloth. He favored that leg terribly as he walked, his puffy jaw clenching with each bent step. The face itself was bruised and swollen, surrounded by hair that was singed in places. Worst of all, in the center of his forehead were instantly noticeable the three circles that marked every V-CIDS person in the camp. Yet the mark on this man's brow was a hideous parody of the common marking; its uneven circles a blistering white.

Despite all that, Olivia knew without question that it was Michael Barris.

The slamming shut of the doors behind Michael drew everyone's attention to the back of the Cathedral. Sharp cries rang out at the sight of him, followed by a ground swell of murmuring voices.

The reverend had stopped.

"Go on," rasped Michael with the remains of his voice, long since screamed into silence. "Read the next verse."

The reverend stood silent, far from Michael at the other end of the hall.

"I know this one," Michael croaked, dragging his right foot across the floorboards as he made his way down the open aisle between the benches. "It goes: 'And the Lord said unto Satan, Hast thou considered my servant Job, that there is none like him in the earth, a perfect and an upright man, one that feareth God, and escheweth evil? And still he holdeth fast his integrity, although thou movedst me against him, to destroy him without cause?' "

Weston lifted his head, his eyes still locked on the broken figure advancing toward him. "Yes, Brother Barris, you remember it well. Please, join us: take a seat."

"Neither, thank you."

Weston was at a loss as to what to do. Bullock was still missing, and he had yet to find Evan Weber this morning. "Well, then—'And Satan answered the Lord, and said, Skin for skin, yea, all that a man hath will he give for his life. But put forth thine hand now, and touch his bone and his flesh, and he will curse thee to thy face . . .' "

Michael painfully moved to stand directly before the dais.

Weston looked down on him with a deep frown. " 'And the Lord said unto Satan, Behold, he is in thine hand.' "

Michael gazed up at him through watery eyes.

"Brother Barris," the reverend said with an infinite patience that filled only a moment, "what do you want?"

Michael spoke slowly and quietly.

"Step . . . down."

Weston was incredulous. "What?"

Michael dragged himself up onto the dais using the altar as a support. Weston turned as the battered man moved around him, his back now toward the congregation of toadies.

"Just who do you think you are, Barris, trying to . . ."

Michael screamed the words at Weston, his face contorted with the animal pain and rage behind it.

"STEP DOWN!"

The sound was majestic in its horror. It was beyond anger or shouting or yelling. It was an anguished soul. It was the sound made by mothers at the death of a child. It was the sound made by husbands as they watch their wives murdered. It was the agony of over a million dead with no end in sight. Weston, shaken by the sound, reeled away from Michael as though struck physically. He stepped backward and, unable to keep his balance, tumbled from the dais into the first row of benches.

"Please hear me," Michael rasped, swallowing hard, trying to clear his throat. "They've been lying to you—they've been lying to us! We aren't doing anything meaningful here. We aren't contributing to finding a cure for ourselves. ERIS has put us here to die, plain and simple. When we don't die quickly enough for them—well, they just pull the plug anyway. The Reverend Weston"—Michael raised his arm and pointed—"has only one purpose here: to help us do our dying quietly like good little sheep. 'Go quietly into that great night.' " Michael drew himself up, grasping both sides of the altar. "Well, brothers and sisters, I *refuse* to die quietly. If I'm going to die, I want someone to know about it!"

Michael shuddered with renewed pain. "ERIS kills our bodies, but Weston's worse—his kind kills our spirit. We have got to find a way out of here before we all die, mind and body, like it or not."

Weston stood up, his bony finger shaking with rage as he pointed to Michael. "Well, brothers and sisters, now we hear the devil speak, after all! 'Follow me' he cries—but to where? He doesn't know! He won't say! All he offers you is doom and death, whereas I offer you life and hope! ERIS is working on a cure—they aren't the demons this misguided soul makes them out to be! *He* is the one who is misleading you! He is the one who wants to take you back into the world where you can destroy others with this terrible plague!"

Weston strode in front of the altar, his voice full and his wrath evident as he pointed to Michael. "This man has been these last few days consorting with the homosexuals in Y block! He has been planning to take over this camp and deliver it into their sinful and perverted hands!"

A perplexed murmur washed like a wave through the congregation.

Weston smiled. "Deny it if he can: his brow bears the mark of the beast!"

Olivia's eyes followed those of everyone else's in the room to the blistered brow of Michael's forehead. The circles that Bullock had fashioned out of wire had not been perfect, the wire loop having extended by necessity into the wood. The result was appalling.

His forehead seemed to be branded with three, crude interlocking sixes—666.

The crowd fell into an awkward silence. Olivia's jaw dropped. Did Weston actually believe what he was saying, she wondered?

Then, instantly, came another thought—would the crowd believe such drivel?

"Listen to me!" she yelled suddenly. The stunned congregation turned at once to face her, searching for some sanity in the room. "This man's brow was clean when he came into this camp. I examined him when he arrived. This is crazy, that's all! Just plain crazy talk!"

"I bear this mark!" Michael yelled, his voice cracking.

"It's the mark of Satan!" Weston proclaimed again, shaking his finger in the air.

"Yes!" Michael shouted back, "because Satan put it there." Michael looked down on Weston standing before the altar. "You, Reverend Quinton Weston, you put that mark there. You ordered Bullock to kill me, but it wasn't enough for him. He had to bring me down first. So you marked me and called me evil." Michael's voice rose suddenly. "You marked me just as you marked everyone in this camp—and probably everyone in your life as well. You don't understand me, you fear me—so you mark me, slap a label on me, and stick me in a box. You don't understand the gays either, so you fear them, mark them with the number of the beast, and feel confident that you'll get to your heaven and they won't. Never mind that every one of them has humanity, that every one of them live lives just as deeply as you do—never mind that your God made them just as surely as he made you!"

Michael straightened to stand as best he could behind the altar. "So, if this is the mark you put on me, I'll wear it proudly, Weston, because it means that *I'm not one of you*!"

Weston turned red-faced back to the congregation. *Where was Bullock!* He felt exposed and vulnerable. He had to get out.

"There you have it, brothers and sisters!" Weston said in a shaking voice. " 'Choose ye this day whom ye shall serve!' I refuse to listen to this vile spawn one moment longer—and if you ever want to get out of this camp, I'll tell you right now that this man is not the one who can do it for you. If you want to live, follow me!"

Reverend Weston walked quickly down the aisle, encouraging people to follow him as he went. When at last he reached the great doors, he threw them open and walked out. His back was straight, confident that his congregation would be behind him.

No one moved.

All eyes were on Michael.

Not a breath was taken in the hall.

A woman stood up. It was Margaret Kelley, the factory requisition manager. "Mr. Barris, even if we could leave here—where would we go? I can believe we could escape the fence; I can even conceive of some of us avoiding getting caught again by ERIS. But, sir, we can't run from the V-CIDS."

Henry Folleson stood on the other side of the hall. "Margaret's right, mister. We can't outrun death. Just where would you have us go?"

Michael gripped the podium, his arms shaking.

He had no answer.

Henry Folleson watched him for a moment, then shaking his head, he turned and walked out of the Cathedral. Sadly, despairing, the rest of the congregation did likewise. In a few minutes, Michael stood alone in the hall.

Except for Olivia, who barely managed to catch Michael as he fell to the dais floor.

"You really are a bloody fool, aren't you?" she said to him as she held him.

"What's left," Michael murmured. "The reverend is crazy, but I don't have anything better to offer this camp than his madness. Who else is there to turn to? God?"

Unexpectedly, in perfect resonance, a quiet male voice filled the room.

"Michael Barris?"

Michael's eyes went wide. "Oh, my!"

Olivia looked up in shock. "That's not God talking, but it might as well be. ERIS has never had communication with anyone in the camp except the reverend and a few of his key people."

Michael spoke up. "Yes, I am here."

"Mr. Barris. My name is—my name is Kestrel. I'm only allowed to use Kestrel over these lines, do you understand?"

"Yes, I understand."

"Mr. Barris, my watch is midnight through eight A.M. every

morning. There is little I can do for you now, but you should know that there are many of us out here who do not agree with what's happening to the camps."

Michael smiled. In a camp of twelve thousand, he suddenly realized how lonely he had been. He was alone no longer. "Kestrel—are you Overlord?"

"No, Overlord is my superior. I am just Kestrel. I am the one here during the night. You can reach me only then."

Then there may be a new player in the game, Michael thought. "I haven't had a lot of luck around here at night. Kestrel—can you help us?"

There was a long pause.

"All I can promise is that if you talk to me—I'll listen."

With that, the captain closed the circuit.

Belly of the Beast

Jefferson Mahonrai Kendall sat leaning forward outside the glass-paned doors to the courtroom, twirling his old Stetson hat in his hands. The wide brim spun in rhythmic precision, like a clock counting down seconds. Yet Jeff Kendall took little notice of the time he spun out from his hands. Waiting had become a way of life, and as Jeff so often said, some things just happen in their own way no matter how much you would like to change them.

So now the hat spun again, marking the trickle of time.

Jeff was one of "Beaver's own." He was born in '65 in the back of an old bright orange Chevy wheeler due to a miscalculation as to the time it took the old truck to both start and get to the doctors. Birth, water, and blood were no strangers to his father, who ran the family farm at 495 East Center. He and his wife took it all in stride, taking care of the necessities and turning the Chevy back for home. They figured the doc would get around to them when he had time.

The fields were out north toward Manderfield, but the parcel in town held the barn, the yards, and the great stand of apple trees to the north. Jeff used to climb those trees, eating too many sour apples for his own good in the late summer or too many fresh peas out of the garden for his mother's liking. When he was quiet—a rare thing—he would sit on the porch in the old metal rocker and gaze into the clouds. Jefferson Kendall was raised on sunshine.

He'd gone to college eventually, but came home more often than most of his high school friends. They had all set their sights on bigger cities and flashier dreams than the open irrigation ditches and curb-less streets Beaver had to offer. Yet to Jeff it didn't matter. The city didn't have any better sky than Beaver, and from what he'd seen, it was a good sight worse. The only hunting going on in New York's Central Park was of other people. The only mountains to climb in Los Angeles were either made of chrome and glass or were machines that never improved your view no matter how high you climbed. The things that made up Jeff's life weren't found in virtual computer simulations. Jeff's life was rock, dirt, evergreen, and white against a blue brilliance. It murmured in cascade. It smelled clean. Jeff's life was *real*.

He was a missionary for two years because it, too, was real and because he had honestly heard God call him. He served his time in the Kobe-Japan Mission, speaking Japanese with that peculiar southern Utah drawl that occasionally thrilled or tickled the people he met in Kobe. Then he came home with wonderful stories, a boxful of slides he never brought out, and a talent for a language that he rarely got to use.

The years came and went. He married a girl he'd met at a church dance soon after getting home—Lynnellen Jacobs. He took her with him to college and brought her back when he was done to take over his sick father's farm. First came the girl, Sarah, who ran the house with an iron will when her mother wasn't about. Then came the two boys, Jesse and Corey, each within two years of each other. It would be five years—which Lynnellen often called the "dry spell"—before the last two, Barbara Ellen and Tyler Woolly, were born.

Then Jeff was made bishop of the LDS Third Ward in '02 and stake president in '06. All the righteous Latter Day Saints in town smiled and nodded their heads at that one. Jeff was about as ideal a Mormon as anyone could ask for.

The world intruding into his family room through the I-Net

video looked like a pretty scary place, and he told his congregation so every first Sunday at testimony meeting. Then when the government shut down the interstate and threw so many people out of work, he reminded them of the Twelfth Article of Faith: "We believe in being subject to kings, presidents, rulers, and magistrates, in obeying, honoring, and sustaining the law." That meant that they had to follow the laws of the land—even if that was martial law.

It came as no surprise when, by the end of the election in '08, a shy and reluctant Jefferson Kendall accepted the post of mayor of Beaver City.

Yet being subject to the current kings, presidents, rulers, and magistrates was easier in theory than in practice. While the town was still running its own services and was in most matters autonomous, the entire area was still under martial law and therefore under the jurisdiction of the ERIS Command Authority. Within the town, Jeff had authority pretty much to do as was needed. Anything beyond the city limits, however, required that he go to the ERIS Command Authority with his hat, often literally, in hand and ask them for help, information, or materials. Sometimes ERIS would comply; more often they would not. Lately, ERIS had become increasingly vague about what was happening beyond those city limits.

. . . And the rumors, quite frankly, had Jeff scared.

"Mr. Kendall?"

"Yes?" Jeff looked up from his still spinning hat into the scrubbed face of an army corporal with crew-cut blond hair.

"Please come in, sir. The lieutenant will see you now."

Jeff stood and walked through the doors into the old courtroom, his boots echoing against the hardwood floor. The beautifully carved railing ran around the room, separating the open floor from the ancient gallery seats. The massive judge's bench, rich in detail, sat on the north side.

The ornate crafted wood of the room was in stark contrast to the three display panels standing about the room and the modern table placed in the room's center. ERIS had needed a command post located in Beaver and had chosen the old courthouse on East

Center Street to house it. The building was a historical landmark but one which, ERIS claimed, was perfectly suited to their needs. Jefferson always wondered if it was the central location of the building that was so perfect for them or the fact that the ancient jail cells were still in the basement. ERIS never clarified that point. The relics and museum pieces were all carefully stored away, and the one-hundred-and-fifty-year-old building was quickly occupied by a staff of twenty and an amazing amount of sophisticated electronic equipment, its cables running along the edges of the halls like information mice.

"Mr. Kendall!" The short man with whom Jeff was all too familiar stood up and walked around the long table. Despite his friendly manner, he didn't offer his hand. Jeff noticed that most outsiders these days rarely offered to shake hands.

"Lieutenant Cummings," Jefferson said with a nod. "Sorry to bother you today."

"Not at all! Not at all!" Cummings said with a bubbling and practiced PR style. "Always an honor to talk to you, Mayor. You remember Corporal Gordon and Staff Sergeant McDonald."

McDonald stood. He was a man of average height with a flat face and small, steel eyes and a body strong enough to bend a pipe around. Gordon had shown him into the room.

"Sure, I know 'em. Gentlemen."

"Wonderful, please sit down!" Cummings motioned to the end of the conference table. It looked stark and out of place beneath the relic chandeliers lighting the room. "So how's Lynnellen?"

"Fine, thank you, sir."

"And that eldest girl of yours—she was in Idaho last I heard."

"At Ricks College, yes, sir. The college is closed now, but she's still up there—at least last we heard."

"Tell you what," Cummings snapped his fingers, smiling. "I think I can get in touch with the operations post there in Rexburg and see if I can't get some word on your girl!"

"Thank you," Jeff said with a kind, calculated smile.

"Not at all! We do what we can." Cummings smiled again but not with his eyes. The game between them was well under way by now, as both men knew. "So what brings you to the old courthouse today?"

"Lieutenant, a group of our local boys apparently had a few too many beers over at the Renegade a few nights ago. They left town heading north in a GMC last Thursday night, and they ain't been seen since."

Cummings flipped open a notebook and clicked his pen. "That's terrible—who were these boys?"

Jeff wondered why Cummings said "were" instead of "are" but let it slide. "Harlan Murphy. Lowell and Louis McNeil was with them and . . ."

Cummings didn't look up. "And Virgil Johnston?"

"Yes." *Now, how did he know that?* Jeff thought.

"I'll just bet Lavonda is fit to be tied!" Cummings smiled again.

Lavonda McNeil was the town worrier. If her sons were missing, there wouldn't be a shoulder in town that hadn't been cried on within a week. Still, Jeff didn't think that Cummings knew the workings of the town that well. He was, after all, an outsider.

"I'm afraid so, Lieutenant." Jeff's face smiled in response. "Anyway, we'd appreciate it if you could find out where these boys are and make sure they haven't gotten themselves into any trouble. They're just good old boys out for a little fun."

"No problem, I'll look into it this morning and get back to you just as soon as I have anything definite." Cummings made a few more notes on his pad, which Jeff couldn't make out across the table despite his becoming quite adept at reading upside down over the years. "Is there anything else?"

Jeff's smile faded slightly as his eyes locked on Cummings. The mayor's voice turned quiet and casual. "Yes, Lieutenant. There's been talk about Milford."

Cummings didn't look up from his writing, but Jeff could see the strain in his smile. Cummings stopped writing and flipped the notepad to a new page. "Really? What kind of talk?"

"They say the army has been killing their own soldiers. They say they've been doing it with firing squads, and they say those squads are getting more frequent. Mostly deserters, they say, and disobeying direct orders. They even say that there's a mass grave west of Milford near the old Star District Ore Mill." Jeff's eyes were calm as he spoke. "That's what they say."

"Those are terrible allegations," Cummings said, looking up

with sleepy eyes. He clicked his pen twice and poised it over his notepad. "Just who . . . *exactly* . . . said these things."

Jeff leaned his chair back on two legs. He had heard it straight from Elmyra Perry, who was working in the housing factory on the western side of Milford. Her husband watched the kids while she worked. She would send back most of her pay in fresh oranges—the Perrys had quickly become the only source of oranges in town and were making a pretty good living bartering the fruit for everything else they needed. The woman had returned to Beaver on furlough only to spend the better part of three days crying. Jeff had been called in by the family to give her a priesthood blessing to comfort her. She calmed down, but not before she detailed everything she had seen to Jefferson.

"Oh, pretty much everybody, you know." Jeff scratched his head. "It's hard to say who exactly . . ."

"Please"—Cummings smiled tightly—"do try."

"I'll check around for you and see if I can find out." Jeff set his chair back down and folded his hands on the table. "So is it true?"

"Mayor Kendall, you know I'm not at liberty to discuss operational aspects of martial law." Cummings held both hands with palms up. "My hands are tied. Look, in any emergency situation drastic and terrible things take place. Even in the army there are occasional criminals who pass the screening into the ranks. These are hard times, and we are under martial law. An occasional trial and execution are to be expected if order is to be maintained."

Jeff raised an eyebrow. "Trials and executions—at the rate of twenty-five to fifty per day?"

Only the faint traces of Cummings's smile remained with him. Jeff glanced at Gordon and McDonald. Both sat board straight in their chairs, their faces a frozen scowl of disapproval. Apparently, some things just weren't talked about.

"Oh, really now," Cummings said softly from behind poker eyes. "Wherever did you get that figure?"

Jefferson Kendall just smiled and blinked. "When you're in a position like I am, things just come your way."

"Well, if I were in a position like you are"—Cummings's voice was a velvet razor—"I'd be more concerned about associating myself with treasonous and seditious gossip. These kinds of rumors have a tendency to grow."

"Well, while we're on the subject—just what are you doing out in the Wah Wah Valley anyway?" Jeff sat back, folding his arms across his chest. He knew he was pushing it, but he had a responsibility to his people—not these outsiders—and he couldn't go back to them without more answers. "I hear that new plant you set up in Milford is turning out housing for about five thousand people a week. All that's going west into Wah Wah. I also hear that you're sending about twenty thousand people each week into the same desert."

"Who is telling you this, Mr. Kendall?"

Jeff ignored McDonald's comment. "Funny thing is, with all those people going into the desert—none of them ever come back out."

Cummings stood up and walked slowly around the table, his hands held behind his back as he walked. "Mayor Kendall, I don't like what you are insinuating—not one bit. Those people we are sending into the Wah Wah are all V-CIDS victims who represent both their own suffering but also a potentially lethal danger to anyone with whom they have contact. They are being quarantined until the day when a cure can be found. Many of them are dying despite our best efforts. I assure you, we are doing everything we can to safeguard the healthy population from the effects of this plague."

Cummings was standing over Jeff, then sat on the corner of the table, looking down on the mayor with an expression and demeanor that was fatherly and threatening. "However, the things you are saying are, quite honestly, seditious and could be clear grounds for detaining you for questioning."

The mayor looked up into Cummings's cherubic face. He could feel the line being drawn in the sand.

"Of course," Jeff said simply, "to do so would be badly misinterpreted by the people in town. Everyone is waiting to hear your reasonable explanation from me and would be understandably upset if I didn't give it to them because you decided to hold me for questioning over something I know nothing about."

Cummings's face relaxed. "Detain you? Oh, Jeff, don't be silly!

Of course, I would never detain you! All this talk is just ridiculous rumor. Go tell your people to relax—and let the army do its job."

Jeff stood up, snatching his hat from off the table. He hadn't learned much. What he did learn, he didn't like.

He was walking toward the door when Cummings spoke again.

"Oh, and Jeff—this town remains under martial law. We are obliged to keep peace in this community."

Jefferson turned. He suspected ERIS was beginning to feel the squeeze somewhere. The original garrison had been housed in the National Guard Armory until three days ago when they had all headed west. If what Elmyra Perry said was true, then they may be pulling manpower in just to keep the whole thing running. Feeling that kind of squeeze could make people nervous. Jeff knew that even without the garrison troops, Cummings could call down enough power to turn his beautiful town into the biggest parking lot this side of Vegas—or anywhere.

A large American flag hung behind Cummings. Jeff decided to speak to the flag rather than the man.

"We are loyal Americans here in Beaver. We willingly submit ourselves to the powers and authorities in the land. We honor, sustain, and obey the law, sir, even if it's martial law. There'll be no loud revolution in Beaver, Lieutenant. You can count on that from me and the entire town."

Remember Me

Friday, April 23 through Wednesday, April 28, 2010
Newhouse Center / 477th ERIS District
Wah Wah Valley, West Beaver County, Utah

Where are you going, my little one, little one?

Amanda screamed. Again. And Again.

"Are you sure we're doing this right?" Virgil said, his brow furrowed deeply with concern.

"Trust me," David Yarrow said firmly. "Children—especially little children get into this power struggle with adults. It isn't that they're mean or bad kids, it's just that they need to know what their limits are—you know, what they can get away with and what they can't. Truth is, that kids don't feel secure until they know what their limits are. It's like being blindfold in the middle of a room. You just don't feel safe until you know where the walls are."

Amanda screamed once more: an earth-shattering, earsplitting scream.

Virgil winced, trying his best to follow the Yarrow man's advice and ignore what the child was doing.

"I jes' wish she'd quiet down." Virgil shook his head. "Barris here needs a little more quiet than Amanda seems willing to supply."

Both David and Virgil glanced at Michael in the opposite bunk. The puffiness in his face had subsided to a montage of bruises that were painful just to look at not to mention the burn scars on his forehead. Nurse Codgebury came to check on him every day—and to keep an eye on Amanda. Michael had spent three days sleeping, and there had been some fear that the concussion would deepen into a coma. Michael awoke just yesterday but still spent most of his time just sleeping off the beating.

"It's especially hard with someone like Amanda." Yarrow shook his head sadly. "The kid's like a wild animal, afraid of everything and without any understanding of what rules to live by."

"She's like a wild animal, eh?" Virgil cocked his head, looking up toward the ceiling. "Kind of like a wild horse being broke, ain't it? I had to wait out a stallion once when I was a kid. My pa said to show it who was boss. Cracked a few ribs in the process, but when he was done, that was the best horse I ever had; damn near the best friend I ever had either." The cowboy looked at David. "So you're saying this is the same thing?"

"Yeah, Virgil." Yarrow smiled through his wince as Amanda let out yet another bellow. "That's about right. She's been in her shell so long, I figure, that coming out must be pretty painful."

Abruptly, Amanda stopped howling. The tears were still there, and she was sobbing but the hysterical tantrum had vanished in the moment.

"Now, Virgil," David whispered.

Virgil turned and looked into the tear-streaked face of the little girl. "Are you all finished, darlin'?" he said softly.

Amanda screwed up her face again and screamed louder than ever.

Virgil turned his back on her again and sat down on the edge of his bunk.

David sighed. "Sometimes it takes awhile."

Virgil pulled a few scraps from under the bedding and began working long pieces of fiber with his hands.

"What's that?" David asked.

Virgil didn't look up, his hands working carefully over the material. "Corn husks. I got it from that hydro-farm woman Janiese McFarlane. Did you know she grows corn in them long plastic sheds of hers from seed to feed in just about a week? Damnedest thing you ever saw! So I just asked her for some of the husks, and she obliged."

Amanda wailed.

David moved closer. "So what are you making out of it?"

Virgil concentrated on the husks. "It's something for Amanda—*if she'll ever hush up*!" He finished loudly enough for Amanda to hear.

The wailing choked off into a series of hiccup snorts. Amanda reined in her tantrum with Herculean effort. Her big watery eyes watched Virgil's hands with a child's curiosity that overcame the fear at the root of her horrendous display. It took a few minutes, but at last Amanda crawled up off of the bunk and moved tentatively, shyly, and still sniffling over to where Virgil continued to work calmly with his hands.

"Watcha . . . making?" she managed at last.

Virgil looked up and smiled at her. Sunshine. "Well, there's my darlin'! Ol' Uncle Virg is making you something for when you're all done cryin'. I was kind a hopin' that would be real soon."

Amanda turned to Yarrow, who was smiling nearby. "Uncle Dave, what's Uncle Virg making?"

David smiled and picked Amanda up. She didn't relax into him like she did with Virgil, but she didn't resist him either. To David Yarrow, it was the most wonderful and painful thing he could remember. "I don't know, dear, but if you're a good girl, I'm sure he'll show you."

Amanda squirmed a little, signaling it was time to put her down. She wandered back over to Virgil and stood silent, waiting with what she personally considered to be astonishing patience in a child her age.

Virgil looked up at her from under a raised eyebrow. "So, Amanda, are you gonna be a good girl and not throw them fits no more? Ol' Uncle Mike over there, he needs his rest so he'll get better, and yer bellerin' ain't been good for him."

Amanda nodded her head, unsure as to whether yes or no was the correct answer but willing to take a chance on it. "I won't 'beller' anymore, Uncle Virg."

Virgil's smile broadened, his large hands now behind his back.

"That's my girl! So you think you're ready for what Ol' Virg has for ya?"

Amanda nodded emphatically.

Virgil drew his hands forward and opened them. There, in his hands, was a corn-husk doll he'd fashioned with care. Not rough nor crude but with a delicate hand and detail that surprised both Amanda and David as he watched from the side.

The little girl reached for the doll.

Miracles.

Amanda smiled.

David Yarrow's lip quivered with electric joy.

"That's my girl," Virgil said, picking up the child who melted into his broad chest.

Where are you going, my baby, my own?
"Uncle Mike, is my mama dead?"

Amanda's small hand clutched Michael's as they walked around the Recreation Field. It was after ten in the morning on Saturday, and things were safely quiet in the camp. Virgil had told her that "Uncle Mike" needed to get out for a bit. She felt a little like she had been asked to walk Uncle Mike one too many times but obeyed her Uncle Virg unquestioningly.

"I suppose that depends on how you look at it," Michael said in that vague way parents talk when they're not sure what the correct answer is. "What do you remember about your mama?"

"We . . ." Amanda hesitated. Even at her age, she knew somehow that some boxes were harder to open than others. "We used to feed the duckies. Down by the water. There was grass and trees, and we would take our sandwiches and eat the insides sometimes and feed the bread to the duckies. They would eat right out of Mama's hand sometimes, and she would laugh and say, 'Oh, you naughty little duckies! You never have enough! You'll be fat little duckies!' She'd wear a yellow dress or sometimes brown pants that felt soft when I'd put my head down on them." Amanda giggled. The sound was like the sun flashes on rippling water. "One time there were even squirrels in the park, and we had some peanuts, and they would come right up and take the peanut if you would hold still enough. They'd climb right up your arm and take it right off your shoulder! I put peanuts there, and every time a squirrel would come and take the peanut, Mama would laugh and laugh. We both laughed. It was fun."

Michael relaxed into the warmth of Amanda's memories. They continued their walk down the slope. Amanda could be a real chatterbox when she let herself go. "What else do you remember about your mama?"

"Well, I remember going to a big 'musement park. Daddy was with us even though he wasn't living with us anymore and he and Mama were still yelling at each other sometimes. We rode lots of rides, and Mama put me in a pack on her back, and I got to lay down in her hair. It was soft and yellow and smelled so good. Mama loved me lots. She always said so."

Amanda finally had gotten quiet. Michael was beginning to feel he'd escaped the original question, but Amanda was better than that.

"So, Uncle Mike, is my mama dead?"

Michael stopped and knelt down, turning to face the little girl who had not yet quite returned to the living. "Darling, I just don't know. I think perhaps she's in heaven with the angels."

"Where's heaven?"

Michael pulled in a breath but wasn't sure of the words to say. Theology was not his strong point. He almost wished that even Weston were around to field this one. "Heaven is up there—up above the sky."

Amanda looked up and frowned. "That's awful far away."

"Well," Michael said. "Maybe your mama isn't so far away as all that, really. You remember feeding the ducks with your mama, right?"

"Yes, that was fun."

"And you remember about her hair and going to the amusement park, don't you?"

"Oh, yes!"

"Then, in a way, Amanda," Michael said gently, "your mama is still alive—inside you."

"Inside me?" Amanda said with wonder, her eyes bright.

"Sure! As long as you remember her and remember all those good things you did together, then all those things stay alive in your thoughts." Michael pointed at Amanda standing in front of him. "If you remember your mama, those wonderful things are still alive inside you."

Michael stood and took Amanda's hand. They continued their walk. Michael wondered if he'd conveyed his thoughts simply enough for the child.

"Uncle Mike, I'm going to remember as much about my mama as I can—then she can be alive a lot!"

Michael was stunned at the thought, unable to think through all the philosophical implications of the child's simple statement. He said simply, "That's good, honey. That would be very good."

Unseen by either of them, a single slim figure watched both of them from the shadows of the Hospice across the field.

Turn around, and you're two, Turn around, and you're four.
Sunday afternoon saw Michael returning from the lunch service to a family room in bedlam.

Men were gathered casually around the walls of the family room. Cliff Harris was blindfolded and chasing after Amanda. Amanda, squealing with delight, was running about the room, fleeing from the clutches of the sinister accountant from Oregon.

"I'm gonna get you!" Cliff would growl in his softest, deepest voice. "I'm gonna get you, Amanda!"

Amanda would squeal again and dash out of his clutches, then stop the moment it looked like she might actually get herself out of harm's way. When she thought she was too safe, she would turn on Cliff and giggle at him through her words.

"No, you won't!"

Cliff would turn, arms outstretched, and lumber with another good-natured growl toward Amanda. The game would begin afresh.

"I'm gonna tickle you, Amanda! I'm gonna get you!"

Squeals and giggles.

"Amanda!" Michael called out. "Amanda!"

The girl turned at his voice and ran into Michael's arms. "Hi, Uncle Mike! Did you bring me anything?"

"Yes, I brought you some extra cookies," he said, lifting her up. "It's time to stop the game for now."

Cliff overheard. Lifting one side of his not terribly effective blindfold, he said, "Aw, Michael, do we have to?"

Michael beamed, holding Amanda up. "Sorry, Cliff, but Nurse Codgebury is coming for a call, and Amanda needs to quiet down a bit before she sees her. We wouldn't want her thinking that she's having too much fun, would we?"

Amanda laughed, bright and honest. "Where's Uncle Virg?"

"He'll be here in a few minutes, honey. He's just finishing up his lunch." Michael kneeled down, setting her on the floor. "Right now, it's story time."

The men around the room suddenly became animated.

"It's my turn to tell the story, Michael."

"Is not! You told her a story just last Wednesday!"

"Hey, I haven't even had a chance to tell a story yet!"

"Yeah, but yours are lame!"

Michael shook his head. "Easy, boys, we've got a schedule. Achmed, it's your turn."

"Yes!" Achmed had just won the lottery. "Yes! Yes!"

"Hey! I want a turn!"

All eyes turned to the voice, unable to mentally connect the phrase with the voice.

It was Sid.

"Well? What are you guys lookin' at?" the barracks supervisor said from behind his shaggy beard. "I got good stories, too!"

Michael smiled. "It's just that none of us thought you knew any stories that were G-rated. You want on the list, Sid, then you're on the list."

Sid grinned at the laughter around him.

Amanda looked up at Michael. "Uncle Mike, remember when you said that my mama was alive inside me?"

"Yes, dear," Michael looked uncomfortably at the barracks men gathering around them.

"Well, I was thinking . . . if the things I remember about my mama are alive inside me, then are the things I forgot all dead?"

Michael looked stunned. "Well, ah, I don't think that they are exactly all dead, but . . ."

" 'Cause if they are," Amanda continued to weave her inexorable chain of childhood logic, "then is my mama just part alive 'cause I only part remember her?"

"No, I don't think that 'partly alive' is right either, honey, it's just that . . ."

"Then, if I remember her all the way, will she be all the way alive again just like . . ."

Amanda coughed.

A deep, croupy cough.

Every man stood frozen in the room.

". . . just like she was before instead of in heaven?"

Michael looked at her.

"How are you feeling, dear?"

"OK I guess." She coughed again.

"Amanda, honey, we'll talk about this later tonight, OK? Right now, Achmed's going to tell you a story." Michael looked up through watery eyes. "Right, Achmed?"

Achmed could only nod.

"Where are you going, Uncle Mike?"

"Just to find Nurse Codgebury, honey. I'll be right back."

Turn around, and you're a young girl, going out of the door.

Sweat glistened off Amanda's face. The fever had raged for two days and showed no signs of dropping off. She'd had a bad night the night before and had slept through most of the day, but now, in the late hours of Wednesday evening, she was awake and in pain. She hadn't been able to keep fluids down since morning. Occasionally, she would go to the bathroom or, more often, vomit violently into the plastic bowl Virgil had appropriated for her out of the Commons Kitchen. In all cases, whether it was urine, stools, or the vomit, there were strong traces of blood. Something was taking the child apart from the inside out.

There was nothing to be done.

Virgil held her in the bunk, swaying back and forth slightly to comfort her the only way he knew how. The cowboy's eyes were fixed forward, angry at what was happening, angry at himself for being unable to do anything about it. David Yarrow stood in the corner inconsolable. Gene Muskat, a teacher from Bremerton, Washington, stood next to David with his hand on his shoulder,

unsure just what to do except be there. Sid took up another corner, frowning deeper than usual, his arms folded across his chest
as he stood stock-still. The doorway was packed solid with men
who spoke in hushed tones. The window was open, despite the
chill in the night to allow air into the warm room. Beyond the
window were shadowed faces peering in to witness this one death
on top of so many others.

Olivia Codgebury was nowhere to be found.

Michael squatted next to the bed, wringing out a cloth in a second basin and dabbing the cool water to Amanda's brow. It was
all he could think to do.

Suddenly, Amanda opened her eyes wide, bright with the fever.
The action caused Virgil to rock even harder, as if the tempo of his
motion could somehow keep her heart beating and her lungs
working. Those bright eyes turned to Michael.

"Uncle Mike," she said in a raspy voice.

"Yes, love," Michael said quietly, "I'm right here. We're all
right here, honey."

"Uncle Mike, I remember my mama."

"Yes, dear, that's wonderful," Michael said huskily.

"Does she live when I remember her?"

Tears burned in Michael's eyes. He fought for control of his
voice. "Yes, dear, she lives when you remember her."

Amanda held her corn-husk doll tightly to her chest. She
blinked, water streaming from her eyes. Michael wasn't even sure
that she was really seeing him.

"Uncle Mike," she said at last.

"Yes, my love."

"Who will remember me?"

Michael sobbed once and choked down his bitter emotions.
"Oh, Amanda, I'll remember you. Uncle Virg will remember you.
We'll all remember you, darling."

"Then, if you remember me, can I still be with you?"

Michael looked straight into the child's bright eyes.

"Yes, as long as we remember you, you will still be alive—and
with us."

Virgil's air left him as though he'd been hit in the gut.

Amanda smiled at Michael. It was the smile that would haunt

him for the rest of his days. She had asked for salvation, and he had given it to her in a way he had only started to comprehend.

Amanda swallowed painfully. "Uncle Mike?"

"Yes, darling."

"Will I be lonely in heaven?"

"No, dear. It's pretty crowded up there right now."

"I hope Mama will be there."

"She is."

Amanda smiled again. "I'll tell her all about my new daddies. I'll remember you all. Heaven is forever, that's what Mama said. So, if I remember you forever, then you'll never die."

Remember me forever, Michael thought, *and I'll never die.*

Amanda Jeannette Delany, age 7, died at 2317 Mountain Daylight Time on Wednesday, April 28, 2010, of complications incidental to V-CIDS infection. Her death was accompanied by the distant rumbling destruction of the Quartz Creek Center to the southwest, the sight of which was obscured by a gathering rain. Amanda was held by Virgil Johnston at the time of her death, who refused to relinquish the body until seven the next morning.

For this reason, Amanda's remains were not among the 204 other bodies on the death pallets that morning.

The Immortals

Heavy gray clouds blanketed the valley, offering no comfort from the leaden light of dawn. A slight morning drizzle, bereft of the strength to cleanse, came and went. A sky of tears, weeping, weak and spent. The desert ground seemed always surprised by these spring storms, both soaking it up thirstily and at the same time, now knowing quite what to do with it, forming small streams to wash its soil away. The rain was in no hurry—it cried without enthusiasm.

Jason Barris, draped in his thick blanket, stood heedless of the damp, chill rain that occasionally fell on him. He stood as he had stood all night gazing into the quarters window of Barracks 7-R, silent and aching. Aching to run away. Aching to go in. Aching for the humanity that burned like an ember in the center of a fire gone cold and dead. Aching to turn his back again on feeling and go back into that frozen blackness that protected him from experiencing anything at all.

So he had stood all night, his soul balanced on the window ledge, suspended between fear and desire—painless refusal to live and the shocking agony of life.

Jason's father moved on the other side of the fogged plastic window, deliberately and quietly. His arms moved with care, working with a blanket, and when at last he was done, he picked up a small bundle from the lap of the cowboy and walked out of the room followed by his companions.

Jason blinked at the empty room. He didn't know why, but he didn't seem capable of moving.

A voice yelled at him, inches from his ear. "Jason Barris, come on down!"

Jason spun around. "Hey! Knock it off!"

Yet the face that suddenly filled his vision wouldn't retreat. Jason took a step back against the wall. There was no retreat. Pressed to within inches of his face, the shaggy beard bristling from the gray skin screwed itself into a gap-toothed smile of P.T.

"What a show! What a band! What a thrill! Step right up, it's the greatest show on earth!" P.T.'s voice whispered conspiratorially. "It's time! The clock has ticked its tock, and the funeral is where it all begins. This ending is the beginning—even you can see it! SEE IT! SEE IT!"

P.T. thrust his carved weathered board into Jason's face, its blank, wooden display screen touching his nose.

Jason slapped the lunatic's hand away, turning his face so as not to look into P.T.'s telling eyes. "Stop it!"

P.T. threw back his head and laughed at the sky. "Ha! Blind! The boy is blind!" P.T. danced away from Jason in a jig that seemed to be dictated by the location of puddles on the ground. "The day of salvation is at hand! The instrument of our resurrection and salvation walks the camps, and the blind boy refuses to see! Be healed, my son, be healed! The word is gone out, Newhouse rises like Lazarus from the grave, and the blind boy wanting not sees not!"

Suddenly, P.T. stopped his dance. He listened.

"What is it?" Jason asked.

"Listen to the thunder, blind boy!" P.T. whispered with electric intensity. "The world is listening. It begins."

Jason listened. From around the corner of the barracks, he could hear sounds approaching. He remained with his back flat against the side of the barracks, turning his head toward the noise.

His father.

Michael didn't see Jason. His face was intent on his path toward the Recreation Field and was at right angles to where Jason stood shivering in the rain. Michael cradled in his arms the blanket from which two small legs dangled. As he passed between the buildings, Jason saw his father reach down and straighten the blanket carefully over the legs to shield them from the rain. In that instant, he passed again out of sight between the barracks.

Then came the procession. The cowboy walked with his jaw set. Then a long-haired, swarthy man and several others Jason had seen through the window passing their vigil the night before.

Still others came. Men from his father's barracks, Jason supposed.

Then, as if by some unspoken shout, the doors from the barracks beyond the procession opened one by one. Strangers stepped into the light sleet and, heads bowed, joined the mourning throng. Word of the funeral—the first funeral known to anyone in Newhouse—had seemed to be carried to every barracks Jason could see.

Jason glanced at P.T.

The crazed man grinned with yellow teeth. "I must run, little blind boy! Don't take too long or you'll miss the show."

P.T. suddenly dashed toward the crowd, pressing his way forward into the flow, yelling all the while something about the heralds going first and preparing the way.

Jason was suddenly aware of motion behind him. He looked the opposite way down the alley and saw more men quietly emptying out of the gray-washed buildings into the damp alleys. He watched them move past him, like a boy standing on the banks of a river, until at last he fell into their stream and was carried with them into the Recreation Field.

The stream had merged with a murmuring sea. Thousands had walked respectfully into the large field, churning the mud with their myriad feet and churning the air with their hushed voices. Jason walked with them for a time and then realized that they were following his father up the hill. Jason began moving quickly, swimming with the current of people, trying desperately to get closer to his father.

Voices fell behind him as he moved forward.

". . . that little girl, doted on by those men . . ."

". . . of our own last week. He's still doing fine, but if anything were to happen to him . . ."

". . . didn't know how painful it was to feel good again about anything . . ."

Jason felt short of breath. Tears were welling up in his eyes unbidden and unwanted. They stung, and he wiped them angrily away. He picked up his pace, pushing past people as he moved.

". . . my own kids. All three died one at a time last year. I never got to grieve . . ."

". . . brother and his wife in the camps last fall. I guess this is their funeral, too . . ."

". . . wish my own father cared as much . . ."

Jason turned around once, trying to get his bearings. The Recreation Field had filled up. He wondered if everyone in the camp was there—there because a few men had loved a little girl. There because his father had loved that little girl.

Jason sobbed. He pushed forward again, tears streaming down his face.

Who knew resurrection would hurt so much?

Michael kicked open the doors of the Cathedral.

Weston, gathered with the Newhouse senior staff at the other end of the building, jumped to his feet at the noise.

"Barris! What is the meaning of this?"

Michael walked down the aisle between the benches, carrying Amanda's body in his arms.

"Get out," he said clearly.

Weston pushed his fists into his hips. "This is a private meeting, Barris! We have a number of camp management posts to fill today and . . ."

"GET OUT!" Michael screamed, crazed. "GET OUT! GET OUT!"

The staff leaped up from their wooden chairs. Michael took no notice of them. His eyes were on the minister governor. Weston didn't move. The reverend stood his ground, feet apart, staring at Michael's forehead. Without shifting his gaze, Weston spoke.

"Brother Weber, will you kindly remove this devil from my sight? Get him out of this holy place."

"Uh, Reverend," Evan stammered from where he stood. "I, uh, I don't think that's such a good idea."

Weston glanced up. The Cathedral doors were packed with people filing in. Even as he watched, the vast hall was nearly shoulder to shoulder full of people.

Sid moved forward from the crowd to stand next to Michael. "Reverend," he said, "we're just going to have a little memorial service for our little girl. We'd prefer it if you'd just leave."

"A funeral?" Weston didn't believe them. "Over a thousand people die in this facility every week, and you want to hold a funeral?"

Sid shoved his hands deep into his pockets and looked at the ground for a moment considering Weston's comment. Then he looked up. "Yes, sir, that's about it."

"This is ridiculous!" Weston shook his head. He looked out at the packed hall. "Brothers and sisters, wallowing in the deaths of our companions is not healthy for us. This basking in misery can only bring heartache to an already painful and horrible situation. I beg you, please go back to your barracks—the administrative council has already adopted a plan whereby . . ."

"Not until we have our funeral," Virgil said, stepping up to stand next to Michael as well.

An angry murmur of agreement rumbled through the assembly.

"Please!" The reverend raised his hands, ignoring Virgil and addressing the crowd. "For your own sakes—for your own sanity—please let the dead go! Let them be lost and forgotten so that you might survive and . . ."

Michael looked to the side of the dais. Olivia Codgebury had been part of the staff meeting. Now she stood with her back against the rear wall of the Cathedral, her lip quivering visibly. *Why didn't you come last night,* Michael thought, *where could you go that was far enough from your own conscience? Or did you just want to let go and forget the bodies of the people who died along the way so that you might live with yourself another day?*

"... cannot bring them back or cure the illness that is taking us all! I implore you—forget the dead that you may live!"

Michael looked into the reverend's face as if for the first time. "I have misunderstood you, Reverend: I thought you were just out for yourself but that was never the case, was it? You are just trying to cope in the only way you know how. You really do think that you are leading as many good people as possible through this hell. You even believe there is an end to this torment other than being hauled out like lumber or smashed flat in one final blast. You're just trying to do the right thing by these people, I can see that now."

Michael stepped up onto the dais. He moved behind the plywood altar and, with a single glance at the reverend, lay Amanda's body on top of it.

"But you're wrong, Reverend. Dead wrong." Michael turned to Margaret Kelley and Henry Folleson, who remained standing motionless on the dais. "You were right the other day. No one is letting us out of here. No one is going to escape. No one is going to outrun the army because none of us can outrun the V-CIDS. We are going to die, and we're going to do it right here inside of a month."

"So," Margaret said, her voice strange and quiet, "just what are you saying, Mr. Barris?"

Michael turned around and faced Amanda, still and cold and blue upon the altar. *Amanda knew,* he thought, *Amanda knew before any of us.*

"What I'm saying is that we all are going to die—but that isn't the crime here. People have been dying for a long time, with or without the V-CIDS. There's no sign that people are going to be giving up on dying soon. Children die, and we feel it's a tragedy. Mothers die, and we think of their poor children. Grandfathers die, and we think that their time has finally come. Murder is a crime, and we are being murdered just as surely as if someone had put a bullet in our brain—but death? No, death is not a crime."

Michael looked up into the faces in the hall. He saw faces of friends, faces of strangers, faces hard, and faces soft. *Who are you? Who remembers you?*

"No," Michael said with conviction, "the crime here is that our lives will pass unnoticed, unsung, and unremembered. We all stand on the bones of our dead. A hundred generations of bones buried and gone in the earth. Plato has long gone to dust, yet we learn from his words. Confucius, Buddha, Mohammad—all dead and gone from us, yet their words influence our thoughts and our actions. Bacon, Copernicus, Galileo, Michelangelo, Fulton, Newton, Edison, Marconi, Farnsworth, Pasteur, Salk—dead! Dead and buried! Yet we stand on the shoulders of those giants with every new invention. How could we do so? Because they left behind them some part of them that was immortal, eternal, and indestructible. Some part of that immortality remains behind with us because *we remember them*! We read their words in books, we hear their souls in their music, and we see them in the images they left behind.

"What about us? Who we are, who we were, what our hopes and our dreams were, what we liked and disliked, what color shirt we wore—all the mundane and wonderful dreams and hopes and desires that make us who we are will vanish in the night. Vanish, I say, in one carefully orchestrated flash that will cleanly, quietly, and quite effectively erase all trace that we were ever here. 'Don't look in the desert,' they say, 'there's nothing out there that you want to see.' 'Don't think about all those victims of the V-CIDS, they are none of your concern,' they say! 'You're dead,' they tell us, and we quietly go into the desert and vanish in the sagebrush and the dust; our dreams, thoughts, art, music, and passion, just so many ashes are scattered by the wind.

"But not Amanda!" Michael shouted, then looked down again at the face of the girl he had so quickly loved and too soon lost. His face contorted in pain, the tears squeezed from eyes that thought they could no longer cry. "She had one last wish."

Michael turned slowly around. He saw Olivia Codgebury crying. *My God,* Michael thought, *I didn't think she could.*

Michael took the broad-tipped pencil she held in her hand and walked to the back of the dais. Grabbing a chair, he dragged it squealing under the large cross that hung there. He stood quickly on the chair and reached up with the pencil.

"No!" Weston cried.

Barris didn't even hear him. He scribbled forcefully so that the letters of his scrawl could clearly be seen on the arms of the cross. *REMEMBER ME.*

Michael turned back to the silent hall. "If Amanda's life is to have any meaning, then we have to find a way that she—that all of us—can be remembered."

It was two in the morning by the time the last of the mourners from the camp filed past Amanda's body. It had been a constant stream all day. Each, Michael knew, held their own thoughts. Some looked on the child and saw their own children. Some looked on the child and saw their brothers and sisters. Some saw the thousands of others, just like them, who had passed before without a single notice. Some looked on the child and saw themselves alone in the cold darkness.

And when each looked up, their gaze fell upon the scrawl on the cross.

REMEMBER ME.

Michael had given it a great deal of thought as well.

The last figure approached the altar. Michael looked up and sucked in a stuttering breath.

It was Death.

Rather, it was Meredith Jernigan, the camp Death Master, her face shadowed by the great dark hood. Yet Meredith hesitated for a moment as she approached the altar and child. In a moment of decision, she pushed back her hood. A cascade of flaxen hair spilled out, radiant even in the dim light of the Cathedral, framing perfectly her charcoal gray eyes.

"Mr. Barris?" she asked.

"Yes," he replied, somewhat unevenly.

"There is much talk in our community about what you have done and the things you have said." The Death Master spoke softly. "They ask what can be done. They ask what you wish them to do?"

Michael sighed. "*I* don't want them to do anything."

Meredith shook her head. "No, Pandora, you have opened the box. It's a little late to close it now. They need someone to lead them. You are that someone."

"Lead them to what?"

"Well," she said, "that actually was my question to you."

Michael gathered his thoughts, then spoke. "We've got to find a way to pass our thoughts and hopes on to those who survive us. Let them know we lived and how we lived and how we died. It need not be just the recording of events but everything that meant anything to us—our art, our music, our crafts, and our dreams. What we thought was funny. What angered us."

"I agree," the Death Master replied, "but all we have available to us to make such records will be destroyed right along with us. No continuance. No continuity. No remembrance."

"Then," Michael said, thinking along with her, "we have to find some way of either safeguarding those records from the blast or getting them out of Newhouse and to a secure place."

"Do you think such a thing is possible?" Meredith asked.

"Yes. I think such a thing could be possible."

"Weston will fight us."

Michael smiled. "Weston doesn't have to know."

Meredith returned the smile shyly. "People have been talking all day about doing something, yet they don't have any one name for what they want do to. What shall we call ourselves?"

Michael looked up at the cross. "How about 'Immortals'?"

Meredith smiled and, pulling her hood back over her head, stepped to the platform. "Then, may death be the first to join the Immortals." She extended her hand.

Michael nodded. "I suppose that makes sense in a way."

She held his hand longer than necessary for their agreement. "Michael," Meredith said softly, "it's time for me to take Amanda."

Michael slowly closed his eyes and nodded. He kept them closed until he heard the robes cross the floor and the side-door close.

When he opened his eyes, he saw Jason standing at the far end of the Cathedral.

"Remember me?" Jason said.

"Is that a request or question?" Michael asked, his eyes red and aching.

"I heard," Jason said as he sauntered up the aisle, "that you had an extra bunk." Jason paused and looked up, his face vulnerable and childlike. "I've already asked Sid, and he said it was OK with him—him and the rest of the barracks family, too." Jason laughed nervously. "Even the Dark Queen gave consent. So—could you use a new roommate?"

Michael slowly walked down off the dais, opened his arms, and enfolded his boy in a long, welcoming, and guileless embrace.

Music

Saturday, May 1, 2010 / 0400 hrs
Newhouse Center / 477th ERIS District
Wah Wah Valley, West Beaver County, Utah

Not even the faintest hint of dawn was in the sky. The chill night was black save for the flat charged illumination panels that every one of the shroud masters carried with them. While she had often cursed their short lives, the dimming glow this late in the evening was to the Death Master's purpose.

She stood next to the main-optics line for the AG pallets, just as she had every morning for the last five weeks. Her cough was worsening this morning into a croupy hack—a bad sign that even she and her iron will had to respect. Meredith knew that her time was running out faster than some in camp. She just wished that she had enough time to accomplish what they had proposed. So she found herself here in the darkness as she had for so many other nights, waiting for the Death Train to pick up its grisly load and wondered what it would be like for her when she rode that train out of camp as yet another piece of lumber.

Still, there was something different this morning in her purpose. To the four shroud teams she had specifically organized this morning, it would have special significance.

All four teams were comprised entirely of Immortals.

With a fatalistic punctuality, the outer marker lights began to flash outside the main gate. Meredith could see the faint outlines of the Death Train hovering in the flashing light of the Perimeter Three gate alarms.

The pallets had come each morning with their wide, flat beds empty, yet this morning, the pallets were covered with bulging tarps pulled tight over crates.

Death smiled.

Carl Emmett had been promoted and accorded all the honors of his new position. He hated it. When the camp factory system had fallen apart, the reverend had called for Preston Duffy to put in an appearance whether he was sick or not. When Preston didn't show up—having been dead for several weeks—Olivia Codgebury was sent to make a determination as to his health. The nurse made the obligatory call, discovered that the man was dead, and promptly assigned an appropriate estimated time of death for the record. Unfortunately, this time was a third time differing from the opposing lottery camp times and called everything into question once again.

Unfortunately for Carl, the dispute was settled amicably, and the loot from Preston's horde was distributed quietly and efficiently. For Carl, the effects were immediate and devastating: without the Preston Lottery Escrow—as he called it—he found himself bereft of the clout that could make things happen anymore. Worse yet, Codgebury dutifully covered her own backside and informed the reverend that Duffy was dead. Reverend Weston, not being one to shirk responsibility, immediately elevated Emmett to the post of Newhouse Settlement Morale Officer. This mostly meant that now Emmett was deprived not only of the wherewithal to accomplish his personal agenda, but that he had to attend staff meetings with the reverend and give his report on the progress of keeping everyone happy in the camp from hell.

With everyone else dying in the camp, why couldn't Weston just crash-out and leave the rest of them to their own misery.

Carl sat against the factory wall, now silent and used mostly for informal gatherings of a less-than-structured nature. It was the "less-than-structured" part that had brought the wrath of the almighty Weston down on his back. True, the recent spate of civil disobedience had put a real crimp in the reverend's dictatorial style, but the man remained the only authority recognized by ERIS in the camp. Weston spoke to ERIS, and ERIS sent the food as long as things ran the way Weston wanted it. It never paid to mess with the man who brought you dinner. So when Weston tells Emmett that the factory gig is up and that he now has around ten thousand people on his hands with nothing to do—well, says Weston, the morale officer had better well come up with *something* to keep these people occupied while they're here. Something organized and lingering. Something meaningful.

Something meaningful?

So Carl Emmett sat with his back against the factory wall and worked hard at thinking of something in this camp that would be considered meaningful.

"Hello, Carl."

Carl looked up, shading his eyes from the sun. "Oh, hello, Barris. Formed any insurrections lately?"

"Well," Michael said slowly as he sat next to Emmett, "as a matter of fact, I thought you might help me with one."

"Oh, great!" Emmett shook his head. "Bad enough your last little stunt ruined my little kingdom—now you want me to join the revolution? Do I have to wear an armband or sing the last chorus of *Les Misérables*? I can quote Groucho Marx better than Karl, but I hope you won't hold that against me."

"No, no, nothing quite so difficult," Michael said easily. "I actually think that my revolution may solve a problem for you. I hear that the reverend is pressing you pretty hard to get everyone active and productive."

"Yeah, you could say that." Emmett was an operator and knew when someone was baiting the hook on him. The question always was just how badly one wanted to get caught. It was time for a judicious silence.

"Well, what if I told you that I could give you structured activities that would keep everyone happily occupied," Michael said with natural ease. "I could get his holiness the reverend off your back and set you up with all kinds of reports that would keep the staff snowed for weeks. How does that sound to you?"

Emmett looked sideways at Michael. "What's in it for me?"

"Just as I said, I get the reverend off your back."

"What's in it for you?"

Michael smiled. "Peace of mind."

Emmett snorted. "Ah, an idealist—those are the dangerous ones."

"All right," Michael said, "let's just say it will forward the cause of the revolution."

"Well, it's not good but I trust it better than idealism." Emmett nodded. "What's the risk to me?"

"None. To everyone it just looks like you're doing your job. All you do is organize the activities in such a way that we can get our business done."

Emmett considered. "All right, just what do you have in mind?"

"Follow me." Michael stood, offering his hand to Emmett.

Emmett looked up and considered. There was danger in this game and all the worse, there was danger that he could not yet fathom. It is always the train you don't see that sneaks up on you as you walk confidently down the track. He knew there was something wrong here and terribly perilous.

He liked it. Risk meant power. Risk meant opportunity. Risk meant change and in all change there was profit. Carl couldn't care less about ideals—he thought that ideals were a crutch that weak people used to excuse their own lack of guts. No: if Michael was on some crusade, then Carl would carry his spear far enough to see the profit in it for himself. When he knew what it was worth, then he'd cash it in. If he was lucky and the stakes were high, who knew?—perhaps even high enough for a "Get Out of Death Free" card? He'd trade a lot of soul just to breathe awhile longer.

Carl smiled as he took Michael's hand.

"Some of our friends have secured a few things to support us down in the warehouse," Michael said, pulling Emmett to his feet. "Perhaps you'd like to join me for a quick look?"

P.T. danced onto the factory floor about midnight. No one saw him—people seldom did. Nor did anyone know P.T. beyond the mystical prophesies he divined from the depths of his carved slab of wood. Where he came from and who he was before the camp was beyond the knowledge even of the Portable Terminal model he had so lovingly carved. Most people assumed that P.T. had been one of those unfortunates who lived their lives plugged into the illusion of cyberspace. When they come suddenly "unplugged"—cut off from the constant electronic tempo and information firehose—they have no connection with reality on which to base any other life. Bereft of any talent or skill in real things, they often disconnect completely. That P.T. was disconnected was evident to everyone.

Everyone was right about P.T. Everyone was wrong.

P.T. quite literally waltzed into the room, his partner a large canvas bag, as he loudly hummed Tchaikovsky's "Sleeping Beauty Waltz" into the vast openness of the factory. He spun with grace between the rows of clean tables. The only other sound was his feet softly rushing across the plank floor.

At least he halted his progress, spinning dizzily to the final triumphant chords of the piece ringing in his mind alone. One table, carefully prepared by his own hand, waited for him. His eyes cleared at once as he saw them. He lowered the shoulder bag and touched them. The water in the carefully prepared basin felt just right to his touch. Cool steel—honest metal, the likes of which he had not seen for an eternity—seemed to sing to him with its bright edges and fitted handles. Glue. Sandpaper he'd made himself the day before as well as the wooden vises and stands.

"A triumph!" he cried quietly to himself, a single tear falling from his tired eyes. "My triumph! My salvation!"

With care, P.T. reached into the canvas duffel and began pulling out carefully gleaned pieces of wood. It would take him three days. Not nearly enough time, he knew, to do the job properly, but had he not pushed the keys and accessed the data from the I-Net? He knew his time was coming but it would be enough. Just enough.

He cut the template from paper and then the wood from the template. He knew the proportions by heart. He ran his hands around the waist of the soundboard. Satisfied, he cut another, this time with beautifully scrolled holes. His hands moved deliberately yet with practiced speed. When the night was done, his work was carefully cleaned. No one knew that he had been here. Indeed, for those days no one knew what had become of P.T.

Until the morning of the third day, when it was finished.

"Mr. Keel! Mr. Keel!"

"Yes," Erik said, looking up instantly. He'd been Martin Keel for so long that the reaction was natural. Being less than natural could get you killed. "What is it, Scott?"

Scott Johnson had almost gotten back to his regular self, although he still heavily favored one leg when he walked. His face may not ever be the same as it was, but it was healing up well. Scott took a great deal of pride in the fact that at least he was still here for the moment while Bullock had disappeared from the camp. People often disappear unaccountably from Newhouse—usually last seen leaving as lumber. Yet if the Death Master had seen Bullock leave, she didn't say.

Scott was one of the few who knew Erik's real name and history. That he was addressing him openly and urgently was uncomfortable. "Mr. Keel, you're needed at the factory—at once."

"I'm sorry, Mr. Johnson, but the factory's closed, and I'm not interested in crafts and—"

"Please, Mr. Keel! At once!"

Erik looked up. There was actual pleading registering in Scott Johnson's eyes.

Erik got up from his bunk at once and began jogging between the buildings of Block Y. He passed the governor's house to the main road. Ahead of him, others were running toward the factory, excited voices in the air. Erik broke into a full run.

He pushed his way through the crowded main doors with Scott Johnson just behind him. Scott was shouting, "Here's Mr. Keel! Please let him through! It's Mr. Keel!"

The listless people parted just enough to allow Erik to pass. He broke through the edge of the crowd to a clearing in the center of the factory floor.

P.T. lay quiet, unmoving on the floor.

"Mr. Keel?" Michael Barris asked.

Erik looked up from the lumber that was P.T. "Yes, I'm Martin Keel."

"We need your help with a bit of a mystery. This man"—Michael's hand indicated the body—"died last night, leaving a note to you. My son, Jason, suggested that we have you come."

"A note? To me? I hardly know the loon."

"Nevertheless, we're hoping you can help us." Michael offered a piece of paper to Erik.

Erik felt suddenly old and very tired as he read.

Dear Newhouse;

This is my triumph! My redemption is complete!

This I leave behind as my Immortal.

Please give my creation to the hands of Martin Keel. He will know what to do with it, if he will. He knows its rightful owner. Tell him we can be the sum of our strengths; not our weaknesses. Tell him we can be one people.

Erik looked up, questioning. "What's all this about?"

Michael stepped aside, revealing behind him a frame atop a worktable.

Erik gasped.

Cradled in the work frame was a violin.

Not a perfect violin. The wood choice had been limited by necessity, and there weren't proper lacquers to finish it properly. Erik's eyes followed the curve of the soundboard around its delicately finished waist. The scroll at the head of the neck was exquisite. It was an impossible thing of beauty in a place where it could never be.

Erik barely heard Michael's voice from a great distance behind him. "The inscription on the back says 'To Erik Simms from Ernest Henderson.' Do you know Erik Simms? Is he in this camp?"

Erik reached down and picked up the bow. The screw mechanism was unorthodox but ingenious. His hands tightened the hair of the bow without thinking. "Erik Simms?" he said flatly. "Erik Simms is a subversive and a revolutionary. Erik Simms is wanted for treason."

Michael's voice took on a strange quality. "Erik Simms was the greatest violinist of our age and a brilliant conductor. I heard him once in San Francisco. His touch was exquisite."

Unbidden, Erik's left hand reached for the instrument, lifting it gently from its cradle. Some part of his mind screamed at the danger that this represented to him. The chin rest flashed upward. The cool wood spoke to Erik, beckoned him on. He plucked at the strings, tuning.

"You know," Michael spoke, filling the awkward void, "P.T. came to me a few days ago demanding violin strings, saying something about there not being any cats around here for him to gut. I wondered at the time what he could possibly want with . . ." Michael suddenly quieted.

The bow was raised.

The violin was unforgiving and Erik's technique had rusted some over time, yet the sweet gentleness that floated out from it filled the room and souls within it. Erik's hands, body, and spirit moved to the stroking of the strings, first tentatively then with growing confidence into the first movement of the concerto he had written for that terrible night so many lifetimes ago. The music soared again, its triumph and tragedy, pain and sorrow again passing through the bow to the strings and into the air in voiced agony and hope. For ten minutes Erik's music had voice once more. Men wept openly, unashamed. Women closed their eyes against the joy too exquisite to express. Erik, too, wept, burning on the altar of those strings the fear and hatred he had clung to as if it were life itself.

At last the final, soft, subtle note drifted through the room. A silence more wonderful than all the applause he had ever heard was his alone to cherish. He looked through his tear-blurred vision at the faces before him. They had sat on the floor at his feet, unable to continue standing under the emotion that he had invoked in them. Their eyes were yearning for what he offered them. They judged him by his work and embraced him. They were not the others "across the line" any longer. For him, the line vanished.

Erik swallowed then spoke, loudly and clearly into the silence. "I . . . I am Erik Simms."

Suddenly, the noise was unbelievable. The silence broken by his own voice, the crowd erupted into a roaring, rolling, majestic cacophony of applause, shouts, and screams. It was joy unbounded. It was hope for a place that their souls had forgotten existed. Erik had forgotten that music was his life. In that moment, Erik lived again.

In the Milford Command Center, one set of ears heard the concert without joy.

"Lieutenant, get me in touch with Weston over in Newhouse. I think we now know why Barris came to Newhouse."

Sappers and Spelunkers

33

Saturday, May 8, 2010 / 1035 hrs
Newhouse Center / 477th ERIS District
Wah Wah Valley, West Beaver County, Utah

"Reverend Weston, is there anyone else listening?"

"No, Overlord, there's no one else here."

"It has come to our attention that Erik Simms, a man convicted of treason against the government of the United States and murder, among a host of other charges, is, in fact, living in your camp under the assumed name of Martin Keel."

"Wonderful, sir! I guess you can stop looking for him, then, can't you."

"Yes. Of course we'll stop looking for him! The difficulty is that I believe Mr. Barris may have come into the camp in an attempt to break this very dangerous person out. Find out what Barris is up to before things get any more bollixed up than they already are!"

"I'd like to point out, Overlord, that the incidence of violence in our community has dropped sharply over the last few weeks, thanks, I think, to our new recreation programs. I can handle Barris. Things here are far better than I think you are informed."

"Cheyenne only takes so many patients, Reverend. There are two pallets that will be making the rounds. One comes through on

Thursday and the other Friday. There's one slot open on the Thursday pallet—feel free to use that as you see fit. Get me the information I need, and the slot on the Friday pallet is yours. We're perfectly clear on this, aren't we?"

"Yes, sir. Perfectly."

"Find out what Barris is up to; stop him and you might just live through this."

The small bunk room was packed with people. Michael wondered, even so, if it would be enough to accomplish what he had in mind. Some present were fanatic about his ideas, others were less than enthusiastic but had the skills Michael needed. He would have preferred a little more cohesiveness to his team but there wasn't enough time for that.

"Ladies, gentlemen . . . Immortals . . ."

A series of chuckles drifted through the room.

"Here then," Michael said as he sat in the center of the floor, "is what I have in mind. You're all basically familiar with the plan. We create a message in a bottle, a time capsule as it were, of the best that is in us. Each person who participates contributes freely those things that they feel would best represent them after we are gone. P.T. finished his, and his gift brought us together in ways that we might not have thought possible."

Erik Simms, kneeling behind where Michael sat, nodded. "He brought us back to life."

Michael smiled gently. "As did your gifts, Erik."

Erik smiled warmly back.

"Now, Carl, how are things progressing with our little crafts project?"

Carl Emmett leaned against the bunk with several others standing between him and Michael. He gazed off through the window in the small room.

"Carl?"

"Right! Sorry," Carl said, his mind coming back into the room. "Every person has been interviewed by the assigned 'crafts councillors' and has chosen their project. Warehouse 1 contains the paper, pens, pencils, and a few specialized items for those projects. It also secures the woodworking tools. Those are kept under constant guard. The woodworking itself is all done in Warehouse 2 during the day while the 'Diversion Squad' keeps the reverend and his bulls busy."

"How are the projects coming?" Michael looked up at Carl.

"We have a number completed. A number of them were started by people in the camp who have since 'crashed out.' Their projects, no matter how far along they are, are stored in Warehouse 3 with the works that are completed. We understand that many of the projects people have chosen are rather ambitious despite our efforts to dissuade people from complex things. Many of those will also not see completion, but it's what the people want. A few have finished their projects—without exception, they have started second projects to add to the tomb."

"What kinds of things are we getting?" asked Jason, who sat cross-legged next to his father.

"You name it, we're getting it," Emmett said. "Mostly, life histories and testaments. We've got about a thousand poems in development and a like number of woodcrafts. That reminds me, there's been a few fights in Warehouse 2 over the shortage of carving tools. Is there anything we can do about that?"

"I'll check with my guardian angel later tonight and see," Michael said. "What else are they creating?"

"Well," Carl chuckled, "there are a number of people who are creating dances."

"Dances?"

"Yes, sir, the problem is that no one we've found knows how to write down a dance."

"Yes we do," Erik said. "Paul Quezada over in Block Z. He was a professional choreographer. I know that he's been working up his own performance dance to express himself and who he is. He's been using standard dance notation to write it down. I'm sure he'd be happy to help anyone else get their dance down on paper—he probably just isn't aware of the need. I'll talk to him."

"Great!" Michael said enthusiastically. "Yours truly has been working on a script for a play . . ."

Surprise bubbled through the room.

". . . What? Why are you people so surprised? Jake Belovich, believe it or not, is writing a cookbook under the title of *How to Feed Twelve Thousand People a Day on Hydroponics and Government Slop.* And we also have about two thousand or so really bad songs being written—including that violin hoedown we heard in the factory the other day."

The realization of what Carl was saying dawned on the group. They whooped and clapped their approval.

Erik just grinned. "You know, I never did write that music down. Thought this might be my last chance."

"Well," Donovan Murdock said, "it's about time!"

"Great"—Erik laughed—"just what I need—a mole with a musical ear!"

Donovan laughed along with the rest of the group. "Fine, you just let us groundhogs do our job." Then Donovan got serious. "Digging isn't the problem—the problem is dig to where?"

"Well," Michael said, "that's why we're here today. All the thoughts, dreams, and hopes we put on paper or into our crafts. None of it will survive if it stays here—it will burn right along with us. We seem in agreement that a tunnel may provide the only means of getting anything out of here, right?"

A ragged chorus of "Right!" rumbled around the room.

"So the question is—where do we put it that's close enough so as not to arouse ERIS yet is secure enough that we know it won't get fried. We have a few options . . ."

As if on cue, Sid handed a large piece of rolled-up butcher paper down from the door where he was standing. Michael unrolled it on the floor while several hands held the corners flat.

"This is Newhouse"—Michael swept his hand over the map not unlike a game show queen—"thanks to Sid's drafting skills. Warehouse 3 was chosen initially because of its proximity to the perimeter and the size of the building. Donovan's team dug a test tunnel to check some of our assumptions about the perimeter fence. Tell 'em what you found, Don."

Don pointed down to the map with a stick. "We angled a shaft down out of Warehouse 3, then leveled off at about ten feet down, shoring the sides all the way. We never did strike the fence projectors—we figure they must be just subsurface. After we went out about three hundred feet . . ."

David Yarrow had been an engineer. He was impressed. "You shored up a tunnel to three hundred feet in six days?"

"Well," Donovan hedged a little, "to tell the truth, it's not a proper tunnel—I mean, you couldn't like drive trains through it or anything. Fact is that the last hundred feet we had to find guys that were a lot less interested in eating than I am, if you get my drift. Anyway, we carved out enough room to go straight up and explore. Sure enough, we came out right between the first and second perimeter fence markers. It looks like the tunnel will work—if we have somewhere to tunnel to."

Meredith Jernigan spoke up. "My group has examined a couple of different sites from on top of the buildings." As Death Master, Meredith could pretty much go anywhere needed in the camp. "Closest to the warehouses are the old foundations we can see north of Gate Echo. The Death Trains pass by those on their way to the furnaces. Unfortunately, none of them appear to have much depth and probably aren't workable for your purposes. Much farther north, however, is a rather large foundation. Probably was a mill of some type."

Virgil spoke up. "That thar was the smelter. This whole she-bang was Sam Newhouse's idea 'round the turn o' the century or so. That thar smelter was supposed to preprocess ore from all them mines up on the peaks. Turned out to be mostly a stock fraud, and people pulled out. I been to that smelter. Them foundations are pretty damn deep and about four feet thick."

"The problem," Donovan said, his thick arms folded across his chest, "is the distance. We'd have maybe two weeks to dig that far, even with us working full shifts around the clock."

"Maybe we don't have to dig that far," Meredith interjected. "Maybe it's enough just to clear the fence and run the stuff over to the foundations above ground."

"What if we just bury the stuff underground?" Sid offered. "Just dig a hole, fill it up, and we're there."

"The problem is that we not only want the stuff to survive, Sid," Erik said, "but we also want it to be found later—and not by the 'hetties' over at ERIS."

"Say, what about your 'guardian angel,' Michael," David Yarrow said. "Couldn't he help us with the problem?"

"I tried that avenue. Sorry—no sale."

"Wait a minute," Jason said. "What about somewhere inside the camp? What about this thing?"

Jason pointed down on the map to the Com Tower.

"Look, it's the only permanent, cement structure in a camp made almost exclusively out of wood. It's not just that: have any of you noticed how the thing is slanted like a sundial toward the center of the camp? This thing is made *specifically* to survive the camp's destruction. If we can find the way inside—then perhaps we have a ready-made tomb for all our memories."

Michael nodded. "Donovan, how long would it take you to tunnel out of Warehouse 1 over to the Com Tower?"

"We would have to move the tools, but we could do it tonight."

"Very well," Michael said, getting painfully to his feet. "The smelter foundation looks like our best bet, but I think we should take a look at this Com Tower first."

In the end, it wasn't necessary to dig the tunnel to the Com Tower. Max Thurmond from Block T and Lucian Carver of Block X took a different approach. Max and Lucian had become friends of the most unlikely sort. Max was as straight a hetro as ever walked into the camp; Lucian was a raging queen of the first water. Two weeks ago, they stood on opposite sides of the line. Now the both of them found each other comical. It was a strange friendship to watch.

Max and Lucian had both cornered Donovan as he surveyed the Com Tower that evening.

"What's so fascinating, Don?" Max asked as both he and Lucian stood to either side of the former factory foreman and followed his gaze up the thirty-foot tower.

"I'm just pondering how to get inside this thing," Don said absently.

"Oh, honey, if you want someone inside," Lucian purred, "you gotta talk to someone who knows how! You thinking of going over or under, baby?"

"Well," Donovan chuckled. "I was thinking of going under."

"Ooh, messy!" Lucian squealed. "Oh, Maxwell, I don't suppose you've ever climbed something that *big* before, have you?"

"Give me some rope, you sissy faggot, and I can climb anything—anything except you." Max chuckled.

"Such brutish talk! Honestly, Donovan, I don't know how I stand to be around him! I'll bet you I can reach the top before the bully can!"

It took them thirty minutes to find a suitable grapple to throw. With a few lengths of rope from the rescue stations near the perimeter fence and a little effort, the two scaled the outer slope of the tower within a few minutes. Donovan didn't know until afterward that the cement to Max and Lucian's friendship was the fact that they were both experienced and fanatical free climbers.

"Excelsior!" Max shouted as he crested the top. He laughed at Lucian. "Hey, butterfly, you aren't floating so good."

"Don't piss me off, Maxwell," Lucian hissed with as much pique as he could muster. "I have had a very bad climb."

"Well, as long as you didn't ruin your nylons!"

Lucian got to the top as well. He'd have beaten the Macho Max if his sneakers had held on the concrete sides of the tower a little better. As it was he'd scraped his knees up pretty badly.

"Well, well, will you look at that!" Max examined the antenna platform. "These antenna aren't real, Lucian! The whole platform is hinged!"

"My, my!" Lucian smiled. "I think we may have stumbled on the secret prize, Maxwell, honey! Did you bring your little glow stick? I'd like to open the box and see what's inside, caramel nougat or peanuts!"

"Lieutenant! We have a Range Safety Alarm at Newhouse Center!"

"What is the alarm, Sergeant!"

"Rail outer shield trip, sir! Look's like the door is open."

"Try resetting the breaker, Sergeant. Those doors have been giving us trouble."

"Yes, sir! Breaker reset. Sir, the alarm is off."

"Thank you, Sergeant. Log the event and let's get on with the security sweeps."

"Yes, sir!"

Lucian stood on the rungs between the three rails that formed the shaft down the middle of the tower. He'd descended enough to allow Max to enter. Max was just above him, wiring the door alarm switch—a continuity contact—permanently shut.

"Keep your eyes peeled for other alarms, Lucian. We're in enemy territory now!" Max quickly closed the heavy steel door above them.

"Hey, Max, I can't see!"

"Sorry, sweetie, but my mother always told me to close the door behind me." Maxwell shook his glow stick and studied the bottom of the door. "A good thing, too, since the Feds probably have surveillance birds watching us, too. We probably don't have much time to explore before whoever was at the other end of that bell gets wise to us. Do you see anything down there?"

"Not yet, sugar!" Lucian tied the glow stick to his waist with his free hand. The support braces for the opposing rails were just like a ladder. "I'm gonna drop down here a little bit and see what there is to be seen!"

"Well, hurry up, will ya?" Max complained. "I feel like an ant that's just climbed into the barrel of a gun."

They both started their descent. Green light from the phosphorus sticks cast strange green shadows that bounced about them with their every move. They had passed down almost fifty feet by their reckoning when Lucian suddenly stopped.

"Oops!" Lucian said.

"What is it?" Max called down from above. "What have you found?"

"You may not believe this, Maxwell, but ol' Lucian just backed his butt onto the point of a bomb."

Max shifted rungs and moved downward, passing up Lucian, who had somehow gotten the crazy notion that if he moved again he might set off the device. Max had been in the army, and though he was certainly no munitions expert, he knew enough that the bomb was safe until activated. He could also read the stencil on the side of the device.

"The thing says, 'U.S. Army RLX-72 "Thorhammer": RG/G Nitromethane Alpha-6 FAE.' Oh, go ahead and move: it ain't gonna bite ya!"

Lucian sighed in relief, moved gingerly, and slipped down the other side of the device. "What does all that stuff mean that you just read?"

"It means that this baby is rail-launched, probably over our own camp. It will mirv little canisters of this nitromethane mix all overhead and then . . ."

"Yes, yes, and then?"

"Well, let's just say your makeup will be the least of your problems."

In the early hours of May 9, 2010, the ERIS camp known as Indian Queen was incinerated by FAE explosives as per the designated pattern. The light from the subsequent fires was witnessed by the Newhouse internees as a glow just over the northern horizon.

By Michael Barris's reckoning, only one more camp would be destroyed before it would be Newhouse's turn. Now it had happened . . . five days sooner than he had expected.

Twenty Pieces

Wednesday, May 12, 2010 / 1920 hrs
Newhouse Center / 477th ERIS District
Wah Wah Valley, West Beaver County, Utah

Michael looked out over the growing crowd in the Recreation Field with a feeling of accomplishment and joy. In the gathering dusk, most of what remained of the entire camp had turned out for the celebration and performance. Each group from all the barracks had selected a representative from among themselves to read, display, or perform their "craft" tonight. Even Weston had approved of the "talent show" as he called it. A clean diversion in the evening air.

Michael's thoughts saddened for a moment—a sadness of the loss of so many. Newhouse seemed spacious now, even empty in some respects. The actual population of the camp, by best estimates, was hovering just above six thousand, nearly half of that which it had originally held when Michael first arrived. He thought of those who had left them, abruptly, with unfinished remembrances and memories yet unexpressed. Oh, there were minor compensations. Those who had died had left an amazing number of bunks vacant. The timber from those bunks had been very quietly busted up and taken down into the tunnel to shore up the walls. So even the dead still participated in the salvation of their ideas and existence.

Now the tunnel was finished, even if the last hundred feet or so were barely large enough to crawl through, and they had barely cleared the last perimeter fence line. They planned to move all the materials into Warehouse 3 that night. The following night, around one o'clock Friday morning, they would make the big move outside the fence and to the smelter foundation over a hundred feet farther down the way. He could only trust that Kestrel would be the eyes on duty that night—and that he could look the other way long enough to secure their epitaph. All that remained then would be to send Virgil back out. Virgil, whose brow was unmarked and who knew the land. He was their best hope for recovery. He was still V-CIDS clear, despite having been in the camp these weeks. He would be the keeper of their memory, the guardian of their legacy.

"It's quite a night, isn't it?"

Michael turned to the sound of Olivia's voice. She stood next to him in the evening air. God had favored them with a warm day and a pleasant evening. The brilliant sunset over the mountains on the west side of the valley had thrilled everyone sitting on the Recreation Field. Olivia's face looked warm in its dying light.

"Yes, it's a brilliant night," Michael answered. "So, are you part of this evening's . . ."

"No," she said abruptly, looking down at the harshness of her own words. "Michael?"

"Yes, Olivia."

"We really are going to die here, aren't we?"

Michael thought for a moment. "Yes, Olivia, we really are going to die here. Did you check the results of my tests?"

"Yes, Michael, I did."

"And I take it that it no longer matters whether I die here or not, does it?"

"No, Michael—you've got it: you're V-CIDS positive now."

"Well," Michael sighed, "at least I'm in good company."

The evening breeze blew a silence between them in the twilight.

Olivia found her voice first. "So, who is in charge of this grand opera tonight?"

"Erik Simms—wouldn't you know it!" Michael shook his head. "The man spends months, literally, keeping a low profile under an assumed name and now, as soon as he claims his name as his own, he simply must be in front again!"

"That's leadership for you." Olivia nodded. "It's like a second skin to some people."

Michael smiled. Yes, he thought, I suppose this was the way things really were meant to work out. He'd come wanting to save these people, somehow, like some latter-day Oskar Schindler. He could only succeed in ways that he had never dreamed of. He would die with these people—his people—but know that they had at least done *something* to change the world while they were still here. Their memories and dreams would live on beyond Armageddon. They would be Immortal.

Some movement caught his eye. Donovan Murdock was running toward him, up the slope from the warehouse. His breath was coming in gulps.

"Mr. . . . Barris!" he gasped.

"Easy, Don, easy!" Michael held the big man's shoulders, half afraid that he might need the support. "Take it slow."

"Yes . . . sir!" Donovan gasped. "You . . . gotta come with . . . me. There's a . . . problem with the . . . in the . . . in the warehouse."

The dust still swirled in the air. Michael choked as he entered the great warehouse, waving his arm before him in a futile effort to clear the air.

"My God," Michael coughed, "what happened?"

"It caved," Murdock said, "we think about fifty feet in. It's a miracle the whole thing didn't go."

"What do you mean?"

"They've been cut—the main cross braces, that is," Murdock moved through the dust toward the tunnel entrance.

Michael wasn't sure he heard Murdock correctly. "Cut?"

"Yeah, someone's deliberately been slicing through the braces." The carefully built disguise in the entrance had been thrown open wide. They could both see dim light flashing back and forth through the dust in the entrance as Murdock continued. "The front nearly came down when we first went in. I told the crew to shore up as they move back."

"You sent someone in there?" Michael was incredulous. "Who?"

"That Yarrow fella's down there—so's Meredith."

"Why send 'em in at all?" Michael called out. He was having difficulty following Murdock into the tunnel.

" 'Cause we heard the son of a bitch screaming when we first got here. They must have cut a little too deep at some point, and the roof came down on them." There was a rage in Donovan Murdock's voice. "And I want to lay my hands on whoever did this."

The dust in the air was even thicker in the tunnel. Michael hacked, his eyes watering. He could hear the creaking of the wood around him as he moved, was aware of the cool mass of earth hanging over his head. He moved slowly, occasionally having to step over the cross-laid timbers and planks that had been set to temporarily stave off further collapse. The columns of light in the dust ahead of him were growing brighter, closer.

At last the ceiling failed utterly, and the maze of braces took on a hideous tangle. The dust-covered forms of David and Meredith were working at the base of a wall of rock, sand, and dust—gray figures in a gray world.

Between them, an arm and head protruded from the collapsed mass. Foam-churned blood wheezed from the open mouth while a matting of blood and dust caked the face.

It was Carl Emmett.

"NO! Let me GO! Let me OUT OF HERE!" Carl screamed at the top of his lungs.

Murdock and Yarrow pinned the raging man against the Hospice examination table. Sid moved quickly, tearing strips of cloth and securing Emmett's arms and legs to the heavy wooden bench. The man's right leg wobbled strangely as he struggled.

"Tie it up higher," Codgebury yelled to him. "Up where it isn't broken—around the thigh!"

Blood oozed from under Carl's shirt. The nurse tore open the shirt. Meredith, struggling to hold the man's head still, looked up into Donovan and David's suddenly blanched faces as they stared down into the gaping wound.

"You two going to be all right?" she asked.

Both nodded with a conviction neither of them felt.

Codgebury worked quickly, reciting to herself the litany of an emergency, since there was no one present who could act on her words. "Multiple abrasions; collapsed and punctured lung; congestion of the bronchial tubes; crushed ribs; massive abdominal wound; internal bleeding—my God, what a mess! Just what am I supposed to do . . ."

Erik Simms rushed into the room. "What's going on in here, Michael? Everyone is waiting and then . . . what is that?!"

Michael turned and pulled Erik back through the door. "Erik, we've got problems. I can't explain them all to you right now, but we've got to keep a lid on this for a while."

"Keep a lid on it?" Erik shook his head in disbelief. "Michael, the entire camp is just outside this building in the Rec Field *right now*! There probably isn't a camp in this valley that can't hear the screams of that guy! What am I supposed to tell them?"

"Tell them anything!" Michael said in a rush. "Tell them that there's been an accident—that much is true enough. Tell them that we're taking care of them as best we can."

"Tell them," Olivia said loud enough to carry across the man's screaming, "that the program will be delayed about an hour!"

"NO!" Carl screamed, "I'VE GOT TO LIVE!"

Michael moved toward the table, looking into the blood-caked face of the man. "Why? Why do you have to live?"

Carl looked up, blinking between Meredith's viselike grip. He began to cry, the tears washing dust in red rivers down around his ears. "Please!" he begged, his voice shaking, "they promised me! They promised I could go!"

Olivia called out, "Sid! Hold this cloth *right here* and don't let up. We've got to try to get the bleeding stopped!"

Michael's eyes held Carl's vision. "Go? Go where?"

Carl blinked. The blood loss had already been substantial. Carl was growing light-headed, his body preparing him for the last sleep he would ever know. "Got to catch the train," he said blankly. "I'm on the list for the train tonight. One o'clock. Just walk out the Main Gate, he says, climb aboard, and I'm on the train to Cheyenne!"

"Who says," Michael pressed closer to the hideous face. "Who says this?"

"Why the right holy reverend." Pink foam spilled from the side of Carl's mouth as he spoke. "Just a little favor, he says, nothing much." The man frowned, his eyes growing cold. "He says you're using us. You just want to escape with that Simms guy. Says you'll subvert the government and take over the country." Carl began to rave again, his voice a hideous screech. "Says you never gave a *shit* about me! Never gave a *shit* about any of us!"

Olivia shouted at Murdock and Yarrow. "Hold him down, damn it! He's bleeding again!"

"Big news man out for his scoop!" Carl ranted, the veins in his neck bulging from the strain. "Get this story, newsboy! I sold you for a ticket out of this death trap! You can die here with the rest of them, asshole! I'm the one who's leaving town! I'm the one—not—not—"

Carl suddenly convulsed. Black blood and vomit sprayed suddenly from his mouth as his back arched backward, straining against the cloth strips that held the contorting and rigid arms and legs. Meredith dived out of the way but there was nowhere to hide. The room was showered with the horrific fountain, covering everyone in the room. It gushed again and again.

Suddenly, it stopped.

Olivia turned, her face coated in the dark ichor.

"Crashed out," she said. "He must have been sick before he ever went into the tunnel."

"Well," Michael said, shaking his now bloody head, "I guess he won't be needing his ticket out of here."

Olivia turned suddenly at the comment. "No, but someone else might use it!"

Michael shook himself in disgust. The liquid covering his face felt cool. "What are you saying?"

"How do you think ERIS knows who they are opening the Main Gate for?" Olivia said urgently.

"Well," Michael replied, "probably the same way they know

who everyone in the camp is—the transponders they plant in everyone's forehead."

"Right! So, if we switched transponders . . ."

"Then," Michael finished, "whoever had Carl's transponder would go to Cheyenne. They'd enter the NIH medical program there."

"Yes," Olivia said, "they'd have a chance of surviving. You need someone to carry the knowledge of where the camp's epitaph can be found. Someone who can be trusted. I could put the transponder into your forehead. A little surgery and you can leave tonight on that one o'clock train!"

Michael shook his head slowly. "No, not me."

"Why not?" Olivia was getting frustrated and angry with the man. She had begun to care about him, and now he wouldn't let her save him. "Get out, Michael! Get out and live! Get out and remember for all of us!"

"Olivia," Michael said softly, "I can't. The people here still need me. I've got to see this thing through. Besides, I can't leave you here to die, and you can't perform the operation on yourself."

Michael Barris smiled suddenly, a single tear winding down his face.

"But I do have someone in mind."

Partings

Thursday, May 13, 2010 / 0035 hrs
Newhouse Center / 477th ERIS District
Wah Wah Valley, West Beaver County, Utah

"Good heavens, Brother Weber, when will this ever be over with?"

"I don't know, Reverend," Evan said sotto voce. "They were three hours late getting the thing started, and they said it might take three hours just to get through everyone. I suspect that the program is running late as it is."

"*Shhh!*" someone urged behind them. "I wanna hear this!"

Weston groaned inwardly but lapsed again into silence. The program was a botched job to be sure—typical of the type of thing one could expect from rabble. First they had started late—something about the Barris boy being badly injured. Now, wouldn't that just be too bad! The reverend had heard the screams from the Hospice. Eventually, they had quit. He guessed the little faggot had died—well, so be it, and the better for it, too! It serves that Barris man right to come and watch his son die after all he had done to destroy the peace and quiet of Weston's camp!

When they finally did get started—after Weston had to convince ERIS to turn on the Rec Field lights so that everyone could see—the program turned out to be just as bad as Weston had predicted: sentimental drivel and worrying about things that these people just hadn't learned to deal without. Home, love, family: what had these things to do with them in the camp? Survival, dedication, honor, commitment, virtue, patience, truth, and right—all the things that Quinton Weston had come to rely on—weren't present in the readings, songs, dramas, and poems set before him and all the camp to see. Worse yet were the queers and the dykes parading about publicly now and displaying their dubious talents. *Well,* he thought, *all of this will end soon. Before this week is out, he knew who would be victorious and whose right would prevail.*

If that weasel Emmett were going to be around tomorrow, he'd chew him out for the sick trash these people had been working on for the last few weeks. It didn't matter now. He'd gotten what he wanted from the little jerk, and now he was going to make good on his promise. It didn't matter now.

Weston looked at his watch: 12:43 A.M. *I really should make sure the snitch gets onto that pallet,* he thought. *Why is this taking so long?*

The barracks buildings stood in sharp relief against the bright glow from the Recreation Field. The sounds from the field occasionally rose with the applause and appreciation of the audience in the distance. There light and warmth prevailed: an island of life in the darkness.

So it seemed from Block W. There the empty building at the far southern end had been cold for weeks, its former residents having either died or moved closer into the camp. The blue-gray walls looked down on the Main Gate with glass eyes like a skull, black and empty—yet not quite empty and not quite dead.

Michael shivered in the black doorway, gazing down the main entrance road of the camp. Block T was opposite him, its own windows now black as well. To the north he could see the sanitation unit—a building with no door that seemed to do its job without any help from the camp—as well as the holding tanks for the effluent. Michael had often wondered about those tanks. They were never emptied, so far as anyone could remember. It wasn't until recently that he realized they didn't need to be. Those tanks were probably just large enough to last for six months. They were probably near capacity right now. *When the crapper is full, then pull the plug. What a way to run a town,* Michael thought.

He glanced to the south. Near him were the twin spikes of the Main Gate, plastic posts rising straight up from the ground that marked the ends of the gate segment of the fence. Every post flared slightly at the top with a barbed-wire ring to discourage climbers even though the poles themselves were in the negative gravity fence and you would be airborne before you ever reached them. It made them look fearsome, if impractical, which must have been the point. At the very pinnacle of the slim pair of minarets were rotating lights: the twin signs in the heavens that the gates were open. Beyond the gate of the Perimeter One, as everyone knew it, were two more pairs of spindly towers to pass the outer two perimeters as well. Michael could barely make out these sentinels. Beyond that, the rolling darkness of the valley floor swept into the distance marked only by the sagebrush, so far as he could tell.

"Where is that damn pallet train!" Michael muttered to himself.

Weston squirmed. His backside hurt from having it planted on the ground so long. Why had that Murdock fellow insisted that he sit right up front. It was an embarrassment, trying to give some stamp of sanction to the entire proceedings, he thought.

With the roaring applause and shouts at the end of yet another in an endless string of recitations, Weston stood up. He began walking in front of the seated crowd, motioning for Evan Weber to stand and follow him. The performer took her bow but, noticing the movement of Reverend Weston, quickly relinquished the performance ground.

"Brothers and Sisters of Newhouse!" Erik shouted as he took his cue and rushed forward onto the stage, his eye on the reverend. "I give you *Quinton Weston!*"

The reverend stopped and turned suddenly at the shouting of his name. Applause burst on cue from thousands in the audience. The sound confused and flattered him.

Erik, looking for all the world like a game show host, applauded politely and smiled with as many teeth as possible. "Reverend Weston! On this wonderful night, could you give us a few words of encouragement?"

"No, I . . . I really must be going. I . . ."

"Oh, please, Reverend!" Erik begged with all the snake oil he could find within him. *Get your fat ass up here, you Fascist bastard!* he thought to himself. *I haven't dragged this thing out just so you could leave at the wrong time!* Erik smiled harder. "It would mean so much to the people in the camp if you would just say a few words. Just a few?"

Evan grabbed the reverend's arm, speaking harshly into his ear. "Reverend! This could be part of Barris's plan! This could be the moment they try to spring Simms!"

"But Simms is right here!" Weston replied. "Look, bring your men in and keep watch on Simms. We'll see who gets away and who doesn't!"

Michael saw them. Three figures emerging from around the corner of Block V, all in a line abreast. The center figure sagged between them, his two companions supporting him as they moved down the road.

Michael stepped into the road as they approached the inner gate. "Did everything go well?"

"Well as you might expect for a minor surgery without anesthetic," Sid said. "We tied him down and bridled him so he didn't make much noise."

"He took it well, Michael," Lucian said on the other side, his voice remarkably quiet. "He's just a little weak is all."

"Weak won't do if he can't make it to the pallets himself. If either of you help him out, the perimeter monitors will pick up your transponders as an unauthorized egress and blow the whistle on us. If I take him out, the gates will let me out but never let me back in."

"That sounds good," Sid suggested.

"It would be," Michael said, "right up to the point where they found me wandering outside and started snooping around. No, he's gonna have to make the last few yards on his own."

Michael reached over and tilted the head back. The bandage on the forehead was bleeding slightly but was beginning to look as though it would stop.

"Jason—can you hear me?"

The eyelids of Jason Barris fluttered open. "Dad?"

"Yes, son. There's not much time, my boy."

"Dad, please don't make me go."

"You've got to, son! The NIH isn't run by ERIS. There's a good chance you'll survive there. If you do, you have to return. Return and find Virgil, we'll get him out and he will help you."

"Return to the tomb?" Jason said, unsure of his own words.

"Yes. Return and bring us home, son."

Jason repeated it. "Bring you home, Dad."

"Right! Now, what do you tell them about that wound to your head?

Jason thought hard. "Wound on my forehead. Some people in the camp found out I was leaving. They tried to steal it from me, but I killed them before they could take it."

Michael sighed. "Yes, son, that's right. Who are you?"

"Who am I?" Jason replied, sounding like he needed a thousand years of sleep. "I am . . . I am Carl Emmett, the camp morale officer from Newhouse."

"Yes, son. Do you think you can make it?"

"Got to," he said groggily.

Jason tried to stand, but his feet slipped out from under him.

". . . a fine effort on everyone's part. You have certainly shown us the spirit of this community and Newhouse's collective determination to see the job through."

Erik Simms stood to the side of the performance area. No fewer than eight of Weber's security men plus Weber himself were standing around him to make sure that he didn't go anywhere. Erik smiled at the thought but was concerned. The reverend's speech was winding down too quickly.

"And so, in conclusion . . ."

The lights atop the inner gate suddenly rotated into life. The light swung around the four men standing at the gate. Their beams illuminated intermittently the road beyond the outer gate—and a single pallet on which several figures sat.

"There's no more time. Son, this is it. You have to go now."

Jason stood shakily. "Dad, please don't make me go. Please don't make me leave you."

"Jason!" Michael took his boy by both shoulders, looking him hard in the eyes. "Jason, you have to leave me. You are my son! No matter what else happened in your life, no matter how different we are, you are my hope, my future! I promised to remember Amanda! I promised to remember you! Now, go, boy! Go and remember us all!"

Sid looked anxiously behind him. "Mike! Hurry!"

"Remember one last thing, son! Remember that I loved you. Now, hurry! Go!"

Michael pushed his staggering son toward the inner gate.

Weston glanced at his watch: 1:00 A.M.

"Thank you all and good night!" the reverend said abruptly, and turned to leave.

Erik dashed from between the security men to Weston's side, grabbing the elder man's arm and swinging him again to face the audience.

"Let's have a big hand for Reverend Weston!" he shouted.

Jason tottered toward the open gate as Michael, Sid, and Lucian watched. The rotating lights continued, waiting and watching for the chosen one to pass between them.

"What happens if the implant doesn't take?" Sid asked.

"What are you saying?" Michael muttered.

"I'm saying that those sentinel towers will probably check that transponder code," the barracks supervisor said. "If the nurse didn't put it back right, they may smell something fishy and do something about it."

Michael took in a series of shallow breaths. He remembered the woman on the road coming in. The explosion of her face. The sound following afterward. He could feel the sights in the mountains, watching, waiting, hoping for some excuse to release all the training and preparation into one cataclysmic act.

Jason, his legs wobbly, stumbled across the inner gate. He picked himself up and walked hunched over toward the second gate.

The lights on the inner perimeter gate died suddenly.

Michael held his breath.

The clearance lights on the second perimeter sprang to life.

Lucian let out a long breath. "Open Sesame, baby!"

Behind them, in the distance, the camp was applauding wildly. Michael smiled. His son was leaving. He'd done what he had come to do—but had found a higher purpose still. Now he was staying to see it through while his son went back to the world to finish the job. It was the first thing he could remember them doing together—and they were doing it apart. Somehow, it all made sense.

Pounding feet sounded behind Michael. Sid pulled suddenly at Michael's and Lucian's arms. The three of them dashed for the empty barracks of Block W, diving into its shadows as the running men approached.

"Jesus!" Sid breathed.

Reverend Weston pounded, out of breath, to a stop just short of the inner gate. Weber and several of his security men stood next to him.

Michael glanced from Weston to his son. Jason had cleared the second perimeter. Its lights were already dying. The exterior was open.

Jason turned around, a black shape against the spinning lights of the gate.

"REMEMBER ME!" Jason yelled.

Michael dared not breathe.

"I WILL FOREVER LOVE AND REMEMBER YOU!"

Michael turned in horror in his hidden blackness to look at the reverend.

"Thanks, Carl!" Reverend Weston called out, waving pleasantly. "We won't forget you either!"

Jason turned and passed the gate. The lights stopped flashing, and the pallets carrying Jason and his new companions whispered quietly into the night.

Michael closed his eyes, listening to the reverend as he walked away down the road.

"Not a bad sort, that Emmett. I hope he has a nice trip."

As every Death Train leaves the camps, a sentry drone hovering over every camp inventories the transponder codes on the pallets before they go to the Ranch Station for disposal. So it was with some small interest that ERIS command noted the passing of Jason Lee Barris, son of Michael Albert Barris.

The remains were cremated at Ranch Station and then combined with the charred remains of the 2,173 other crematorium subjects from the Wah Wah ERIS Centers and shipped via the daily designated pallet train to be dumped at the disposal facility in Long Valley.

The reverend had a special condolence in mind for later in the day.

Groundhog Day

Friday, May 14, 2010 / 0732 hrs
Newhouse Center / 477th ERIS District
Wah Wah Valley, West Beaver County, Utah

The bowl of the sky was a brilliant blue. Morning had come clear with a gentle wind out of the southwest, bringing warmth across the valley and thawing the bones in the camp with its gentle life. Such changes in climate were not unknown to the valley. It was May, and weather hung in a wildly gyrating balance act of chaos, undecided as to whether spring should reign or the skiffs of snow, so cold you would swear the air itself had crystallized. Fate had taken a hand this morning, for the day dawned gloriously, gentle and warm.

Michael stretched at the main door of his barracks, taking the air in as one continuous sniff. "What a day, Virgil! What a day!"

"Yep," the cowboy said, his crumpled hat bent over, his eyes intent on something he was working over in his hands.

"Murdock should be about finished clearing the tunnel by now. We'll use the crafts period to move everything from Warehouse 1 through the day into Warehouse 3. By tonight, everything should be just about ready." Michael seemed unreasonably happy this morning for a condemned man. "You given any thought as to how you're gonna get this done?"

"Yep," Virgil said distractedly.

"Yep?" Michael repeated.

"Yep."

Michael shook his head. After all these weeks in the same bunk room with this tall man, Michael "Mr. Communication" Barris was still baffled by the unspoken codes of Virgil's speech.

"So, give!" Michael said. "What are you gonna do?"

Virgil looked up from his work, his eyes fixed into some place far beyond the sky. "Well, ol' Mister Fairfield fixed up a little wheelbarrow kind of a thing over at the wood shop that jes fits through that rabbit hole you dug. I reckon I can use that to haul most of the stuff over to that thar foundation. I'll cover it up, jes like you said, so's the rain and snow and stuff won't bother it much. Then I'll get my ass home and come back fer it when times is more cordial."

"Yes," Michael said, trying to find with his own eyes the vision that had so enraptured Virgil in the bright blue above. "Any thoughts on how you're going to get home?"

"Yep."

"How?"

"By not lettin' them som'bitches catch me."

Michael reflected. "Yeah, I guess that's as good a plan as any." He looked down at Virgil's hands. "What are you working on there, Cowboy?"

Virgil glanced sideways at Michael, then continued to work as he spoke. "Thar's someone in this here camp that didn't get no chance to put somethin' on your pile of memories. I jes figured that they needed remembering, too."

Michael suddenly recognized the corn-husk doll forming in Virgil's strong, agile hands.

" 'Course, she took hers with her—the Death Lady made sure of that. But this one is just the same, and I figured she'd want to go along for the ride, too."

Michael slapped a hand against Virgil's back, raising a small cloud of dust. "We're gonna miss you, Cowboy. We owe you a lot."

"I reckon you do," Virgil said, keeping his eyes averted, purposely not looking toward Michael's face.

Michael smiled. Maybe he understood the big man more than he thought. "I guess you're going to miss us, too."

Virgil began blinking his eyes quickly to clear them of the sudden, unwanted tears caused, no doubt, by the strong sunlight.

"Yep," he said, handing over the finished, perfect doll.

Michael whistled merrily with each step, ignoring the pain that was increasing in his joints. He had begun feeling the stiffness just two days earlier but had not considered until today that it might be a symptom of anything more than the amount of hard work he had pressed himself to do. The work was not yet done but close enough to completion that he didn't have to worry about the aches that were slowly taking over his limbs. "One more day," he told himself, "just one more day and we're all home free."

The paper box in his hands held the first of their treasure, their spirits, and their hope. Letters, manuscripts, songs, journals—all written with loving hands and without the supposed benefits of sound/word processors and electronic editors. They were imperfect and homegrown. They were alive in his hands. He could feel the love and craft against his chest.

In a few minutes, others would follow with similar cargo to be carried down the single line of escape from the confines of Newhouse Center. The tunnel was their umbilical cord to a life that lay beyond the perimeter fence, beyond the line of death that ERIS had drawn in the sand.

Michael hooked his foot around the bottom corner of the Warehouse 3 door and pulled it open far enough to allow him passage. Slivers of light streaked the floor from the gaps in the wall planks made by the slowly weathering wood. The back of the warehouse held the last of the dirt from the tunnel. Murdock and his group had apparently worked through the night as promised. There was considerable concern that the tunnel might have caved farther down the drift than they could clear. By dawn, however, word had reached him that the frames had held beyond a thirty-foot section of caved timbers and that the shaft was clear again. Although, Donovan wouldn't vouch for the elegance of the work they had done to shore up the caved region.

Michael staggered slightly under the weight of the box as he moved into the room. His brow slipped into a slight question as he looked about for a place to set the box down. The cover to the tunnel was again left open, the lights in the sloping access ramp shining down into the tunnel itself.

"Hey! Murdock! You left the door open again!"

Michael sensed movement in the shaft. There was no reply. He continued to cast about for a place to set the box, found a place at last where it looked like the ground was reasonably well packed and bent down with the heavy box.

"Murdock! Is that you?" Michael called over his shoulder. The lack of reply suddenly troubled him. "Murdock?"

A shadow moved toward him from the tunnel. Wispy white hair drifted in the light from behind him as though the figure moved through water. Flashing from the shadows were dark emerald eyes.

The apparition spoke from the depths of the earth. " 'God is jealous, and the Lord revengeth; the Lord revengeth, and is furious; the Lord will take vengeance on his adversaries, and he reserveth wrath for his enemies.' "

Reverend Quinton Weston approached like some terrible perversion of the dead rising from the grave. Michael stood, uncertain. After Carl's activities the night before, the Immortals had posted watches on the tunnel. Only now did he realize that the watch was not present.

"I've been waiting for you, Brother Barris," the reverend's smile dripped poison.

"What are you going to do?" Michael's voice was dry.

"What am I going to do?" The reverend's face was a mask of barely controlled contempt. " 'For the day of vengeance is in mine heart, and the year of my redeemed is come.' Your little game is over, Barris. There will be no escape for you now—not you or anyone else!"

"I never intended to escape," Michael said carefully.

" 'Never intended to escape' you say?" The reverend sneered. "Such a good little boy who is so wrongly accused! What, did you expect your escape to be some sort of accident? 'Oops, I escaped by accident through this tunnel I just happened to find! Oh, and look, Erik Simms, the most sought-after subversive in the United

States just happened to escape with me!' " Weston's face turned suddenly cold. "No, Mr. Barris, no one is leaving this camp to start a revolution!"

Michael snorted with astonishment. "What? That's what you think this is all about? Some pointless political revolution? You myopic, shortsighted, stupid . . ."

"I'm not blind or stupid, Barris!" The reverend's eyes flashed a brilliant green in the shattered light. "You have mocked all that is honest and good! You have trampled authority and consorted with all manor of harlots and sinners!"

"As did Christ." Michael set his jaw as he spoke.

"Christ did not incite riots, as you have!"

"No, He merely beat the living crap out of the money changers in the temple until they fled before him!"

Weston's face flushed bright red. "You mock the Holy Bible!"

"No, Reverend," Michael said. "I mock you."

"You are evil," Weston breathed.

"No, you are blind." Michael spat. "Where in you is the sweet peace of the carpenter's son you claim as your own? You use the words of Christ like a foil with which to cut an enemy to ribbons. You force those you fear to submit to you through intimidation and guilt. 'By their fruits ye shall know them,' He said. Well, I've seen your fruit, and it is a bitter and vile mouthful!"

"Blasphemy!" Weston shouted. He drew in a deep breath, suddenly rigid with the effort to control himself. At last, the tension flowed out of his body. "Nevertheless, I shall exact justice, and I shall put an end to you. Am I right in this, Brother Weber?"

Michael turned again to the tunnel. Evan Weber was walking out of it, his hand clasped around a small cylinder with a cross handle on the top. An electronic fuse.

"Oh, God, no!" Michael whispered.

"You aren't the only one who sends for unorthodox supplies," the reverend taunted.

Michael turned to the grinning, triumphant Weston. "Don't do this, Reverend! No one wants to escape—you yourself said there would be no where for anyone to go."

"Nice try, Mr. Barris, but I don't trust . . ."

"Wait!" Michael had suddenly remembered a piece he had

done on the Anaconda Mine explosions in '03. He began backing at right angles away from the entrance to the tunnel, his hands up submissively. "If it's me, then just take me! Kill me! I'm V-CIDS positive now—ask Codgebury, she'll tell you! I haven't got much longer with this flu I have coming on. Just—just let those people save some of their dreams! All those crafts, stories, and music they've been writing have been for this moment! All they ask is that they be allowed to put their dreams and memories out of harm's way! No one's mortal self is going beyond these walls— please, let them save something of their souls!"

"No," Weston said. "You talk well, but I don't trust you."

Michael's hands dropped. It wasn't until that moment that he realized he had been begging. " 'And fear not them which kill the body,' " Michael murmured, " 'but are not able to kill the soul: but rather fear him which is able to destroy both soul and body in hell.' "

"What?" Weston said absently.

"Matthew 10:28, Reverend. I'm surprised you haven't read it." Michael said sadly.

"Then perhaps you'll like this one, Mr. Barris," Weston rumbled. "It goes, 'Vengeance is mine, thus saith the Lord.' Destroy it, Brother Weber."

Michael dove for the ground, cupping his ears in both hands, his mouth wide open.

The old C-4 explosive in the canisters had begun to sweat a little from age and was barely stable yet did its job well. Four small canisters had been tied by Evan Weber at even distances down the tunnel. ERIS command had given the security chief adequate instructions as to how to set, wire, and arm the charges. It had all seemed very simple.

Unfortunately for Evan Weber, he was smart but not experienced. He expected the blasts to be neat, little things like in the holo/vids where a little smoke and a little flash cause just as much damage as you think you need. He was wrong.

Explosions expand air. It is the force of this expansion that does the damage. When an explosion goes off in the open air, it radiates out until the force dissipates into the atmosphere.

Long ago, however, miners discovered that explosions underground were a different story. The blast has two possible directions underground: either shattering some rock face as it should or following the earlier path through the open tunnels. Blasts underground do their job, but mostly they shoot straight back up the shaft.

In the case of Murdock's tunnel, the side expansion forces of the four simultaneous blasts shattered the timbers and flexed the tunnel walls enough to achieve their purpose. The ceiling collapsed for the entire length of the tunnel.

But, like a cannon, the main force of the explosion shot up the tunnel—and into Warehouse 3.

Evan Weber's body stood at the entrance to the tunnel. In an instant, the force of four C-4 canisters blew rocks, splinters, and debris through him as though he barely existed. It picked up the riddled form and drove it with a roar of other jetsam through the south doors, shearing his limbs from his body in ragged gashes. Slivers rocketed through the air with him still as what was left of him slammed into the north wall of Barracks U-2 along with several hundred pounds of rock and wood moving at bullet speed. Evan Weber was beyond recognition—and would never care again.

The full impact of the blast had missed the reverend by a few feet, but it was enough. The old man had been picked up and thrown through the wall, which yielded only after his passage, and into the street with terrible force, bouncing against the hard ground arm and shoulder first. The brittle bones crushed at once from the impact, his upper arm and left shoulder becoming a useless gelatin mass in the moment. His eardrums were shattered as well, blood pouring from them. There he lay screaming incoherently.

Michael was deafened by the sound and shaken by the intensity of the blast. He crawled out through the dust and was wondering if he had lost his direction when he emerged into the light. Hacking out the dust coating his throat, he looked up. The south wall of Warehouse 3 was completely gone, its roof waving and creaking with the sudden loss of support.

Sid appeared next to him. "Barris, my God! What's going on?"

Michael shook Sid's hand loose from his shoulder and ran between the warehouses to their north side. Murdock, Jernigan, and several others began appearing with him, all staring to the north.

"It took us three weeks just to dig it." Murdock's voice was unsure and choked. "We've run out of time."

A wide, concave rut had appeared in the desert floor. It ran straight under the three perimeter lines toward a distant, almost invisible foundation.

The tunnel was forever gone.

Ghost Train

Friday, May 14, 2010 / 0750 hrs. and
Saturday, May 15, 2010 / 0400 hrs
Newhouse Center / 477th ERIS District
Wah Wah Valley, West Beaver County, Utah

David Yarrow summed it up. "Now what?"

Michael's hearing was slowly returning. He was still shaken but understood all the ramifications of the question. He turned to answer as best he could but was captured by a remarkable sight beyond Yarrow.

It was the entire camp. They had rushed to the warehouses at the sound of the blast—the adrenaline rush and fear from the initial explosion still bounding in their veins. Now, dazed and in shock, their collective hopes dashed, they stood gaping and listless.

"Brothers and sisters!"

Everyone, including Michael turned toward the sound.

Incredibly, Reverend Weston stood up.

His wispy white hair was matted red and slick against his balding pate. His body was twisted, like steel that had mangled in a vicious accident—strong but completely wrong in form. The left sleeve of his shirt was a crimson mash beginning at the neck. Weston used his right arm to hold the left forearm against his body. It looked as though that action was the only thing keeping the arm attached. The right eye had small shards of something protruding from a bloody mass that was difficult to look at.

It spoke.

"Brothers and sisters, stop him!"

Not *"help me,"* Michael thought incredibly.

"He is evil! He has lied to you! He has misled you!" Weston screamed the words, barely intelligible, as he twisted his body around to address the crowd gathering in a wide circle about him. "He was going to leave us! He was going to abandon us! He was going to escape!"

Someone picked up a charred rock. Then another.

Weston's good eye saw the motion. "He's got you confused, brothers and sisters! There's no salvation in this world for the rebellious! No immortality for those who question! Follow me and I shall lead you in the ways of righteousness! We can yet be victorious! We can . . . we can . . . we can yet . . ."

Ten hands. Hundreds of hands. All found shards of the mountain behind them. All eyes looked at Weston and saw his tomb.

Weston took it all in through the pain. "You fools!" he yelled, hoarsely through the liquid frothing in his mouth. "I am the power here! I hold your lives in my hands! You are wayward sheep! Sheep bleating to the call of this false shepherd! After all I have done for you! After all that I've given to you—do not turn on me now!"

A silence descended on the camp. In the distance above, a crow cawed.

"If there be any among you that is without sin," Weston sneered, "let them cast the first stone."

Miriam Barns stepped into the clearing around the minister. Weston had gotten around to giving her the news of her murdered husband two weeks before. Then she watched her sons both taken slowly by the flu. Each had died in her arms.

Miriam threw.

Her stone was badly thrown, striking the reverend in the chest. It bruised him slightly. A minor injury considering the reverend's other far more serious injuries at the time. Yet it was enough.

For her stone was followed by another. Then another. Then a cascade of stones.

Michael yelled for them to stop. Shoved. Pleaded. No one heard him nor paid him any notice.

Weston fell beneath the shower of stones. Soon all evidence of him disappeared under a small mountain of rock. Weston's tomb.

In the last moments left to him, the reverend gave thanks to God that he had endured the hardships and scorn of the world. With his last breath, Weston knew he had been right.

They gathered in the blown-out warehouse. The structure was hardly safe, but the chances were good that any optics bugs that had been planted there to spy on them would have been either fried or distorted in the blast. ERIS was watching always. About five thousand people needed to talk in private.

Michael stood, surveying the rubble-choked tunnel entrance. He didn't need to check with Murdock or anyone else for that matter. Even if they could clear the tunnel, the overhanging dirt would be so unstable as to make it impossible to shore up again.

When he turned around, he saw the entire camp staring at him. Waiting for him. Pleading silently with him.

They've chosen me, Michael realized. *They want me to save their memories. They want me to save their souls.*

Virgil stepped up. Of all people, his was everyone's voice. "Well, Mr. Barris, what the hell do we do now?"

Walk away, the voice within Michael said. *You are not the savior of these people. You owe them nothing.* Yet he knew that he did owe them. It was why he had come. He had watched the world unravel in a Babel of speed, misinformation, manipulation, and control that was an illusion at best. They were his penance. They were his own salvation as surely as he was theirs.

Michael turned to David Yarrow. "Dave! Find Murdock and anyone else that remains from the senior staff. Keep 'em quiet about this. If they want to cooperate or they're one of us, fine, tell them to keep their mouth shut about Weston. If not, lock 'em away. We've got to take control of the camp and we have to move quickly to do it. Lucian! Get some people together right now to help him."

David and Lucian began pulling people out of the crowd to help them.

"Everyone else, please!" Michael called out. "Please get back to your barracks. We have an alternate plan that will accomplish our goals. In an hour, someone will be by each of your barracks to explain the plan. Each of you will be crucial to its success, and your part will be explained to you then. Please! Get back to your barracks so that we can get our plan implemented. Virgil, Sid, Meredith—you stay with me."

Good Lord, Michael thought with a chill, *I sound just like Weston.*

The crowd slowly dispersed. Virgil shoved his hands deep into his Levi's and waited. Meredith folded her arms and looked away, her thoughts her own. Sid couldn't keep still. He bounced on the balls of his feet, his hands working nervously.

"Great!" Sid said, his breath short and his eyes twitchy. "So, like, you have this incredibly brilliant alternate plan to the tunnel."

"Well . . ." Michael said slowly.

"So what's the hour for?" Virgil asked lazily.

"To come up with the incredibly brilliant, alternate plan," Michael said.

"Oh, great!" Sid became even more agitated than he had already been. "You want to move, like, a couple of *tons* of paper and crafts out of here unnoticed, and you figure you've got less than a week to do it?"

Michael was getting irritated. "Look, there's got to be some way out of the camp!"

"Yep," Virgil said, "there sure is."

"What?"

"Die."

"Well now, that's very helpful, Cowboy, and thank you *very* much!" Sid's sarcasm had an hysterical edge to it. "Just what the hell is that supposed to mean?"

"Wait a minute," Meredith said. "The cowboy might have something. The food's stocked through next week. ERIS told the reverend that there wouldn't be any more food trains until the first of June. We can assume that's a lie, if your date holds true. And I was informed this morning that tomorrow morning would be the last Death Train for a few days."

"The last Death Train?" Sid said. The adrenaline was beginning to wear off and he was calming down. "What the hell do they expect us to do with the dead?"

"All I was told was that there were some scheduling problems, and that it would take a few days for them to straighten them out. In the meanwhile, I'm supposed to empty out the factory and use it as a temporary morgue." Meredith shrugged. "Just stack 'em like cordwood, they said."

Michael nodded. "Right. The factory's right in the center of the camp. It would be near the center of the blast—that only makes sense."

"So," Sid asked, turning back to Meredith, "what's your point?"

"My point is that tomorrow morning, a five-pallet train is supposed to leave the camp with our last shipment of dead," Meredith explained. "If we could somehow 'procure' one or two of the pallets out of the middle of that train—fool ERIS into thinking that the train was still intact—then perhaps the cowboy here could drive them up into the hills."

"Is that possible?" Michael was not yet convinced.

"Look," Meredith explained patiently. "These are government sleds they're using. They're built to government specs. That means that they are both made by the cheapest bidder and built with unnecessary redundancy. I've had plenty of opportunity to look at those pallets—every one of their A/G lift nodes has an emergency power backup connected to it. That's so that the whole sled won't dive for the ground when its main power and guidance get shut off. I'd be willing to bet that those backups are about five times more powerful than they need to be. Field redundant. When Uncle Sam wants to send his boys into some ground war in Australia, he wants to be sure his boys can keep going."

Virgil smiled. "I follow! If we could strip some of them other train cars . . ."

"Pallets," Michael corrected.

"Fair enough, then, . . . strip some of them other pallets of their power backups, unhitch a couple, and load 'em up, then I could ride 'em outta here when the gates open for the train."

"Whoa, Cowboy," Sid held up his hands. "What about transponders on the pallets themselves—let alone the dead? What about finding some way to steer these things even if we can get it to work? What if ERIS catches on to us before we're ready? There are so many different ways this could be fucked up . . ."

"Hey!" Virgil yelled, pointing his finger in warning at the building supervisor, "I warned you once about using that kind of language! Thars a lady present, and I won't abide such talk!"

Meredith giggled. "Why, thank you, Virgil. Death has rarely had such a compliment!"

Michael thought for a moment, his chin resting in his right hand, his shoulders slumping under an unseen weight. "Yes, it really may be our only other chance. Spread the word that we have another way to get our memories out of the camp, but that we will need everyone present at 0400 tomorrow morning to make it happen."

Meredith smiled. "I guess we really are going to let the dead bury the dead this time, aren't we?"

The colonel, otherwise known to the camps as Overlord, retired from the command post at 2230 hours. The Quartz Creek riots had started up again earlier in the day. The colonel had considered blowing the camp on the spot, but his attention was soon diverted by an urgent message from ERIS Central. Two armored infantry battalions had joined with revolutionary forces against the government positions in Vegas. Nellis Air Force Base remained secure while heavy armored fighting was reported along the southern end of the Strip. A call for government reinforcement and additional command and control had occupied the colonel through the day.

So it was that the colonel did not have opportunity to see how that "Weston fellow" in Newhouse had done with the little explosives he had sent him. He retired as soon as possible with a vow to ask about it first thing in the morning.

In the absolute darkness, the rotating lights marking the inner Main Gate at Newhouse sprang to life at 0100 hours. Beyond the outer markers, two pallets with V-CIDS internees paused on their trip to Cheyenne, Wyoming.

The inner gate lay open, its sensors tuned to the transponder signature of Quinton A. Weston.

Thirty minutes later, the gate shut automatically, and the pallets departed with no additional weight.

The long watch was half over. The captain with the code name of Kestrel leaned back in his chair, his feet up on the command console. It was a moment's break from the boredom of the watch. The coffee was hot and strong.

"Captain." The intercom rattled to life. "The body train is approaching Newhouse."

Kestrel rubbed his eyes, trying to rid them of the numbness and the fatigue. "Very good, Lieutenant, run the ingress autosequence on the Main Gate." He sipped judiciously at the edge of his cup. The monitor showed the motion of the five pallet transponders through the perimeter fences, each in sequence. The pallets continued into the compound under the direction of the Death Master in the camp. Usually, they stopped next to the sanitation plant, but tonight they moved farther down the line, finally coming to rest next to the warehouses.

"I wonder what that's all about," Kestrel muttered to himself. He reached forward and flicked on the infrared overlay.

It flared brilliantly into life. The entire camp was awake. Newhouse looked like someone had just kicked an anthill.

Every portable light in camp was shining, their panels aglow in concert to banish the deep night. Thousands of people scurried about the pallets, some carefully piling the night's dead—over two hundred of them—onto the first three of the pallets. Others, having formed a great human chain, were passing materials, journals, arts, crafts, and the sum of their existence, hand to hand, person to person, from the depths of Warehouse 1 to the trailing two pallets.

Now the dawn was beginning to show itself as a faint outline of the eastern peaks. Michael looked at his watch. They had less than half an hour to make this work.

"Max!" Michael called under the pallets. "Where are we with this thing?"

Max slid out from under the hovering flatbed of the pallet. "Virgil's been pulling the power packs from the forward sleds and tying them onto the rear two with whatever he can find. He's about done with that. Those packs should activate on their own when Virgil separates from the forward sleds. He won't do that until he's cleared the last gate—no sense wasting the batteries when ERIS will give us a ride."

"How does he drive it?" Michael asked.

"We've already disconnected the train controller from the front and moved it back here," Max said. "We can start the whole deal from here—enough to get it started toward the gate. ERIS takes it from there. Virgil just pulls the pin, and he should be able to steer it by sitting up on top. Me, my problem is a bit more difficult, so if you'll excuse me, I'd like to . . ."

"Why?" Michael was spooked. Every little thing looked like a disaster. "What's the problem?"

"No problem, boss." Max held up both hands as if to soothe Michael's fears. "The transponders on all of the pallets need to be moved. We're spacing them evenly—five transponders evenly covering the first three. We hope it'll be enough to fool whatever ERIS is monitoring with."

"Colonel!" The captain jumped up from his chair, his third cup of coffee sloshing hot onto his hand.

"As you were, Captain," the colonel said in a quiet voice.

The captain sat back down slowly. "Sir, we weren't expecting you until change of watch."

"I just couldn't sleep, Captain. Something was nagging at me, and I just had to wander down here and see who it was."

Who it was? The captain's awareness increased at once. "Sir, everything seems to be proceeding normally. Conditions, with the exceptions noted in the shift logs, are nominal. Those exceptions pose no threat to the integrity of this command, sir."

"Indeed, Captain," the colonel said with an almost distracted voice. "I would hope not. What is the current location of the NIH people that were picked out last night?"

The captain flicked a monitor to life and moused to the requested data. "Sir, they are currently approaching the Tooele Processing Center. They should be there in about five minutes."

"Show me on the board, Captain."

The large display map on the main wall monitor in the large room beyond them swept upward away from the valley until it encompassed the entire state. It then zoomed downward to show the location of the train.

"Tighter, Captain. I want to ID everyone on that railcar."

"Sir, I can give you the manifest—"

"If I want the damned manifest, Captain, I'll ask for it! Do it!"

The captain moved. The map leaped closer. Thirty-two names with indicator lines flashed on the screen.

"He's not there," the colonel muttered to himself. "Captain! Give me a location on Quinton Weston!"

The map pulled back far enough again to include both the train that was still selected, and a new indicator for "Weston, Q." The marker pointed to the Wah Wah Valley.

"Tighter, damn it, Captain. Tighter!"

They seemed to fall into the map. New details flashed into existence as the scale grew larger. The county, the valley, the camp. The indicator pointed to a spot just south of the warehouse buildings.

"He could be there to see the Death Train off," the captain offered.

The colonel didn't acknowledge the remark. "Does that drone maintain transponder logs?"

"Yes, sir!"

"Captain, plot a position trace for that transponder ID for the last hour." The colonel's face looked grim. They both watched the screen. Nothing changed. "That's all? Go back two hours."

"No change, sir."

"Six hours. Twelve hours!"

"Sorry, sir, the target is stationary."

The colonel shouted. "Stationary for twelve hours?" He reached for the console and hit the overlay mode active, then punched the I/R camera on-line.

The signal remained. No heat.

"The man's stone-cold dead." The colonel blinked at the swimming lights on the screen. "But the rest of the camp is a goddamned beehive! What the hell is going on in that camp?"

Michael grabbed Virgil by both shoulders. He needed the cowboy's attention. It was time.

"Virgil, we're all counting on you."

"Yes, sir, Mr. Barris, I know." Virgil was watching the last of the bodies being loaded onto his pallets. Blankets had been laid over the epitaph and bodies carefully set on top of that. Virgil would have to play dead for a while. "Do you think them bodies is necessary?"

"You have to look like a Death Train—at least until you get out the gate. Nurse Codgebury has taken the transponders for those people out of their heads and laid them on the first three pallets. That way, they can't trace you after you leave the track. After that, Virgil, cut loose and don't stop until you're in the hills. Find someplace safe to put our things."

"Yes, sir, I sure will, sir."

"One last thing you have to do, Virgil."

"Yes, sir?" Even the cowboy was nervous now.

"You gotta live."

"Oh, I intend to, damned right I do!"

"No," Michael said, looking into his eyes. "You *must* live. You're the only one who can bring us home."

"Yes, sir. I understand."

The lights on the inner Delta Gate began to rotate. The pallet train had already begun to move northward and out of the camp. Virgil shook Michael's hand and then bounded up onto the pallet.

A huge cheer rose from the crowd. Virgil waved, then lay down gingerly among the dead, their bodies covering the collection of the spirit of Newhouse and the Immortals.

The inner gate light stopped rotating. The Perimeter Two gate lights flashed as the gate opened. The pallet train moved through. One gate left.

* * *

"What have you done, Captain?"

The captain looked up in shock. "What have *I* done, sir?"

The colonel's face was uncomfortably close to the captain's. "I know all about those diverted supplies, Captain, and that little incident with the compound lights a few weeks ago. You've been playing fast and loose with me, mister, but now it's gone too far. I don't know what friends you think you have in that Newhouse Camp, but they won't help you now, boy! Who's on that train? Tell me!"

"Sir!" the captain bleated. "Dead people—just dead people so far as I know, sir!"

"Visual!" The colonel shouted through the intercom to the lieutenant in the situation room beyond. "Give me drone visual on Newhouse!"

The overhead shot appeared on a side monitor.

"Close-up of the pallet train!"

The pallet train leaped closer. Bodies covered five pallets. The outer gate had just opened. The pallets were leaving the last perimeter ring.

"Superimpose ID on the pallets."

The screen was suddenly jammed with two hundred and fifteen names.

All the indicators pointed to the first three pallets.

The colonel straightened up as he spoke. "Lieutenant, go to Omega on Newhouse."

"Yes, sir!" came the electronic voice.

"Colonel!" the captain cried out. "That camp isn't scheduled for termination until—"

"That camp," the colonel cut in, "is not going to trouble me anymore." The colonel pushed the intercom button. "Lieutenant, prepare to turn safeties key."

"Affirmative, sir."

"On my mark: three, two, one, turn!"

"We have a red light with safeties off on November-Charlie."

The cheering was still going on. The pallet train had just passed the outer gate when a loud bang was heard from the Com Tower.

Michael looked up. The cheering stopped.

A loud whump sound thundered through the camp. Michael's heart went suddenly cold. A large, dull green cigar-shaped casing leaped from the concrete tower, arching into the sky, heading to its carefully predetermined point five hundred feet directly over the center of the camp.

Talons

Saturday, May 15, 2010 / 0542 hrs
Newhouse Center / 477th ERIS District
Wah Wah Valley, West Beaver County, Utah

The great bullet shape curved darkly against the brilliant sky, its own bulk still shadowed by the mountains to the east. It was a sudden and terrifying death knell.

People screamed. The entire camp began to run. Nearly a quarter of them dashed headlong into the inner perimeter A/G fencing and were lifted into the air, the fence itself humming perceptively under the strain of levitating nearly a thousand souls. Others dashed into the camp itself, down its alleys or into its doors. Mindless panic gripped them all at once.

Michael simply watched in despair and fascination.

Where could he run?

The outer casing exploded away, exposing the inner mechanism. Stage one. The loud popping of an aerosol ejector was heard by everyone in the camp.

Olivia Codgebury was next to him. Michael sensed that she was kneeling. In those last moments, he wondered why he had never considered her particularly religious.

Michael held his breath and waited.

The great weapon, devoid of its shielding, began to tumble through the air. It somersaulted three times over, pitched downward, and with a terrible shattering of lumber and siding it demolished the communal toilet building in the center of Block J. It bounced there and continued through the west wall of Barracks J-16 where it lay hissing for some time.

Michael opened his eyes.

Nothing happened.

The only sound he heard was behind him. Max and Lucian were high-fiving each other and whooping to the clouds.

"Lieutenant! What the hell is happening!"

"Colonel, we have a launch confirmation from the tower, and the control circuits are confirming a detonation."

"THEN WHY IS NEWHOUSE STILL THERE!"

The lieutenant's life was flashing before his eyes. "Sir! There must have been a malfunction in the mechanism, sir!"

The colonel wheeled suddenly on the captain, who was still shaking. The older man grabbed Kestrel by his uniform tie and hauled him with a single hand up out of his seat. "This is *your* fault, Captain! You did this, you and your revolutionary friends!"

"Colonel!" The captain regained his own footing but only a portion of his own composure. "Surely, the colonel is not suggesting that anyone in this command would be able—let alone willing—to enter that camp and sabotage the destruct mechanism."

The colonel released the captain with a shove backward. "No, but that hasn't stopped you before from breaking protocol with that camp, has it! I've gone just about as far with you as my friendship with your old man allows. I think it may be time for a lesson."

The colonel turned back to the console, opening the intercom mike. "Lieutenant! Call the field and have them prep Angel 1 for immediate release. Tell them that the captain and I are personally coming down to take care of this one."

The captain straightened his tie. "Sir?"

"It's time to get in some flight time, son!"

* * *

"*Hoo-wee!* What a party!" Lucian was dancing in the street amid the stunned crowd. "Brothers and sisters! Working together! Payday, girl! It's payday!"

Max was no less enthusiastic. "Hot damn! We pulled it off, baby! All the way! Touchdown!"

Michael smiled with wonder. "What have you two been up to?"

"Just a little surgery, honey!" Lucian slapped Michael lightly on the shoulder. Then he reached down to pull Olivia up from the ground. "Oh, girl, we're sorry—we didn't mean to butt in on your racket!" Lucian laughed almost hysterically again.

"What?" Michael said.

"Well." Max smiled. "We couldn't kill the dog so we decided just to pull its teeth. Lucian and I have been climbing that tower for the last week—a little late-night recreation, you understand. We found the maintenance winch inside the tower, managed to get the shroud casing off in one piece, and started pulling the individual canisters out. We just finished two nights ago, and we weren't all that sure we got them all."

"Good Lord," Michael said, "you disarmed it? Where did you put the canisters?"

"Well, we've been sliding 'em under the reverend's house," Lucian explained. "We figured they'd be safe there."

Olivia smiled. "You two probably just soiled about half the underwear in this camp. I don't know whether to kill you or kiss you."

Michael shook his head. "There's going to be little time for either. If they pushed the button once, they'll find another way to push it again. Erik! Get some people organized to pull those people out of the fence! I'm going up to see what's happened to Virgil!"

The captain pulled the old A-10 in a steady turn to the west, leaving the wings into a steady ten-degree climb as the gear came up. The morning sun lit the San Francisco peaks ahead of him like fire, the sky beyond the HUD a clear and brilliant blue. The desert rolled quickly below him as he nosed down slightly and steadied the craft at 5,500 feet MSL, not clearing the ground below by more than 500 feet. Sagebrush and dry gullies flashed past him.

The A-10 was ancient. It was a thirty-year-old machine designed for a different time. It had been fitted with auxiliary A/G packs to give it vertical takeoff and landing—VTOL—capabilities, although just barely. The A/G packs were unstable in maintaining a launching or attack platform so the A-10 did its work the old-fashioned way: it flew to its target and destroyed it. The colonel might have preferred the late model A-21 Raptor with its coordinated attack and flight systems, but in his business you take whatever they give you. What he got was the A-10. Ungainly, ugly to the bone, it still sucked aviation fuel into its twin turbofans and delivered. This one was mounted with four sets of uprated Rockeye Mk 30/NGD Nul-gravity delayed cluster bombs, each bomb itself containing over two hundred small canisters essentially identical to the ones that should have exploded over Newhouse earlier that morning. Any pair of those bombs would devastate a camp quite effectively. Inboard of these were mounted two sets of six AGM-65A Maverick air to ground missiles. Television guided, these were for more precision work against moving ground targets. The A-10 was designed to kill things on the ground. It was still very good at its job.

"Angel 1: Level at 5-5," the captain called through the mask. Their A-10 had been a two-seater: a trainer. The captain turned his head as best he could with the helmet. "May I assume the target you have in mind, Colonel?"

"You know damn well where we're going, Captain!" the colonel replied from behind him, though the voice carried through the helmet intercom. "What's the time on target?"

"Time on target is ten minutes, sir, including the approach run," the captain replied coolly. He had entered the aircraft first but had nevertheless noticed the colonel enter the backseat sporting a 9mm sidearm. "I am electing to make my run on the target from the south." There was a pause. "Colonel . . . what's the rush in blowing this camp?"

"Open your eyes, Captain!" the colonel's voice rattled in the captain's helmet. "There's more at stake here than the lives of a few revolutionaries and perverts! There are people in this country who would like nothing better than to stop us now—people who don't have the vision or the sense of history or the downright guts to make it happen. We've heard what the people of this country want, boy, and we're going to give it to them!"

This has to end, the captain thought. *Somewhere this has to end.*

Michael emerged through the roof of the three-story known as Barracks 16-U. The shadow of the mountain he could clearly see cast halfway across the valley—the promise of warmth later under the afternoon sky.

Olivia Codgebury climbed into the open air after him, her voice filled with concern and excitement. "Where is he? Where is he?"

"There," Michael said. "There to the north."

From their vantage point, they could both see beyond the wreck of Warehouse 3 and the fence lines in the sand. The three pallets of the Death Train itself had turned westward and could be seen dropping down toward the Ranch and its constant pillars of furnace smoke.

Other movement, however, had caught Michael's eye.

Two pallets to the north. They moved eastward, up the slope, skimming the sage as they moved. In front of their piled burden, a lone figure stood, waving a broken straw cowboy hat in the air.

"Michael," Olivia said quietly behind him. "They're coming."

Michael turned, following her outstretched hand pointing to the south.

Some great, dark predator was crossing the sky.

"The problems of this country are vanishing," the colonel said. "Vanishing into the night and we're all part of that magical act. The people have spoken, Captain! The fabric of our moral society is being weakened, they cry: we eliminate the perverse among us. The poor are draining the resources of this great nation, they moan: we eliminate the poor. Think of it, Captain, a nation whose dross and refuse have been cleansed, purged, expurgated from among us. We pass through the fire, Captain, the impurities melting away in the bright light until all that is left is the strong, the moral, the driven. We are going to come out of this a nation of strength, boy, like the world has never seen.

"And make no mistake, Captain," the colonel ranted on, his words fast and excited in argument both with the silent captain and his own conscience, "this is not just a war of blood and bone, but a war of ideas. It's not enough that we purge our society of these weak individuals—we have to purge it of their misguided and weak ideas, thoughts and practices. They must not only be gone, but forgotten as well."

Captain Gregory Murrow knew in that moment that he could no longer live with such madness. He had been playing with the idea of taking his stand and knowing that it would be futile. He would die for his attempt and nothing would change. He had bent the rules as far as he could—which was not far enough—to help the people in the camps. Still they died and nothing had changed. Yet now he knew it was time to reclaim his humanity. He had to do something that would make a difference. He had to live long enough to make it happen.

Behind him, Captain Murrow knew, was his colonel, who was quite prepared to put an end to the captain's ability to do anything ever again. They had come out here to prove some point of sanity on the part of the colonel. Perhaps the colonel needed to prove it again to himself. In either case, Captain Murrow was getting an entirely different point.

"Now, Captain," the colonel said calmly, "you will be an instrument of that policy. The mission is as follows: you will drop one pair of the Rockeye Mk30s on Newhouse Center, setting detonation at 500 feet AGL directly over the Commons factory building. You will destroy the camp and all its occupants. Then you will hunt down the five death pallets and destroy them either with the AGM-65A's or the cannon."

"Colonel," Captain Murrow said, "I don't see how blowing up pallets of dead people . . ."

"Not a single virus must escape, Captain! Just one can infect the whole system."

"Are you talking about the disease, sir," Murrow asked, "or just men in general?" The captain didn't wait for the reply. He had cleared the Squaw Springs canyon and was already over the Antelope Springs Camp. He was so low that he could clearly see the people running in the camp. Men, children, women, all breathing and all dead. *Let the dead bury the dead.* He pulled the A-10 into a sharp right turn back toward the peaks and set up his attack run. "Time to intercept two minutes. A-G weapons select to Rockeye. Safeties off. CCIP in the HUD to active. We are beginning our run."

Captain Murrow pulled back on the stick, popping the aircraft up for the dive on the camp. As he did so, unnoticed by the colonel, Murrow reset the release proximity safeties to zero.

The great condor wings wheeled in the sky to the south, leveled and soared directly toward Michael and Olivia. The sound of the engines rumbled closer from across the valley.

"Where's Virgil?" Michael said.

"Nearly to the canyon, but I can still see him," Olivia answered. "Michael?"

"Yes?"

"We haven't always . . . I mean, we aren't . . . look, I'd just like someone to hold my hand."

Their fingers intertwined. They were real. They were alive.

"I'm set for a dive approach." The captain nosed the A-10 down sharply, blood rushing to his head, but at least he hoped the colonel behind him was taking it harder than he was. The ground tilted below them. Newhouse Center appeared in the heads-up display at the western foot of the mountain range. Up front, Murrow saw the death pallets crossing the valley toward the Ranch crematorium. His eye also caught movement up the canyon east of the camp. *See the man. See the man run. Go, man, go!* "Radar target lock. CCIP is operating."

"Captain?" The colonel was suspicious. The dive was steep.

Just play along for a few more seconds, Colonel. "Stand by for release. Three, two, one: mark!"

Murrow pickled the release on the HOTAS hand controller. The releases snapped open.

Murrow pressed the stick forward.

"Captain! You son of a bitch!" The colonel screamed behind him, fumbling for the duplicate controls in the back.

The captain countered the colonel's commands. He had only a moment to glance sideways. The bombs he had just released were drifting off either side of the A-10. He was flying down with them, his course and speed identical to their free fall. Murrow smiled. *It had to end. It had to end here—and it had to make a difference. Come with me, Colonel! Come with me and let us stand before the judgment bar of God together. I really want to be there with you.*

The 9mm bullet exploded the back of his brain, but it was too late. The A-10 and its formation of cluster bombs were already passing the 500-foot level. Murrow didn't get to enjoy the sights the colonel saw: the A-10 ripping past the suddenly decelerating bombs while the casings exploded around him.

A single, merciless instant.

Erik Simms missed his violin. He had placed it with care atop the pallet just before it had left. He had sent his life with it, and now he felt hollow and alone.

He had watched Michael and a few others hurry into 16-U, but he didn't follow. For him, it was done—finished. There was nothing left to say, nothing left to do, no music remaining to be heard. It worked or it didn't.

So resigned, he turned instead and wandered into Block Y coming at last to stand in the center of his barracks—the court of the Dark Queen. The building was deserted now. Erik sat on the floor in the single shaft of light pierced by the darkness from high overhead. So many friends gone. Such a waste of time and energy. Yet even now he knew that it had been a life well lived.

In the silence, he thought he heard a gentle, familiar voice. For a moment, he knew that he was not alone.

"Martin?" he called out.

Then the distant rumble intruded on his thoughts. They are coming, Erik thought. It is finished. He slowly closed his eyes and waited.

A single, merciless instant.

Sid Jarolscowitz's nose was bleeding, and he couldn't stop it.

Worse, his heart had begun to race. He knew his blood pressure must have shot up through the roof. The V-CIDS was taking him, right here and now. He dropped down on all fours, trying to catch his breath.

Suddenly, it made him angry. To have lived through so much and to be conquered by the disease short of everyone else in the camp. He saw himself stumbling just yards short of the marathon's finish line, which he used to love running in another life—that life before the camps. He saw himself fall and watch the other runners pass him as he lay there helpless on the ground.

Sid was a runner. He wouldn't just lie here and die. In agonizing pain he stood up, blood streaming from his nostrils, and took a step into the Rec Field. Another step, then another, each more sure than the step before. He would cross the finish line. He would finish the race. He threw his arms high in victory, his face turned upward to the sky, his eyes wide open to the huge shadow falling directly toward him.

A single, merciless instant.

David Yarrow could hear the screaming roar overhead, but his attention was elsewhere. Not ten feet from him, a four-year-old boy stood crying and alone in the wailing crowd. David knelt down, smiled at him, and opened his arms wide. The boy smiled, too, tottering toward him happily. Both were oblivious to the fury descending on them from above. David's soul soared. His last act, he knew, would be one of kindness.

A single, merciless instant.

Meredith Jernigan couldn't stop crying. After all the weeks she had moved through the camp, quietly and dispassionately collecting the dead, the sight of the living in their last moments moved her. The tears were hot, coming with a wailing despair from deep within her that carried all the feelings she had never allowed herself to express.

Death looked on the camp and wept.

A single, merciless instant.

Olivia turned to Michael on the roof of 16-U.

"Did you know that I put a poem on that train?"

Michael turned to face her, smiling. "You? An Immortal?"

She smiled at him shyly. "I guess so."

The roar overhead was rapidly coming closer.

"Tell it to me," Michael said, looking into her eyes, still holding her hand.

Nurse Codgebury smiled back and began reciting:

> *Withering traces of my wood, my lumber*
> *Here in the soul-soaked dust*
> *I lay with brothers, sisters bones*
> *Confused and lost.*
> *Home, thou hast forsaken me*
> *But Immortals we, our minds live on.*
> *Here in the soul-soaked . . .*

Michael never heard the end of the poem.

A single, merciless instant.

The A-10 passed the falling Rockeyes, leaving the area clear for their dispersal of cluster bombs. The casings blew apart then scattered canisters over the area of the compound. The weapons were general-purpose weapons, not carefully calculated for the specific target like the ground-launched FAEs in the towers. These weapons were prudent. They covered a larger area than the camp.

That would have been sufficient, but the unfeeling gasses that dispersed suddenly had much more to work on than just the usual wood and flesh. The A-10 had not even reached the ground before the fire spark ignited the volatile mass that the atmosphere had become. The fuel and weapons stores of the four remaining Rockeyes, still in their mounts, as well as the warheads and propellants of the six Maverick missiles liberated their energy into the reaction mass as well. As the buildings collapsed and the population was crushed beyond recognition, the canisters that Lucian and Max had so carefully removed were liberated as well.

The footprint of the explosion extended a full half mile beyond the boundaries of the camp, the earth itself raised into a hellish maelstrom. Even the concrete tower, designed specifically to withstand the destruction forces of the camp, crumbled under the chaos that was suddenly unleashed. In a merciful, merciless instant—Michael Barris and Olivia Codgebury holding hands on the rooftop, Sid Jarolscowitz smiling as he raised both fists to the sky, David Yarrow comforting a small boy in his last moments, and Erik Simms slowly closing his eyes against the inevitable—all ceased to exist with such force that even their bones were gelled into an unrecognizable mass boiling away in the calculated heat of the incendiaries.

The A-10 never hit the ground. Captain Gregory Murrow would have found it glorious.

In the foothills of the San Francisco Range, far from the eyes of man, Virgil Johnston cried like a baby.

The destruction in Newhouse Center was outside the established norms for the camps. It would take an additional two weeks to rebuild the abort tower, turn the ground, grade it, tamp it, and reset the perimeter fences and power conduits. The usual week would then follow where the buildings, prefabricated in the continuously operating factory just west of Milford, would be levitated into place, clean, fresh, and new.

It was projected that, since the camp was blown early, it would be fully operational again by the first of June—right on schedule.

No change was required in the scheduled flow of internees to the other camps.

Ferrets

Wednesday, May 19, 2010 / 2130 hrs
195 North 2nd West / ERIS District 6
Beaver City, Beaver County, Utah

The banging at the door was insistent. Quietly insistent. Jefferson Kendall told the video to pause and got up from the overstuffed rocker in the front room.

"Now, who could that be at this hour?" Lynnellen Kendall called out from the kitchen. She was punching bread down by hand in the kitchen. It was late, but the smells of baking bread were comforting to Jeff. If Lynnellen had it in her mind to do serious baking for the Relief Society, then there was a good chance that she would make some thick noodles and chicken soup. It was one of the things that Jeff most looked forward to in life.

Jeff passed out of the living room and through the dining room to get to the small alcove that served as their entry. The architecture was a bit strange: the house had been remodeled several times over its long life even to the extent that a second floor had been removed from the top while other rooms were added where porches used to be. There was even one bedroom in the back of the house that could only be entered by going through one of two other bedrooms. It didn't bother Jeff—the house had belonged to the town banker for many years. Now it was Jeff's. He'd built quite a nice barn in the field out back, despite it being close to the center of town. Jefferson guessed that he didn't have any more sense of design than anyone who had lived in the home before. It didn't matter. Design was nice, but practical was better. "Don't bother, Lynnie," he called affectionately to his wife, "I'll get it."

Jefferson looked through the small glass window in the old-fashioned door.

"Oh, Lordy!" he whispered to himself. "Virgil!"

Jeff twisted the brass knob on the dead bolt. It was all the invitation Virgil needed. The cowboy pushed the door open in a rush, tripping on the stoop and spinning into the dining room. Jeff grabbed him by the shoulders, trying to look into the man's face. Virgil wouldn't hold still: he was as nervous as a cat full of coffee.

"Please, President Kendall!" Virgil was as close to begging as Jeff had ever seen him. "You gotta help me!"

"Hold on, there, son! Quiet down!" Jeff continued to hang on to Virgil. The cowboy had called Jeff "President Kendall"—not uncommon in these parts. As leader of the LDS Stake in Beaver, his title was president. It was considered by most folk in town a more important and certainly higher calling than that of merely "mayor." Most folk, for that matter, would call him Jeff before they would even mention the word mayor. Virgil, when he deigned to call him anything at all, would simply use Jeff.

Yet Virgil had called him President Kendall and in doing so had passed a subtle code between them. *I am one of you. We are of one church. We are of one community—and I am appealing to you for help by cashing in on that oneness between us that no outsider can understand.*

"Jeff?" floated a voice from the kitchen. "What's wrong?" Lynnie.

Jeff looked quickly over Virgil's shoulder. Lynnellen was still too intent on her bread to actually turn around from her work. Her back was to them. *Thank the Lord,* Jeff thought, then said, "Nothing much, Lynnie, just an interview I'd forgotten. I'll take it in my office." As stake president, one of the most pressing things

Jeff did was to take care of a constant stream of one-on-one interviews with people regarding everything from asking folks to accept a religious calling to be bishop of one of the local wards to
dealing with the moral transgressions of Sister Marybell Kincade's
wayward daughter. There were so many interviews to be done that
he was grateful that the mayor job didn't take up much of his
time—at least until recently. The lines between church and state in
Beaver had never been an issue for most people—they preferred
church to *be* state. Jeff was beginning to wish that things were a
bit more clearly divided.

"Virgil, get yourself through the door on the other side of the
living room. Sit down there and wait for me . . ."

Virgil shook his head vigorously, his eyes wide. "You don't understand, President, they're—"

"Virgil!" Jeff said, his voice a tone that meant unquestioned
command and obedience. "Sit in that room for one minute while
I take care of some business and then we can take care of your
problem!"

Jeff watched Virgil's staring eyes. The distrust and resentment
of a lifetime were still there—but some fear was outweighing it.
After a long moment, Virgil looked away, and nodded. Jeff led him
into the office, made sure that the door to his bedroom was closed,
and then left the cowboy sitting in a chair across from his
masonite-topped desk. Jeff walked back out to the living room,
carefully closing the door behind him.

Lynnellen was just emerging from the kitchen, wringing her
hands in a towel to dry them. "Jeff, who is it?"

"Where are the kids, Mother?" Jeff asked evenly.

"They're in bed, you know that!" Lynnellen's face clouded. He
never called her Mother. "Jeff, what's going on?"

"Get the kids, Mother. I think you all should spend the night
over at Sister Hansen's."

"Why, Jeff?" There was a worried edge to Lynnellen's voice,
not panic—never panic from Lynnie. "Who's in your office?"

"Better you didn't know." Irritation was growing in Jeff's voice;
irritation and the hint of fear that his wife had never seen before.
"Now, do as I say, Lynnellen."

He had spoken her name. She knew he meant what he said.

She turned at once, passing into the small intersection that passed for a hall in the center of the house. Jeff could hear her waking Tyler and Barbara, gently but insistently. Jeff turned to the small table that sat to the side of the arch separating the dining and living rooms.

Jefferson Kendall picked up the phone and punched in the number on the Touch-Tone pad.

"So that's the story, President. Gawd's honest truth. I spent the last month or so in one o' them prisons they been building over thar. Got out and had to stand around watching while ever' one o' the people I met there was blowed clear to hell by them army som'bitches."

Jeff sat across the desk from Virgil. The stake president leaned forward, his hands folded on the desk. The desk lamp was the only light in the room, casting deep shadows into the corners.

The old clock on the wall ticked several times before Jeff spoke. It was 11:17 P.M. Virgil had talked and answered Jeff's occasional questions for nearly two hours.

"Virgil Johnston, this is the damnedest story I've ever heard," Jeff said at last. "So what did you do with all their things—their memorial? And how did you end up on my porch three days later?"

Virgil looked down at his hands, listening to the clock for a moment. "Well, President, them batteries lasted quite a while. I'd thought I might put it all down the Cactus Mine, but she'd caved long ago and weren't worth the trouble. I rode them pallets over the pass."

"So," Jefferson said quietly, "where did you put them?"

"Well"—Virgil looked up, his eyes turned suspicious—"that ain't no concern right now. I worked my way through the hills and passed south of Milford over to Minersville. I ran into a little trouble there."

"A little trouble?" Jeff prodded.

"Well"—Virgil fidgeted slightly—"I sorta ran into the army by accident and needed to leave Minersville in a hurry."

"A hurry?" Jeff prodded.

"Well, I sorta—borrowed a truck."

Jeff's head sank down into his hands.

"It's Allen Godburr's truck—hell, he don't mind and I lost them army bastards somewhere's around the fairgrounds," Virgil said, somewhat hurt. "I didn't know where else to go, President."

"Virgil." Jeff shook his head. "I'm not sure what I can do to . . . do you hear that?"

Something was rolling through Beaver. Something big.

"That ain't no farm machinery," Virgil said in hushed tones.

Jeff stood up and parted the curtains behind him. The noise grew louder by the moment. Beneath the street lamp, a pair of Hummer Mark IV's skidded around the corner and stopped in front of the house. A moment later, an armored personnel carrier slid to a stop at the intersection, kicking up dust from the street as it rotated on its gravity fields to look directly back at Kendall.

"Shee-it!" Jeff muttered, gauging that this might be an appropriate moment for his rare use of the traditional Southern Utah expletive. He then turned to Virgil, moving quickly around the desk. "Let's go, son! Follow me!"

They passed through the back bedroom and then the girls' room. Light suddenly poured through the curtained windows in a white, false dawn. Jeff glanced out back. Another APC had taken up a position in his own barnyard. Just who did they think he had in here with him? Someone wanted Virgil very badly.

Jeff turned sharply in the small hallway and opened a door. A thin staircase of ancient wood descended into the small, damp basement. The walls were concrete in some places while the thick lava rock and mortar of the original foundations still protruded in spots. Virgil quickly ducked onto the stairs, his worn boots slipping. He slid down four steps before catching himself.

"Don't make a sound!" Jeff said from the lighted hall above. He suddenly shut the door.

A shaft of brilliant light entered the cramped, low-ceiling room from a single, dust-coated window that was far too small for Virgil to fit through even if he had wanted to. A single glance around him at the workbench, shelves, and old junk of the room confirmed his fears.

The only escape from the room was back up those stairs.

Jeff walked casually over to the front door, allowing the banging to go on for a while before he appeared.

"Good evening, Lieutenant Cummings! What brings you and the entire garrison to my house at this late hour of the night?"

Cummings had lost a good deal of his charm to the night. He said simply, "May we come in?"

"Would my answer make any difference?"

"No," Cummings said, shaking his head slowly.

"Then, by all means, please make yourselves at home," Jeff said, standing aside. Cummings entered quickly, his 9mm sidearm drawn and ready. Behind him, the ubiquitous Sergeant McDonald was holding an AAR-21 Accelerator Assault rifle across the chest of his combat jacket. He remained at the door.

"Sorry to disturb you so late in the evening." Cummings's purr seemed to have acquired an edge. "But we are hunting down a very dangerous man, and I understand that you may be able to help me in this matter. By the way"—Cummings looked around—"where's Lynnellen and the kids?"

"Oh, they're over at Kimmer Hansen's. Kimmer's got a touch of the flu and wanted a little help with her kids tonight is all. So," Jeff said, pointing at the gun, "you gonna shoot me or what?"

Cummings smiled, slipping into the PR mode that was like a second skin. "Sorry, Jeff, but this guy's a dangerous one. Positively psycho. Virgil Johnston—remember, you were asking about him last month?"

"Yes," Jeff said, then indicated the couch under the big window in the living room. The stake president could see that the APCs had all disgorged their armed contents, men who now were cordoning off his home from the outside world. "Please sit down, Lieutenant, you're making me nervous."

Cummings smiled, holstered his weapon, and sat on the couch. Jeff sat down opposite him in his overstuffed rocker.

"Now, what's all this about Virgil?" Jeff said easily. "Virgil may be a little unusual, but I've never thought of him as crazy."

"He's a killer, Mayor. A killer pure and simple." Cummings shook his head. "You remember when Johnston, the McNeil twins, and Harlan Murphy disappeared last month?"

Jeff nodded. "Sure." The living room was directly over the cellar, and he'd never gotten around to insulating it well. Every word being spoken, Jeff knew, was falling through the thin floor to the ears of Virgil below them both. "Who could forget. Lavonda comes and cries on my desk just about every day my office is open."

"Well, the news isn't much better. One of our security teams found her boys and Harlan Murphy out in the desert west of Milford." Cummings shook his head again. "God only knows what they were doing out there in the first place—it's all restricted due to the epidemic. Still, they got in somehow, I guess. Anyway, the search team finally found the boys."

"Dead?" Jeff said grimly.

"Yes, sir, I'm afraid so." Cummings was the perfect balance of sympathy and indignation. Well practiced. "Worse yet, our investigation proves that all three were murdered by Virgil Johnston. Harlan had been shot once in the back of the head—pretty much fatal within seconds. The McNeils, however, were both gut shot and left to die on their own. They may have survived for an hour or so before they finally succumbed. I can't imagine the horror they must have endured."

"You're sure it was Virgil?" Jeff said, thinking through everything being said.

"I'm afraid there's really no doubt," Cummings said. "We've got the forensics evidence and the gun itself that he used. It really is an open-and-shut case—one which I have opened here and which I intend personally to shut."

Cummings stood suddenly. "You tell me that your people are supporters of the government. I've read your articles in the *Beaver Press* on supporting our leaders in this time of crisis. Well, here it is, Jeff, a real-live crisis. We've got to stop this murderer, and I need your help to do it. Now, we know he was in Minersville today, and we've had reports that he was in town tonight. We got an anonymous phone call that said we should ask you about him. Do you have any idea where he might go?"

Jeff laughed. "Of course I do, Lieutenant! He came straight here!"

Mountain Man

"What?" Cummings was dumbfounded.

"Yes, sir, the boy came straight here to me. Showed up here right around nine-thirty or so. Started telling me some darn-fool story about 'death camps' out in the Wah Wah Valley. Now that you've told me your story, it all makes sense. The boy must have been all liquored up when he took them boys out into the Wah Wah and shot 'em dead. When he'd sobered up, he probably had to come up with some wild story just to cover his ass. It didn't make much sense to me, Lieutenant."

"Of course," Cummings said quietly. "No sense at all. So, where is Virgil Johnston now?"

"Gone." Jeff waved his hand casually toward the night beyond the picture window. "I threw him out about an hour ago! Told him to take his lies packing before I had the town string him up. Now that I know what you've told me, I suspect the town will do just that if he ever shows his face around here again!"

"Where did he go?" Cummings said quickly.

"Said something about Manti. Last I saw he was driving off to the north in a truck—stolen now, I suppose." Jeff stood up. "I'm sorry, Lieutenant, I wish I could be more help to you. If you hurry, you might be able to catch him; that truck didn't look like it was moving that well."

"Thank you, Mayor," Cummings said hastily, rushing toward the door. "You've been of invaluable service. Sergeant! Mount 'em up! We're going north!"

"Don't mention it, Lieutenant!" Jeff yelled, waving to him from the front door. "And if you ever find that murderous bastard, you call me first thing!"

Two men rode out before dawn.

There was nothing unusual in their appearance. They had driven out of Beaver trailing a large horse rig behind the beat-up wheeler truck. They started out along the old Manderfield High-way for a short while before turning off onto the North Creek Road. When the rig reached North Creek itself, they opened the doors of the rig and saddled up just as dawn began giving its first blush in the blue-black sky. With practiced ease, they settled the packs on the third animal.

The waters of the North Fork were swollen with the late spring runoff. The snows on the eastern peaks were thawing out and de-livering their usual thread of life to the valley far below. It was into these waters that the riders moved, the hooves of their ani-mals making slow progress up the icy creek bed. Only when neces-sity demanded did they move up to the banks and return to the waters as soon as possible. The waters washed their trail, cleans-ing it of their passage.

They took the southern fork of the stream called Pine Creek, passing Rattlesnake Peak on their south as they moved beyond the foothills and onto the towering mountains themselves. Sagebrush gave way to scrub oak and quickly thereafter to towering pines. The riders knew the twisting confluence of the mountain like a hymn, and both could recite the names of each creek in their sleep: Iron, Bosman, Lion, Gorilla, Sweetwater, and—in the rarefied air of the Wasatch Range—finally, Blue Lake Creek.

The riders looked on Shelly Baldy Peak to the south and Mount Baldy to the north. The climb had leveled into a box canyon that was as near to heaven as either man had ever hoped to know. The

pines formed a wall of green around the dead-end canyon, the tim-
berline within sight above them. Grass carpeted the canyon floor
and set like a brilliant gem; in the center of it all lay the placid
waters of Blue Lake itself. Six mule deer suddenly raised their
heads, their ears swiveling forward at the water's edge. They could
sense the approaching riders. The riders themselves reined in to a
stop. They both knew it was time.

"Virgil," Jefferson Kendall said, turning in the saddle, his heavy
coat rustling with the motion, "I guess my best advice is to take
'em over the top somewhere this side of Mudd Lake and then
down on into Bullion Canyon. There's no roads into that canyon
above Bullion Falls and plenty of places for you to hole up.
There's some mines down Warnick Gulch—you might use them.
Hunting's not bad, and you can always cross back this side if you
want to get a little fishing in. If you have any real problems, you
might have to drop down into Maryvale, but on the whole I think
this is the best you can hope for."

"Yep," Virgil replied, eyeing the mountain like an old friend, "I
reckon that's as good advice as I've gotten in a long time."

"Just stay up here, Virgil," Jeff warned. "This ain't no game
anymore. Cummings will expect me to string you up by your pri-
vates if you come back into town, and I'm telling you right now
that I'll do it, too. He wants you dead, son, and I'll be obliged to
help him kill you if you come back."

Jeff turned to look back up the peaceful canyon. He tilted his
old Stetson back on his head before he continued. " 'Course, if
you got the V-CIDS, then you ought to come down. Then it won't
matter if we kill you or not. We'll send a few boys up here now
and then to check on you and make sure you get resupplied."

"I sure do appreciate it, President," Virgil said with a husky
voice. "It ain't just fer me anymore, you know. I got the trust of
a whole lot of people who are countin' on me to remember
them—and where their souls are kept, so to speak."

Jeff smiled. "We've all got things that we need to remember—
and things we've got to do. All you gotta do is wait it out now,
Virgil. Just wait it out. Things are changing, son. The Constitution
may be hanging by a thread, but we'll save it yet. And when the
night's over, we'll get word to you. Then you can come home."

"Then," Virgil said, "we'll all come home. They ain't dead, you know, President—all them people from out in the desert. They're all just sleepin'—and I'm the only one who knows right where they sleep, too."

Virgil clucked at the horse quietly. The animal began to move, the packhorse in tow.

They hadn't gone more than a dozen yards when Virgil turned around. "President, you know the story of King David?" he called out.

Jeff looked perplexed. "Yes, I do."

"Ain't he one o' them Jewish kings from the Bible?"

Jeff looked puzzled. "You know the Bible, Virgil?"

Virgil squinted into the bright sky. It was nearly noon, and he had a long trail to make before he could bed down. "Seems to me he weren't always the straightest shooter when it came to Gawd. He'd been a good kid and got blessings and stuff from the big man upstairs, but in the end he just flat screwed up. Ain't that right, President?"

Jeff chuckled. "Yes, Virgil, I suppose that's pretty much it. In the end he murdered Uriah the Hittite just so he could cover up his sin with Uriah's wife Bathsheba."

"You know, President," Virgil said, "when I think of David, though, I think of the kid with a sling standing up mighty brave before that there Goliath—not some murdering, lying, wife stealer. Maybe in the future you'll think of me and think of all them people that died out there, and you'll think of ol' King David."

Jeff shook his head. "I don't understand what . . ."

Virgil looked Jeff in the eye.

"When you think of us—you just remember King David."

With that, Virgil turned the horse about and vanished into the Tushar Mountains.

Epilogue
Phoenix

October 9, 2013 / 1235 hrs
Grampian Mountain / Former Star Mining District
Above Frisco Ghost Town, West Beaver County, Utah

The wind never stops.

It blew across the desert sands when two miners, Ryan and Hawkes, first discovered the great silver ore body in the mid-eighteen hundreds. They had been prospecting up the Grampian Mountain and walking back to their camp near Squaw Springs on the eastern edge of the Wah Wah Valley. Each day they would sit below an outcropping of rock to rest in its shade. One day they happened to bring along a prospector's pick and chipped away at the ledge.

The surface fell away—and uncovered a vein of silver so pure you could scratch it with a powder horn and see its shine.

Men came to the eastern slope of the Grampian, the southern peak of the San Francisco Mountains, to take the silver from the ground and build their fortunes. The railroad came with no other purpose than to carry those riches back to more civilized lands. The mine boomed. The town of Frisco grew up at its feet, boasting two streets and twenty-five saloons—quite an accomplishment in the Mormon-controlled territory. The Saints in the east half of the county may have owned the ballot box, but the mines had the wealth.

Then on February 14, 1882, the great Horn Silver Mine, queen of the silver mines in all the west, came to an end. After weeks of rain followed by days of snow, the mine was heavy with water. The stopes—vast man-made caverns where the miners had removed the precious ore and tried to replace it with huge scaffolds of supports—were straining under the pressure of the water-soaked ground above. Just as the graveyard shift was about to enter the mine, the stopes gave way. Inspectors had to be hauled out of the vertical shaft with lowered ropes when the lift cage was caught in the collapsing walls. Just as the last of them reached the surface, the stopes gave way.

The sound shattered glass as far away as Milford.

The mine had glory-holed. The vein of pure silver was never found again.

The wind blew on unheeding these events. It never gives. The wind only takes.

By 1912 others were willing to give it a go. Even as Sam Newhouse was building his mine community on the western slopes of the Grampian in Wah Wah, another mine was sunk on the eastern slope. North and slightly higher than the Horn Silver's original site, the idea of the new mine was to sink a vertical shaft between three hundred and a thousand feet deep and then tunnel south in the hopes of striking the original Horn Silver vein.

They called the mine the King David.

Its shaft eventually dropped thirteen hundred feet straight into the earth.

It never found the vein. The treasure it sought was never there.

The wind blew on.

The Lulu, a mine based on the same idea but this one to the south, fared no better than the King David. The glory was lost and not to be recovered. Frisco died a slow and quiet death. Bawly Sacket's livery stable, the Slaughter General Store, Lawrence's Saloon, the Hotel Southern—all of them vanished under the relentless summers, harsher winters, and constant, unrelenting sand and wind. By 1960 most of the buildings had disappeared. By 1990 only a few of the foundations and stone kilns could be discovered.

By 2010, only the commemorative plaque could be seen from the road, the town of twenty-five thousand no longer even scarring the desert sands. Even the grave markers had been wiped clean.

Yet the miners' souls who had worked and dreamed so hard on the mines might have taken comfort that their King David mine had yet one more treasure to give up.

Dust filtered down on him as he fell, slowly, controlled and silently into the darkness below. The square of light far above him receded as the ancient, rotted timbers lining the shaft slipped by, one by one. The original lift rails were rusted beyond recognition, their dark, dried-blood color running as a wavering line down into the abyss. The light from above, even though the middle of the day, would only penetrate the shaft so far. Darkness was enveloping him.

There was no bottom in sight.

Jason checked the readout panel on his left forearm, forcing himself to breathe evenly through the respirator. There was plenty of oxygen flowing through the re-breather, and it looked like he'd have nearly three hours available—more than enough time.

His descent was drifting slightly to his left. Jason adjusted the controls of the levitation pack. The AG plates responded, centering him better in his descent. The less he disturbed even the gas-filled atmosphere in this place, the better chance he had of surviving. For all he knew, it was the weight of the air alone that kept this shaft open after all these years. Jason had outlived V-CIDS, the civil war, the chaos following the Collapse, and the establishment of the new government. He wasn't about to die by making a stupid mistake in a hundred-year-old mine shaft.

He reached down carefully to activate the halogen torch hanging at his belt but stopped for a moment, falling in the darkness. He thought of earlier in the day. The sun beating down on him with unnatural warmth as he walked again the black circle of earth that had been Newhouse. He gazed up at the mountains he had longed to reach. He hesitated at the boundary where the gravity fence had stood. He paced off the distance and stood where Barracks 7-R had once stood—where he had bunked with his father and come to know and love him. In his mind, he reached down again and plunged his hand into the soft black earth. He touched the bodies and souls trampled and seared into the ground. He felt them there still. He wondered then if his father had stood in this same place when the end came . . .

Tears stung his eyes again at the thought. He blinked them away and touched the pad on the torch. Light sprang to life below him. He had to see.

Like an angel on invisible wings, Jason drifted softly down to the bottom of the shaft at the head of a column of light. He could see that the years had not been kind to the mine; the base of the shaft was filled with broken timbers and debris that had fallen from the shaft itself and had otherwise made its way into the mine.

His treasure, though, was not buried. He caught a quick breath.

In the pool of his torch, the two pallets could be seen. Virgil had said that he had brought them here, guided them over the shaft one at a time, and then adjusted their AG panels down so that they would float to the bottom, first one and then the other. The first had fallen on top of the debris at the bottom of the shaft, settling gently as the power in the pallet's batteries eventually failed. The second had only missed falling directly atop the other and had settled listing heavily to one side.

Jason dared not press his weight on the debris around the pallets. The perfection before him required that he float lightly around them.

He drifted silently forward, lifting the blankets that had remained in place. The natural gases that filled the mine had long ago pushed out most of the oxygen, permeating the contents of the pallets with a naturally preserving mixture. Nothing had faded. Nothing had rotted.

It was there. *They* were all there.

Erik's music, crafted onto the paper by his own hand and secured in place by P.T.'s final gift—the violin; Olivia Codgebury's "Home Where Art Thou"; David Yarrow's dance diagrams; Miriam Barns's letters to her lost family; Lucian's folk songs; and a thousand more like them speaking to him from the dead— speaking to his memory.

A single manuscript, bound with tied cloth caught Jason's eye. Tied to the stack of paper was a corn-husk doll.

Amanda's doll.

Jason picked up the manuscript and brushed the dust from the cover, the title burning his eyes with its hand-lettered script.

"For Jason: I Remember."

Jason folded the manuscript to his chest. The tears streamed down his dirty face. His father was here. His father, who he only knew in death.

Jason's cry thundered up the shaft, echoing into the empty tunnels and reverberating into a cry of a thousand voices. His own voice. Their voices. Rising up from the earth. Rising up from the bottom of the grave. Cries of death. Cries of triumph.

Holy and unholy. Death and living still.

Lazarus.

Part of Jason wished to stay here, buried in the earth, joining as one with others that had died who should have lived.

A voice. Father's voice.

"Remember me."

A voice, His voice.

"I will forever love and remember you."

Jason gave a long shuddering sigh into his respirator and carefully placed his father's manuscript in his own hip-pack. Then working with practiced ease, he moved around the pallet, replacing the long-exhausted batteries with the fresh ones he had brought with him.

Jason activated the AG plates on the pallets. When they both were hovering evenly over each other, he tied them together to stabilize their ascent. At last all was ready. Jason stood atop the memorial, atop the memories and hopes that had so long fought to survive. He increased the lift control.

The pallets began lifting Jason toward the light high above.

"I'm taking you home." Jason smiled through his tears. "We're all going home."

AFTERWORD
Stranger Than Fiction

April 26, 1995 / 0830 hrs
Twinpines
Flagstaff, Coconino County, Arizona

This book is not about AIDS. This book is about forgiveness and compassion. It is a book about our souls.

This book also has history.

I had wanted to write this book years ago, but could find no one who was interested in publishing it. My name had been made in fantasy and science fiction, I was told—why would I want to write something so obviously serious as this? It wasn't the right time, some said. It wasn't commercial, said others.

During that time years ago, while riding to the airport, a couple I had known—who were old friends—asked me what I was going to work on next. I told them I wanted to write a near future book about AIDS concentration camps. They were vehement in their response: they thought it was a terrible idea. Their words both shocked and saddened me. "Do you really want to write a book about homosexuals?" they asked me. "Won't people who read your work be influenced toward sin?"

I notice that I don't hear from them much lately.

Meanwhile, the AIDS epidemic continued to rage barely checked. The disease had become politicized. The great American majority (whoever they are) believed it was a disease that "other" people got—"other" people *meaning people other than the "Majority,"* who were supposedly decent and good. Occasionally, one of the *majority* would get the disease through some terrible accident. It frightened. It angered. Yet it remained a gay disease, a drug addict disease, a promiscuous disease, and therefore, many reasoned, it only touched *others*—never *them.*

Thousands died. Millions suffered. Not nameless, faceless others either, but people that I knew. People that you knew. Family. Friends.

I don't pretend to know why some people are gay and others are not. I don't know why some people have AIDS and others do not. All I know is that Christ said "judge not that ye be not judged" and added no codicils to that injunction. Miriam Barns may have cast the first stone in this story—but we may not.

Beaver City, Milford, the King David Mine, and the Wah Wah Valley all actually exist. Stop by and visit. You'll find the natives genuinely friendly. My own father—who was born in Milford—was Beaver-raised and many was the summer and holiday that I've spent in that beautiful little town, both in Jeff Kendall's home and that of Virgil Johnston. I've walked the halls of the courthouse (which my grandmother helped to renovate) and where my father used to produce plays during the summer months. I've listened to the stories of the Grampian Range and the Horn Silver Mine from my grandfather and grandmother, standing all the while in the ghost-town ruins where my great-grandmother's general store once stood in Frisco. I've walked the ground at Newhouse as you may want to do, felt the wind in my hair, and gazed in reflection across that barren valley that is so picturesque, lonely, and deadly.

Don't go poking about the mines—stay well away. Most of them are owned by the Anaconda Copper Company and are posted—with good reason. They are almost universally over a hundred years old and are unquestionably death traps for even the most experienced miners.

While the places are real, the people live only in my imagination. They come from pieces of folks that I know or knew or thought I knew. Any similarity between them and actual folks is purely coincidental.

In part of my reading for this book, I ran across the following little tale told to David Black by Colleen Johnson in his book *The Plague Years: A Chronicle of AIDS, the Epidemic of Our Time.*[1] It goes like this:

> Colleen told me about a man with AIDS, who had given the disease to his wife. She was pregnant, and her baby was born with AIDS. The only one in the family who was healthy was their five-year-old daughter—who asked her mother, "Are you going to die?"
>
> "Yes," the mother said.
> "Is daddy going to die?"
> "Yes."
> "Is the new baby going to die?"
> "Yes."
> "Can I come with you?" the girl asked.

Child, please stay with us just a little while longer. Grow up and remember. Remember your mother, your father, and remember the baby who had lost life's battle before even having a chance to fight it. Sing for them, weep for them, and honor them in your living memory.

Whatever their fate may be beyond this life, let us remember them here.

For in us, they are immortal.

[1]*The Plague Years: A Chronicle of AIDS, the Epidemic of Our Time.* David Black. 1986 Pan Books Ltd.

The typeface used in this book is a version of Sabon, originally designed in the 1960s by Jan Tschichold (1902–1974) at the behest of a consortium of manufacturers of metal type. As one who began as an outspoken design revolutionary—calling for the elimination of serifs, scorning revivals of historic typefaces—Tschichold seemed an odd choice, but he met the challenge brilliantly: The typeface was to be based on the fonts of the sixteenth-century French typefounder Claude Garamond but five percent narrower; it had to be identical for three different processes, working around the quirks of each, such as linotype's inability to "kern" (allow one character into the space of another, the way the top of a lowercase *f* overhangs other letters). Aside from Sabon, named for a sixteenth-century French punchcutter to avoid problems of attribution to Garamond, Tschichold is best remembered as the designer of the Penguin paperbacks of the late 1940s.